MW00478854

DREAM
WORLD

Book Two of The Dream Waters Series

Erin A. Jensen

Dream World is a work of fiction. Names, characters, places and incidents are the products of the author's imagination or are used fictitiously. Any resemblance to actual events, locales or persons, living or dead, is entirely coincidental.

2016 Dream World
Text copyright © 2016 Erin A. Jensen
All Rights Reserved
Dream Waters Publishing

ISBN: 0997171243
ISBN 13: 9780997171242

First and always, to my soul mate. I never would have gotten this far without you Chris.

To Missy for being right there with me through all the ups & downs on this journey.

To Michelle Baker for boosting my confidence when I sorely needed it, loving my first book before the edit & editing it into the final polished version.

To Kate, Amy, Emilie & Al for being the most amazing bunch of beta readers that any writer could ever hope for.

To everyone at the Newark Wegmans Pharmacy for all your support and encouragement.

To Matt Morano, Sandy Fronefield, Ron Smith & everyone at Wegmans for selling my first book in the store, advertising the heck out of it & organizing an incredible book signing. Wegmans truly is the best company to work for.

Deep into that darkness peering, long I stood there, wondering, fearing, doubting, dreaming dreams no mortal ever dared to dream before.

—Edgar Allan Poe / The Raven

1

CHARLIE

It was a Tuesday. The day my life changed forever. Just another ordinary day for the rest of the world. I hit the power button on the television as I passed the hotel dresser, but I didn't bother looking at the screen. I was way more interested in the grease-soaked paper bag in my other hand. Plopping down on the queen-sized bed, I shrugged out of my jacket, kicked off my shoes, tossed the room key to the bedside table and tore into the bag like a wolf tearing into fresh prey. Practically salivating, I unwrapped the first double bacon cheeseburger and an almost orgasmic moan escaped my throat as my teeth sank into it. I leaned back against the headboard and looked at the television across the room. The middle-aged man onscreen was proclaiming the wonders of a food processor that no kitchen would be complete without. My eyes darted to the bedside table and did a quick visual sweep of the bed. Then I spotted the remote on the desk across the room and let out a defeated sigh. I was already feeling way too lethargic to get back up. After stuffing in a second burger, a large order of fries and a chocolate shake, I sank back against the pillows, closed my eyes and tuned out the infomercial salesman's obnoxiously cheery voice.

In under two weeks, my life had changed so drastically that it was almost too much to process. I'd gone from being a mental patient in a long-term care psychiatric facility to a lonely hotel patron with nowhere to go and nothing on the horizon. I was diagnosed at a young age as a schizophrenic suffering from paranoid delusions, my *delusions* being the fact that I see things and remember things that other people can't. Unlike the rest of the world, I remember the Waters that carry everyone to the Dream World each night while their bodies sleep. I remember the world where everyone takes an alternate form and lives an alternate life. I can see people flip to their Dream forms in this world and I can jump in the Waters and travel to the Dream World whenever I want to. A few weeks ago, a gorgeous new patient had walked through the door in the middle of a group therapy session and though I didn't know it at the time, her entrance was the first in a series of events that'd change my life forever.

At an almost mindboggling speed, Emma Talbot became the closest friend I'd ever had. And it wasn't long before an elderly fellow patient opened my eyes to the fact that I wasn't the only Dream Sighted person in this world. She opened my eyes to a lot of things, including the fact that my new best friend was constantly shadowed by a second Dream form, an enormous fiery-eyed dragon. After several unsuccessful days spent trying to figure out why Emma had a dragon for a bodyguard, I met the man who was going to change my life—the dragon, Emma's husband, David Talbot. When I first realized he was Emma's dragon, I attacked him full force in the middle of the common room during visiting hours and he knocked me out cold with the flick of a wing. I woke up in the Dream World inside a cave in the Dark Forest, where David patiently explained that he was also Sighted. And that I was also a dragon.

When I woke in the facility the next morning, Emma was already gone. Her husband, who also happened to be a big shot lawyer, had gotten a judge to let her go home under house arrest and be treated by a live-in psychiatrist. He convinced the judge that another patient at the facility posed a threat to Emma's safety, and I wholeheartedly agreed. I'd watched that other patient flip to a writhing man-shaped swarm of insects and go after Emma. I also watched the dragon that shadowed Emma lunge at

Frank the bug-man and melt his hand to a lump of charred flesh, but I was the only one who'd been able to see that.

Opening my eyes, I extended a leg and dragged my jacket up from the foot of the bed with my toes. I pulled an envelope from one of the pockets and for about the thousandth time, I opened it and slid out the sheet of expensive-looking pale gray stationary. **David Talbot Attorney at Law** was engraved in thick silver letters at the top of the page. The note was written in black ink and the handwriting was elegant, but not in a girly way.

> *Dear Mr. Oliver,*
> *Please accept this small token of my gratitude for protecting what I hold most dear. Use it to forge a new path for yourself.*
> *Best of luck in your future endeavors,*
> *David A. Talbot*

No phone number. No address. Unless you counted the office information that was engraved at the bottom of the page. But I didn't. When I met David Talbot in the Dream World, he asked if I'd be interested in joining his "family" of Sighted employees. He'd offered a glimmer of hope that I might actually belong to a family that didn't dismiss me as a lunatic but if he'd really wanted me to join the family, wouldn't he have done more than leave an envelope at the facility with instructions to give it to me when I was discharged?

David Talbot's business card from the Law Offices of Talbot and Associates had been tucked inside the letter. No more contact information than the stationary. No private number. No "call my office and tell the secretary you were invited to join the family."

A prepaid credit card with no mention of how much it was worth had also been tucked inside the letter. I used it to buy a few necessities at a corner store, gum, toothbrush, six-pack of soda. When I asked the cashier if she could tell me the balance, her eyes grew three times wider as she whispered the amount. I asked her to repeat it. Twice. When I decided to get a hotel room until I figured out what to do with my life, I got a similar reaction from the guy at the check-in desk.

I turned the business card over in my hand a few times, stupidly hoping to find something new. The silver engraving glinted when it caught the lamplight, but that was it. Tucking the card in the pocket of my jeans, I yanked the blankets up over me and sank back against the foreign comfort of the hotel mattress.

I was used to being alone. Even my own mother wanted nothing to do with me, the woman I'd always believed to be my mother anyway. David said it wasn't possible for an Unsighted mother to give birth to a dragon child. Dragons were only conceived when both parents were Sighted, either way, I was used to going solo and I'd never let myself hope for better or believe that I was worth something. I'd always aimed to convince everybody, including myself, that I was a smart ass who didn't give a crap but for some moronic reason, I'd let David Talbot get my hopes up. For a brief moment I actually believed I was special, but it was all just a bunch of bullshit. He'd enchanted Emma with a dragon bodyguard and he'd used an enchantment to chain me to the floor of the cave. He'd probably just used magic to make it look like I was a dragon. Since the day we met, I'd spent hours in the Dream World trying to turn back into the dragon he'd shown me to be, but the reflection staring back at me was never anything more than a human idiot who'd gotten suckered into believing in a fairytale. And now being nothing hurt like hell because I'd let David Talbot convince me to care.

There was a new infomercial on television for a bead-maker that no self-respecting crafter should be without, but I had even less energy to get up and grab the remote after all the fast food I'd wolfed down in a pathetic attempt to stuff down the hurt. As I steadily slipped into a grease-induced food coma, I closed my eyes and let the Waters take me...

...I groggily lifted my eyelids and found myself curled up on a soft patch of earth. The Water was only a few steps away and the sun was lazily sinking toward it. Behind me, the cries of awakening nocturnal creatures echoed through the forest. Rubbing my eyes, I stood up and headed toward a weathered dock that jutted out over the Water a short distance from where I'd slept. I had no idea where I was. Since I didn't see any point to jumping in the Waters lately, I'd been falling asleep naturally like the rest of the world and each time I drifted back to the Dream World, I found myself someplace new. I stepped up onto the dock and the boards groaned in protest as I made my way to the end of it. I took a deep breath, filling my lungs with the earthy evening air, and sat down on the edge of the dock. Forgetting I wasn't in the other world, I reached in my pocket and pulled out the card. Then I realized where I was, and that the card shouldn't be there. I turned it over in my hand a few times. Just the same boring law office business card. It didn't say anything new, but what the heck was it doing in my pocket in the Dream World?

"Penny for your thoughts." I jumped at the nearness of the unfamiliar voice. I guess I'd been too engrossed in studying the stupid card to hear him walk up behind me.

I twisted sideways and watched the old man who belonged to the voice take the remaining steps to the end of the dock. Old bones and weathered boards creaking in protest, he sat down beside me. White-haired, bearded and dressed in a simple dark blue tunic and matching pants, he considered me with a kind smile, waiting for an answer.

"Yeah. Uh," I stammered. "Just admiring the sunset."

His smile widened. "And here I thought you were wondering about that card in your hand."

I glanced down at the card. "Nah. This's nothing important."

His pale blue eyes twinkled with amusement. "Of course. Invitations from the Sarrum are just everyday occurrences."

"I'm sorry?" I looked down at the card, then back at him. "The what?"

He chuckled softly to himself. "I heard you were lost. But I didn't imagine you'd be quite this lost."

No longer finding his smile quite so kind, I scowled at him. "Who exactly are you? And why do you think you know me?"

His smile grew faintly apologetic. "Names aren't important, Charlie. But if you must call me something, call me Arthur."

"Okay Call-me-Arthur, how do you know my name?"

He shifted, trying to make his aged body more comfortable on the wooden planks. "Everyone knows your name. It isn't every day that a lost dragon is discovered."

"So you're Sighted?"

"I am," he agreed with a half-smile on his lips.

Yeah. So far this conversation was annoyingly pointless. But he knew about the card. *An invitation from the Sarrum.* "How do you know about the business card? And what the heck is a Sarrum?"

Call-me-Arthur's gaze shifted toward the Water. "News travels quickly through the Dark Forest. Everyone's quite curious about you, you know."

"No. I don't know. Why don't you enlighten me?"

He looked away from the Water and studied me curiously. "I wouldn't dream of stepping on the Sarrum's toes. He's already offered to do just that, hasn't he?"

If he wasn't an old man, I'd have been sorely tempted to knock the smug smile off his face. "Seriously, what the hell's a Sarrum?"

Raising an eyebrow, he replied, "I believe you know the Dragon King as David Talbot."

"The Dragon King?" I raked a hand through my hair. "David Talbot is the king of the dragons?"

Another soft chuckle escaped his wrinkled lips. "No. David Talbot is the king of Draumer."

I resisted the urge to growl at him. "And Draumer is what? The Dream World term for dragons?"

His grin faltered slightly. "No. Draumer is the Dream World term for *Dream World.* It seems the rumors are wrong. You aren't more man than beast. You're more beast than man. Honestly, how could you live your entire Sighted life without even knowing the name of the world you inhabit?"

Who the hell was this guy? I didn't have to take this. "Listen, I'm not really in the mood for company. So why don't you move along?"

He let out a lingering sigh. "I meant no offense, Charlie. Why don't we start over?"

I looked away from him and turned toward the sunset. "Okay. Start."

"I came here to offer advice before you accepted the Sarrum's offer."

I glanced down at the card. "Then you wasted your time. He didn't give me an offer, just a generic thank you note."

Call-me-Arthur cleared his throat, prompting me to look at him. So I did. "That's no generic thank you, my boy. That piece of cardstock is worth more gold than you could possibly imagine."

Well that definitely peaked my interest. "How do you figure?"

He reached out and took the card from my hand. And worthless as I believed it to be, I snatched it right back. "It only appears ordinary because you haven't accepted the Sarrum's offer."

I traced a finger along the edge of the card. "How exactly do I do that? Call the law office and tell the secretary that the Sarrum of Draumer offered me a job? That'd earn me a one-way ticket back to the loony bin."

Eyes narrowed, he studied me curiously. "You aren't embarrassed about your stay in a mental facility?"

"Why should I be? My closest friends were in that facility. Including my best friend, the Sarrum's wife."

The cordial grin slipped from his face. "You'd best keep that to yourself. Dragons do not share their treasures. She's not yours. She's his. And if you'd like your heart to keep beating, you won't forget that."

Seriously, who the hell was this guy? "Thanks for that totally obvious piece of advice."

"If it was obvious, you wouldn't ever refer to her as *your* anything. Not even your friend. She's his. And only his. Period."

I returned my gaze to the Water and the sky above it. The sun was just barely visible above the horizon and the air was already starting to cool. I opened my mouth, hoping something clever would pop out.

But he didn't give me the chance. "Yes, I know. You aren't stupid. But we've gotten off topic. To accept the Sarrum's offer, you have to toss that card in the Waters."

"Toss something worth more than I could possibly imagine?" Seemed like a pretty stupid suggestion to me.

He answered in a softer voice, as if our whole conversation had taken place in a completely different tone. "It's the invitation that's valuable. Not the piece of cardstock."

Somehow his change in manner softened mine. "So what advice did you come to give me?"

He grinned, more to himself than me. "Your life is about to change dramatically, Charlie. I just thought you should know that not everyone believes the Sarrum walks on water. There are those who don't think he deserves to sit the throne."

I studied his amused expression, unsure what to make of him. "Are you saying I shouldn't accept his invitation?"

Call-me-Arthur's brow furrowed. "No. You'd be a fool not to accept. There is much that the Sarrum and his followers can teach you. You won't find a better education in all the Sighted world. I'm simply suggesting that you keep an open mind, remember not everything they teach you is set in stone and consider what else the world has to offer before you blindly pledge yourself in service to the Sarrum. If you'd like, I could provide a different point of view when you need one."

I absently traced the raised silver letters on the card with my index finger. "What am I supposed to do? Bring you with me and tell them I'm not sure if I can trust them?"

A humorless chuckle erupted from the old man's throat. "No. I'd prefer that my heart keep beating. I'm no friend of the Dragon King."

The sun had disappeared completely and the air was cooler, but still pleasant. "Why is that?" I wondered aloud, genuinely curious.

He regarded me with a sorrowful smile. "Because the last time I saw the Sarrum, I tried to take his life."

"Yeah," I muttered, wondering whether that should make me fear him or the Dragon King. "I guess that would get you kicked off the holiday guest list. So why'd you try to kill him?"

His pale blue eyes misted as he whispered, "Because he'd just killed my sister."

For the first time, I wondered if I would've been better off staying lost. "Go on."

He cleared his throat and blinked the tears from his eyes. "I've got nothing more to say on that subject but you must understand that the traditional way of thinking for a dragon, especially a royal one, is that women are property. And the primary function of a Sighted female is to bear a dragon child."

Dread knotted in my stomach at the thought of what that meant for Emma, but he clearly didn't intend to elaborate. "How would I contact you if I had questions?"

He reached into a pocket and pulled out a softly glowing white stone. Then he held his hand out, offering it.

The glow intensified as I took it from his hand. It felt surprisingly cool to the touch. "What is it?"

"A moonstone." He cleared his throat. "I've taken up enough of your time. I'll leave you to your thoughts. If you have questions, hold the stone in your hand when you jump in the Waters and it will take you to me. I only ask that you not mention me to the Sarrum or his men."

"I won't." I looked up to thank Call-me-Arthur. But he was gone. I stroked a finger over the stone's smooth surface, then stuffed it in my pocket and turned my attention to the card in my other hand. *A business card worth more gold than I could possibly imagine.* Muttering, "What've I got to lose," I tossed it in the Water...

...Another infomercial for knives sharp enough to slice through metal was playing as I opened my eyes. Sitting up, I tossed the covers off me and fished for the business card in my pocket. It was still there. I pulled it out with a disappointed sigh. The same generic information was engraved on its surface. Honestly, what had I expected?

Feeling like an idiot, I tossed the card to the bedside table and it landed blank side up. Only, it wasn't blank anymore. Heart racing, I snatched it off the table. A phone number was penned in perfect handwritten numbers on the back. Just a number, but it hadn't been there the thousand other times I'd studied the card. I stood up and moved to the desk across the room, clutching the card worth more than gold.

Hand trembling, I lifted the hotel phone off the receiver.

2

BENJAMIN

I t was exactly the sort of evening that I relished slipping into. No moon, no stars, just the pitch black of the eternal night sky and the air that sweltered thick and hot enough to rob the breath from your lungs. I sat down on a boulder beside the seemingly bottomless pool of Water and watched the Water cascade into it from the rock high above. Dark and powerful, the Water fell without a sound. In fact, not a single sound emanated from the forest. Nothing dared make a sound in my presence. I sank into the darkness, merged with it, became it. Then I looked to the top of the canyon a short distance from the Waterfall and knowing black eyes blinked in the darkness, vowing to take my place as soon as I stepped away.

I turned as a creature noiselessly emerged from the forest. Dressed in a heavy black cloak, beads and potion flasks and the teeth of various beasts strung around his neck and waist, he walked upright like a man. But beneath his cloak, the creature sauntered toward me with the bestial grace of a predator. His skull and facial bones were the bones of a man, but no flesh covered them, just pure white bone gleaming in the darkness. A wiry tuft of black hair grew from the top of his skull and eyes darker than the starless sky searched for me through fleshless sockets.

Though he couldn't see me, he stopped just inches from my feet. "How are you, my old friend?"

I stood and let the darkness slip away from me. "That depends on whether you can help us."

The corners of his mouth lifted into a disconcerting smile. "Still the same ray of sunshine, I see. I'm well, too. And my journey was uneventful. Thank you for asking."

I took a step toward him, and he instinctually took two steps back. "I'd lose that smile if I were you. And save the cleverness for your potions. No one here is in the mood for jokes."

He shook his bony head. "I've missed you too, Darkness. You always were the life of the party."

I narrowed my eyes at him and he took another step back. Then I gestured toward the Waterfall. Dropping the smile, he stepped into the pool of Water and waded through the bottomless darkness toward the Waterfall.

I turned and nodded to the shadow on the ledge. Another blink confirmed that he'd head down to take my place. I waded into the Water as the witchdoctor stepped through the Waterfall. A moment later, I followed him.

He was already halfway across the black marble floor when I stepped out the other side. Darkness huddled in the corners beside the entrance, beyond the reach of the candlelight that illuminated the great hall. Sinking into that darkness, I watched the doctor approach the Sarrum. Wings tucked regally behind his back, the Dragon King stood at the base of a wide set of marble steps at the far end of the hall. His eyes briefly darted to me, then returned to the visitor. As the doctor reached the foot of the steps, the Sarrum ascended them in human form. Sitting down on his throne, he gestured for the visitor to approach.

Nodding, the witchdoctor climbed the steps and settled into the chair beside the throne.

The Sarrum greeted him with a warm smile. "You're looking well, old friend."

The witchdoctor's bony mouth curved into a grin. "As are you, Sarrum. It's been far too long."

I stood quite a distance from them, but I heard every word as clearly as if I stood between their seats.

The boss nodded. "I'm sorry we aren't meeting under more pleasant circumstances."

The doctor dropped his freakish smile. "As am I, my King. But I'm honored that you seek my help."

Eyes narrowed, the boss sank back against the ebony cushions on his throne. "Then I trust you're aware of what I seek your help with?"

The doctor cleared his throat. "I believe I am."

The boss raised an eyebrow. "And?"

Shifting nervously in his seat, the doctor cleared his throat again. "I willingly pledge myself in your service, Sarrum. And I'll gladly do whatever you ask of me but I must confess, I am troubled by the rumors I've heard recently."

The Sarrum's stare intensified. "To what rumors are you referring?"

Clearing his throat a third time, the doctor squirmed in his seat. "The rumors of what became of the other doctors who displeased you."

A low growl rumbled in the Sarrum's throat. "Entirely different circumstances. I should hope you'd have no reason to fear such consequences."

The doctor dipped his head. "Of course, Sarrum. Forgive me for bringing it up."

The boss smiled. A smile so cold, it'd freeze a traitorous heart. "Not at all. You were right to be concerned. I will not accept failure. But the solution is simple. Don't fail me."

The doctor swallowed. "I don't intend to."

"Good. Then let's get on with it and discuss the terms."

The doctor's body relaxed a little. "I'm at your disposal. Just tell me what you want me to do."

I stopped listening. I knew what was expected of the doctor and I knew exactly what had become of his predecessors. Old friend or not, we wouldn't hesitate to do the same to him. Failure was not an option.

They shook hands as their business concluded and I slipped from the shadows as the witchdoctor made his way back across the room. He didn't smile when he reached me this time. Instead, he eyed me warily. I gestured toward the Waterfall. Heart racing, the doctor nodded and exited the hall. With a nod to the boss, I stepped through the Water after him.

3

CHARLIE

The brick building across the street made me think of gingerbread houses and old money. An odd combination, I know. But for some reason that was the vibe I always got from stately old houses like fifty-five Sycamore Lane. I rechecked the address I'd scrawled on the back of the business card of unimaginable worth. This was the place. When I dialed the number that appeared on the card, a voice I didn't recognize had answered. "Hello, Charlie. I was beginning to wonder if we'd be hearing from you." I'd been too nervous to ask who he was and he hadn't volunteered the information. The conversation had been very brief and to the point. He gave me an address. I scribbled it down. He instructed me to go there in the morning. Then he hung up.

The building didn't look like an office. It looked like a home. In fact, the whole neighborhood looked residential. And wealthy. A decorative steel fence surrounded the huge perfectly manicured lawn. Everything about the estate was elegant and perfect, and I was feeling sorely underdressed. I'd actually gone out to buy some respectable things to wear after the brief phone conversation, a pair of khakis and a button down shirt. And I felt downright proper until I got out of the taxi and got a look at the house. I was wearing sneakers. Why didn't I buy a pair of loafers? Or maybe a suit? Shit. Why did I even care what I was wearing? I'd never given a crap about that sort of stuff before. Shit. Maybe I should've gotten a haircut. Seriously, what the hell was wrong with me?

I stepped off the sidewalk and slowly made my way across the quiet side street. Was this the Talbots' house? Was David in there? Or Emma? Or somebody waiting to throw a burlap sack over my head and drag me to my death? Benjamin's face came to mind. David Talbot's right hand man. I'd never seen Benjamin's Dream form, but the guy was a walking talking nightmare in this world. The one time I met him, it was all I could do to keep from pissing myself when he spoke to me. Shit. I'd never been this nervous before. About anything. Ever. Taking a deep breath, I walked through the gate, traversed the brick pathway and climbed the front porch steps. Another deep breath and I moved to the door. No going back now. I lifted my hand to knock. But the door opened before I touched it.

The man who answered looked to be in his early forties. He had a polished clean cut look about him, the kind of look that made women take notice without being pretty-boyish enough to make men hate him for it; light brown hair spiked in a messy-on-purpose style, lively gray eyes and a carefree smile. Height-wise, he was on the shorter side. But what he lacked in inches, he made up for in biceps and triceps and whatever muscles made a man look like he belonged on the cover of a romance novel. I knew the type. He was the jock who would've stuffed me in a locker in high school, the frat boy who would've made my life hell if I'd gone to college and every young cheerleader's wet dream. To my relief, he was dressed even more casually than I was; untucked t-shirt obnoxiously snug enough to show off his muscles, jeans and bare feet. As he moved to the center of the doorway, my eyes were immediately drawn to a tribal-style tattoo that spanned the length of his right arm. Inked all in black, it began with the head and extended claw of a dragon on his inner arm above the wrist. The rest of the beast's body snaked up his arm, wings drawn back, clawed limbs tensed like the creature was maneuvering its way down his arm. Its spiked tail coiled around his well-defined upper arm and disappeared beneath the sleeve of his shirt. "Charlie. It's nice to finally put a face with the name." He extended the inked arm and shook my hand, a firm welcoming greeting accompanied by a genuine smile, and I immediately decided that I liked him.

"Sorry. You've got me at a loss," I confessed. "Who're you?"

"Brian Mason. I'm your new housemate." His grin widened as he stepped aside and motioned for me to come in. As I moved into a foyer that was easily twice the size of my bedroom back at the facility, Brian shut the door. "Welcome to fifty-five Sycamore."

"Thanks," I muttered, taking in the cathedral ceilings, ritzy décor and works of art that looked like they belonged on the walls of a museum. A living room full of classy leather furniture branched off to the right of the foyer. On the far side of the room, there was a minibar and a huge flat screen television that would've made my friend Bob at the facility drool with envy.

Brian ushered me toward the living room and I looked down at my sneakers. Was I supposed to take them off before stepping on the carpet?

"Don't worry about the carpet. Make yourself at home." He flashed me a beaming smile as he stepped into the room and I followed, feeling like I'd just won the lottery. He sat down on the couch but as soon as I settled into the chair beside it, he clapped his hands on his thighs, hopped to his feet and moved to the bar across the room. "Can I get you a drink? Wine, beer, single malt?"

"It's a little early in the day." *Crap. That sounded rude.* Would I ever learn to filter what came out of my mouth?

Flashing his frat boy grin, he stepped behind the bar. "It's my day off and I intend to enjoy it." Grabbing a glass and a decorative bottle of scotch from beneath the counter, he poured himself a drink. "Sure you don't want one? It might help you relax a little and I guarantee you've never tasted anything like this."

"Yeah. On second thought, I will take one." Frowning, I watched him pour a drink that I probably couldn't have afforded to buy. "Is it that obvious I'm nervous?"

Brian sauntered back across the room, handed me one of the drinks and sat down. "It probably wouldn't be to most people, but I'm pretty good at sensing that sort of thing." He sunk back against the couch cushions. "I'm sure it doesn't help that I know all about you, and you didn't even know my name till a minute ago."

I nodded then took a tentative sip of the scotch. The buttery liquid slid down my throat, leaving warm hints of caramel, vanilla and honey on my tongue. Holy shit. He wasn't kidding. The stuff was amazing.

His grin widened. "What'd I tell you? It's a mouthful of heaven."

"You'd know all about that," Benjamin's deep Dark voice thundered from the foyer as he stepped in the house.

Suppressing a reflexive urge to piss myself, I downed another swig of scotch.

Brian grinned at me. "Don't mind him, Charlie. Benji's bark is worse than his bite."

Yeah. Somehow, I doubted that.

Benjamin's nightmarish glare fixed on Brian. "Call me that again and you'll be eating your meals through a straw for the next month."

Apparently not the least bit intimidated, Brian stood up, headed to the bar and poured another drink. Then he walked it over and handed it to Benjamin as he settled onto the other end of the couch. Sinking back into his own seat, Brian turned to me. "By the way, Benji's serious about the nick-name. I wouldn't call him that."

Since my mouth was full of scotch, an involuntary snort of laughter burst from my nose. Benjamin's glare shifted to me. And I cleared my throat. "Sorry."

Ignoring my apology, Benjamin returned his attention to Brian. "How much have you two discussed?"

Brian casually smoothed a wrinkle on his shirt. "Not a damn thing, Benji."

Benjamin's eyes narrowed. "Keep it up. I'll fuck up that pretty face of yours."

But Brian just grinned at him. "The ladies love a tough guy."

Benjamin actually *smiled*. "That'll be me. You'll just be the pathetic bastard with the busted face."

"And the ladies will still love me," Brian chuckled.

Dropping the smile, Benjamin took a sip of his drink. "We've got company coming soon. You should start orienting the virgin before we put him to work."

Brian stood up and grinned at me. "Come on Charlie, let's go start your orientation before the principal gives us both detention."

I hopped to my feet and looked at Benjamin, then Brian. "Uh…for the record…I'm not a virgin."

Brian answered with a nod. "In our vernacular, a virgin is a Sighted individual who never learned of our ways as a child. I know you aren't a virgin *sexually*."

"Excuse me?" I muttered, more than a little disturbed by that last statement. "How exactly would you know that?"

"I can smell a virgin a mile away," Brian replied matter-of-factly, like that was a perfectly ordinary skill.

Benjamin snickered at the baffled expression on my face. "He means that literally, but I'd put money on it being closer to a two mile radius."

Benjamin was *smiling* and *joking*. And my new housemate had just declared himself a walking virgin detector. It was enough to make me consider checking back into the loony bin.

Brian dropped to the arm of the couch. Numbly following his lead, I sat back down and took another sip of the drink I was now really glad I'd accepted.

"Let's start with a few basics," Brian suggested. "Then you and I can go out back, get some air and continue our lesson."

I managed a stiff nod.

And Brian began my first lesson. "Sighted vocabulary employs a lot of Unsighted terms. It makes it easier for us to talk in the waking world, which is our term for this world by the way. If an Unsighted person overhears us, our conversation won't sound like total gibberish. So first off, our forms in the waking world are referred to as *bodies* and our forms in Draumer are referred to as *souls*. With me so far?"

Nodding uneasily, I muttered, "So what kind of soul can smell a virgin?"

Ignoring Benjamin's laughter, Brian answered, "There really isn't a cut and dry classification for what I am. Lots of creatures aren't purely one type of soul. The basic distinction is that every creature is either a creature of Light or a creature of Darkness. The specific labels used to describe most creatures actually originated in the waking world and just sort of made their way into our vocabulary because they loosely described a particular type of soul. Creatures of Light have been called all sorts of things, angels, fairies, pixies, elves. And creatures of Darkness are generally referred to as demons but there are plenty of specific labels for Dark souls too, trolls, imps, giants, dragons. And lots of us don't fit neatly into a single category. My Unsighted mother was an elf and my Sighted father was an incubus."

"An incubus?" I'd heard the term before, but I wasn't exactly sure what it was.

Brian nodded. "Mythically speaking, an incubus is a male demon who seduces women while they're sleeping and a succubus is the female counterpart. In actuality, there are very few souls who can resist the advances of an incubus or succubus. The demons can literally charm the pants off almost any creature and talk them into doing just about anything, sexual or otherwise. My Sighted father used his charms to steal the heart of my Unsighted mother and I'm a Dark creature with both elf and incubus characteristics—"

"Which means the son of a bitch is graceful and confident and pretty to look at," Benjamin interrupted. "And he can charm almost anybody into doing whatever the hell he wants them to. It's a skill set that makes him a dangerously persuasive lawyer and an even more dangerous romantic suitor with a spot-on accuracy for sniffing out virgins."

"I also throw a pretty unforgettable party," Brian chimed in, winking at me.

Scowling disapprovingly at Brian, Benjamin shook his head.

The scotch in my belly gave me the liquid courage to look Benjamin in the eye and ask, "So what kind of soul are you?"

Eyes locked on me, Benjamin propped his feet up on the coffee table. "I'm the shadow moving in the periphery of your vision, just beyond what you consciously see. The monster that you knew was in your closet when you were a child. The feeling of dread that fills you when the lights go out and you're all alone in the dark. Your worst nightmare in the flesh. A terror so great that you dare not utter its name."

I was ready to piss myself by the time Benjamin finished, but Brian just laughed. "And Benjamin just taught you your first Sighted nursery rhyme."

"What the hell kind of nursery rhyme is that?" I muttered. "Do Sighted parents enjoy scaring the crap out of their kids?"

Benjamin grinned at me, and the temperature in the room dropped at least ten degrees. "Have you ever considered the words to the nursery rhymes and lullabies in this world?"

Ignoring both of us, Brian continued my lesson. "Benjamin is what some refer to as a boogeyman, a shape shifting demon who elicits fear. But the proper term is *shadow*. More specifically, Benjamin is the Sarrum's shadow. In Draumer, Benjamin is referred to as *the Darkness*."

"You said most Sighted terms originated in the waking world. Are shadow demons named after the silhouettes that objects cast in the light in this world?" I wondered aloud.

"No," Benjamin replied icily. "Those were named after us."

Did this guy ever utter a sentence that didn't make you want to piss yourself?

Brian cleared his throat, drawing my attention back to him. "Most of the fairytales in this world are based on actual creatures and events in Draumer. Remember the story of Peter Pan? He flew into the Darling children's window because he was chasing after his shadow. Shadows are powerful souls all on their own, but they're capable of bonding with another individual and a bonded shadow is stronger than an independent one. He inherits a lot of the qualities of the creature he's bound to and vice versa. When I say that Benjamin is the Dragon King's shadow, I mean it literally. He's bound to the Sarrum and since the King is the most powerful creature in all of Draumer, you really don't want to get on either of their bad sides."

"I figured that much out already," I muttered. "How permanent is the bond a shadow forms with another creature?"

Swinging his feet off the coffee table, Benjamin stood up. "As permanent as the bond between your head and your body. It's for life. So it isn't a choice we make lightly. Now if you'll excuse me, I've got a lot to do today." At that, he moved to the foyer and headed upstairs.

"Let's go talk outside." Brian stood and started walking. As I followed him down the hall, he gave me a quick tour. "Kitchen's on the left. Help yourself to anything you find in there. Dining room's just past the kitchen. Bathroom's across the hall. Benjamin's office is the door after that. You'll probably want to stay out of there."

"Not a problem," I muttered.

Brian let out a chuckle as he opened a set of French doors at the back of the house. "Benjamin's an acquired taste. You'll get used to him. I'd say he drops the whole scary-as-hell thing once you get to know him, but he really doesn't. You just get better at interpreting which death glares you can ignore and which are about to earn you a broken nose."

I followed Brian onto a large deck that overlooked an immaculately landscaped backyard. To our right, there was a huge grill that looked like an outdoor stove, a bar and a table and chairs. Basically, an open-air kitchen. To our left, cushioned furniture was neatly arranged around a low table beside an outdoor fireplace. "Do the Talbots live here?"

"In this shack?" Brian grinned at me as we settled into two cushioned chairs. "No. The Talbot house is much more impressive."

"This is the nicest house I've ever been in," I muttered. "How does all this work? Are we expected to

ERIN A. JENSEN

pay rent? Because I'm pretty sure this is out of my price range."

Brian shook his head. "Room and board are perks for the Talbot employees and you're basically a trainee at the moment."

I shifted uneasily in my seat. "What exactly am I training to be?"

Brian waved his hand to shoo a dragonfly that seemed intent on landing on his arm. "Well for starters, we'll be teaching you all the stuff you should've learned from a guide when you were younger."

"A guide?" The dragonfly flew toward me and I waved a hand in the air until it changed direction. "David mentioned something about being Emma's guide when we spoke in the cave, but I don't get why she needed one. She's not Sighted."

Brian cleared his throat. "I'm probably not the right person to explain their relationship to you, but a guide is the adult responsible for teaching a child about Draumer and the ways of the Sighted. When a child is born, the Sighted person closest to the family is responsible for determining if the baby is Sighted. If the baby is, that person is expected to see to it that a suitable guide is appointed. Obviously if one of the parents is Sighted, the job's theirs. If not, the closest Sighted relative usually becomes the guide and if there isn't one, the duty falls to the closest friend of the family. That person can either take on the task or appoint someone else. You're a Sighted virgin, which means you slipped through the cracks somehow and were never appointed a guide. So, we'll be giving you a crash course. I'll be guide number one and my job will be to teach you the basics. After that, you'll move on to more advanced lessons with other guides and we'll determine what type of work you're best suited for, but I'll always be around to answer any questions you've got along the way. After all your training's done, you'll probably be offered the opportunity to make this arrangement permanent and come to work for the family."

There had to be some fine print he was glossing over. Call-me-Arthur warned me not to blindly pledge myself in service to the Dragon King. "I've got a couple questions."

Brian flicked the persistent dragonfly off his arm. "That's what I'm here for. Fire away."

"How can you tell if a baby is Sighted?"

"Same way you determine if anybody's Sighted, unmask and see if they shine."

"Yeah…uh." I downed my last sip of scotch. "I have no idea what you just said."

"Sorry." Brian flashed me an apologetic smile. "This whole guide thing's new to me. The words are such a part of my vocabulary that I don't even think about it. *Unmask* means to reveal your soul. In fact, it's actually where the expression 'bare your soul' came from."

"So unmasking is flipping to your Dream form," I muttered. "Got it."

Brian extended an index finger and watched the dragonfly crawl onto it. "Those are made up terms. If you don't want to be referred to as a virgin, you should start using the proper ones."

"You said you unmask to see if they *shine*. What does that mean?"

Brian flipped his hand over and the dragonfly moved to his palm. "*Shining* is the involuntary brightening of the eyes that occurs when a Sighted person sees someone unmask."

"Uh," I muttered, feeling stupid despite Brian's patient teaching style. "I've never seen that happen."

He looked up at me as the dragonfly traveled up the tattoo on his arm. "Makes sense. You haven't been around many Sighted people. Just unmask and watch my eyes."

I cleared my throat. "I don't know how to unmask."

"You'll learn," Brian whispered, standing from his chair. "Follow me." I followed him through the French doors, back to the foyer and up the stairs. Benjamin was just stepping out of a bedroom when we reached the second floor. Eyeing us, he pulled the door shut.

"You heading downstairs?" Brian asked.

Benjamin glanced at me, then nodded.

"Good. I need you for a demonstration." Brian turned around and headed downstairs without waiting for a response, and I followed with Benjamin close behind me. As we stepped into the living room, Brian flashed me an encouraging smile then turned to Benjamin. "I need to demonstrate what shining looks like and our new friend doesn't know how to unmask yet."

I cringed internally, waiting for Benjamin's icy glare to belittle me. Instead the shadow's expression softened as he looked at me. "Step closer and watch my eyes."

Numb from the shock of Benjamin's kind words and probably also from the scotch, I did as he said. I was a little relieved Benjamin would be demonstrating the shine and not the unmasking. I wasn't sure I was ready to find out what a shadow looked like.

Brian stepped toward us and Benjamin put a hand on my shoulder. "You're going to feel him unmask and you'll want to turn and look, but the shine's just a quick flash. Keep your eyes on me so you don't miss it."

Nodding, I looked into Benjamin's eyes and an involuntary shiver crept down my spine. Benjamin's gaze shifted to Brian and I felt him unmask, but I stayed focused on the infinite Darkness of Benjamin's eyes. A flash lit the darkness, wringing his iris with bright light. An instant later it was gone.

I stayed focused on Benjamin's eyes, waiting for him to give me the okay to look away. When he nodded, I turned to look at my number one guide.

Brian still basically looked like Brian, except for the fact that his ears were pointy. He was dressed all in black, heavy black boots, black pants and a black sleeveless shirt with decorative stitching that was also black. The dragon tattoo still snaked up his right arm and a second dragon was inked in black on his face. The beast's head and front claws were above his left eyebrow and its body snaked down his temple and along his cheek with its spiked tail extending to just below the corner of his mouth. He looked less like a clean cut frat boy and more like a no-nonsense warrior you'd definitely think twice about pissing off.

"Nice ink," I muttered. "You aren't required to get tattoos when you join the family, are you?"

"That *ink* is the mark of the Sarrum," Benjamin growled. "And it is definitely meant to make someone think twice about pissing him off."

So the mind-reading thing wasn't limited to the Dream World and Benjamin could do it too, maybe because the Sarrum could? Brian did say the bond allowed them to share some abilities. I took a step back from Benjamin. "Sorry. I didn't mean to be disrespectful."

Benjamin just stared at me, his expression utterly unreadable.

And Brian re-masked or whatever the opposite of unmasking was. "You didn't sound disrespectful and you aren't required to get tattoos when you join the family. Mine served a very specific purpose when I got them. They were part of the uniform for my first assignment."

"I've got to get to the airport." Benjamin moved to the foyer and opened the front door.

I watched the door close after him, wondering what type of assignment would require you to permanently ink your body.

4

EMMA

Panic gripped me as the Water dragged me under. *How did I end up in the Water?* My lungs were burning, begging me to breathe. *And it was so cold.* This was how it would end. I was going to die, frozen and alone, terrified and forgotten. Unable to resist the urge, I sucked in a desperate attempt at a breath, filling my lungs with ice water. I wanted to scream, but I couldn't. There was nothing I could do to stop this. This was *supposed* to happen. *I was meant to die in the Waters...*

...Warm lips planted a chaste kiss on my forehead, rescuing me from the nightmare. I kept my eyes closed as he drew back the covers and listened as his bare feet padded across the floor to the bathroom. When the door clicked shut, I opened my eyes and rolled toward it. A warm breeze wafted from the window and I shivered, more because of a feeling I couldn't shake than the temperature. It was a sink-ing feeling, like everything was wrong with the world and it'd never be right again. It'd settled in the pit of my stomach the day I came home from the facility. *Home* was supposed to feel comfortable, like slipping into your favorite sweater. Only it didn't fit right any-more. Everyone was keeping me at arm's length, as if there were secrets I didn't deserve to know. And I hated the new housekeeper, but not just because she wasn't Isa. I could see the fear in her eyes when she looked at me and she acted like David was a monster. I got why she hated me. Who wouldn't hate the wom-an who'd stabbed her predecessor? But what reason did she have to fear my husband?

David had been extremely patient with me since I'd come home. He'd moved himself into the guest bedroom across the hall before I even set foot in the house. It was a cautious gesture, so I wouldn't feel pressured, but he hadn't spent a single night in that guestroom. I still hadn't sorted anything out. The man behind that door could be an adulterer. He might even be a murderer. I probably should've pushed him away, but I'd spent too many nights ly-ing awake in an empty bed at the facility. I needed to feel him next to me, his warm breath, his strong arms, but he never assumed. He always waited for my invitation, though it didn't have to be spoken. He just knew, like he'd always known. He hadn't done anything more than hold me in his arms. He hadn't even attempted more because he knew I didn't want him to. *Honestly, who was I kidding?* Even that gentle kiss on my forehead had roused every nerve in my body. And yet, I couldn't let him touch me, not if his hands had touched someone else. How could I stay with him if that was the case? I slid the covers off my legs and grimaced at the ugly contraption strapped to my ankle—my house arrest ankle bracelet. I couldn't leave David even if I was absolutely certain I wanted to. I was literally a prisoner in my own home.

Behind the door, the water started running in the shower. I slid out of bed and walked across the hall to the guestroom. I needed to use the facilities and I couldn't look at him just yet, not before coffee and definitely not when he was standing naked in a glass-walled shower just a few feet away. Swallowing the lump in my throat, I shut the guestroom door behind me. I *ached* to go back over there and join him. I didn't want to think anymore. Thinking hurt too much. I just wanted to feel his skin pressed against mine and taste his beautiful mouth. That was the only thing I *was* sure of. I stepped into the bathroom and closed the door.

I used the facilities, washed my hands and splashed some water on my face. Then I exhaled an unsteady breath, tugged off my tank top and slipped out of my pajama shorts and panties, letting them drop to the floor at my feet. I *ached* for the feel of him. It'd been so long. I stood there for a minute, naked and vulnerable, my brain warring with my body and my heart. Fighting back tears, I slid the shower door open. *I will not go over there.* I stepped in, slid the door closed, turned on the water and ice cold water came pouring down on me. Good. Maybe the cold would snap me out of this. I adjusted the temperature, turned and tipped my head back into the stream of hot water. I let it run over me and tried not to picture David standing naked in another stream of water right across the hall. Combing my fingers through the tangled strands of my wet hair, I turned around and reached for the knob but I stopped myself before turning off the water. *You will not go over there.* Maybe if I said it to myself enough times, I'd stop being so weak and pathetic. Fingers shaking, I picked up the shampoo bottle but the sound of a door opening made me fumble with it and it slipped from my hands. I looked across the room. The bathroom door was still shut. It was the bedroom door that'd opened. I drew a deep breath. David was out there getting dressed. I shouldn't desperately want him to walk through the bathroom door. I shouldn't be aching for him to yank the shower door open and step into the shower with me. But the thought of it, the possibility of him bolting through that door and possessing me with his hands and his mouth and melding his naked body to mine, just the thought had my body throbbing with need. I sagged against the shower wall, needing to be touched and hating myself for needing him. A painful urge to touch myself where I needed him to touch me had my body trembling and I dug my nails into the palms of my hands, fighting it, denying myself even that slight release. My life was such a hopeless mess. How could I keep doing this? Seeing him every single day, lying beside him every night, feeling the heat of his breath on my skin and not touching him. He might've betrayed me, hurt me in the worst possible way, but my body couldn't stop wanting him and neither could my heart.

I hastily finished showering and wrapped myself up in a towel but by the time I worked up the nerve to open the door to the bedroom, he was gone.

"...Emma?" Dr. Song's gentle voice was tinged with sadness. I met his eyes, brown and warm like always, but there was sorrow in them today. He smiled, but it only made his eyes look sadder. "This is our last session together. Are you going to tell me what's on your mind?"

I smiled back at him and whispered, "Does it matter? You'll be done with me after today."

The doctor exhaled a slow steady breath. "You'll like Dr. Price, Emma. His credentials are a hell of a lot more impressive than mine."

The sinking feeling grew a little heavier and I let out a laugh that sounded more like a sob. "Sure."

I'd lost the only person I could really talk things through with, and I'd left the facility before Charlie was even allowed out of wherever they'd taken him after he attacked David. I never got to say goodbye or ask what made him go after my husband.

Dr. Song stood from his chair and walked past me to the window. He drew back the curtains and slid the window open, and the scent of salt water and the sound of crashing waves wafted in with the sunshine. Rolling his sleeves up, he passed my chair and sat down in his.

I wasn't going to cry. It wasn't Dr. Song's fault that he was abandoning me. He had no more say in the matter than I did, and I had no say at all. He hadn't really helped me work through anything, but he made me feel calmer. Our sessions were a comfort. But David was replacing Dr. Song. Feeling calmer wasn't good enough. David needed to fix me, so he'd sent for another doctor with more impressive credentials.

Dr. Price was the Talbot family's physician over in England. He was also an old college friend of David's. They'd come to America to attend college together. David liked it so much that he never went back, but Dr. Price had gone home to take his expected place caring exclusively for the Talbot family. I'd never met the man and I didn't really want to. Having him treat me was just another way for David to control my life. My therapy sessions were supposed to be confidential, but I doubted that would matter to David's old friend. He was a spy, coming to tell David what was going on inside my messed up head, coming to fix what was wrong with me but I was too broken to fix. David should've just let me die the night I slit my wrist. I looked down at my wrist and absently traced a finger over the scar.

"Emma?"

I jumped at the sound of my name.

Dr. Song let out a sigh as he placed his hand on top of mine. "It *will* be alright, Princess. Dr. Price is going to help you."

I shivered and felt myself sink a little deeper. *Princess?* That was David's pet name for me. *Why would the doctor call me that?*

The doctor squeezed my hand and smiled, but there was so much sorrow in his eyes. "I promise you, Emma. It will be better soon."

I closed my eyes as his words wrapped around me like a warm blanket. "It has to be. I can't do this anymore."

"Soon you won't have to," he whispered, and warmth flooded through me with his words.

5

I let myself into the boss's house from the garage. A heavy silence hung in the air, exaggerating the echo of my footsteps as I stepped into the foyer. I headed to the dining room, not really expecting to find anyone there. Things were pretty strained between the two of them but if they were eating breakfast together, they'd at least be attempting to have a conversation. I stepped through the archway into the dining room. A platter of pastries and fresh fruit sat on the table and the smell of coffee still lingered in the air, but only one of the plates had crumbs on it and only one cup had a cold forgotten sip of coffee at the bottom. The second place setting hadn't been touched.

Her thudding heart informed me of her presence before she made any external sound. I turned around slowly so I wouldn't spook her. The imp was a skittish creature. You had to be careful not to make sudden moves around her, especially if you were me. I suppose I should've given her props for never pissing herself in front of me, although there had been a couple close calls. She was such a quivering bundle of nerves. I usually went out of my way to avoid her, but it was too late for that. I should've known she'd be hovering somewhere nearby.

Her beady eyes met mine, which was a monumental improvement over our first encounters. "Good morning, sir. Can I get you a cup of coffee?"

"Yeah. I'll take a cup." Her timid squeak was like fingernails on a chalkboard. It wasn't hard to see why she irritated the crap out of the boss, but he didn't exactly have loads of applicants lined up to be his new housekeeper after what happened to the last one. A pang of sorrow gripped me at the thought. If Doc couldn't heal them… How much longer could things go on the way they were?

With a subservient nod, the imp scurried back to the kitchen. "Cream and sugar?" she squeaked from the other room.

"No. I take it Black. Same as yesterday." *And every other fucking day.* How many cups of coffee did she have to pour me before she remembered that? *Black, like my eyes and my skin and my soul, for fuck's sake.* How hard was that to remember?

"Of course," she squeaked. "Sorry, Sir."

I bit down on my tongue. I was on edge. We'd been in limbo for too fucking long, all of us. But the imp in the kitchen wasn't the one to take it out on.

Cup clinking against the saucer with the tremor of her hands, she stepped out of the kitchen but she didn't meet my eyes.

I met her halfway across the floor and ignored the way she cringed when I took the cup from her. It was time to make my exit before she lost the battle with her tear ducts or her bladder. "Where's the boss?"

Her heart was beating so damn fast, I half expected it to explode. That'd be just what we needed, another death to explain. "In his office," she squeaked without looking up.

"Thanks for the coffee." I started toward the boss's office without waiting for a response.

The boss called, "Come in," from behind the closed door of his office before I even had a chance to knock.

Opening the door, I found him at his desk with a cup of coffee in hand and a case file spread across the desktop. He swiveled his chair toward me. "Morning."

I closed the door and settled into the chair in front of his desk. "The imp's getting braver. She didn't spill my coffee on herself today."

The boss grimaced. "I'd almost rather do the housework myself at this point. We really ought to fire her and put her out of her misery, but I'm not sure how we'd explain her dismissal to Emma."

I sipped my coffee and closed my eyes, savoring it for a second before answering. At least the imp made good coffee. "Emma can't stand her either. Do you really think she'd care?"

Brow furrowed, he leaned back in his chair. "She'd assume it had something to do with what she did to Isa."

I took another slow sip and considered that for a second. "Tell her she quit because I made her piss herself."

He answered with a faint smile. "I suppose that's believable enough but I think we're changing enough as it is for now."

I sat my cup on the edge of the boss's desk. "She'll warm up to Doc soon enough and once he fixes everything, she'll understand."

He exhaled and an elegant wave of blue smoke wafted from his nostrils and swirled through the air, filling the room with his scent. "*If* he fixes everything. I'm not fool enough to assume that's a sure bet. He's skilled, but we're asking him to work miracles."

I grabbed my cup and downed another sip. "He *has* to work miracles. We don't have any other options."

The color drained from the boss's face, just for a split second but it was enough to make me regret my words. My edginess was nothing compared to his.

It was foolish of me to forget that. "What time does their flight get here?"

I glanced at my watch. "Three hours from now. I'll be there in two."

Looking more through me than at me, the boss nodded. "Bring him by after they get settled. I'll be here all day."

"No appointments?"

"A few, but they're meeting me here." He shot a sideways glance at the door. "I'm not comfortable leaving her yet."

There was so much heartache in his eyes. It wasn't like him to let that show, even if it was just me. This was starting to take its toll on him. For Doc's sake, I hoped he could make good on his promises. Hell, for everyone's sake. "It's good that you're here. She needs to know you're close by."

He let out a humorless chuckle. "I'm not so sure she'd agree with you, but that's beside the point. I need to be here."

I dropped my voice to a whisper, "I know."

He cleared his throat, banishing the sorrow from his expression. "Did the lost dragon show up this morning?"

I lifted my cup for another sip, realized it was empty and sat it back down on his desk. "He did."

The boss raised an eyebrow. "And?"

"There's not much to tell. He's about as virginal as it gets, doesn't even know how to unmask." I couldn't help breaking into a grin. "Speaking of virginal, Brian freaked the hell out of him by telling him he could smell a virgin."

I felt a bit of satisfaction watching the boss crack a smile. "Sorry I missed it."

"I'll keep you posted on his progress, but I don't think you need to clear your schedule anytime soon. He's got a lot to learn before he'll be ready for any lessons from you." I looked down at my watch. "I'd better take off. I want to check on Isa before I head to the airport. I'll text you once everyone's settled."

He nodded.

And I left the room and exited the house in stealth mode. I'd already used up all my patience for the day. If I heard one more squeak out of that imp, I'd lose it and it was too early in the day to deal with the smell of piss.

6

CHARLIE

I had no idea how long I'd been sitting in the overstuffed armchair, staring at the layout of my new bedroom. If I weren't Sighted, I'd have been pinching the hell out of myself and expecting to wake up back at the facility. After Benjamin left the house, Brian had taken me upstairs to check out my room. He said he had some business to attend to and told me to make myself at home. I'd already checked out every inch of the room. The closet was full of clothes, really nice clothes. I couldn't decide whether to be impressed or creeped out by the fact that they were all my size. The bed was amazing, even more comfortable than the one at the hotel. I had my own bathroom, fully stocked with towels and more bathroom products than I knew what to do with. And I had a desk with a brand new computer. It all seemed a little too good to be true.

Call-me-Arthur's warning kept knocking around in the back of my head. I could see why people would *blindly pledge themselves in service to the Dragon King.* There were a lot of perks. I made a mental note to pay Call-me-Art a visit sometime soon. I needed a reality check. There had to be a downside to all this.

Brian was awesome, but I was a little disappointed that I hadn't seen the Talbots yet. Maybe I was an idiot, but I'd figured David would be the one teaching me. Brian did say I'd move on to *more advanced lessons* later on. I suppose the Sarrum had more important things to do than teach some Dream Sighted *virgin* a bunch of stuff he should've learned when he was in diapers. To be honest, I was really disappointed that Emma wasn't around. I was dying to see her again. She was falling apart when I last saw her at the facility. She didn't know if she could trust her husband. He might've cheated on her, he also might've murdered the woman he cheated with and now Emma was stuck with him no matter what. They'd taken her from the facility and put her under house arrest. I was seriously worried about her, and the way Brian changed the subject when I asked about Emma and David's relationship wasn't exactly reassuring.

No matter how cool my new room was, I didn't feel like sitting alone anymore. Brian did say to make myself at home. If he was still busy, I could always check out the monster television in the living room. I hopped up and made my way downstairs, feeling a little like a trespasser in the unfamiliar house. I grinned at the sound of pots and pans clinking together in the kitchen. Hopefully, Brian was the one making all the noise. I couldn't exactly picture Benjamin doing anything domestic. It was a lot easier to picture him tearing into the flesh of a helpless animal he'd killed with his bare hands.

Brian looked up as I walked in the kitchen. "Perfect timing. I could use another set of hands."

I let out an unintentional snort of laughter. "I doubt anybody would want to be subjected to my cooking."

Brian raised an eyebrow. "How much cooking have you done?"

"Not much," I answered with a shrug. "They didn't exactly have culinary classes at the nuthouse, and my mom was always afraid to let me near the knives."

Looking genuinely saddened by my response, Brian frowned. "Well the joke's on all of them because I'm going to teach you how to cook like a champ."

I stepped up to the counter beside him. "A cooking champ?"

Brian flashed his frat boy grin and shook his head. "Shut up. You know what I mean. Forget about all that crap from your past, Charlie. You aren't crazy. You're a freaking *dragon*. It doesn't get any cooler than that."

I couldn't stop myself from grinning like a cheese-ball. "I knew there was a reason I liked you. But seriously, you're gonna have to give me some guidance. I'm clueless in the kitchen."

He tossed a few plastic bags of fresh vegetables at me. "So we'll take it slow. You can start by washing these."

"*That* I can do." I grabbed the bags, carried them to the sink, turned on the water and started dumping the vegetables in. "This is a lot of food. How many people are we cooking for?" I knew it was stupid to get my hopes up, but I really wanted him to say that Emma was coming.

"Emma's not coming." Did he read my mind? Or was I just that obvious? Abandoning the potatoes he was peeling, Brian walked over to me and shut the water off. "You won't be seeing her for a while, Charlie. She's got a lot going on right now and seeing you would just confuse her."

"What the hell does that mean?" I turned to him, searching his eyes for some hint of an answer. "What's she got going on? And how would I confuse her?"

Brian let out a heavy sigh. "I get it. I'm pretty close to her too and we're all worried about her, but there's a lot happening that you don't understand and I'm not the right person to explain it to you."

I knew it wasn't Brian's fault and he did seem genuinely sorry, but I couldn't stifle the rage that was simmering inside me. "Yeah. You said that before. What happened to all that *I'll always be around to answer your questions* bullshit?"

"Look, it's not my place—" Brian didn't get a chance to finish his sentence.

He was interrupted by the sound of the front door opening, lots of stomping feet and dull thuds that sounded like heavy things being set down. *Luggage?* When Benjamin left the house earlier, he said he was off to the airport.

Benjamin's voice thundered from the foyer, "Down the hall, first door to your right."

And a sweet feminine voice answered, "Thank you."

Brian elbowed me and whispered, "Let's go meet our house guests." There was a look of regret on his face, a look that made me feel like an asshole for jumping down his throat.

But I was so out of my element with everything that was happening, I didn't really know what to say. So I just nodded and muttered, "Sorry for being an asshole."

Brian smirked at me. "Are you kidding? I live with Benjamin. You're a freaking ray of sunshine. You want to see an asshole? Finish the last of the coffee in the house and watch him come into the kitchen in the morning."

I did my best to stifle my snort of laughter. For all I knew, Benjamin could read our minds from the foyer. At the very least, I was guessing he had the hearing of a hawk. "Thanks for the warning. I'll be sure never to drink the last of the coffee."

"Fuck you both," Benjamin grumbled from the foyer. *Yup. Hearing of a hawk.*

Brian winked at me as he headed out of the kitchen and I followed him to the foyer, wondering who the heck these houseguests were. *Wasn't I the guest?*

Benjamin glared at me. "No, asshole. Orientation's over. Now earn your keep and help us get these bags upstairs."

"Yeah, okay," I muttered, wondering what'd happened to the semi-friendly guy who demonstrated what shining looked like earlier.

Benjamin narrowed his eyes at me. "Never joke about depriving me of coffee. There's nothing funny about that."

A black man in his mid-fifties with a bald head and a graying goatee walked through the door as Benjamin finished his sentence. He was wearing black-rimmed glasses and a black suit jacket over a dark gray button down shirt, and the leather bag in his arms was practically bursting at the seams. Dark eyes dancing with laughter, he spoke in a soft jovial voice with a British accent, "There's nothing funny about anything as far as this old bastard's concerned."

A low growl erupted from Benjamin's throat and the man took a step backward, but his friendly smile never faltered. "Come on, Benjamin. Let us in the door before you get all pissy on us."

Still growling under his breath, Benjamin shut the door and motioned for the man to move to the living room. Grinning, the man dropped his bag at Benjamin's feet. "Your hospitality is mindboggling, Darkness."

The three of us followed our new guest into the living room, and Brian extended his inked arm in greeting. "Welcome to our house, Dr. Price. My name's Brian Mason. Please make yourself at home here."

The doctor's grin widened as he took Brian's hand. "Good to meet you, Brian. It's nice to see someone has some manners around here." Dropping Brian's hand, he turned his attention to me. "And you must be the virgin dragon I've been hearing so much about."

Just as he said it, a girl who looked to be in her early twenties stepped in the room. She was thin and couldn't have been much more than five feet tall, but she seemed to fill up the space around her more than she should. Her jet black hair was shorter in the back and it swung forward just below her chin, creating a frame for her delicate face. Her doe-like eyes were a rich chocolate brown and her skin was the color of coffee with just the perfect amount of cream. Her youthful features looked vaguely Hispanic, and her cheeks blushed a deep shade of pink when she heard the doctor call me *the virgin dragon.*

I could only imagine how red my face must've been. Seconds after her eyes locked with mine, her gaze dropped to the floor. *Great. Awesome first impression. Thanks, Doc.* I turned back to the doctor. His hand was out, waiting to shake mine. I took it, realized I should probably say something and muttered, "I'm Charlie."

Grinning like he knew my attention was focused on the girl behind him, he turned and motioned for her to join us.

As she timidly approached us, her eyes met mine with a look of nervous hesitation that made my insides tingle.

The doctor put an arm around her shoulder and didn't seem to notice the way she shrunk at the contact. "This is Isabella's daughter, Rose."

Brian nodded without extending his hand. He'd obviously picked up on her reaction to being touched. "It's nice to finally meet you, Rose. We're glad to have you here."

She barely met Brian's eyes. "Thank you. It's nice to be here."

Her eyes darted to me, and I nodded. "Hey. I'm Charlie." *Duh. You said that already. Now I was a virgin and a moron.*

She answered with a shy grin. "Nice to meet you."

"Likewise." *Likewise? Great. I was a tool, too.*

Benjamin cleared his throat, and the look on his face almost stopped my heart. It was like a flashback to the day I first met him. That was how he'd looked at me when he saw my arm around Emma. *But all I did was say "hi."* Rose seemed much more nervous around Brian and the doctor. So why was Benjamin glaring at me?

As soon as I finished the thought, Benjamin's glare shifted to the doctor. And his arm dropped to his side like Rose's shoulder had given him an electric shock. *Okay. So it wasn't just me.* I waited for Benjamin's glare to shift to Brian.

Grinning, Brian winked at me as he moved toward the foyer. "Come on. Let's help get these bags upstairs."

I followed Brian and hoisted a hefty suitcase off the floor before Benjamin could call me an asshole again. Then I lugged it upstairs, wondering who these new people were and what I'd done to piss Benjamin off.

7

EMMA

I managed to make it till evening without running into David. I'd waited to eat until after my session with Dr. Song to avoid him at breakfast and the rest of the day was just a blur. I'd moved aimlessly through the house, lost in thought. David had been working from home since I'd come back. He'd stop anything he was doing at the drop of a hat for me. I didn't doubt that for a second, and I'd spent the better part of my day talking myself out of going to him.

My aimless wandering had eventually taken me out to the terrace, where I curled up in a lounge chair with a blanket wrapped around my legs and a book in hand. I'd been staring at the same page for so long that the sun was beginning to set. I shut the book as absently as I'd opened it. I needed to see him. It was an aching desperation that gnawed at my insides. I'd been fighting it all day, but I needed to feel his arms around me. A mental picture of Sophie's naked body tangled up with his flashed through my head and I tossed the blanket and book aside, raced across the terrace and yanked the French doors open.

I hurried down the hall and rushed into the bathroom as the contents of my stomach barreled up my throat. Dropping to my knees on the tile in front of the toilet, I coughed and retched until every vile chunk of my breakfast came up. Another vision of that whore's body writhing on top of my husband's flashed through my head and my empty stomach clenched and heaved bitter yellow bile until there was nothing left to expel. Sucking in an acrid breath, I wiped my mouth with the back of my hand and stood on shaking legs. I moved to the sink, turned on the water and cupped it in my hands to rinse my mouth. *He was such a bastard.* With a ragged sob, I turned off the water, dropped my head in my hands and wept over the sink. *I hated him so much.* I needed to scream at him, and throw things, and hit him until he understood, until he hurt like I hurt. Without consciously registering what I was doing, I marched out of the bathroom and headed toward his office. I was a clammy trembling mess and my breath reeked of vomit, but I didn't care. David didn't deserve any effort from me. He deserved my rage and my hatred. He deserved to hurt.

Muffled voices were conversing behind the door to David's office as I neared it—David's strong confident voice, Benjamin's deep voice and a new voice I didn't recognize. *What was I doing?* Did I really want to barge in there and make a scene in front of Benjamin and whoever else was in there? Another wave of nausea gripped me and I started to back away, but the door opened. David stepped out and shut the door behind him. Heartache and longing flared in his eyes as they locked with mine for a few pounding heartbeats. Then his features settled into the familiar mask, perfectly calm and controlled. *Always in control.* I tried to cling to the rage I'd felt marching over but it slipped away as he looked at me, patiently waiting for whatever I'd come to do. If I screamed and threw things and hit him, he'd stand there and take it. I could see it in his eyes. Another wave of nausea washed over me and my eyes welled with tears. *Damn it. He wasn't supposed to see that.*

He let the mask slip away as he stepped toward me. And I melted, trembling and sobbing and reeking of vomit. Without a word, he wrapped his arms around me.

Hands balled into fists at my sides, I fought the urge to sink against the warm comfort of his chest. "Don't touch me," I sobbed in a broken whisper.

He just stood there and held me, knowing how badly I needed his touch.

"I hate you," the words barreled from my throat as reflexively as the vomit had.

He drew a sharp breath, but he didn't say a word. He just tightened his hold on me. Unable to resist, I sunk against his chest and a tightness loosened inside me. For several minutes, we just stood there in silence.

He was the one who finally spoke. "Have you eaten dinner?"

I cleared my throat but my voice still came out gravelly, "I'm not hungry."

He tilted his head back to meet my eyes. "You need to eat, something light if your stomach isn't up to more." I didn't know how he could think about food with the foul stench of my breath in his face. Suddenly self-conscious about my vomit-breath, I dropped my head to his chest but he reached down and gently took hold of my chin. Then he tilted my head up and brushed his lips against mine, a tender whisper of a kiss. Wrapping his arm back around me, he whispered, "Don't hide from me, Princess. Don't ever hide yourself from me."

I turned my head toward his office. "Is Dr. Price in there?"

David's slow exhalation heated the nape of my neck, sending a warm shiver through me. "He is. Would you like to meet him?"

"No."

"Then let's go get something to eat." He started down the hall, gently sweeping me along with him.

I glanced over my shoulder. "Aren't you going to tell them you're leaving?"

Slipping his arm to my waist, he whispered, "They'll figure it out."

※

I excused myself to freshen up while David was telling Sara what to fix us for dinner. I'd brushed my teeth and swished with mouthwash twice. Now I stood at the mirror, barely recognizing the pathetic girl staring back at me. Had I always been this weak? *No.* I'd been stronger. *Before.* Before what? Something had changed. And then everything had changed. And I hated my husband for it. But it wasn't just the incident with Sophie. Horrible as that was, there was something else. Something came before that night. The ground had already been crumbling out from under me. *But why?* It almost felt like a dream I'd woken up from. I couldn't recall what'd happened but the feeling of dread had stuck with me. There was another reason to hate David. *A reason to fear him.* I was sure of it but for the life of me, I couldn't recall what it was.

I drew a deep breath and opened the bathroom door. I was being ridiculous. The incident with Sophie was more than enough reason to hate him. *But not to fear him.*

As I stepped in the dining room, David smiled at me and something in his eyes melted the fear and hatred inside me as he watched me cross the room. How many times had he watched me like that? Too many to count, but it never stopped affecting me. That look in his eyes was all the foreplay I needed. A twinge of arousal flared inside me and my body was instantly aching for him. I hated that he could still do that to me. *Had he looked at Sophie like that?* I couldn't give in to it, no matter how much my body begged for him. *I wouldn't give in.*

He slid the chair beside his back from the table and I sat, willing the beat of my heart to slow down. I fought the primal thrill that surged through me as he pushed my chair in. Turning to face him, I slid my chair back several inches. A mix of pain and anger and lust was brazenly visible on his face as he pivoted toward me. *No mask. Not perfectly in control. Just him.*

His raw display of emotion was like a match striking inside me. I sat there staring at him, breathing too loud and too heavy. I knew I should cling to the heartache and rage I'd felt earlier, but I couldn't. Nothing registered but the flames that licked at me from the inside, heating the places where I needed him to touch me. God help me. I needed to feel him, pressed against me, moving inside me.

He didn't say anything but his hand gripped the tablecloth, bunching the fabric beneath his fingers as he sat there watching me. I wanted those fingers to fist in my hair. I wanted him to knock all the dishes off the table and lift me onto it. He leaned forward, and my body throbbed for him—

"This soup is very mild," Sara announced as she stepped through the door with a steaming crock of soup in her pot-holdered hands. "There's nothing in it that might upset the stomach."

Her voice was like a slap to the face, startling me back to my senses. I slid my chair back.

And David's mask snapped back in place.

I stood on trembling legs and muttered, "I don't think I'm up to it." Without meeting David's eyes, I turned and raced for the door.

The sound of a fist slamming on the table and a startled yelp echoed down the hall as I headed for the terrace, but I didn't slow down. I needed air. David's muffled growl was audible as I reached the French doors but I didn't catch his words. Yanking the doors open, I stepped out onto the terrace. The words didn't matter. It was all in his tone. He was furious that Sara had interrupted us and he was making that abundantly clear. I closed the doors and moved to the book and blanket I'd left lying on the floor. I sat the book on the table beside the lounge chair and folded the blanket in half. Still aching for my husband's touch, I clutched the blanket to my chest and dropped into the chair.

A moment later, the French doors flew open. David stormed through them and slammed them shut. Then he moved toward me, drawing deep hungry breaths.

I tensed, wanting him to leave and needing him to stay.

His pace slowed. So did his breathing. When he reached me, he sat down on the foot of the lounge chair. I waited for him to say something, not really sure what I even wanted him to say. But he just watched me. The mask was in place but I could see the tension in his jaw muscles.

A hundred times, I almost told him how much I needed him, how much I missed the feel of him. But I stopped myself a hundred times, waiting for him to speak first. *He was so beautiful. Why couldn't I just give in?*

With a wistful sigh, he stood and kissed my forehead. "You should eat something." Then he moved to the doors, yanked them open and left me alone before I could ask him to stay.

I wrapped the blanket around me, vainly trying to stifle a shiver that had nothing to do with the temperature. Then I curled up in a ball and cried myself to sleep.

8

I only moved a few paces down the hall from the doors to the terrace. This was slowly killing her. And watching it, being powerless to fix it, was killing me. Benjamin kept cautioning that I was depleting myself too much, but I'd gladly give every breath in my body to bring her back to me. I'd been criticized incessantly for wedding a non-dragon, a creature of Light no less, a creature who required a constant drain of energy to survive in the Darkness. Keeping her in the Dark, draining her body of Light was a selfish choice, but dragons do not part with their treasures and there was nothing I treasured more than Emma. I could never have stopped myself from taking her. One could argue that she was never mine to take, but she'd be the first to disagree...

...I looked down at the bouquet in my hand and brushed a fingertip over a pale pink rose petal. The air

inside the elevator was too stale and thin. I loathed being caged in small spaces and the fact that I had little interest in the task at hand certainly didn't help. The elevator doors opened and I stepped out with a resolute sigh. A few steps down the sterile hallway, I found myself at the nurse's station.

I cleared my throat and three sets of female eyes lifted, a middle aged woman with graying hair and an expanding midsection, a wiry black woman with intricately braided hair and a petite young thing who couldn't be much more than twenty. "Hello, ladies. Could one of you please direct me to Judy Reed's room?"

Three bodies heated at the sound of my voice and the youngest one's cheeks blushed an obvious shade of pink that rivaled the ribbon on the bouquet in my hand. She eagerly hopped to her feet. "Of course. Follow me."

I nodded to the other two, ignoring the scent of their arousal. It was a blatant odor that didn't mingle well with the fragrance of the flowers in my hand. Frankly, I didn't want to be there and I had no interest in any of these women.

I followed the exaggerated swing of the hips in front of me, itching to get the hell out of the sterile facility. The place reeked of disinfectant and flowers and wet cunt. The swinging hips halted at a closed door and the girl turned and flashed what she believed to be a seductive smile. Without taking her eyes off me, she knocked on the door.

Judy's cheery voice answered, "Come in."

And the nurse motioned for me to go in, but continued to stand there blocking my entry. "If there's anything else I can do for you, please come find me."

Nodding my thanks, I reached around her to open the door, stepped into the room and promptly shut the door in her face.

"David!" Judy greeted me with a beaming smile from her hospital bed. Then her eyes dropped to the tightly swaddled bundle of pink in her arms.

Jumping from the chair at his wife's bedside, Albert swiftly crossed the room, took my hand and shook it. "Thanks for coming, buddy." His grip was a little too tight and the tension rolling off of him was palpable.

"I wouldn't have missed it for the world."

Albert took an awkward step toward the door and smiled at the mother of his newborn child. "I think I'll step out for a bit now that David's here to keep you company."

"Sure," Judy answered in a strained whisper. "I'll see you later."

Without another word, Albert opened the door and left. He could be such a clueless ass.

Smiling warmly, I moved toward Judy's bed.

She looked down at her precious child and her smile grew more genuine.

I hated this. But it had to be done. As the Reeds' closest Sighted friend, it was my responsibility to determine if their newborn was Sighted. This was all well and good, except for the inconsolable crying that'd accompany the shine if the infant happened to be Sighted. It seemed cruel to test her with my face, for the first unmasked face that she encountered to be the face of a dragon. That was the true cause of colic. The inconsolable crying had nothing to do with intestinal distress and everything to do with a Sighted infant's exposure to an unmasked Dark creature and the Darker the creature, the harsher the reaction. As if that wasn't bad enough, Albert and Judy were both fairies—pure creatures of Light. If this child were Sighted, she'd spend her entire infancy traumatized by this brief encounter. But it had to be done and the rules were clear. I had to be the one to do it. I stepped closer, kissed Judy on the cheek and took my first look at the child. A perfect cherubic face peeked out from a bundle of pink blankets. She was sound asleep, and waking her would make the whole experience that much more jarring for her. I just hoped to God the infant wasn't Sighted.

Judy smiled up at me. "Would you like to hold her?"

I might as well get it over with. There was no sense in drawing this out. "I'd love to. But I have to warn you, I'm not very good with children. I'll probably hand her back in tears."

Judy rolled her eyes as she held her newborn out to me. "I'll take my chances."

I took the fragile creature from her. She breathed the sweetest contended sigh as I cradled her to my chest, and a pang of guilt gripped me. "What's her name?"

"Emma." Judy whispered the name like she was sharing a precious secret.

"Emma," I repeated, increasing the temperature of my breath just enough to rouse her from sleep.

The baby's eyes popped open, and my heart stopped beating. Her eyes were the most magnificent shade of green. She was absolutely striking, a product of pure Light. I hesitated, uncertain whether I could bring myself to do it, but skipping it would be doing the child an unforgivable disservice if she was Sighted. She had to be tested. "Emma," I breathed the name once more like it truly was a precious secret. Then I unmasked, and I stood there with this newborn creature of Light in my claws and watched those gorgeous eyes shine for the very first time.

But the crying never came.

She just laid there looking up at me, perfectly content to be in the clutches of the world's Darkest creature.

And I fell in love...

...I waited in the hall until the Waters took her. Then I plunged in after her, transported her safely to our clearing in Draumer and left without lifting my eyelids.

Back in the waking world, I returned to the terrace. I picked her up, still bundled in the blanket she'd wrapped herself in, carried her to our bedroom and gently placed her on the bed. As I laid down beside her, she let out a contented sigh and instinctively pressed her body against mine.

Drawing her into my arms, I made my way back through the Waters to her.

9

CHARLIE

After ten minutes of vacantly surfing through channels on the monster television, I settled on a movie about zombies. I honestly didn't care what I watched. I just needed some mind numbing alone time. Dinner had been painfully awkward. Brian had tried his best to make small talk. But Dr. Price was clearly preoccupied. Rose shrunk whenever she was put on the spot to answer a question. I hadn't wanted to call too much attention to myself because I still felt like an imposter, and part of me was afraid they'd realize they'd made a big mistake and I didn't belong. And Benjamin was...well, he was Benjamin. As soon as the meal was over, Dr. Price and Benjamin left the house. Rose excused herself and hadn't left her room since. Brian said he had to call it a night after we finished cleaning up because he had a date to get to, then he marched upstairs and closed himself up in his bedroom. So, either he had a woman tied up in his room or the date wasn't in the waking world. Given what I knew about him so far, both possibilities seemed equally plausible. I didn't feel like closing myself up in my new room just yet, so I'd poured myself a tall glass of soda, popped some microwave popcorn and plopped down in front of the monster television.

"Mind if I join you?"

I'd been so lost in my thoughts, I hadn't even heard Rose come downstairs. I sat up a little straighter and turned down the volume. "No. Not at all. I'd love some company. This place was feeling kinda empty."

With a timid smile, she sat down on the opposite end of the couch and curled up with her feet tucked beside her. "I know what you mean." She shivered, and I handed her the fleece blanket I'd carried down from my room and watched her wrap it around her small body with an appreciative grin. "Thanks."

Mentally reminding myself to think before speaking so I wouldn't sound like an idiot this time, I nodded and sat the popcorn bowl on the couch between us. "So, Dr. Price said you're Isabella's daughter. Is that the Isabella who works for the Talbots?" I gave myself a mental pat on the back for not asking *is that the Isabella that Emma stabbed?*

Rose nodded. "The Sarrum is hoping I can help bring her out of the coma."

I chewed the popcorn in my mouth, considering what to say next. "How long's it been since you saw her?"

"I haven't seen her since the day she gave birth to me." Rose took a few kernels of popcorn and daintily popped them in her mouth.

"She gave you up for adoption?" I whispered, hoping the question wasn't offensive.

Rose nodded. "I was raised by the Sarrum's aunt."

"Did you know you were adopted?" For some stupid reason, I felt a little jealous. According to the Sarrum, I was adopted too. The Unsighted woman who'd raised me couldn't possibly be my birth mother because dragons could only be born to two Sighted parents. It probably wouldn't have made any difference if I'd grown up knowing I was adopted, but it would've been nice not to be kept in the dark about it.

"Yes," Rose whispered, eyes misting.

Damn it. "Sorry. Sore subject?"

"Not really. I was lucky enough to be raised by the most royal of all the dragon families."

I didn't know anything about the royal dragon families, but I was self-conscious enough about being the *virgin dragon*. I didn't want to cement that by admitting just how little I knew, so I just nodded.

She smiled like she was responding to something I'd said. *Could she read minds too?* "Dr. Price said you were a virgin?"

I cleared my throat. "Yeah. Uh. Until recently, I'd never met another Sighted person, so I never learned about the ways of the Sighted."

"Oh," she muttered, dropping the smile. "Right."

I shifted to face her. "Did I say something wrong?"

"No," she whispered, shifting toward me.

"Then why the sad face?"

Rose lowered her eyes to the popcorn bowl. "Can I trust you, Charlie? Something in your eyes makes me think I can, and I could really use a friend."

"Yeah." I reached out to give her hand a comforting squeeze, but chickened out and grabbed a handful of popcorn instead. "You can trust me. What's up?" I popped the kernels in my mouth, hoping she hadn't noticed that I'd started out reaching for her hand.

"I just thought..." She glanced toward the foyer. Then her eyes drifted back to the popcorn bowl. "Well...when the doctor said you were a virgin dragon... I thought he meant you were like me."

"Like you?" I whispered, hating the sorrow in her eyes.

Rose nodded. "A virgin dragon."

Oh. Shit. Did she really just tell me she was a virgin? The kind that Brian could sniff out? I cleared my throat but my voice still came out too deep and throaty, "You mean a *virgin* virgin?"

She looked up at me with a shy smile. "Yeah. The kind that's never had sex."

"Oh. Right." *Don't be an idiot. Don't be an idiot. She's just a friend confiding in a friend. But why did she feel the need to share that?* "And, uh…why are you telling me this?"

She took a deep breath like she was working up the nerve to say something, and I grabbed my soda and took a long slow sip so she wouldn't feel rushed to answer.

"Do you think the Sarrum plans for you to put a dragon in my belly?"

I half-coughed half-choked mid-sip and soda dribbled out of my mouth and nose and spilled down the front of my shirt. *Way to act casual, dumb ass.* "What?"

She was so lost in her own thoughts that she didn't seem to notice my coughing drooling mini-freak out. "Louise, the Sarrum's aunt, believes the Sarrum brought me here to impregnate me. The Dragon King needs to make an heir to the throne and his princess is weak and not a dragon. But when the doctor said you were a virgin dragon, I thought maybe he meant for you to make a dragon for him."

"What?" Apparently, I wasn't capable of saying anything else. When Benjamin said they needed to orient me before they *put me to work,* that wasn't exactly the sort of work I expected. A primal part of my brain suggested that there were worse jobs, but I mentally kicked myself for even thinking it.

Both our heads swiveled at the sound of a key turning in the front door. Benjamin opened it and he didn't take more than a step in the house before fixing me in the death glare to end all death glares.

Shit. Did he hear any of that from outside? Or read it from my mind?

Dr. Price followed Benjamin into the foyer and shut the door. As Benjamin moved toward us, his eyes shifted to Rose. "Why don't you go upstairs and wait for me?"

Don't piss yourself. Don't piss yourself. I mentally chanted over and over as Rose jumped from the couch and hurried upstairs. *What the hell did Benjamin want with her upstairs?*

"None of your fucking business," Benjamin growled in a guttural tone that turned my stomach.

"What is Rose waiting upstairs for?" I insisted, sounding every bit as terrified as I felt.

Benjamin let out a low growl. "Watch yourself, virgin. Stay the fuck out of matters that don't concern you." He took a few steps toward me and everything went dark.

Swallowed by a void of darkness and fear, I lost control of my bladder.

I woke up in the bed in my new room, still dressed in the same clothes and relieved to find them dry and free of piss stains. The room was dark and the sky beyond the gauzy curtains was speckled with stars. Should I look for Rose and find out what the hell Benjamin wanted from her? *No.* A gut feeling warned me that looking for Rose and checking up on Benjamin would be a stupid thing to do and unlike my days back at the facility, I didn't want to act stupid in this house. *What the hell was I even doing?* Should I trust these people or get the hell out while I still could?

It was definitely time to pay Call-me-Arthur a visit, but how exactly was I supposed to do that? He said to jump in the Waters with the moonstone in my hand, which was great, except the moonstone didn't exist in the waking world. Needing to do *something*, I called to the Waters. They immediately appeared and I took a deep breath and plunged in.

As the Waters knocked me around and chilled me to my bones, I thought of the shore where I met Call-me-Arthur and pictured the weathered dock. The Waters pummeled me, trying to knock the thoughts from my head, but I'd been bullied enough for one night. I wasn't going to take any shit from the Waters. *Take me to that shore and that dock! And stay the hell out of my head!*

I rocketed to the surface and was surprised to discover that I could see clearly, even though I'd forgotten to keep my eyes shut. It was sunset, just like last time and the dock was just a few feet to my right. As I waded toward it, I reached in my pocket, felt the oddly cool surface of the moonstone and pulled it out. Did I need to step out of the Water? I was supposed to jump in the Waters with the stone in my hand, right? Feeling kinda stupid and not at all confident it'd work, I hoisted myself onto the dock. Then I walked to the end and smoothed my thumb over the stone's cool surface. *Here goes nothing.*

I squeezed the stone in my hand, closed my eyes and jumped off the edge of the dock, but I didn't hit the Water. My body just kept plummeting. Confused, I opened my eyes and found myself rocketing through a tunnel of Water. *Water that wasn't touching me.* I could breathe and I could see the Water all around me but even though nothing was holding it back, the Water didn't touch me. As I barreled past a face watching me from the other side of the tube, things started getting brighter. *Did I just see a face in the Water?* The question was quickly forgotten because suddenly, I wasn't plummeting down. I was plummeting *up.*

I breached the surface, expecting to emerge near a different shore. Instead, I was standing on dry sand. I was perfectly dry and my eyes were already adjusted to the light. I looked around. There was no Water, anywhere. A rush of panic twisted my stomach. How would I get back to the waking world if there wasn't any Water to jump into?

"What kind of host would I be if I didn't provide my guest with transportation home?"

I spun around and found Call-me-Arthur sitting in a generously cushioned chair a few feet away from me. "What is this place?"

He motioned to a chair beside his, that I could've sworn wasn't there a second ago. "Just a safe place to meet. Somewhere off the radar."

I moved to the chair that hadn't been there and sunk against the overstuffed cushions. "Why won't anybody give me a straight answer today?"

Pale blue eyes twinkling, Call-me-Art chuckled. "If you must know, *this place* is a mirage."

"A mirage?" I echoed. "Something you see that doesn't really exist? Like water in the desert when you're dying of thirst?"

He nodded. "Something like that. It's a created space. It does exist but you could walk straight past it without detecting it, if you had no business being there."

I let my head drop back against the cushions. "Huh?"

"If the space wasn't created by you and the creator didn't want you there, you'd never detect the mirage."

I raked a hand through my hair. "Couldn't somebody who wasn't invited walk right through it?"

"No." Call-me-Art picked up a pitcher full of an iced red drink from a table that wasn't there a moment ago. He lifted the pitcher and raised an eyebrow, wordlessly questioning whether I'd like some.

I nodded and he started pouring into the glass in my hand. *What the hell? Where did the glass come from?* "The magic that creates a mirage wards it. Anyone who wanders there uninvited feels an overwhelming need to change course."

I took a sip of the red drink. It was thick and sweet and a little bit spicy, unlike anything I'd ever tasted before. "Can the people inside a mirage see someone outside it?"

"No. That's the beauty of it, total privacy. You can't see in or out. It's a created space that exists but doesn't exist, the perfect place to meet when you don't want to be overheard or keep something you don't want found."

I took a big gulp of my drink and relaxed a little. "How does a person create a mirage?"

Call-me-Art grinned like he was appreciating a private joke. "A *person* doesn't."

"Okay." I took another sip of the red stuff and waited for him to elaborate, but he didn't say anything more. "Can you expand on that?" I was starting to feel like I was talking to my friend Nellie back at the facility. Cryptic answers were her specialty.

"Only dragon magic can weave a mirage." He lifted the pitcher.

And I held my glass out for a refill. "Does that mean only dragons can create mirages?"

He refilled my glass, then sat the pitcher back on the table. "Yes. That's what I said."

I reminded myself that there was no point in arguing. "So are you a dragon?"

Art sat his glass on the table as he locked eyes with me. "That is a very impolite question."

I sipped the red stuff again. My insides felt curiously warm, like someone had stoked a fire in my belly. "It is? Why?"

He shook his head. "I say you're being rude and instead of apologizing, you ask more questions."

"Sorry." *I felt amazing. What was this stuff?*

Art sat up a little straighter. "Asking what lies beneath the mask is as offensive as asking someone to strip in the waking world, because you want to see what they look like without their clothes."

Brian and Benjamin didn't tell me I was being rude when I asked what they were.

He raised an eyebrow. "That's because you're a virgin and it's their job to teach you."

I sat my glass on the table a little harder than I meant to. "I wish everyone would stop calling me that."

"You take offense to the proper term?"

"I take offense to what everyone assumes it means."

His brow furrowed. "And how do you know what others assume?"

"Well for starters, the new house guest flat out *said* it." I paused to pick up my glass and take another sip. "She also told me she was a *virgin* virgin and she asked if the Sarrum wanted me to *put a dragon in her belly.* There's not really a wrong way to take that."

Art shifted in his chair. "Who was this female guest?"

"I don't know. She's a dragon and she's Isabella's daughter, and she's under the impression that the Sarrum wants to knock her up. Why would she think that? And why did she say his princess is weak?"

"Common knowledge," Art replied softly. "The Princess isn't a dragon. She's a creature of Light who was never meant to be kept in the Darkness."

Kept? My stomach knotted at the word. "You say that like she doesn't want to be there. From what I've seen, she's pretty in love with her husband."

"Stockholm syndrome," he whispered, more to himself than me. "Keeping her the way that he does is criminal. But who's to punish him? He's the King after all."

The knot in my stomach tightened. "What do you mean *the way that he does?* How does he keep her? You make it sound like she's a prisoner."

Art let out a troubled sigh. "Think of it this way, the Sarrum is like a naughty little boy who saw a beautiful butterfly and decided to keep her. How do you keep a lovely winged thing from flying away after you capture it? You rip off her wings and stick her in a jar. Visiting her every day and filling her jar with pretty things doesn't make it any less terrible.

The Princess is the stuff of fairytales, locked away in a dragon's lair, his most precious treasure."

The red stuff seemed to curdle in my stomach. *Rip her wings off and stick her in a jar.* Emma had scars on both shoulder blades. He couldn't mean that literally. *Could he?* I cleared my throat and choked back the urge to vomit. "Why does everyone call Emma *the Princess?*" I wasn't sure why, but my stomach knotted every time someone said it.

Call-me-Art nodded. "You're starting to get it, aren't you? The perversity of it all. Tell me Charlie, what do you call the wife of a king?"

The knot tightened again. "You call her a queen." *Pedophile.* That was my first impression of Emma's husband. *A man old enough to be her father.*

He nodded again, looking proud for some sick reason. "And what relation is a princess to the king?"

My throat felt too dry so the words came out hoarse and broken, "A princess is the king's daughter."

"Yes, she is. He took her from her parents the day she was born, Charlie. She was so beautiful that he just had to have her. He kept her locked away in the Darkness and raised her as his own child. As if that wasn't perverse enough, when she grew older, he took her as his lover, then he married her. The sick bastard married his own daughter and his followers still refer to her as his child."

My stomach clenched and everything started spinning. "I don't know what to make of any of that."

"What have they told you about the King and his little Princess?"

"Nothing," I muttered, wiping the sheen of sweat off my forehead. "Brian changed the subject when I asked about them and he said that seeing me would confuse her. I should get the hell out of there, shouldn't I?"

"No. You should stay close. How else will you ever be able to help her?"

"I don't know." I felt really hot and dizzy. I needed to leave before I threw up. "I don't understand any of this." *Nellie had those same scars on her shoulders, she was petrified of dragons and she said she'd fallen in love with one.*

Call-me-Art nodded. "Yes. It's probably time to pay your friend Nellie a visit."

10

I woke up feeling exquisitely sated. *He made love to me in the rain on a sweet bed of grass.* I tried to cling to the dream and the utter bliss I'd felt, but it was already starting to fade. God help me. I didn't want David to keep his distance. I needed him near me, and he knew it. Somehow, he always knew. I waited in bed, lingering in what was left of the sated bliss while he showered. Then we ate a leisurely breakfast together. We didn't say much, but we didn't need to. I just needed him there. Dr. Price was still settling in at the house on Sycamore so he wouldn't be coming over until later in the day, which was fine with me. I wasn't exactly anxious to meet him. With no plans for the next few hours, I decided it was the perfect time to sneak in some yoga. Tense as I'd been lately, I needed a release. So I changed into workout clothes, rolled my yoga mat out on the living room floor and popped in my favorite yoga DVD. Since David was in no hurry to go to his office, he'd settled onto the couch behind me to read the morning paper.

I tried to focus on the music and let go of the tension knotting my muscles. *But it wasn't the release I needed.* I had to rid those thoughts from my mind. What I *needed* was to clear my head and concentrate on the poses. This was the *only* release I'd allow myself but the more I stretched and contorted, the more I realized having David in the room wasn't such a great idea. *He was what I needed, not the stupid stretches.* I tried to banish those thoughts by focusing on the instructor's voice as I shifted into downward dog pose, arms stretched out in front of me, legs pulled back, bottom in the air like a silent invitation. God help me. This wasn't relaxing anything. I needed him, and he was right behind me. *Touch me. Please.* I was desperate to feel his hands on me. *I need you to touch me.*

I didn't hear him get off the couch but as I dropped to my hands and knees, I felt the warmth of his body as he crouched above me. His lips grazed my ear as his hands slid under my tank top, setting the blood beneath my flesh on fire. He dragged my shirt up and slipped his hands inside my sports bra. With a sigh of resignation, he yanked the shirt and bra over my head, peeled them down my arms and tossed them aside. *I should push him away.*

"Shhh," he rasped in my ear, igniting a lick of fire inside me. His hands explored my breasts reverently, as if he'd never touched me before and the pads of his fingers caressed my nipples with a tenderness that made me ache for him until I couldn't keep my hips still. Then his hands slid down my sides. "Tell me to stop," he whispered hoarsely as his fingers traced the flesh above the waist of my yoga pants, "and I will."

I whimpered, but it wasn't a *please stop*. It was more of an, *if you stop now I'll die.* A slow hiss escaped his mouth, heating the base of my neck as he slid his hands beneath the waistband and peeled my pants down at a torturously unhurried pace. When he reached my lace panties he hooked a thumb on either side and tugged them down my thighs with the pants, baring my bottom half to the cool morning air. A shiver convulsed through me as his hands stopped moving. *Don't stop. Please. I need to feel you inside me.* As if reading my mind, he lifted me, yanked the clothing off and tossed it aside in one deft movement that left me breathless. *Don't stop.* His hands slid between my legs and traveled down my inner thighs, coaxing them apart. One broad palm moved to my stomach and the pressure of his fingers low on my belly made every nerve ending in my body tingle. *Don't stop.* His free hand slipped between my legs. A tentative fingertip circled the flesh that burned for him and the room started spinning. "Do you want me to stop?" he rasped in my ear, dipping the tip of a finger inside me.

"Don't stop," I whimpered.

He removed his hands and pulled back from my body but before I had time to protest, he was on his back beneath me with his head positioned between my legs. A low growl rumbled in his throat as he reached up and captured my waist. In one swift motion, he lowered my hips, lifted his head and slid his tongue inside me. A gush of heat flared between my legs and I dropped my head with a startled moan. He drew my hips down with him as he lowered his head to the floor, his tongue never leaving my flesh. He worshipped me relentlessly with his mouth and the world blurred. Nothing existed beyond the heat of his tongue and the fire it ignited inside me. He gripped my hips possessively, devouring me and savage groans of agonized pleasure escaped my lips. Unable to bear the intensity, I tried to pull away. But his iron grip kept me pinned in place until I had no choice but to melt against his mouth and grind my hips in time with the movement of his tongue. *This was torture, sweet…agonizing…torture.*

My body began to shake convulsively as I writhed against his mouth. Thought escaped me…then sight…then fingers hotter than any flame were thrusting deep inside me. A cry filled the room, echoing wild and feral against the walls. *My cry.* Too lost in sensation to move, my body stilled. But his tongue and his fingers kept working their magic while his other hand braced my hip. Moans more animal than human escaped me as I lost myself in an endless wave of ecstasy and he didn't relent until he'd drawn every last feral whimper from me, until every last shudder of pleasure had passed.

With one final lingering stroke of his tongue, he drank me in. Then he slid out from under me and flipped me to my back, cushioning the blow with his hands. Still fully clothed, he crouched above my naked body as I drifted back to consciousness. When I met his beautiful blue eyes, his mouth dropped to mine and I tasted my own arousal on his tongue as he kissed me slowly and deeply until my body was throbbing for him all over again. As he broke the kiss, his lips moved to my ear. "You are mine."

I closed my eyes and murmured, "I'll always be yours."

He drew a deep breath, breathing me in through flared nostrils. Then his body shifted away from me. I propped myself up on my elbows as he stood from the floor. *Where the hell was he going?* There seemed to be a question in his eyes as he backed away. "Come find me later, after your session with Dr. Price."

My heart was aching as I nodded. I was desperate to say something that'd keep him from leaving, but I couldn't beg him to stay. If he didn't want to make love to me *after that,* what on earth could I say? *Was it all just for me?* I fought back the tears that threatened to fill my eyes. This was embarrassing enough already. I couldn't let him see me cry.

As I lay there naked and panting like a pathetic fool, he moved to the doorway. He didn't open his mouth when he turned back to look at me and his lips didn't move to form the word *MINE,* but I heard it clearly in my head. His voice, confident and strong. And possessive. *MINE,* his voice growled inside my head again.

Then he left the room.

11

CHARLIE

When I woke up, it was morning. I wasn't in any hurry to run into Benjamin, so I took a long hot shower and tried to make sense of all of it…of *any* of it. *What the hell was I doing?* I should be running as fast and as far away as possible. But where would that leave Emma? My stomach knotted thinking of what Art said about her relationship with the Sarrum. He was right. I needed to pay Nellie a visit soon, but I couldn't hide in my room all day.

I got dressed in a button down shirt and a new pair of jeans from the closet. If jeans were good enough for Brian, I figured they must be okay, especially since I wasn't the one who put them in the closet. I stepped back in the bathroom, ran a comb through my hair and took a deep breath. *Time for more fun.*

The house was eerily quiet as I made my way downstairs, but an eager grin spread across my face as I reached the foyer. Somebody was obviously awake because the smell of fresh coffee hung in the air, luring me down the hall toward the kitchen. Praying I wasn't about to run into Benjamin, I stepped through the door and headed straight for the coffee pot.

"You look like hell." I stopped and turned toward the archway to the dining room. Brian was sitting at the dining room table, dressed in plaid pajama pants and a slightly less fitted t-shirt than the day before. Swinging his bare feet off the chair beside his, he greeted me with a wide grin.

"I'm not much of a morning person," I muttered, eyeing the second cup of coffee and plate of food beside his. "Is your date joining you for breakfast?"

Chuckling, he motioned for me to come in and sit next to him. "Nah. She's home having breakfast with her husband with a dopey satisfied grin on her face. This is for you."

Perverts. I was stuck in a house full of perverts.

He pulled the chair beside his back from the table. "Ask me."

I obediently moved to the chair and sat down. "Ask you what?"

"Whatever questions you're dying to ask."

I picked up the coffee Brian had poured for me and took a sip, considering what to ask. *Is Emma the Sarrum's prisoner? Is the Sarrum just a massive per-vert? What did Benjamin want with Rose last night? Is Benjamin going to kill me? And oh yeah, did the Sarrum invite me here to knock up some poor sweet dragon girl and make him an heir?* If Brian could read my thoughts, his expression gave nothing away. I sat my cup back on the table and settled for, "Can you teach me how to unmask?"

Brian shoved what was left of his breakfast to-ward the center of the table. "That's a tough one. It's like asking someone to teach you how to take a piss. Unmasking is just basic instinct."

"Great. I'm so stupid I need somebody to teach me how to take a piss. I'm just not trying hard enough, is that it?"

Tapping his fingers on the side of his coffee mug, Brian shook his head. "No. I think you're trying *too* hard. You just need to relax and let it happen naturally."

"Right. I've spent my whole life not knowing how to do it, but now I'm supposed to relax and it'll just happen?"

Brian slid his chair back from the table. "Maybe you just need a breather. Why don't we take a fieldtrip today?"

I chewed and swallowed my mouthful of egg be-fore asking, "A fieldtrip where?"

"Is there anywhere in Draumer that you've always wanted to visit?"

I laughed at his feeble grasp of just how little I knew. "How am I supposed to answer that? I don't know about any places I've never visited."

Brian swirled what was left at the bottom of his coffee cup. "Well, what sections of the forest have you been in?"

"I don't go into the forest," I muttered. "It's not safe in there."

A massive grin spread across his face. "You mean you've never left the fringe?"

I dropped my fork to my plate with an aggravated sigh. "I don't even know what the fringe is."

Brian seemed unfazed by my frustration. "You've never left the Water?"

Always keep the Water in sight, Charlie. Never stray from it and never go into the forest. When I was a boy, my father traveled with me in Draumer. We'd lived a nomadic life, never staying in one place for too long. He'd warned me never to go so far that I couldn't see the Waters, never go so far that I couldn't *escape* through the Waters and *never* go into the forest. "It's not safe in the forest," I muttered. *I was never alone in Draumer until the day my father died. How could I have forgotten that?*

Brian grinned at me as he hopped to his feet. "Finish your breakfast. We're definitely going on a fieldtrip."

"Where?"

"Where else?" He grabbed his plate and cup and headed into the kitchen. "We're going into the forest."

"It's not safe," I muttered, not really sure I believed it anymore. *But my dad wouldn't lie to me.*

Brian sat his dirty dishes in the sink, then moved back to the doorway. "The person who taught you that was Unsighted, right?"

"Yeah," I mumbled around a mouthful of egg.

Brian stepped back in the dining room. "That's what the Unsighted have always been told. It's safer for *them* to keep to the fringe but you aren't Unsighted. You're a freaking *dragon.* What do you think is in there that *you* need to fear?"

I swallowed my food and shrugged. "I don't know."

Grinning, Brian collected my half-finished breakfast and coffee and carried them into the kitchen. "We're definitely going on a fieldtrip. I'm gonna take you to meet my brother."

I wasn't finished with the food but I didn't even care. I narrowed my eyes at him as he stepped back into the room. "Okay?"

"Let's get outta here." With that, Brian walked out the door without waiting to see if I'd follow.

But of course, I did follow him down the hall, up the stairs and into a room that I hadn't been in yet. It was furnished with two couches and three chairs with lots of fluffy pillows and a few fleece blankets draped over the backs. "What're we doing?"

Brian plopped down on the couch closest to the door. "I told you. We're going on a fieldtrip."

A fieldtrip to Draumer. I sat down next to him. "Are we supposed to hold hands or something?"

Amusement danced in Brian's eyes as he flashed his frat boy grin. "I don't think I'm your type."

"How do you know that?" I wasn't exactly sure why I'd asked, since he wasn't.

Brian's grin widened. "When we met, what was your first impression of me? Before we shook hands?"

"I thought you were a jock-frat-boy-asshole." *Crap. Was that too much honesty?*

Still grinning, Brian nodded. "If you had any homosexual or bisexual tendencies, you would've seen me as everything you've ever wanted in a man. But since you don't swing that way, you saw me as your notion of every girl's dream man."

"Huh," I muttered, "and that's part of the whole incubus thing?"

"Yup." Brian propped his feet up on the coffee table in front of us. "We don't need to hold hands. You go. I'll find you."

"I don't even know where I'm supposed to be going."

He rapped his knuckles on my temple. "Now you do."

"Ouch! What the hell?"

"Figured you'd be more comfortable with that than a gentle caress."

I rubbed the side of my head. "Yeah. You're probably right."

Looking totally on the verge of sleep, Brian dropped back against the cushions. "So go on already."

I still didn't have a clue where I was headed, but I figured Brian must know what he was doing. So I closed my eyes and silently called to the Waters. They instantly appeared and I took a deep breath and plunged in.

Ignoring the cold, I tried to focus on wherever I was supposed to be going but nothing came to mind. Maybe the Waters sensed how weak my grip on the information was. Or maybe Brian's knuckle trick just didn't work on me. The Waters still spit me out fairly quickly, sopping wet and extremely disoriented. I wasn't in any Water. I was standing on dry ground, and the forest ahead of me looked unnervingly dark and foreboding. *Shit.*

"What the hell took you so long?" Brian stepped up beside me, inked and pointy-eared and dressed all in black. *And totally dry.* "Shit, Charlie. You're soaking wet."

I took a deep breath, then realized I wasn't out of breath. "I just came through the Waters. Of course I'm wet."

Brian shook his head. "Yeah. We'll have to work on that."

"You mean I don't have to come out sopping wet?" If there was ever a trick I wanted to learn, that was it.

"You can't let them push you around like that. You're a freaking dragon." He started toward the tree line before I could ask who *they* were.

Taking a deep breath to steel my nerves, I followed him. The closer we got to the forest's edge, the louder my heart was pounding. Brian stepped through the trees and I swallowed the lump in my throat and stepped in after him. It was too dark and too quiet, and something in the air made the hairs on the back of my neck prickle. I wanted to turn around and run. The only thing stopping me was the utter calm of the pointy-eared warrior in front of me. Each step deeper into the forest felt a little more *wrong*. The air seemed too thin and my head felt like it was on the verge of imploding. I was about to ask him to stop so I could take a breather, but the melodic chirping of songbirds and the sunlight funneling through the trees up ahead suddenly made the walk more bearable. In a few more steps, Brian was stepping out of the trees.

I stepped out after him and almost shit myself. There was a whole *village* in front of us, a scene straight out of a fairytale. Cobblestone streets. Brick houses and storefronts with wisps of smoke wafting from every chimney. A fountain in the center of the square. And people, and lots of creatures who weren't people, laughing and talking and moving in and out of quaint little shops. I turned to Brian and muttered, "Holy crap."

"I figured my brother's village would be a good place to start." Brian nodded toward a pub with a wooden sign lazily swaying in the breeze. A black silhouette of a dragon was painted on the sign and the name of the pub was painted in gold letters beneath it. *The Dragon's Lair.*

I followed Brian toward the stone building. "Is your brother a dragon?"

"Nope," Brian chuckled. "Catchy name though, right?"

"Yeah," I whispered, following him through the front door.

The spacious interior of the pub was full of jovial rosy-cheeked creatures. A roaring fire crackled in a massive stone fireplace off to the right. Booths and tables full of patrons were scattered about the room in no apparent order and at the far end of the room, there was a long wooden bar with hordes of customers milling about and mingling in front of it.

Once he caught my eye, Brian started toward the bar. "Come on, let's find my brother."

A cluster of waifish fairies stood to our right, their gauzy wings glistening in a dazzling display of constantly changing colors as they reflected the light from the fireplace and the chandeliers. The nearest one turned toward us as we passed by. "Hello, handsome." She was obviously talking to the chiseled warrior I was walking beside. I might as well have been invisible next to him. *Not to mention the fact that I was still dripping wet like an idiot.*

Brian dipped his head in greeting. "Ladies."

The fairy beside the one who'd spoken first eyed me curiously. "Who's your soggy friend?" I would've thought she was mocking me, if it wasn't for the heavy-lidded expression on her face.

"My friend is the lost dragon," Brian replied in a dreamy tone.

The heavy-lidded fairy winked at me.

But Brian shook his head. "Sorry ladies. No time for talking." He started moving again and I reluctantly followed. Behind us, the fairies made disappointed pouty sounds and I hated Brian just a little. He might get that kind of reaction all the time, but I sure as hell didn't. Would've been nice to savor it for a minute or two. "Trust me," Brian whispered, "I'm doing you a favor."

I rolled my eyes at him. "Wow, thanks." I was about to say more, but the horde of creatures milling about in front of the bar parted a little and I forgot how to speak. I didn't have a homosexual bone in my body. Brian said so himself. But the man behind the bar made me wish that I did. *What the hell?*

"It's normal," Brian murmured. "I forgot to mention that my little brother is pure incubus. It doesn't matter what your sexual preferences are. He could make you forget that you've ever wanted anything but *him*."

"Shit." The room suddenly felt too hot and it only grew hotter as we moved closer to the bar. Brian's brother made marble sculptures of Greek gods look like fat ugly slobs. His bone structure was exquisitely chiseled. His eyes were a sparkling shade of green that beckoned you to jump in and swim in them and lose yourself forever. His flawless skin was a delicious mocha color. His head was shaved so there was nothing to obstruct the perfection of his face. And his body... he was dressed in a black leather vest and the magnificently toned muscles in his arms rippled as he wiped the glass in his hand with a cloth. *I'd like to be that glass.* Shit. *What was happening to me?*

"Totally normal." Brian's calm voice barely registered as we neared the Adonis behind the bar.

Brian's brother practically blinded me with his dazzling smile as we stepped up to the bar and I focused like hell on not getting a hard-on. *Not gay. Not gay,* I reminded myself.

"I won't hold that against you," Mr. Adonis murmured. His voice was like liquid silk and his smile melted my insides. I sat down on a barstool, afraid my legs might give out. The Greek god turned to Brian. "Hello, brother. It's been a while since I've seen you in here."

Brian shook his head. "Turn down the charm, Tristan. You're freaking my buddy out."

"I have to amuse myself somehow." Tristan hit me with that smile again and my cheeks flamed as a bead of sweat dripped down my brow. "And I do love a challenge. It's too boring when they beg for it."

Holy. Fucking. Shit.

"Easy lover boy," Brian growled. "This is the lost dragon." I think Brian meant that to cool his brother off.

Instead, Tristan cranked his dazzling smile up a notch. "Did somebody forget to tell me it was my birthday?"

I kinda tuned out at that point. Actually, I think I might've fainted.

12

EMMA

I had no interest in returning to my yoga after David left the living room, so I gathered up my clothes and headed to our room. I probably should've worried about running into somebody, but I was too frustrated to even consider the possibility of bumping into Sara or Benjamin or my new doctor while I was marching naked through the house with a wad clothes in my arms. Honestly, I didn't care what Sara thought of me. Benjamin probably wouldn't even notice. And impressing my new doctor wasn't exactly high on my priority list. I was supposed to be a crazy woman, right? Might as well act the part.

When I got back to our room I took a long hot shower, replaying what'd happened in the living room over and over in my head. *Why did David leave so abruptly?* The old us would've made love for hours, but he left the room still fully clothed as soon as he finished giving me the release I'd been desperate for. *Was it all just for me?* It'd never occurred to me that he might've moved into the guestroom because he wanted to. Was I just so broken and needy that he didn't have the heart to tell me? *I was such a fool.* I'd been so busy worrying about whether I could trust David. It'd never occurred to me to worry about whether he even cared.

I stepped out of the shower, dried off and changed into faded jeans and a comfy t-shirt. Feeling incredibly stupid, I crawled into bed. Pathetic as I felt, I still curled up on David's side. His pillow smelled faintly of him and even after everything that'd happened, his scent was a comfort. It made me feel safe. Tugging the blankets up to my chin, I closed my eyes and fell apart. And when I had no tears left to shed, I drifted off to sleep...

...*I was drowning again.* No. Not again. *I'd never stopped drowning.* Everything else had been a dream. I'd never been anywhere but the Water. *Not since that night.* No... That was a dream too. None of it had ever been real. No one had hurt me. I hadn't witnessed anything horrible. It was all just a nightmare. *This was real.* The Water. The cold. The fear. This was where I belonged. *Where I'd always belonged.* I was the Water's and the Water would never let me go. I'd stay until my heart stopped beating. *This was where I was meant to die...*

... "Emma," his voice echoed from far away. "You are mine." *No. I'm the Water's.* "You belong to me, Princess." *I belong to the Water.* "OPEN YOUR EYES."

Gasping for breath, I sat up and looked around. The room was dark and my heart was racing. *Where was I?*

His arms wrapped around me and I sunk against his chest. "You're with me, Princess."

My eyes couldn't seem to adjust to the dark. So I closed them and focused on the steady beat of his heart. "I'm with you."

His arms tightened protectively. "Yes. And you're safe."

"My heart hurts," I whispered. "I don't think I belong here anymore."

"Shhh." His head dropped to my ear and the heat of his breath lessened my panic. "You'll always belong here. You belong with me."

The ache in my heart sharpened. "Why can't I see anything?"

He crooked a finger under my chin and tilted my head up. "You can see me."

I could. His eyes blazed bluer than the purest sapphires. I dropped my head back to his chest, needing the comforting beat of his heart. "I don't know what's real anymore."

"I'm real," he whispered. "You're mine, and I'll never let you go."

"Promise?"

He exhaled and his scent filled the air. "I promise you, Princess. I will not let you go. Just cling to that. You're mine and I'll never let you go."

"But you don't love me anymore," I sobbed against his chest.

Another breath, hotter than the last, bathed me in his scent. "Why do you say that?" There was so much sorrow in his voice.

"I miss the feel of you so much."

"I'm right here," he whispered, heating the side of my neck. "I've always been right here, but you need to wake now. The doctor is coming. He's going to help you."

"No. I don't want to go back in the Waters," I whispered. "Please. Don't make me go back."

"Wake Emma." He kissed my lips…

… I opened my eyes. *I must've dozed off.* I dreamt of being in his arms. That made sense. I fell asleep on his pillow breathing in his scent.

Someone knocked on the door, and I sat up and rubbed my eyes to shake off the grogginess. "Come in, Doctor."

The door opened and a black man with a bald head and a graying goatee stepped in the room. He wore black pants and a black suit jacket over a crisp white shirt with no tie. Behind his black-rimmed glasses, his eyes were as dark as Benjamin's but his brimmed with cheer and compassion. A smile lit up his face as he approached me. "Hello, Emma." He stopped beside my bed and held his hand out for a handshake.

"Hello, Doctor," I whispered, taking his hand.

His handshake was firm enough to instill confidence, but gentle and warm enough to make him seem likeable. "Your husband and I are old friends. I don't see any need for us to be so formal. Please, call me Jeremy."

Nodding, I let go of his hand. "Alright, Jeremy."

"That's much better. I never was one for formality." He glanced around the room. "I've been told I have a pleasant bedside manner but I'll admit, this is the first time I've actually met a patient at her bedside."

As much as I'd been determined not to, his warm smile and gentle voice made it hard not to like him. "Sorry. I guess I dozed off. We could go somewhere else."

He sat down on the opposite side of the bed, swung his feet up and crossed them at the ankles. "No. I like this. It's much less stuffy than some sterile office."

I propped David's pillow behind my back. "I'm not sure David would be thrilled with our choice of meeting places."

The doctor shot me a knowing grin. "Yes. There are plenty of things your husband wouldn't be thrilled with. He and Benjamin always were the stuffy ones. I'm sure he'll get over it."

I raised an eyebrow. "It's not often I hear some-one talk about either of them like that. Most people are sort of intimidated by them."

He blew out a breath that was part exhalation, part chuckle. "That's because they both have very large sticks up their asses and most people feel the need to kiss up to them, but that wasn't in my job description. The only feelings I'm the least bit concerned about are yours."

I wasn't sure what to say to that, so I just bit my lip and waited for him to say more.

"So tell me, how long have you been cooped up in this house?"

"Too long."

Dark eyes twinkling, he grinned at me. "Then we should go for a walk."

I lifted my pant leg to reveal the house arrest ankle bracelet. "I can't walk very far."

"Why don't we walk the beach and see how far that lovely piece of jewelry allows you to go?" Jeremy hopped off the bed and held a hand out to me. I took it and he gently tugged me to my feet. "If the police show up, I'll just explain that we were testing the boundaries. We can call it an exercise in learning your limitations."

I shook my head. "I know exactly how far I can go."

"Well then, what've you been waiting for?"

I dropped my eyes and toyed with a loose thread on the hem of my t-shirt. "I guess I just haven't felt much like leaving the house."

"I can't say I'm surprised," Jeremy whispered. "You've had nothing but Dark souls with sticks up their asses for company, but you my dear...you need sunshine. It's a crime to keep you locked up in this place."

13

CHARLIE

"How long's he been like that?" Benjamin's Dark voice thundered somewhere distant.

"Not long." *Brian's voice.* "Half an hour at the most."

"Why the fuck did you take him there?"

"He needed a break," Brian's voice echoed. "If you weren't so damn scary—"

"Did you accomplish anything useful before you lost him?"

"I found out he doesn't know how to pass through the Waters without getting wet," Brian answered. "We've got our work cut out for us. Did you take Doc to meet the Princess?"

Benjamin's hazy silhouette nodded. "I'm heading back to pick him up in a few minutes. He thinks we should bring the virgin over for a visit."

Brian let out a loud sigh. "What do you think?"

"I think if we can drag his sorry ass to the car we should bring him and leave it up to the boss."

"My sorry ass can walk," I muttered, more anxious about seeing Emma than nervous about facing Benjamin."

"Then get the fuck up," Benjamin growled. "What're you waiting for? An engraved invitation?"

As soon as I stood, the room started spinning. I groaned and squeezed my eyes shut. "What the hell happened to me?"

"You got such a hard-on for Brian's brother that you passed out," Benjamin answered with a disturbingly terrifying grin.

"Don't listen to him, Charlie." I turned toward Brian just in time to see him scowl at Benjamin. "Tristan was being an ass."

"Let's go to the car," Benjamin barked. "You two can suck each other's dicks on the way over."

Awesome. Now Benjamin could belittle me for being a virgin *and* a closet homosexual.

Benjamin raised an eyebrow as we headed downstairs. "The way I heard it, you were pretty *out* of the closet."

"Do you have to keep reading my mind?" I snapped, before thinking about *who* I was snapping at.

Benjamin chuckled, pretty much the most horrifying sound I'd ever heard. "It's kinda hard not to when you holler all your thoughts."

"I do?"

"Yeah," Brian agreed behind me. "We'll have to work on that."

"Great," I muttered as we stepped from the house and moved into the garage. "One more thing that I suck at. I *think* too loud."

The drive to the Talbots' house was pretty quiet. Everybody seemed lost in their own thoughts and I mostly just focused on trying not to think too loud. Before long, we were approaching a massive gate with a security guard sitting in a booth beside it. He nodded to Benjamin and the gate opened. The stone house that we headed toward looked like a freaking castle. There was a wide staircase in front that led to a huge front porch, there were balconies all over the place and beyond the house was the beach. Not just a little shared beachfront, a sprawling piece of property with God only knows how many acres of private beach.

We pulled into a huge garage full of cars that probably cost more money than I'd ever see in a lifetime, and Brian and I followed Benjamin through a side door into the house. The foyer that we entered made the one at fifty-five Sycamore look like a broom closet. I could've comfortably lived in that space alone. Benjamin motioned for us to follow him and we walked to another room that I would've gladly taken up residence in. There was a well-stocked bar with nothing but seriously impressive top shelf liquor, a mahogany pool table, a monster television that was even bigger than the one at fifty-five Sycamore, a massive stone fireplace and lots of classy leather furniture that looked too expensive to actually sit on.

"Hello, my new dragon friend," a voice like melted chocolate murmured behind me. "Can I pour you a drink?"

Shit. Shit. Shit.

"That's not much of a greeting."

Thinking as many cold-shower-thoughts as I could call to mind, I turned around. "Sorry." Tristan was dressed in a charcoal gray suit, pale blue shirt and a blue and gray striped tie. I didn't need to see the label to tell his suit cost a fortune. The tie was silk, the shirt probably was too and even in a suit, you could tell the body underneath was spectacular. *Shit.* He was every bit as perfect in the waking world. When my eyes finally made their way up to his gorgeous green eyes, he winked at me.

"You're not going to pass out on me again, are you?" He took a step closer. "Give me a little warning so I can catch you this time."

Holy shit. He smelled good enough to eat. *Did I really just think that?* "No, man," I rasped in a voice that was *way* too throaty. "I'm good. Really."

Tristan flashed me a dazzling smile. "Alright then. How about that drink? Name your pleasure, dragon."

Shit. Shit. Shit. "No. Thanks. I'm good."

"Suit yourself," he murmured.

Brian stepped up beside me, almost protectively. "Mind if I cut in?"

"Cut in, join in, *watch*, whatever makes you happy, brother." Extending a hand, Tristan grinned at his older brother as they exchanged a handshake and a manly clap on the shoulder.

"Go talk to Benjamin," Brian ordered with a nod toward the shadow.

Tristan grinned and winked at me again. "I'll catch up with you later."

"Sure," I croaked.

As I watched him walk away, Brian murmured, "Don't worry. He'll stop toying with you soon. The less of a rise he gets out of you, the quicker he'll get bored."

"Great. Thanks for *that* choice of words. What exactly does Tristan do? Does he work for the Sarrum?"

Brian nodded. "Yep. He's a lawyer. He works with me at Talbot and Associates, and he can charm a jury like nobody's business."

"I'll bet," I muttered, watching Tristan pour a drink for Benjamin.

"I got Tristan a job working for the Sarrum back when I was first hired," Brian continued, "he helped me with my first assignment."

I finally managed to peel my eyes away from Tristan and look at Brian. "The assignment you got the tattoos for?"

"That's the one."

"Mind if I ask what the assignment was?"

"Not at all," Brian answered, eyeing his brother. "We were assigned to guard the Princess during her college years. The tattoos were a warning that I wasn't to be messed with and neither was the Princess. The Sarrum paid for law school for my brother and me. My course schedule was identical to Emma's, and Tristan's was pretty damn close. She never went anywhere on campus without at least one of us."

I was going to comment about the fact that Emma wasn't a lawyer, but something else about Brian's story was far more confusing. "The Sarrum let the two of *you* guard Emma?"

Tristan stepped up beside me as Benjamin left the room. "Why's that so surprising?"

"Uh...well...I kind of get the impression the Sarrum's the jealous type. It's a little hard to imagine him hiring two Greek gods to hang out with the love of his life all day."

Tristan let out a chuckle. *Even his laugh was sexy as hell.* "Why would that be a problem?"

"Was it…not an issue," I muttered, hoping I wasn't about to offend him, "because you're gay?"

Another laugh escaped Tristan's perfect lips. "What makes you think I'm gay?"

"Uh," I muttered, raking a hand through my hair. "Now I'm just confused."

"I'm no gayer than you," Tristan murmured.

"I'm not gay at all," I insisted, maybe a little too emphatically.

He flashed me a devilish grin that made my insides quiver. "I know. It's just too much fun to mess with you. You don't have to react to me at all, you know."

"Huh?"

"Dragons," Tristan whispered, "can resist the charms of an incubus or succubus."

"Then what the hell's my problem?"

Tristan shrugged. "I don't know. Maybe you don't know how to block it."

"Fabulous," I muttered. "One more thing that I suck at."

"Don't be so hard on yourself," Tristan murmured. "It's got to be pretty overwhelming having everything be so new all at once."

I blew out a breath. "Yeah. It sorta is." *But I was still stuck on the perfect male specimens for bodyguards thing.* "Can fairies resist the charms of an incubus too?"

Tristan grinned at me. "Not at all."

"Then why would the Sarrum be okay with Emma hanging out with you two?"

"Are you kidding?" Brian chimed in. "Emma barely noticed us."

"How is that possible?"

"Have you ever seen the way she looks at him?" Tristan asked.

I pictured the way Emma looked at her husband when he came to visit her at the facility, and the look on her face whenever she talked about him. "Yeah. I have."

"He's the *Dragon King*, Charlie," Brian reminded me. "How could a couple of incubi compete with that?"

"Honestly," I whispered, "I don't get it."

Tristan cocked his perfect head to one side. "What's not to get?"

"Am I seriously the only one who thinks David Talbot is a massive pervert?"

"Charlie." Brian shook his head.

"No. *I mean it.* Why am I the only one who has a problem with the Sarrum being a pedophile?"

Brian shook his head again, and Tristan just stared at me with a cautionary glint in his eyes.

"I mean he *kidnapped* her, kept her locked away, raised her as his daughter. Was it always his plan to make her his sexual plaything? And what, he was just such a gentleman that he played daddy until her age hit double digits? Or did he even wait that long?" I was too lost in my rant to pay attention to their subtle headshakes. The more I thought about it, the angrier it all made me. "It's just so freaking *sick*. Why isn't anybody else bothered by what a massive pedophile the Sarrum is?"

It was the instantaneous rise in room temperature that finally got my attention. As the wall of heat slammed into me, I shut my mouth and looked at the two incubi in front of me. Tristan's eyes were unnaturally wide and Brian wouldn't even look at me.

"Please," snarled a voice too deep and thunderous to be human. "Don't stop on my account." The voice wasn't loud. It was low and furious in a calm sort of way that made my stomach drop and the hair on the back of my neck stand up. *Fuck*.

"Go on," the Dragon King snarled behind me. "I believe you were enlightening everyone about what a deviant I am. *Please continue*." I heard him step closer and the heat at my back intensified as if I was getting dangerously close to a roaring fire. He took another step as his voice thundered inside my head, "TURN AROUND AND FACE ME."

The rage in his voice made my heart pound harder than it ever had before. I didn't want to turn around. I wanted to run and never stop running but, without consciously intending to, my body spun around like someone or something had turned it.

The Sarrum was standing a few feet away from me, and Benjamin and the doctor were behind him.

No one was close enough to have actually touched me. *This is it. I'm about to die.*

David Talbot took a step closer and raised his hand slowly and furiously, and my body flew back and slammed against the wall several feet behind me. "Nothing more to say?"

I couldn't have answered even if I wanted to. Something massive and bony was crushing my throat. *It felt like a claw.* As I thrashed in its invisible grasp desperately fighting to draw a breath, I realized my feet weren't touching the ground. Horrified, I looked up at the Dragon King. I *felt* his sneer like a throb of pain in my chest. And *his eyes.* His body was still in human form but deep blue flames flickered in his rage-filled eyes.

He stepped toward me and I felt myself fading. Those terrifying eyes were only inches from my face as the claw tightened its grip around my windpipe. *But he still hadn't touched me.* Everything in the room started to blur, everything but his rage and those flames in his eyes. I heard faint voices. Brian's. Benjamin's. The doctor's. But the only voice I could focus on was the one that thundered inside my head, "IF YOU ALREADY KNOW SO FUCKING MUCH, GET THE FUCK OUT OF MY HOUSE!"

I fell to the floor, sucking air through a throat that felt brittle and dry. I couldn't talk. I couldn't move. I just lay there like an idiot staring up at the Dragon King. Nostrils flared, he exhaled and I felt my flesh roasting. "GET OUT OF MY SIGHT!" he breathed the words as if they were fire, and they thundered aloud and inside my head. Then he turned and left the room.

I sat there gasping, too stunned to move.

But Benjamin yanked me to my feet and growled, "Move." I sped through the house, more dragging behind him than walking with him. I wanted to ask him to stop, or at least slow down, but before I knew it, we were back in the garage and he was dragging me into the car. I wanted to protest but my throat was too raw to talk.

"It's time for us to go." He touched my arm as he fastened his seatbelt and a chill ran down my spine. Then he started the car. Everything seemed blurry and out of focus as we pulled out of the garage and made our way down the long driveway. The gate opened as we approached it and Benjamin kept driving without slowing down or even nodding to the guy in the security booth. "You really fucked up, kid."

Yeah. Thanks. I got that.

"It's time to stop acting like a moron," Benjamin growled, "and grow the fuck up." The car was moving too fast, but Benjamin just kept accelerating and I couldn't seem to get my mouth to form the word *stop.* "We've got real problems. We don't have time to waste on your bullshit!" Benjamin roared as the car sped onto a narrow bridge. "Do you get that?"

Stop! Stop! Stop! I finally managed to choke out the word, "STOP!"

Benjamin turned his head and glared at me. The car skidded sideways and slammed into the side of the bridge, then we were flipping over and the next thing I knew, we were plummeting toward the water.

We hit the water with a deafening thud and then we were sinking, with my screams echoing through the car's interior until we hit the bottom. *I don't want to die! How the hell do we get out?*

"You're the dragon," Benjamin growled. "Figure it out!"

"What?"

"Command the water!" Benjamin demanded. "And get us the fuck out of here!"

Was he serious? "You're insane!" As I screamed at him, hairline fractures started forming on the windows and as the cracks widened, water started seeping in.

"This is a new suit!" Benjamin roared. "If it gets ruined I'm going to fucking kill you!"

"What the hell is wrong with you?" I screamed. "We're about to die! And you're worried about getting your suit wet?"

"CONTROL THE WATER AND GET US THE FUCK OUT OF HERE!"

Ice cold water was flooding the floor of the car and I could barely feel my feet anymore, but that was the least of my worries.

I was going to die in a car next to a maniac.

14

DAVID

I ignored the doctor's protests as I marched from the lounge, but he hurried after me and continued to babble like a lunatic. Barely able to contain my rage, I spun around and stepped up to him. The doctor's eyes widened with comprehension but the rest of him just stood there frozen with panic. Brian rushed out the door, grabbed him by the arm and dragged him back into the room. Seething with fury, I continued down the hall. That insolent fool had picked the wrong day to piss me off. My muscles had already been coiled with frustration, just itching to spring. Rage coursed through my veins, boiling my blood, burning in my chest. I'd been patient for far too long. I was done tiptoeing through my own home. *And I was done holding back.*

The imp stepped into the hall as I neared the door to the living room. She took one look at me and a terrified squeak sprung from her lips as she bolted back into the room. The beat of my heart thundered maddeningly in my ears as I moved to the staircase and bounded up the steps a few at a time. My patience was spent. There was an unquenchable fire in my belly. My body was aching from the weight of everything I was fighting to hold together. My wife looked at me through a stranger's eyes—seeing me, but not truly seeing me. I was done being patient. *She was mine.* And it was time to remind her of that.

I stepped onto the second floor and followed her scent down the hall to our bedroom. I threw the door open and found the room empty. Breathing in the heady scent of her, still potent from her arousal, I moved to the bathroom and opened the door. The sight of her stopped me dead in my tracks for a moment. She stood at the sink, eyeing her reflection in the mirror. Her eyes were so full of sorrow. She looked so lost and confused, as if the face of a stranger was staring back at her. If I could fix it, I'd have done anything, no matter the cost. But there was nothing I could do, no way for me to get her back. Her eyes met mine through the mirror but she didn't turn around, almost as if she wasn't certain I'd be there if she did.

I kept my eyes on her reflection as I stepped up behind her. Then I dropped my chin to her shoulder and unmasked. It was stupid really. I'm not even sure why I did it. I suppose some foolish part of me hoped that if I did it enough times she'd recognize me. I watched her eyes shine and hurt a bit more when she didn't react. *See me, Princess. You're dying without me. Why can't you see that?* I let the mask fall back in place, brushed the hair from her neck and kissed her.

She closed her eyes and sighed as I brushed my lips over her smooth flesh. When I looked back at her reflection, there were tears in her eyes.

I slipped my arms around her waist. "No more tears."

Her reflection looked confused and slightly angered.

I pressed my body to hers, pushing her against the sink, letting her feel how much I wanted her. "Hate me if you need to," I whispered. "But no more tears. This morning was for you. Now this is for me."

The scent of her arousal flooded the room as I ground against her backside and dropped my mouth to her neck. She let out a startled gasp as my hands slid under her shirt, possessively touching what belonged to me. Her eyes drooped shut and her head fell back against my shoulder as I yanked her shirt over her head and tossed it to the floor. "Open your eyes," I demanded. And she did, watching with lowered lids as I unclasped her bra and ripped it off. "Mine," I whispered, teasing her nipples between my fingers. "Do you hear me? You are mine."

"I'm yours," she agreed in a throaty whisper. She closed her eyes and moaned as I toyed with her breasts, brushing my thumbs across the nipples until her hips were rocking and her backside was grinding against me.

"Open your eyes," I growled in her ear, pinching her nipples.

She obliged with a delicious moan, her lids even heavier as she watched me fondle her in the mirror. Her backside pressed against me, desperate for more attention but I stayed focused on her breasts, keeping her needy and wanting. Her hands reached back and anxiously attempted to tug at my shirt but I ground against her, pinning her body between mine and the sink until she was moaning and lowering her eyelids.

"Eyes open," I growled.

She opened them wide and watched hungrily as I undid the button on her jeans and tugged down the zipper. She writhed, desperate to turn around and touch me but I kept her pinned in place as I slid her pants down, leaving her little pink panties in place, knowing full well it'd frustrate her. Lifting her off the floor, I tugged her pants off and kicked them aside as her eyes began to droop again.

"Don't close your eyes," I rasped in her ear, slipping a hand down the front of her panties. She looked almost helpless to comply as my fingers slid lower and caressed her in slow circles, working her into a whimpering frenzy. "Look at me," I growled, watching her eyes pop open as my fingers pushed inside her.

She cried out, clearly struggling to keep her eyes open as I slid my fingers in and out of her, stroking her in circles and grinding against her backside in time with the movement of my hands.

"You are mine," I growled in her ear, thrusting my fingers in harder.

"Yours," she gasped as her body began to spasm. She kept her eyes open and locked with mine as I teased her orgasm further and further until her body went limp from sated exhaustion.

Without waiting for her muscles to finish spasming, I tore off her panties and spun her around. She cried out as I lifted her onto the sink, pushed her legs apart and positioned myself between them. Then she tugged off my shirt and undid my pants, eagerly sliding them down my legs with her toes. Kicking them aside, I grabbed her by the waist and pulled her toward my hips as I buried the length of myself inside her. "Mine," I growled, covering her mouth with mine and pushing my tongue between her sweet lips as I moved inside her.

She clung to me, clawing my back, biting my earlobe, screaming my name until we came in unison, a perfect harmony that seemed to last forever. It'd been far too long since I'd been inside her.

"Mine," I growled as I slowly pulled out of her. I moved to the shower, started the water running, then scooped her into my arms and carried her in. "And I'm just getting started with you."

15

CHARLIE

Benjamin's booming voice sounded distant and everything around us was starting to blur. I would've been better off if I'd never left the facility. David Talbot's fucked up *family* made my fellow mental patients seem rational and sane.

"You need to focus!" Benjamin shouted. "Save the soul searching for another time and get us the fuck out of this Water!"

"You're a lunatic!" I screeched in a panicked voice that didn't sound remotely like mine. "We're both going to die because of you!" This maniac's face was the last face I was ever going to see. I'd never see Emma again. I'd never get the chance to visit Nellie. I'd never find out what the Sarrum planned to do to Rose.

As the certainty of my impending death struck me, my life started to flash before my eyes...

...First came visions of a happy childhood with a father who kept me safe and taught me how to survive in the Dream World...my father teaching me how to fish... him pointing out constellations as we lay on tattered bedrolls beneath a starry sky...us building a fire to warm up beside at the end of a weary day...

..."Never leave the Water, Charlie. And always be ready to escape through it." There were tears in my father's eyes. "Bury it, Charlie. Never let them see what you are and never let the Water out of your sight."

I wanted to act brave and make my father proud, but I couldn't stop the tears from falling. How could I leave him behind?

"Promise me," he whispered. "Promise you'll keep it hidden."

I shook my head. "Let me stay with you."

He choked back a sob as he pulled a little blue vile from his coat pocket. "Drink it." He pressed the vile into my hand. "And stay hidden."

"We can both jump in the Water," I whispered, tears streaming down my cheeks. "We can get away together."

A tear slid down my father's cheek as he shook his head. "I love you, Charlie. Never forget how much I loved you. I promised your mother that if there ever came a day when we couldn't get away, I'd have you drink this and escape through the Waters."

"I don't understand." Heart in my throat, I ignored the hoof beats that shook the ground beneath our feet and

the unholy shrieks echoing from the forest.   "Why can't you jump out of here with me?"

He sighed and hugged me to his chest.   "We'd just come back to this same spot tomorrow, and they'd be waiting for us.   There's no escape for me, Charlie.   Not this time.   But if I stay behind, you can wake wherever you want tomorrow.   Just remember to concentrate on staying away from here.   The Waters will listen to you, Charlie.   And if I get away, I promise I'll find you."   He grabbed the vile from my hand, uncorked it and poured it down my throat, and I was too terrified and confused to fight it.

A deafening chorus of shrieks rose from the forest, and my heart froze.   The heavy flapping sounds of monstrous wings filled the air and giant hoof beats shook the ground so hard that my teeth chattered.

"Go!"   My father gave me an urgent shove toward the Waters.

But I shook my head, refusing to budge.

"I love you, Charlie.   Keeping you safe has been my life's goal since the day I met your mother.   Let me take my last breath knowing I kept my promise to her."

I should've argued, but a monstrous growl just inside the trees spooked me and I ran to the Waters and left my father to die...

...My mother's eyes were dull and lifeless as she opened the passenger door.   I stepped out of the car, and she shut the door and started toward the hospital without *waiting to see if I'd follow. "This is for the best, Charlie. You know it is."*

I fought back the tears. There was no point in crying. She didn't care about my tears, and the other patients would see it as a weakness. I couldn't show any hint of weakness. I wouldn't stand a chance in there....

...I was sitting on a folding chair half-listening to Bob's ranting and Frank's whining, when the most beautiful girl I'd ever set eyes on walked through the door. There was so much sorrow in her gorgeous green eyes. I wanted nothing more than to put a smile on her perfect face...

...A smack upside the head snapped me back to the present, back to the car filling up with water, back to the conclusion of my sorry little life.

"Charlie!" Benjamin delivered a second smack to my head.

"What the hell!" I shrieked. "What? Killing me isn't awful enough? You have to hit me while I wait to die?"

Benjamin grabbed me by the shoulders. "Do you want to die?"

"Of course not! What the hell kind of question is that?"

"THEN FOCUS!" he growled. "The Water will listen to a dragon, but you can't give it any wiggle room. You have to COMMAND it to release you! If there's any doubt in your mind about whether it'll work, it won't."

"What?" *Why was I even arguing?* If I was a goner, what was the harm in humoring him? And if there was even the slightest chance he was right, how could I not give it a shot? Ridiculous as it sounded, what did I have to lose?

"That's not good enough!" Benjamin roared. "The Waters won't listen to a whiny *maybe*! OWN IT! Make them see that you're the boss and they'll have to listen!"

You're a maniac.

"And you're a fucking coward!" Benjamin gave my shoulders a shove as he let go of me. "You thought it yourself. What the hell have you got to lose? But you're still sitting here wasting your last few breaths. Wasting *my* last breaths! IT'S TIME TO LET YOUR BALLS DROP AND BE A MAN! BE A FUCKING DRAGON!"

Screw it. "LET US GO DAMN IT! I COMMAND YOU TO LET US GO!" *Yeah. So... nothing happened.*

Benjamin glared at me, but he still looked way too calm for the current situation. "That's it? One fucking try and you're calling it? TRY AGAIN! HARDER!"

I knew we were about to die, but he was seriously pissing me off. And I was wasting *his* last breaths? "I DEMAND THAT YOU LET US GO! YOU HAVE NO RIGHT TO KEEP US! WE DON'T BELONG TO YOU! WE BELONG TO THE SARRUM! SO LET US OUT OF HERE BECAUSE IF YOU RUIN THE DARKNESS'S NEW SUIT, YOU'LL BE IN

SOME SERIOUS TROUBLE! LET US GO RIGHT THIS FUCKING INSTANT!"

The car rocketed toward the surface so quickly that I could barely process it. *Holy crap! It actually worked!* The car sunk a few feet, and Benjamin growled at me. *Right. Focus. Total confidence. Of course it worked! I'm a dragon! And I work for the Dragon King! (At least, I did before he tried to strangle me to death.)* The car sunk deeper, and Benjamin smacked me upside the head again. *I'm a dragon. And this is the Darkness. The Water has no right to keep us!* A rush of power surged through me as the car broke the surface.

I sucked in a deep breath and took a look around. We were still in the car, and the car was still parked in David Talbot's garage. I turned and scowled at Benjamin. "WHAT THE HELL JUST HAPPENED? WAS ANY OF THAT REAL? OR WERE WE JUST SITTING HERE THE WHOLE TIME?"

Benjamin slipped the car in reverse and grinned at me as he backed out of the garage. "What if we were? What difference would it make?"

"WHAT DIFFERENCE WOULD IT MAKE? I just watched my life flash before my eyes! I thought I was going to die!"

"But you didn't," Benjamin replied calmly.

"SO?"

"So how fucking amazing do you feel right now? You just cheated death and you made the Waters listen to you. How do you feel?"

"I, uh…" I stopped to consider that for a second. My heart was slamming in my chest. I'd been sure the Sarrum was going to kill me earlier, then I was sure I was going to drown next to a seriously mental shadow and now, I was sitting safe and dry inside a car. "I feel pretty great actually."

We didn't speak for the next several minutes. I think Benjamin was giving me time to process everything.

Eventually, Benjamin broke the silence. "I know you think you can hold your own with the Sarrum because you're a dragon. Part of you thinks if push came to shove, you'd stand a fair chance against him. Don't deny it. Remember, I can read your fucking thoughts."

I couldn't deny it. It had crossed my mind once or twice.

"You need to understand that the Sarrum isn't *just* a dragon. The Sarrum is the most powerful creature in existence. He's the product of generations of pure royal dragon breeding. The Talbot marriages have always been carefully arranged. The most potent dragons from all the royal families throughout the world have been strategically mated with them. They bred each generation to enhance the most desirable qualities and strengthen the Talbot blood and the Sarrum is the strongest dragon the world has ever seen. Everything that you've witnessed is only a miniscule fraction of what the Dragon King is actually capable of. Are you familiar with the story of Atlas?"

"Yeah," I muttered, wondering why we were transitioning into Greek mythology.

"Atlas shouldered the weight of the sky and kept if from falling. *That* is how you should think of the Dragon King. What you see is just the power that's left over, while he's simultaneously shouldering the weight of the sky. He's holding more together than you could possibly fathom. Imagine Atlas holding up the sky and still fighting battles at the *same fucking time.* If the Sarrum ever dropped that sky, you couldn't begin to imagine the full potency of his power. The day we first met, I warned you that you didn't want to make an enemy of the Dragon King. Remember?"

"How could I forget?"

"*I meant* it. You have no idea how powerful he truly is."

"Point taken." I'd already majorly pissed off the King, enough for him to strangle me and kick me out of his house. So where exactly did that leave me?

"Tonight," Benjamin growled, "I'm taking you on a real field trip."

"Okay." *Just please tell me we don't have to hold hands to get there.*

It was dinnertime when Benjamin and I got back to the house on Sycamore. Dr. Price was extremely quiet during the meal and he fidgeted whenever anyone tried to make eye contact with him. Brian still hadn't returned from the Sarrum's house. And Rose didn't come down for dinner. In fact, I hadn't seen her all day. Then again, my schedule had been pretty full, what with making the Sarrum want to strangle me to death and almost dying in an imaginary car crash.

After dinner, Benjamin informed me that it was time for our fieldtrip. I followed him upstairs, wondering where he was heading and where exactly he was taking me on this fieldtrip. When we got upstairs, Benjamin moved to my bedroom door and opened it. I raised an eyebrow, afraid to ask where this was going, afraid to even *think* it, but I'm pretty sure the look on my face still conveyed my concerns.

Benjamin gestured for me to get the fuck in my room. Yeah. His facial expressions were pretty clear too, complete with curse words. Besides, the word *fuck* was used as punctuation in practically every sentence that came out of his mouth.

I stepped in and Benjamin followed, then shut and locked the door. Again, I wondered where the hell this was going.

"Relax, asshole," Benjamin growled. "What've I ever done to make you think I'd be interested in holding your fucking hand? Or crawling into your bed?"

Right. He had a point. "What are we doing then?"

"Lay down on the bed," he demanded in a low growl that made my stomach drop.

As much as I didn't want to, I immediately flopped down on the bed. I wasn't sure whether he'd scared me into doing it or somehow forced me.

"Relax," he growled as he settled into the arm-chair across the room.

Nice and distant. Good.

"You're starting to piss me off."

"Sorry," I whispered so softly I barely heard myself, which was enough, since Benjamin could hear things I didn't say out loud.

"Sleep," he growled.

I instantly found myself in the Waters. I hadn't called them and I definitely hadn't jumped in them, but there I was. I looked around as the Waters pummeled me, but I didn't see Benjamin anywhere. Did I somehow mess this up?

"Charlie," a distant voice growled. Then something grabbed my arm.

The next thing I knew, I was standing in total darkness. It was hotter than hell and eerily silent. The *something* grabbed my arm again and I let out a startled scream.

"Way to make an entrance," Benjamin growled.

"Sorry," I whispered. "Where the hell are you?"

"I'm right here." He didn't add *dumb ass* to the end of that sentence, but I was pretty sure it was implied. And there he was, standing right in front of me. He didn't look any different than he did in the waking world, except he was dressed in a head-to-toe black getup that made him look like a badass pirate or vampire, someone you'd never consider messing with.

"I don't need an outfit to give off that vibe."

No. He seriously didn't. "Where are we?" I whispered.

"What the fuck are you whispering for?" Raising an eyebrow, he looked me up and down and rolled his eyes. "I'm glad to see my lesson in the car had such a profound effect on you."

I looked down, wondering what the heck he was talking about. *Damn it. I was totally sopping wet.* "Sorry."

"Forget it." He touched my arm and I could see clearly in the dark, like he'd given me night vision goggles. "Virgins," he muttered, shaking his head as he took a few steps forward.

That's when I saw the huge Waterfall cascading from a cliff high above us. "Why can't we hear the Water rushing down?"

"Because it's silent," he grumbled, shoving me toward the pool of Water at the base of the Waterfall.

"Thanks," I whispered. "It all makes perfect sense now."

"What the fuck are you whispering for?"

I made a conscious effort not to whisper, "I don't know. I have no idea where we are and this place is seriously creepy. It feels like anything that goes bump in the night could just sneak up on us. You know?"

He looked at me like I was an idiot. "No. I don't know. What the fuck could be out here that's scarier than me?"

"Good point," I whispered, then remembered I didn't need to whisper. "So where are we?"

"This is the entrance to the Dragon King's lair. Now get moving. I don't have all day." He gave me another shove, pushing me into the bottomless pool of dark Water.

But it wasn't bottomless. It was actually surprisingly shallow. I looked at Benjamin and he motioned toward the Waterfall. "What? Am I supposed to walk up to it?"

"Walk through it," he growled.

Sure. Why not? I trudged through the dark Water, trying not to freak out about not being able to see my feet or whatever might be in the Water with me. When I got to the Waterfall, I looked back. Benjamin was standing just a few inches behind me. He nodded, and I stepped into the rushing Water. After two steps, I came face to face with solid rock. *Was this some stupid joke to see how gullible the virgin dragon was?*

A hand reached through the Water and grabbed my arm. "Do I seem like a practical jokester to you, asshole?"

Now that he mentioned it. No. Not so much.

Benjamin's hand yanked me back through the Waterfall, but the dark pool of Water and muggy darkness weren't on the other side anymore. I took a step forward and shook my head in disbelief. We were in a massive elegant room with a black marble floor. Thousands of candles lit the place. Across the floor, there was a wide set of steps leading up to a giant throne covered with black cushions and all along the walls of the great room, silent Waterfalls toppled down from nowhere, flowing into nowhere without a sound. I turned to Benjamin.

He eyed me and shook his head.

I looked down. *Dripping wet. Again. I was hopeless.*

Benjamin moved to the nearest Waterfall. "Come on. It's time for you to see what happens when you make the Sarrum your enemy."

I didn't like the sound of that, especially since I'd sorta fast tracked myself in that direction, but I followed without commenting.

Benjamin stepped through the Waterfall and I followed close behind him. When I stepped out the other side, we were in a damp poorly lit corridor that smelled like a God-awful mixture of mold, stale piss and blood. I had no idea why I was so sure of that. It wasn't like that was an odor combination I smelled often, or ever. Benjamin started down the corridor and I followed, unable to shake the feeling that I was wandering deeper into a nightmare.

As we made our way down the foul smelling corridor, creatures started whispering. And the farther we walked, the louder they got. Soon it wasn't just whispers—whimpering and moaning and wailing echoed in my ears, but the sounds didn't seem to be coming from anywhere. As far as I could tell, there was nothing but solid wall along either side of the corridor. The voices seemed to be coming from *inside* my head. "What the hell is that?" I whispered, not even caring if Benjamin would mock me for whispering.

"Enemies," Benjamin growled without looking back.

Shit. I really didn't like this.

In a few more steps, another silent Waterfall cascaded across our path. Benjamin stepped into it and I hurried after him, terrified that I might end up somewhere different than he did.

I breathed a sigh of relief when I bumped into Benjamin's back on the other side.

"Charlie?" a weak voice croaked.

I stepped beside Benjamin. We were in a stone cell. It was even darker than the corridor so I couldn't make out much detail, but it stunk of stale piss and vomit. Dried stains and wet stains splattered the stone floor. I didn't even want to speculate about what they were.

"Charlie?" the feeble voice croaked again. "Is that you?"

I squinted, wishing my eyes would adjust to the darkness and Benjamin touched my arm, restoring my night vision. *Shit.* Dr. Spenser from the facility stood shackled against the far wall with his arms chained above his head. Of course he wasn't in human form. He was in his Dream form, or *soul form*—a toad-like creature with long protruding fangs like a saber tooth tiger's, bulging eyes and a grossly distended stomach. "What is he?"

"He's a sorrow eater," Benjamin growled, glaring at the toad. "A demon who feeds off the misery of others. We usually call them sorrows for short. The majority of them work as psychiatrists or grief counselors or funeral directors, or any other occupation where they'll encounter a lot of sorrow in the waking world. The noble ones use their appetite for sadness to lessen the grief of sorrowful souls, but nasty fuckers like *this one* cultivate the sorrows of the grieving. They magnify and intensify their pain so they can keep gorging on it."

"Shit."

"Charlie," the toad croaked. "Please. Help me."

"Yeah," I muttered. "That's not gonna happen." I'd always hated Spenser. The fact that he feasted on people's sorrow wasn't a shock. I knew that already. The slimy bastard made Emma miserable during her stay at the facility. She usually left her sessions with him in tears.

Benjamin took a step toward Spenser, and he let out a pathetic whimper. "No. Please. Not again."

"Is that what your victims said to you?" Benjamin snarled. "You get what you deserve, you nasty bloated fuck."

Piss streamed down the toad's legs as he looked to me for help. "Please, Charlie."

Benjamin grabbed him by the throat. "Feast on this, sorrow." A murky dark vapor began to seep from Benjamin's mouth and the toad clamped his mouth shut, but Benjamin pried his mouth open, wrenching his jaw much wider than it was ever meant to go. Then the Darkness exhaled again and the murky vapor oozed from his mouth and funneled down the doctor's throat. Spenser thrashed and whimpered and pissed some more, but Benjamin just kept pouring the dark vapor into him until he grew silent and still.

The Darkness released the toad's throat and jaw and let his limp body slump to the floor. Spenser's muscles twitched as he sagged from the shackles around his wrists that were clearly anchored too high above his head. His scaly wrists were raw and bloody, and his arms appeared to be dislocated from his shoulders.

"This piece of shit tortured the Princess while she was at the facility," Benjamin growled. "And he denied the Sarrum the right to visit his own wife." Benjamin yanked the toad to his feet and struck him across the face. The contents of my stomach curdled as the crunching sound of breaking bone echoed against the stone walls of the cell. The doctor let out a pitiful shriek, and the Darkness wrapped his fingers around his throat. "Beg for mercy."

"Please," the toad croaked in a frail broken whisper. "Show me mercy."

The words were barely out of the doctor's mouth when Benjamin slammed the toad's head against the stone wall behind him. A trickle of blood-tinged mucous dripped from Spenser's fat lips as his eyes rolled back in his head.

"Stop," I whispered. I hated Spenser, and he deserved to be punished for all the misery he'd caused, *but this was too much.* I could barely keep my dinner down. "Please stop."

Ignoring my plea, Benjamin slammed the toad's head against the stone again and a fresh stream of piss gushed down his legs as his body went limp. Benjamin released his throat with a satisfied growl and left him drooping from the chains at his bloody wrists. Without a word, the Darkness crossed the cell and stepped out through the Waterfall.

I followed him into another section of moldy corridor where another silent Waterfall spilled like a fluid curtain across our path. I focused on keeping my voice steady as I asked, "Is Spenser Sighted?"

"Yeah," Benjamin growled. "He is." Without waiting to see if I had other questions, he stepped through the Waterfall.

I swallowed the lump in my throat, stepped in after him and stepped out in another stone cell. A swarm-of-bugs-in-the-shape-of-a-man sat crouched on the stone floor across the cell. He rocked slowly back and forth as a nauseating buzzing sound emanated from every twitching insect that formed the shape of his grotesque body.

"Frank?" The bug-man was a fellow patient at the facility. He went after Emma, mumbling that she'd "offered herself" but he never actually laid a hand on her. The dragon enchantment that guarded Emma melted Frank's hand the second he reached for her, but I doubted the fact that he didn't get to finish the job mattered to the Dragon King. I turned to Benjamin. "What's wrong with him?"

The Darkness eyed Frank with distaste. "He's locked in a place much worse than this cell."

I raised an eyebrow.

"He's trapped inside his own head, reliving every horror that's locked away inside."

I wasn't sure how to feel about that. "What is he?"

"He's a pestilent," Benjamin answered in a low growl.

"What? Like a plague?"

"Kind of, I suppose." Benjamin narrowed his eyes, like he was considering Frank in a new light. "Like the plague of locusts in the Bible. Most pestilents are diagnosed as schizophrenics in the waking world because if creatures whisper in their ears while they're sleeping in Draumer, they hear it in the waking world. Other demons love to take advantage of that. They tell them to do wicked things over and over until their minds eventually snap. When schizophrenics claim that the voices in their head made them do something unthinkable, they're usually telling the truth."

"Did demons in Draumer tell Frank to go after Emma at the facility?"

Eyes still glued to Frank, Benjamin nodded. "Yeah."

"Is he Sighted too?"

"No," Benjamin growled as he stepped back through the Waterfall.

I took one last look at the rocking plague of locusts. It almost didn't seem fair to punish him for something he'd been tortured into doing. The Sarrum obviously had no compassion for any creature who messed with Emma, regardless of the circumstances. Part of me respected that. The other part couldn't help feeling sorry for Frank, but I didn't want to wait too long to follow Benjamin and end up stuck in the cell with him. "Sorry Frank," I whispered as I stepped into the Waterfall.

When I stepped out, we were back in the corridor and another Waterfall noiselessly sliced through the path in front of us. The second I reached him, Benjamin stepped into it.

I followed and stepped into a damp cell that stunk of spoiled meat. A man with a scraggly beard and filthy matted hair stood chained against the far wall. His lips were cracked. His face was badly bruised. One eye was swollen shut. His pants were soiled and his body drooped from wrists that were shackled too high above his head. But that was hardly the worst of it. A gaping gash had been sliced across his shirtless chest from his left armpit to his right hip and the guts that spilled from it were rancid and pussy. *There was no way this guy should be alive.* But he lifted his head and looked at me.

I turned to Benjamin, because I couldn't stand to make eye contact with him. "Who is this?"

Benjamin glared at the man who should be dead. "Tell him who you are, traitor."

The man coughed and a thin stream of blood trickled from his cracked lips. "I'm a traitor," he echoed in a thready whisper.

I forced myself to look him in the eye. "What did you do to end up like this?"

"I betrayed the Sarrum's trust," he whispered, "and I hurt the Princess."

Rage flared inside me, my chest tightened and the cell suddenly felt too hot and cramped. "The Princess is a friend of mine. What'd you do to her?"

The man's head drooped, his open chest rising and falling as he gasped for air.

"What'd you do?" I demanded, no longer caring what they'd done to him.

"I stood by while others attacked her and after the Sarrum saved her—" his voice broke off in a fit of gasping and coughing, and it took a full minute for him to catch his breath enough to continue.

"When the Sarrum summoned me to help her, I blinded her."

Blinded her? *Emma wasn't blind.* Benjamin exited through the Waterfall before I could ask any questions. Then it hit me. When I met the Sarrum, he told me he was Emma's guide when she was a child. At the time, it made no sense because Emma wasn't Sighted. *Shit.* Emma *was* Sighted, and somehow this son of a bitch *took* her Sight. Fighting an overwhelming urge to walk across the cell and rip the man's guts completely out, I followed after Benjamin.

I stepped out in a new corridor. This one was clean and lit by hundreds of scented candles that made the hall smell like an intoxicating blend of exotic spices. At the far end of the corridor, another Waterfall spilled from ceiling to floor.

But I was still battling the urge to go back in the last cell and make that bastard hurt even more. Chest heaving, I looked at Benjamin. "What the hell's happening to me?"

"Something that's been asleep for a very long time is beginning to wake," Benjamin murmured. There was an unfamiliar note of approval in his Dark voice.

I looked back at the Waterfall behind us.

"He belongs to the Dragon King now," Benjamin growled. "And I promise you, he's nowhere close to finished with him."

The tightness in my chest loosened a little. "How is he still alive?"

"The Sarrum heals him every morning."

"Why?"

"Because dying would bring an end to his suffering," Benjamin growled. "So every morning, the Sarrum heals his wounds. Then he rakes a claw across his chest, causing just enough trauma to leave him in agony while keeping him conscious till the next morning. Then he starts all over again."

"Message received," I muttered. "Don't piss off the Dragon King."

"There's one more place I need to go." There was an edge of sorrow to Benjamin's words. "And I don't have time to take you back. So keep your mouth shut and be respectful, or I'll find an empty cell to stick you in." With that, he walked to the Waterfall at the end of the corridor and stepped through.

I moved toward the Waterfall, certain there was nothing that could shock me at this point. Then I stepped through and realized I was wrong.

16

BENJAMIN

It might've been too soon to let the virgin see her, but I wasn't about to skip visiting because we'd spent too much time on his fieldtrip. I stepped into the Waterfall and grimaced as the familiar prickling sensation washed over me. Then I stepped out the other side, cloaked in the ridiculous form I'd been confined to since the Princess was a toddler. I tensed as the virgin stepped through behind me. *So help me, if he uttered one disrespectful syllable I'd stick him in an empty cell for the night.* He blew out a breath but he didn't say a word.

Across the room, Rose sat in a chair at her mother's bedside with her hand on top of Isa's and her head resting beside it. It looked like she hadn't moved an inch since I brought her to see her mother the night before. I crossed the room and put my hand on top of hers, and she sat up and smiled.

On the other side of Isa's bed, Doc sat at the bedside table he'd fashioned into a workbench. He was hunched over a leather-bound volume of potions and spells, surrounded by a clutter of vials and a peculiar assortment of ingredients. He was so engrossed in his reading that he didn't notice me until I rounded the bed. When he looked up at me, the corners of his mouth twitched, but he didn't crack a smile. He was smart enough to know that wouldn't end well for him. He dipped his head. "Darkness."

"How's she doing?"

His fleshless face grimaced. "No change, I'm afraid, but I won't stop looking until I've found a cure."

I didn't respond. He knew the stakes, and I hadn't come to threaten. I'd come to see her.

Exhaling loudly, the witchdoctor stood up and stretched. Then he walked to the virgin, and I dragged his chair to Isa's bedside and sat down.

Across the room, Doc cleared his throat. "Hello, Charlie." When the virgin didn't answer, Doc raised his voice. "What's the matter? Cat got your tongue tonight?"

With a stone cold expression of respect on his face, the kid shook his head. Then he looked at me.

"You can talk. Just keep it down."

Nodding, Charlie turned to Doc. "Hey, Doc. Sorry. I was told not to speak before we came in here."

"Understandable," Doc whispered. "But now that you are here, do you have any questions? We are supposed to be teaching you, after all."

Charlie's thoughts echoed so loudly through the quiet room that he might as well have shouted them at us. *Yeah. What the heck is going on in here? Why are you guys hanging out at a doll's bedside? And oh yeah, why did Benjamin turn into a sock monkey when we walked in?* "Thanks," he whispered. "But, uh... I don't really know what's going on in here. So... I wouldn't even know what to ask." *Besides, I'm not so sure the Sarrum still wants you to teach me after what happened this morning.*

I suppressed a smirk. The kid was learning—not to block his thoughts, but to be respectful. It was a start.

"Mmm," Doc whispered. "Well, let's start with a simple explanation of what's going on in here and then we'll take it from there."

The kid nodded. *There's a simple explanation for all of this?*

Doc just kept pretending he couldn't hear every thought going through the kid's head. "First of all, the space that we're in right now is very special. Benjamin must be quite pleased with how you're progressing to bring you here."

Not really. I just didn't have time to take him back first.

Doc suppressed a chuckle by turning it into a cough. "This space is heavily enchanted. It was woven with a special kind of magic that would allow a creature of Light to dwell here in the heart of the Darkness."

He's talking about Emma. This is Emma's cage.

Clearly uncomfortable with the kid's unspoken comment, Doc cleared his throat. "The magic that wove this place shaped things quite specifically when the Princess was a toddler. Benjamin was the Princess's primary guard. I'm sure you can imagine what a frightening caretaker the Darkness would've been for a young child, so a special form was assigned to him and to Isa, when she joined him a few years later. In the waking world, the Princess had a sock monkey and a doll that looked identical to these two. They were gifts from the Sarrum, and he bound her guards to those forms so she'd feel more at ease when she was alone with them. Undoing the magic that confined them to those forms would require undoing the entire protective enchantment the Sarrum wove for his Princess, and I'm afraid that'd be quite unthinkable. So here they are—two brave guardians of the Dragon King's most precious treasure, forever bound to the forms of a child's playthings."

As Charlie quietly processed that, I reached out and took Isa's hand. *Your daughter hasn't left your bedside, Isa. She's incredibly anxious to meet you. It's time for you to find your way back to us. Doc will help. I won't let him rest until he does.*

"So that doll on the bed is Isabella?" Charlie whispered. "The housekeeper that Emma stabbed?"

I lifted my head and glared at the virgin. "She's no more a *housekeeper* than I am a driver. Isa is the Sarrum's sorceress. Show some respect for fuck's sake."

The virgin cringed. "Sorry. I didn't mean to be disrespectful."

I gave Isa's hand a squeeze. "You didn't know. Now you do."

"Right," Charlie whispered. "So Doc, you're here to heal Isabella? And Rose is here to visit her?"

"Yes," Doc answered softly, "among other reasons. And quite soon, I'll require your help in healing Isabella. Rose's too."

Charlie and Rose both raised their eyebrows but neither of them said anything.

"I suspect," Doc whispered, "that the two of you possess a knack for potion-making and sorcery, and I believe your help will be invaluable to my efforts."

"Why would you suspect that?" Charlie wondered aloud.

Doc looked at Rose and smiled. "Sorcery is in Rose's blood. Her great grandmother was a legendary sorceress, as is her mother."

Rose dropped her head to Isa's hand to conceal her smile.

Then Doc turned to Charlie. "And I have a very strong suspicion that potion-making is in your blood, young man."

17

CHARLIE

Doc wanted to give Benjamin and Rose some alone time with Isabella, so he asked me to join him for a drink and offered to answer any questions I might have. We left the room through the same Waterfall I came in through but when we stepped out the other side, we weren't in the candle-lit corridor that smelled like exotic spices. We were on a balcony overlooking the Dark forest. The top of the huge Waterfall that we'd entered the palace through was several feet below us, yet we weren't anywhere near the top of the palace. There were lots of other balconies and spires much further above us. I moved past a wrought iron table and chairs and stepped up to the railing for a better look at the silent Waterfall. "Why couldn't I see the palace when we were down at the bottom?"

The doctor crossed the balcony and leaned his forearms on the railing beside me. "Because this isn't on the other side of the Waterfall."

"What does that even mean?"

He turned toward me with a patient grin. "Space isn't the same in this world as it is in the waking world. You can't necessarily get from point A to point B by moving in a straight line."

A gentle breeze made the Dark forest's sweltering heat a little more bearable. It also kept blowing my hair into my eyes. Raking it back from my face, I frowned at Doc. "So that's why we walked out the Waterfall in Isa's room and ended up somewhere different than where I walked in from?"

Doc nodded. "Locations aren't linear in this world. Water is the primary means of travel from one place to another. In fact, there are many places that can *only* be accessed through the Waters." Doc moved to the table and chairs and motioned for me to join him.

I walked over, slid a chair back from the table and sat down. "So all the places Benjamin took me tonight? If the Waterfalls weren't there, those rooms wouldn't be connected?"

Nodding, he pulled an ancient-looking bottle of wine and two glasses from the pockets of his cloak, and I was too distracted thinking about the Waterfalls to even wonder how he did it. He lifted a glass and his creepy eye sockets widened. When

I nodded, he poured me a drink. "That's correct. The rooms of this palace are not spatially connected. They actually exist quite separate from one another."

I took a sip of Doc's pocket wine. It tasted like apples and a weird combination of spices that I wasn't entirely sure tasted good together but I didn't want to be rude, so I'd probably finish it anyway. "That's pretty wild."

Doc poured himself a drink and took a sip before answering, "It is indeed pretty wild. But you must have other questions. Now's your chance to ask someone who won't growl and swear at you for asking."

I choked on the wine in my mouth, trying to stifle a laugh. "Yeah. The Darkness can be kind of intense."

"He certainly can," the doctor agreed with a grin. "But I suppose we shouldn't expect someone who's earned a title like that to be all rainbows and sunshine."

"Good point," I muttered, sliding my fingers along the stem of my glass. "I do have a couple questions."

"I'm all ears." Doc took a slow sip of funky apple wine, then leaned back in his chair.

"The last man Benjamin took me to see..." The tightness flared in my chest again, and I had to stop and breathe through it for a second. "He said he blinded the Princess. Emma used to be Sighted, didn't she?"

Doc hesitated for a second, then nodded. "Yes. She was Sighted."

"Who was that guy?"

The doctor started fidgeting with a corner of the label on the wine bottle. "He used to be the royal healer here at the palace."

"That's why the Sarrum asked him to help Emma after someone tried to hurt her."

Doc nodded but said nothing.

"How did he blind her?"

"She'd just been through something quite traumatic. He gave her a potion to drink and told the Sarrum it'd help calm her down. Instead, it trapped her in the Waters and she was stuck between the two worlds for too long. The Waters intend to strip our memories of the world we leave behind. For the Unsighted, it erases those memories almost entirely and any fragments they do remember, they just assume were dreams. For those of us who are Sighted, the Waters still attempt to strip our memories but we're able to resist it."

I nodded and waited for him to go on.

"The Princess was in the Waters for far too long. It's a wonder she even survived the ordeal, especially considering she'd just gone through a trauma, which I suspect made it easier to strip her memory. There were fresh memories that she didn't want to hold onto."

I got the impression Doc was skipping over a lot of details. "So how did she get out?"

Doc downed the last sip of his wine and poured himself a refill. "The Sarrum dove in after her."

"And the Waters listened to him because he's a dragon?"

Doc cleared his throat. "Yes. Something like that."

"You said it's a wonder she lived through it. How did she survive?"

"The Sarrum healed her as much as he could, but he couldn't restore her Sight." Doc paused to down a hefty sip of wine. "She does have a residual bit of memory left, just a flicker really. The reason that Brian said seeing you would confuse her is that you're partially responsible for the deteriorated state she's in now."

The tightness in my chest intensified. "Me? How?"

"You spoke of this world with her when the two of you were at the facility, and that residual flicker of memory was just enough to remind her that she should know things she doesn't remember. It's much like an Alzheimer's patient becoming agitated when people speak of things they realize they should know but can't recall."

"Shit." I pushed back from the table and moved to the railing. "I had no idea. I never would've intentionally done anything to hurt her."

Doc angled his chair toward me. "Everyone knows that, Charlie. You wouldn't be here if they didn't. We also know that Emma cares for you and she misses you, but the Sarrum is concerned that seeing you would confuse and upset her right now. How would we explain the fact that you're training with us? Why would her husband hire the crazy fellow who attacked him at the mental facility?"

I let out a frustrated sigh. "Yeah. I see your point."

He stood up and joined me at the railing. "Brian believes a visit from you would be beneficial and I'm inclined to agree. We'd planned to discuss it with the Sarrum at his house this morning."

"But I pretty much fucked that up."

"Yes. I'm afraid you did. I think it'd be best to table that conversation for a bit. In the meantime, I'd like you to begin training with me."

I raked my hair back from my eyes. "Why do you think I'd be good at making potions?"

"I have a knack for detecting those sorts of talents," Doc answered with a bony grin. "I can smell it in your blood."

"Am I the only one who *can't* smell weird things you shouldn't be able to smell?"

Doc's grin widened. "Who determines what you should and shouldn't be able to do? The Unsighted? All the rules have changed, Charlie. Once you awaken the dragon inside you, you'll be amazed at the things you're able to do."

I liked the sound of that. "So when do I start training with you?"

Doc started toward the Waterfall we'd come out through. "I'd begin today if it were up to me. Unfortunately, it isn't. We'll begin as soon as Benjamin decides you're ready."

18

EMMA

It'd been so long since we'd made love and David seemed determined to make up for every lost moment—in the shower, against the bedroom wall because we couldn't make it all the way to the bed and once we did make it, the rest of the day was just one magnificent orgasmic blur. Eventually, I drifted off to sleep, sated and blissfully sore from his relentless attention and I dreamt that we were making love on a fragrant bed of grass beneath a star-covered sky.

When I woke, a few hours had passed. The sky was getting darker and there was a subtle chill to the breeze wafting in from the open window across the room. Sitting up, I pulled the comforter up from the foot of the bed and snuggled closer to David as I tucked it under my chin. His eyes didn't open, but he turned toward me and pulled me to his chest.

I closed my eyes with a contented sigh. I'd missed this—lying pressed against his chest with the beat of his heart sounding in my ear. This was where I belonged. I never wanted to leave our bed.

Then I plummeted back to reality. *What the hell was I doing?* It was like David had flipped a switch inside me when he stormed into the bathroom. As soon as he touched me, I couldn't think straight and I became powerless to resist. Sure, part of me knew I should've pushed him away, but the pounding of my heart and the ache between my legs had silenced that part. I'd convinced myself that none of the reasons for keeping my distance really mattered. *But they did matter.* Nauseated by my utter lack of self-control, I slid away from David, sat up and clutched a pillow to my chest.

David let out a groggy exhalation as he sat up beside me. He swept a stray tendril of hair from my face and smoothed it between his fingers. "What's wrong, Princess?"

Why did I let myself forget all the reasons I shouldn't have let him touch me? And how could he still affect me that way after everything that'd happened? I was so weak and pathetic. Fighting back tears, I shifted toward him. "Did you kill Sophie?"

He let my hair drop as his gaze shifted to the window. "Let's not talk about that now."

Rage coursed through my veins at his words. I threw my pillow across the room, just narrowly missing a vase of fresh flowers. "Let's not talk about the woman who said she was your lover? About how she said you were tired of playing daddy while I cried on your shoulder and you enjoyed being with a woman who knew more than just the tricks you'd taught her? Or how about the fact that she *knew* I'd never been with anyone but you? Sure! Let's not talk about any of that! Let's just pretend none of it ever happened! That I didn't come home from the party and slit my wrist! And I didn't stab Isa when she tried to stop me from slitting the other one! Let's not talk about how Sophie just happened to die after I told you what she said to me! Talk about it! Damn it! I want you to talk about it!"

He'd been so patient for so long. I'd almost forgotten how passionate my husband's reactions could be, but something inside him seemed to snap as I was screaming at him. His jaw clenched and his nostrils flared as his eyes locked with mine. "You want to talk about it? Fine! Let's talk about it! Sophie Turner was a whore! She'd screw anything with a pulse and it *killed her* that I didn't want to fuck her!"

The contents of my stomach curdled as he spoke.

"And she didn't just proposition me that night! She did it all the time! But when she propositioned me at the party, I grabbed her by the arm and spun her toward you. You were across the room, laughing with Brian and Tristan. I pointed at you and asked her what the hell she thought I'd ever want with her, when I had you. I pissed her off and she took it out on you, but if you think I fucking touched her you need to open your eyes!"

I wanted to believe him, more than anything. *But he still hadn't answered my question.* Heart pounding, I screamed, "Did you kill her?"

"What do you think? Look me in the eyes!" Something primal flared in his eyes as he leaned toward me and it frightened me a little, but it also made my heart ache. "Do you believe I killed her?"

The ache in my heart deepened as I jumped off the bed and whispered, "Yes." I rushed to the chair across the room, grabbed my bathrobe, slipped it on and tied it as I headed to the door.

My hand was on the doorknob when he came up behind me, slammed a palm against the door on either side of me and growled, "You aren't going anywhere!" My heart was racing and I was furious, but his feral growl beside my ear spread like wildfire through my body and I was instantly wet for him. *What the hell was wrong with me? How could I be so pathetic?* "You wanted to talk! So talk! Hit me! Scream at me! Just turn around and face me!"

I did what I always did, exactly what he told me to. Caged between his arms, I turned. His face was just inches from mine. He was breathing heavily, angrily. Something about it felt so familiar, like we'd done this before. *After he rented the horror movie my mother wouldn't let me watch.* White hot pain flared in my head and I squeezed my eyes shut.

"Look at me," he growled, more command than request.

I opened my eyes and locked them with his. "Why should I believe you?"

"Because," he snarled. "I haven't looked at another woman since…"

"Since what?"

He exhaled slowly. "Since the day you were born."

Something tightened in the pit of my stomach. "When I told Charlie about us, he called you a pedophile."

"Yes, I know," he answered in a low growl.

I wasn't sure which ached more, my head or my heart. "What?"

"He was here at the house this morning. I was going to offer him a job to thank him for looking out for you at the facility but as I was walking in to speak with him, he was saying precisely that."

Voice wavering, I asked, "What did you do to him?"

"Nothing he couldn't walk away from." His growl was low and furious as he added, "Show more concern for your new friend than for me, and I'm apt to take it out on him."

"He didn't do anything to you," I muttered. "Take it out on me."

David pulled his head back and narrowed his eyes at me. "Do you actually think I would harm you? Is that how you see me now, as a pedophile and a murderer?"

My throat felt too tight as I whispered, "I don't know what to think of you anymore."

His nostrils flared and his muscles tensed. And for a second, I actually thought he might hit me, but he took his hands off the door and stepped back. "Go, before I do something I'll regret."

Heart slamming in my chest, I whispered, "No."

He took a step closer, touched his forehead to mine and stroked my cheek with his fingertips. "You don't see me at all anymore. See me, Princess. You have to see me." *The ache in my head was unbearable.* "I can't hold back much longer. You need to fight through this before it kills us both." He tenderly brushed his lips against mine, a faint whisper of a kiss. *And the pain in my head intensified.* Then he stepped back and opened the door.

I wanted to shut it. I wanted him to kiss me again. I wanted to go back to bed and wake up all over again, so none of this had happened. But I saw it in his eyes. He wanted me to go.

So I turned around and left.

19

DAVID

I watched Emma march halfway down the hall before I raced up behind her and wrapped an arm around her waist. "That's not how this ends!"

She tried to pull away and when I wouldn't let her, she let out a frustrated scream. "Let me go!"

"You're mine," I rasped, keeping her firmly pinned against me. "I won't ever let you go."

She smacked my arm and tried to pry it from her waist but when I tightened my hold, the scent of her arousal hit me like a shockwave. Maddened by the scent, I lifted her off the floor, carried her back to the bedroom and slammed the door shut.

"I hate you," she whispered, each word a dose of poison. If enough of those words escaped her lips, my heart would stop.

"No," I murmured, setting her on her feet. "You don't."

Blinking the tears from her eyes, she muttered, "Well…I wish I did."

"No." I stepped away from the door, making it clear that she could exit if she chose to. "You don't." She hadn't wanted to leave in the first place. I'd left her little choice by opening the door.

A tear slid down her cheek as she looked up at me. "I think we're too broken to fix."

I took another step back. "I refuse to believe that."

She crossed the room and sat down in the chair by the window. "I can't take this anymore." A humorless chuckle escaped her lips as she lifted the ankle with the house arrest bracelet. "But I don't even have a choice. I'm stuck with you."

I moved to my dresser, grabbed some fresh clothes and slipped them on. Then I sat down on the bed and waited for her to continue.

She dropped her eyes to the floor. "You should've let me die that night."

Heartache and fury and grief warred inside me as I opened my mouth to respond, but there was nothing I could say to fix this. "It would've killed me too."

She looked up at me, a vacant shell of who she should be. "Maybe that would've been for the best."

I knew I ought to keep my distance. She felt trapped and she needed space, but I couldn't stop myself from moving to the chair and kneeling at her feet. "You can't mean that."

Her smile was like a knife to my heart, so cold and distant. "I do. I wish I was dead." A tear slid down her cheek as she twisted the knife. "And I wish you were, too."

I leaned forward to wrap my arms around her, but she recoiled and struck my cheek. "Get away from me! Can't you see how much I hate you?"

"Go ahead," I whispered. "Let it all out. I can take it."

She swung her hand back and struck me a little harder than the first time.

"I love you," I whispered.

"Please leave." Her voice was so cold and hollow.

I stood and moved to the door. "Get dressed. Dr. Price is here to see you."

She crossed her arms over her chest. "I don't care."

"If you don't keep up with the therapy, they'll send you back to the facility."

"At least then I'd be away from you."

Smoke billowed from my flared nostrils. But what the fuck did it matter? My wife couldn't see it. "Fine. Don't get dressed. I'll send him up anyway."

"Don't sleep here tonight," she whispered, as I opened the door. "I don't want to see your face."

I carefully restrained my anger and answered without turning around. "Then you won't." Making a conscious effort not to slam the door, I stepped from the room and marched toward the staircase to fetch the doctor. *If he didn't fix this...*

Jeremy felt me coming and met me halfway up the stairs.

"Fix her," I snarled. "Soon."

Beads of sweat glistened on his brow as he dipped his head. "I'll do my best."

"Not good enough!" I grabbed him by the collar and ignored the way he flinched at the heat of my breath. "I will not accept failure!"

The second I released him, he rushed toward my bedroom with a flurry of apologies and whimpered promises.

I stormed to my office, locked the door and dropped into the chair behind my desk. I needed an outlet for my rage...

... The stench of purulent organs assaulted my nostrils as I entered the dank cell. The moment the traitor met my eyes, I unmasked and willed the shackles to release him. And he pissed himself as his hands dropped to his sides.

I crossed the stone floor and wrapped a claw around his throat. "I am not leaving this cell until you hurt worse than I do." I backhanded his face, a howl of pain accompanied the crunch of splintering bone and I grinned at him. "So you're in for a very long night."

"Please," he pleaded through a dislocated jaw. "Just let me die."

I tightened my grip on his neck, and sweat dripped from his blistering brow as I breathed my response in his face. "How interesting that you should say that tonight." I gripped his neck a little harder, and a pitiful wheezing sound emanated from his throat. "That's what the Princess just said to me." I squeezed a little tighter, the wheezing stopped and his flesh took on a sickly blue tint. "She said she wished I'd let her die that night."

I released his throat and he fell to the floor, gasping for breath through a partially crushed windpipe. *That was Sophie's fault.*

"Really?" I stomped on his left arm and he let out an agonized shriek. "You take no responsibility for that night?" I stomped on his right arm and ground the bones beneath my heel, but his feeble whimper was insufficient. "I believe we've neared your breaking point, traitor." Stepping off his crushed limb, I breathed life into his broken body.

His cracked ribs and dented windpipe mended and his breathing normalized. A sigh of relief hissed from his broken jaw as I put his organs back in order and sealed the gash they'd spilled out through. Once his jaw was healed, he sat up and whispered, "Thank you for your mercy, Sarrum."

My laughter thundered inside his head. *There will be no mercy for you, Doctor. Not ever, and certainly not tonight.* Ignoring his tears, I stepped back to the

Waterfall, reached in and sensed the sorrow's frantic movements on the other side. The wet sound of tearing flesh and the snapping of brittle bones bled through the Water as I tore him from the chains and yanked him through. I tossed his fat body to the stone floor beside the freshly healed traitor and he landed in a puddle of his own making. Two weak hearts raced as I stepped toward them.

"What is this?" the sorrow whimpered.

"I figured you could both use some company." I stopped just outside the sorrow's puddle of piss. "I know the Darkness has been taking fine care of you but I must confess, I regret being such a neglectful host. You must be famished."

"No," he whispered. "Please...no."

I swung a wing and knocked his bloated body backward. "I offer you nourishment, and you decline the offer? Is that any way to thank your King?"

"I'm sorry," he sobbed like a frightened child. "I didn't know who you were when Emma was at the facility."

I leapt forward, crouched above him and dipped my head so that we were face to face. "Don't you dare lie to me, you miserable piece of filth!"

"Please!" he sobbed. "I don't want to die!"

I filled his head with my laughter until it neared the point of bursting. "You won't die tonight, not if you do as I say."

"Anything," he whimpered.

"Your new cellmate has much to grieve over and he'll soon be in a world of hurt. Cultivate his despair all you like in my absence."

A twisted smile spread across the sorrow's face. "Why would you give me such a gift?"

"Because his transgressions were worse than yours. In a few moments, I'm going to break him and I expect you to tend to his suffering while I'm away. In exchange for this service, you may feast on his misery to your foul heart's content."

Ignoring the traitor's sobs, I lifted the sorrow by the neck. "But first, you'll feast on mine."

It didn't take long for the sorrow's howling to turn the traitor's stomach but I continued to pour my misery down the sorrow's throat, and I didn't stop until several minutes after he lost consciousness.

I tossed his bloated soul to the stone floor, and he let out a pitiful moan as my venom gushed from his swollen lips.

Then I stepped toward the traitor. "I'm done playing, and you've had sufficient time to heal. Now it's time to break you."

20

EMMA

I ignored his knocking the first three times. The fourth time, the doctor's gentle voice accompanied the knock on my bedroom door. "I'm coming in now, Emma. Are you decent?"

I tried to steady my voice as I answered, "Go away, Doctor!" He didn't need to know I'd been crying, and I certainly didn't want to discuss it with him.

"I've been instructed to let myself in if you won't open the door, but I don't think it needs to come to that." When I didn't answer, he turned the knob and pushed the door open. He smiled at me as he stepped in the room but behind his black-rimmed glasses, dark eyes studied me with hesitant concern.

I pulled my legs up and tucked them beside me on the chair, being careful to keep my robe closed. Ignoring David's suggestion to get dressed didn't seem like such a great idea, now that I was stuck in nothing but a bathrobe for my therapy session. "I don't have anything to say to you," I muttered in a hoarse voice that made it abundantly obvious I'd been crying.

"Alright." He shut the door and walked across the room to me. "Why don't you start by getting dressed? Then we can find a more suitable place to talk."

I drew my knees up to my chest and wrapped my arms around them, making sure the robe stayed in place. "What's wrong with this room? We met here the other day."

"Yes," he agreed with a nod. "But today, the room reeks of sex and you're barely clothed."

I hugged my legs a little closer. "Did you really just say that to me?"

Chuckling softly, he leaned against the wall. "Yes, I believe I did. I don't mince words, Emma. That's just a waste of everyone's time. I'm not about to sit on that bed. It's obviously been well used. Go get changed. I'll hunt down Sara and ask her to change the bedding. Then you and I can find a quiet spot elsewhere."

"I told you," I whispered. "I don't have anything to say to you."

The doctor moved to the pillow I'd thrown on the floor, picked it up and tossed it on the bed. "We could discuss the reason you're so angry or how you feel about spending half the day in bed with a man who you suspect cheated on you, a man you also suspect of murder."

Resting my chin on my knees, I muttered, "That's *your* old friend you're talking about, Doctor."

"Yes." He moved toward my chair. "And *your* spouse but all of what I said is true, is it not?"

"No comment."

"And stop calling me Doctor. It's too stuffy. Call me Jeremy. If you won't relocate, why don't you take the bed and offer me the chair?"

"Because I don't want you here, Jeremy."

He grinned as he approached my chair. "Sleep, Emma."

Then I was sinking...

...I sat up and tried to get my bearings as I groggily surveyed the room. I couldn't remember lying down or even coming to my room for that matter. *So how did I end up in bed?*

"I brought you here," said a Dark voice in the corner.

"Who are you?" I whispered. "And where's the Sarrum?"

The creature who belonged to the voice stepped from the shadows. "I'm the new royal healer." Something between a man and a beast, the healer wore a heavy black cloak that seemed unnecessary given the heat. His face was a mask of bone with a wiry tuft of dark hair sprouting from the top, and strings of beads and different sorts of teeth were strung around his neck and waist.

"Who gave you permission to enter my chambers, royal healer? And you didn't answer my second question. Where's the Sarrum? I find it hard to believe that he asked you to sneak in here while I was sleeping."

A creepy grin spread across the healer's face. "I told you. I didn't sneak in. I brought you here. You were wandering around the palace corridors quite disoriented, and the Sarrum is busy tending to other matters."

"Then where's Benji? Or Isa?" A burst of pain exploded at my temples and I dropped my head to my hands.

"There it is again," the healer murmured. He covered my hands with his and warmth seeped into my head, dulling the pain. "That's how I found you, standing in a corridor with your head in your hands. You couldn't tell me who you were or why you were there, so I brought you here and stayed to keep an eye on you."

"Thank you," I whispered as the pain subsided.

"There's no need to thank me. That's what I'm here for. But since you did, you're quite welcome." The healer dragged a chair to my bedside and sat down. "Tell me, when did you first experience the ache in your head?"

Something twitched inside my head, a threat of future pain. "I'd rather not talk about it."

The healer crossed his legs and shifted in his chair. "What would you like to talk about?"

"Can you please just tell me where Benji is?"

"I'm afraid he's busy at the moment."

"I'm sorry," I whispered. "I don't mean to be rude, but I really don't feel like talking right now. Could we do this another time?"

"The sooner we speak, the sooner I'll be able to heal you, Princess."

"I don't need healing," I muttered, wincing as the pain flared again.

"Yes. Yes." The healer placed his hands back on my head. "Of course. This is perfectly normal. No need to take away this ache in your head, then?"

"Please make it stop," I sobbed.

"Shhh." Heat pulsed from the healer's fingers and the pain became a little more bearable. "It's alright, child. Just relax."

"I'm not a child."

"Tell me, Princess," he murmured as his hands moved over my scalp. "Who is the Sarrum to you?"

"What?"

"Father? Teacher? Husband?" His hands stopped moving on a particularly tender spot. "*Captor?*"

The pain sharpened and the room began to blur. *Why was he asking me that?*

"It's a simple question," he murmured.

I didn't even know this man. For all I knew, he was lying about being the royal healer. "I'm sorry," I whispered, pushing his hands away. "Newcomers are generally not welcome in this space and I don't want to continue this conversation. Whoever you are, please leave. I need to find the Sarrum."

"I told you Princess, the Sarrum is busy. And if I wasn't welcome in this space, how would I be standing here at your bedside?"

"I don't really care," I muttered. "Will you please go?"

"We'll never make any progress if you refuse to speak to me in both worlds."

The pain gripped me, consuming me, and I clutched my head and doubled over on the bed.

The healer touched the base of my skull. "My apologies, Princess. My back is against the wall. I have no answers and questioning you is my only means of figuring this out."

It felt like someone had set the inside of my head on fire. Everything was spinning and the healer's hands didn't even begin to alleviate the pain. "Where's the Sarrum?"

"He's busy, Princess. I told you that already." As the healer spoke, his hands explored the back of my head and the ache seemed to move with his fingers.

Everything was spinning. My world was spinning out of control, and I was terrified. "Get out of here,"

I whimpered. "And get the Sarrum. I don't care if he's busy."

"Shhh," the healer whispered. "Just try to relax, Princess. I'm here to help."

He wasn't holding me down but in that position, face down on the bed, doubled over on my knees, it felt like I was suffocating. "I want the Sarrum," I whispered. "Where is he?"

"Busy," the healer murmured.

I heard movement on the other side of the room but I didn't need to look up. I knew who it was. The air felt hotter and heavier and the scent of Dark spices had begun to leak from my pores. "Take your hands off my wife, witchdoctor."

The healer's hands immediately broke contact. "Of course, Sarrum."

"Now...get out."

With a mumbled, "Yes, my King," the healer scurried across the room and exited through the Waterfall.

I didn't lift my head as he moved toward me. I was too afraid that moving might intensify the pain.

The mattress sunk beneath him as he sat down beside me. *Form of a man, weight of a dragon.* He breathed in and my pain subsided. Then his scent washed over me, bathing me in warmth. When I still didn't move, he gently rolled me to my back and slipped a pillow under my head. "Better?"

"Yes." I did feel better physically. *But why did I still feel so hopelessly lost?*

Lying down beside me, the Sarrum pulled me close and tucked my head beneath his chin.

"The healer said you were busy attending to other matters," I whispered, pressing my ear to his chest and calming at the sound of his heartbeat.

He kissed the top of my head and stroked my hair back from my face. "I'm never too busy for you, Princess."

21

CHARLIE

If I was Unsighted, I would've wondered what I ate before bed that gave me such bizarre dreams. But I was Sighted and all of it had actually happened—going on Benjamin's fieldtrip, seeing Spenser and Frank and that doctor who'd blinded Emma in those stone cells, watching Benjamin turn into a sock monkey to visit a doll in a coma and learning that Doc smelled a knack for potions in my blood.

A newspaper pegged me in the back of the head, and I dropped my spoon in my cereal bowl and turned toward the culprit.

Brian flashed his mischievous frat boy grin as he stepped into the kitchen. "What planet were you just on?"

I picked the paper up off the floor and tossed it back at him. "One where scary shadows turn into sock monkeys to visit injured dolls, where people walk through Waterfalls to get from room to room and witchdoctors tell me they smell a knack for potions in my blood."

"That's my favorite one." Dropping into the chair across the table from me, Brian grabbed the cereal box, buried his arm up to the elbow, pulled out a handful and popped it in his mouth.

I shoved my half-eaten bowl of cereal aside. "How bad did I screw up with the Sarrum yesterday?"

Brian frowned as he sat the box back on the table. "Honestly?"

I nodded and braced myself for the ugly truth.

"It was pretty bad." Brian leaned his elbows on the table and propped his handsome semi-groggy face on his hands. "But I don't think you did irreparable damage. You just set yourself back a little."

I let out a frustrated sigh. "Doc said the Sarrum was going to talk to us about me visiting Emma?"

Brian nodded without lifting his face off his hands. "Among other things. We were going to discuss your progress, where we thought your talents might lie, who would be teaching you what. We'll just have to table all that for a while, but there are plenty of lessons we can work on while we wait it out."

"Alright. So what's next?"

Brian reached across the table, grabbed my half-eaten bowl of cereal and shoveled a spoonful into his mouth. "I think we'll work on staying dry when you go through the Waters today."

I rolled my eyes and muttered, "Excellent."

"What's with the sarcasm?" Brian asked around a mouthful of cereal.

"Sorry. It's a lesson I really want to learn. It's just... didn't Benjamin tell you how much I suck at it?"

Brian tipped the cereal bowl to his lips and drained the milk into his mouth. "Benjamin's old school. He's a firm believer in the 'throw someone in the water and they'll figure out how to swim' method of teaching. That's not really my style."

"So...you don't think I'm totally hopeless?"

Brian hopped up, opened a cupboard near the sink and grabbed three coffee mugs. Then he set them down in front of the coffee pot and filled all three. "I think you can do whatever you put your mind to."

He carried the mugs to the table. I took one, nodded my thanks and savored a big sip before asking, "Who's the third cup for?"

"Didn't my brother mention that I'd be helping with your lesson today?" a voice richer and more delicious than my coffee murmured from the hallway.

"Nope." I took another sip and concentrated on not being attracted to Tristan as he stepped in the room dressed in black and gray plaid pajama pants that hung a little lower than his black silk boxer shorts. *Not gay* I reminded myself as I admired his spectacular shirtless chest and washboard abs. *So… not…gay.*

Grinning at me, Tristan took the third cup of coffee from his brother and sat down between us at the head of the table. "You're getting better."

I focused on *not* letting his smile dazzle me into unconsciousness. "Better at what?"

"Exactly what you're doing, blocking my charm."

I sipped my coffee and leaned back in my chair. "Is charm a technical term or are you just really full of yourself?"

"Both," Brian answered before his brother could swallow the coffee in his mouth.

Unfazed by Brian's comment, Tristan yawned and extended his arms to stretch. I tried to ignore the thrill that coursed through me as I watched his muscles flex. "You haven't mastered the whole dragon thing yet so it makes sense that you're still affected, but you're doing a pretty good job of fighting it."

"I sat my cup on the table. "So…dragons aren't affected by the charm at all?"

"They can be," Tristan murmured, milking his chocolaty voice for all its worth. "But it's a conscious choice. If they don't want to be charmed, they won't be."

"Why would somebody *choose* to be charmed?" I wondered aloud.

Grinning, Tristan leaned forward. "Remember the effect I had on you when we first met? You were drooling all over yourself and focusing like hell on keeping your dick soft, even though you don't swing that way."

I sipped my coffee and pondered that for a second. "Thanks for that painfully accurate recap. Was there a point you were trying to make? Or do you just enjoy embarrassing the hell out of me?"

Tristan cranked his smile up a notch and I fought the urge to squirm in my seat. "A little of both, I guess. Point is, if I can affect you like that, imagine what a *succubus* could do."

"Shit."

A burst of laughter trickled from Tristan's perfect lips. "*There's* my point. You can see why somebody might decide *not* to block that, right?"

"Yeah." *God help me if I ever ran into a female version of Tristan.* "Do any succubi work for the Sarrum?"

Brian and Tristan exchanged awkward glances, and Brian cleared his throat. "There was one. She was a phenomenal divorce attorney, but she isn't with us any longer."

Isn't with us? Something about the way Brian phrased it made it all click. "You're talking about Sophie Turner, aren't you?"

Brian nodded and Tristan dropped his eyes to his coffee cup.

"Emma said Sophie claimed to be having an affair with the Sarrum. Was she? Not knowing if it was true was killing Emma."

Tristan hopped up and cleared all three cups from the table without asking if anyone wanted a refill. "You need to stop questioning the Sarrum's relationships. Know your boundaries, Charlie. Their personal business is off limits." With that, he crossed the room and placed the cups in the sink.

Brian stood from the table, stretched and motioned for me to follow him. "Come on. Let's go start your lesson."

I vacantly followed him down the hall and up the stairs. It didn't sit well with me, the way everybody kept changing the subject whenever I asked about the Sarrum's relationships, or the way they all cowered at the Talbot's house when I called the Sarrum a pedophile. *Okay. The fact that he was standing behind me probably had something to do with it that time.* But that was beside the point. Sophie was a female version of Tristan. How could the Sarrum resist *that*?

My first attempt to stay dry in the Waters was a miserable failure, so were my next six. But I had to hand it to them, Brian and Tristan both had the patience of saints.

"We could take a breather," Tristan suggested as I waded to shore sopping wet for the seventh time. "Why don't we go to the Dragon's Lair for a drink?"

Brian put his hand on my shoulder and magicked me dry for the seventh time. "Or we could keep working on it."

Tristan's gorgeous lips turned down in a seductive frown. "Come on. Give the poor guy a break."

Brian scowled at his brother. "We don't have time for one of your breaks right now. How's he going to focus in that place?"

"Trust me." Tristan grinned as he tugged on my shirtsleeve and Brian's inked arm. "I think it'll help."

Brian let out a frustrated sigh. "Fine. But this'd better be a quick stop. Doc's antsy to get Charlie's training underway and Benjamin won't let that happen until we've taught him the basics."

"Trust me," Tristan murmured, pulling us both by the arm.

It was just a short walk down a dirt path through the forest to get to the Dragon's Lair. As we stepped out of the forest and neared the entrance, the tavern's wooden sign swung from its chains in the breeze like it was welcoming us in.

Tristan pulled the door open, and Brian and I followed him into the tavern's boisterous interior. A beautiful bird-like creature with snow white feathers and long gray lashes was playing a melancholy tune on a piano near the door. The room was full of cheery characters, laughing and drinking and filling their bellies, but as the three of us stepped in, the music stopped. And every-one stopped what they were doing to watch us walk across the floor.

With that many eyes on us, I wanted to disappear but Tristan just raised a hand in the air. "Carry on folks. We're just here to recharge."

The music started up again, and most of the pa-trons returned to laughing and talking and drinking as Brian and I followed Tristan to a circular booth tucked in a corner by the fireplace. It was occupied by two female fairies who were giggling and drinking bubbly pink drinks from long-stemmed glasses. One was a little plumper than the other, with rounder more voluptuous curves. Her skin was a gorgeous olive color and her orange and yellow wings blazed with fiery brilliance, reflecting the light from the fireplace. The other fairy was thinner with a pale porcelain complexion and wings that glistened like dew-drenched rose petals. As we neared the booth, they both stopped talking.

"Hello, ladies," Tristan murmured, laying his chocolaty voice on nice and thick.

The plumper fairy lowered her eyelids and bit her lip as she looked up at Tristan, drinking him in. "What can we do for you boys? Share our table? Buy you drinks? Take you to bed?"

Damn. She sure was forward. It took me a few sec-onds to realize that she probably wasn't. I raised an eyebrow at Tristan. *Is that the charm talking?*

Tristan winked at me as he slipped into the booth beside the full-figured fairy. "We're on duty, ladies. But if we weren't, I'd say yes to all three of those offers."

The plumper fairy giggled, and the waifish one's cheeks blushed a deep shade of pink that matched her wings beautifully as she eyed Tristan with a mischievous smile.

Tristan winked at her. "Maybe we could meet up later?"

"Which of us?" the waifish one asked in a breathy whisper.

Tristan reached across the table and brushed a fingertip over her knuckles. "All of us."

Shit. She's gonna pass out. I hopped in beside the rose petal fairy, just in time to catch her before she smacked her head on the table.

Tristan beamed at me. "Nice reflexes!"

Nudging me over, Brian sat down next to me as I slid the pink fairy closer to her fiery-winged friend. "Yeah. Just great. We don't have time for this."

I tried to rest the rosy fairy's head against the back of the booth, but she flopped toward me and would've landed face first in my lap if I hadn't caught her.

The plumper fairy giggled. "Why'd you catch her?"

"We're here on business, remember?" Tristan murmured in her ear. The orange fairy's cheeks blazed as she slipped out of consciousness and fell into Tristan's arms. He shot me a dazzling smile. "How do you feel right now?"

"Uh…" I shifted and propped the thin fairy's head on my shoulder. "Awkward… and hungry."

"Perfect," Tristan whispered.

"Perfect?" I caught the rose fairy's head as it slipped off my shoulder. "What's perfect? If we were in the waking world, I'd be pissing myself, worrying that we'd get arrested for slipping these two roofies."

Brian grinned at his brother. "Nice."

"Am I missing something?" I muttered, bracing my palm against the pink fairy's forehead because it wouldn't stop slipping off my shoulder. "What's nice?"

A female troll wearing a stained apron over a puke-green dress stepped up to our table and blew Tristan a kiss. "Hello, beautiful. What're you doing here on your day off?" Apparently, sitting in a booth with two unconscious girls draped all over you didn't even warrant a second glance if you were with Tristan.

Tristan blew the warty troll a kiss and shot her a dazzling smile. "Working. You remember my brother?"

The troll's eyes moved to Brian and mentally un-dressed him. Then she smiled. "Of course I do. You brothers are hard to forget." Her beady eyes shifted to me. "Who's your new friend?"

"His name's Charlie," Tristan murmured. "He's the lost dragon."

Troll girl raised her eyebrows. "Well, holy fucking shit!"

What was I supposed to say to that? "Uh. Hi."

The troll giggled, flashing a mouthful of grimy teeth. *So much for being hungry.* "Incubus brothers and a freaking dragon. It must be my lucky day."

"We didn't come to play," Brian grumbled, but the way that he said it made me wonder if they sometimes *did* come to play.

"Well, muscles," the troll answered, "What did you come for?"

Brian shrugged. "No idea. Ask my beautiful derelict brother."

She giggled, flashing those nasty teeth again. Then she turned to Tristan. "Well derelict? What can I do for you boys today?"

"Nothing, gorgeous," he answered in a velvety whisper. "We got what we came for."

Troll girl giggled again and finally seemed to notice the two unconscious fairies. "These little twits? Want me to wrap them up to go for you?"

Tristan planted a kiss on the orange fairy's forehead as he slipped out of the booth, and she let out a contented sigh as she toppled against her rosy friend. "No thanks, my warty little angel." He reached in one of the pockets of his perfectly fitted pants, pulled out some money and tossed it on the table without counting it. "Just keep an eye on them for me until they wake up. Make sure nobody messes with them."

Following Tristan's lead, I slid out of the booth after Brian and propped the rose petal fairy against her orange friend, but I skipped the kiss.

The troll picked up the money and stuffed it down the front of her dress between her saggy breasts. "Anything for you, Tristan."

"Thanks." He cranked up the dazzle factor on his smile and planted a kiss on her leathery cheek. "See you tomorrow."

I didn't say anything as we crossed the crowded room and exited the tavern. In fact, I stayed quiet until we were back in the forest and far enough down the winding path that the tavern was out of sight. "What was the point of that?" I muttered as we turned a corner, not far from the Water.

"Practice," Tristan murmured.

I raked a hand through my hair as I followed Tristan out of the forest. "For what exactly? Date raping fairies?"

Brian smacked me upside the head, not hard but enough to let me know I was out of line. "Not funny."

"Sorry," I muttered, rubbing my head. "I wasn't serious."

"Serious or not," Brian growled. "We don't joke about a thing like that."

I cleared my throat to say something, but couldn't decide what the appropriate something would be.

Tristan stopped walking as we reached the Water. "It's kind of a touchy subject for us. You've seen what we can do. The effect we have on people?"

"Yeah," I whispered.

"We could make almost anyone do almost any-thing we wanted them to—with us, to us, to others while we watched. And not all incubi and succubi concern themselves with what is or isn't moral. I might tease a lot, but I respect the actual wishes of the individuals I affect."

"Sorry," I muttered. "I didn't realize. But how do you know what an individual's actual wishes are, when everyone just throws themselves at you?"

"You know," Brian growled. "And you respect those boundaries."

Know your boundaries. That's what Tristan said at breakfast when I asked about Emma and David. No, I'd asked about *Sophie* and David. My stomach turned. Were they touchy because Sophie *did* cross those boundaries? "Seriously," I muttered. "I really am sorry."

"Forget it," Tristan murmured, clearly less both-ered by my comment than Brian was. "It's time to give the Water another try."

"Why will this time be any different?"

"Because," Brian answered, stepping beside his brother, "you're getting a lot better at blocking."

"Blocking what?"

"Things that shouldn't affect you." Tristan grinned at me. "When I asked how you felt in the tavern, you said hungry and awkward."

"Yeah. So?"

"So," Brian answered, "Tristan was laying it on as thick as it gets and you didn't let it affect you. You were too distracted watching how charmed everyone else was to get charmed yourself."

"And that helps me, how?"

"If you can block me," Tristan murmured, "you can block the Waters." Before I could answer, he shoved me into the surf and the Waters swallowed me.

Shocked and freezing, I tried to remember where I was supposed to meet them. Where the hell was I going? I could feel the Waters tugging at the memory. *FUCK OFF!* I hollered mentally, remembering Benjamin's lesson. *No wiggle room. Own it. IF YOU CAN ACCESS MY MEMORIES, TAKE ME WHERE I'M SUPPOSED TO GO! YOU HAVE NO RIGHT TO KEEP ME! AND DON'T YOU DARE SPIT ME OUT SOPPING WET! I'M A DRAGON! AND I DON'T WANT TO SEE A DROP OF MOISTURE ON ME WHEN I STEP ONSHORE!* Confidence. Own it. I had this. The Waters hurled me toward the surface, and I felt that same rush of power that I'd felt in the car with Benjamin.

I opened my eyes and found myself sitting in the grass beside the Water.

"Tell me I'm a genius," Tristan hollered as he and Brian walked toward me.

I looked down. *I was bone dry.* "You're a genius, Tristan! I could kiss you!"

"You could, but you don't really want to." Tristan laughed and planted a kiss on the top of my head.

A shiver of pleasure shot through me as I stood up. I was afraid to even extrapolate what *more* than a kiss on the head would be like. "I seriously LOVE you right now, Tristan." I clapped him on the shoulder, then wrapped my arms around him in an appreciative bear hug. "I so fucking love you!"

Brian put a hand on my shoulder. "Easy there, tiger. Let's not get carried away."

I let go of Tristan. "What's the big deal? I'm not gay. And neither is Tristan."

"I'm not anything," Tristan murmured beside me.

"What exactly does that mean?"

"It means I'm as open-minded as it gets. You might say I'm Omni-sexual." *His charm seemed to be getting stronger.* "You name it," Tristan murmured. "If it's sexual, I'm into it. And I've done it. And I've watched others do it."

I swallowed and took a deep breath. "Did you just crank up the charm?"

"Nope," Tristan whispered. "I'm guessing part of your block involved thinking that I wasn't interested in you. Guess I should've mentioned that *dragons* are on the top of every incubus and succubus's bucket list because they're immune to our charm. We all want what we can't have."

"Shit." I was so focused on *not* getting turned on, it took me a minute to think about Sophie's bucket list. *We all want what we can't have.* There was a stupid part of me (the part that wasn't gay but was trying like hell not to react to the gorgeous incubus beside me) that understood why David Talbot might've succumbed to the succubus's charm, and it made my heart break for Emma.

22

ISABELLA

I couldn't see anything but the Waters and most of the time, I couldn't hear anything at all. There was a morbid tranquility to this Watery grave of mine, but too much tranquility can drive you insane. Still, I never forgot to be thankful. By all rights, I should've been dead. In fact, I should've died a long time ago but that's another story for another time.

Before this solitary existence began, I was the royal sorceress. I was also one of the Princess's guards. I had been since she was a child. The Princess and I had a lovely symbiotic relationship. I'd given my own daughter up at birth, a necessary decision but that didn't make it any less heart wrenching. And the Princess's mother had never loved her, not the way that she should've anyway. Emma and I were like two puzzle pieces. We'd both lost the puzzles we were meant to fit in. But by some miracle, we discovered that we fit—maybe not as perfectly as we would have with our original puzzle, but enough to help fill the void. I dried Emma's tears, read her stories and watched over her while she played. And I watched her grow into a beautiful young woman that any mother should be proud to have for a daughter. It broke my heart when she lost her Sight. It broke all our hearts. Every day, a little more of her went missing and there was nothing we could do to fix it.

The succubus had always been trouble. When the Princess lost her Sight, Sophie saw it as an opportunity and she swooped in for the kill. Maybe the Sarrum should've seen it coming, but he was too riddled with guilt to notice. He just couldn't forgive himself for lying to the Princess all those years or for the horrible way she'd discovered the truth. It traumatized her, broke her, made her question everything she'd always trusted to be true. But that wasn't good enough for Sophie. She didn't just want Emma broken. She wanted her gone.

I blamed myself for what happened next. When Benji brought the Princess home from the party that night, he told me she was in rough shape and asked me to watch her while he went back to get the Sarrum. If I'd gotten to her sooner, maybe I could've talked some sense into her but there was no reasoning with her by the time I reached her. She'd already slit one wrist. I figured sneaking up and grabbing the knife would be the best way to stop her, but it didn't work out the way I intended. I startled her and she was so far gone, I don't even think she saw me. The eyes that looked at me were the eyes of a stranger. Whoever it was that stuck that knife in my chest, it wasn't Emma.

I should've bled out on the kitchen floor that night, and I suspect the Princess should've too. If it wasn't for the Sarrum, we'd probably both be dead. By the time he got home, I was too far gone to heal. So, he tethered me to my last fragile breath and suspended me in the Waters, and that's where I remained—trapped between two worlds, preserved in a bubble, clinging to my final breath. My true life support wasn't those machines at the hospital, it was the Sarrum's magic. It was a precious gift, but I could feel how much it cost him. Keeping me from dying was a constant drain on the King.

Eventually, I discovered that I could move closer to the surface if I focused hard enough. I couldn't break through but I could occasionally hear my loved ones. Sometimes I'd reach the surface and hear the repetitive beep of a heart monitor, the chatter of nurses, an authoritative voice paging staff overhead and once in a while, I'd hear my son amidst those sounds but he didn't visit very often. And the hospital sounds depressed me, so I mostly stayed near the other surface. I was never alone there. My soul mate came as often as he could and I heard the witchdoctor's voice all the time, so I knew I was in the best possible hands. Rose sat at my bedside almost constantly. She held my hand and told me she couldn't wait to meet me, and she begged me not to leave before we ever got a chance to speak. More than anything, I wanted to tell her it'd be alright. *It had to be.* I couldn't let my life end without explaining why I'd given her up. She needed to know that she'd always been in my heart.

I'd been near the surface for hours. My soul mate's voice had lured me there. Rose was sitting on my left and he was on my right. Neither of them spoke, but I could feel them and I desperately longed to tell them both how much I loved them.

Rose was the one who eventually severed the silence. "Benjamin?"

I heard his head rise from its resting place beside my hand. "Yes?"

"What was my mother like?"

"What *IS* she like," he growled. "She's still with us. Don't speak as if she were gone."

My daughter choked back a sob. "Sorry."

Benji let out a heavy sigh. "I'm the one who should be sorry. I shouldn't have snapped at you."

"It's alright," Rose whispered. "Would you please tell me something about her?"

"Like what?" he grumbled, practically a tender whisper for the Darkness. If it'd been anyone other than my daughter, he wouldn't have let them off the hook so easily.

"I don't know. How did you meet? What's she like? Anything. I just want to know something more than what I've read in letters or heard from Aunt Louise."

"Aunt Louise?" Benjamin whispered. "You don't call her mother?"

"No. She never pretended to be my birth mother. She's my dragon mother, although she despises that term. She always says that a foolish lost girl soiled it, but she never says more. Do you know anything about that?"

"Yes," Benji answered in a hoarse whisper. It was a subject we rarely brought up. He didn't like to talk about her. Neither did the Sarrum.

"Is that all you'll say?"

"On that topic, yes," Benji growled. "But I will tell you about your mother. What would you like to know?"

"Tell me how you met," Rose whispered. "Or when you fell in love with her."

I heard Benji shift in his chair, settling in to tell my daughter a story, and I'd never loved him more. If only she'd had a father like him. Life could've been so different for us.

"Those stories are the same," Benji whispered with a tenderness that only crept into his voice when he spoke to me or Emma, and now my Rose. "I fell in love with your mother the day I met her."

"Did she know that?"

"Probably not. Expressing emotion was never my strong point, unless the emotion was rage. Your mother came to the palace with her grandmother Rosa, the woman you're named after. They never should've found the entrance to the Dragon King's lair. No one could without an invitation, but somehow those two did. They marched right up and asked the guard for an audience with the Sarrum. I'm still not sure how they convinced her to let them in. But they did. When I walked into the room, your mother was terrified but despite her shaking voice and hands, she was brave. If I weren't capable of smelling fear, I probably wouldn't even have noticed her trembling. Isa looked me right in the eye and pleaded for our help to keep you safe."

"The shadow... who fathered me?" Rose whispered. "He meant to take me after I was born, didn't he?"

"Yes," the Darkness replied in a harsh whisper, "but I promised your mother I wouldn't let that happen."

"She mentioned you in her letters a lot."

Benji gave my hand a squeeze. "Did she?"

"Yes. She obviously loved you," Rose stopped to clear her throat. "I mean *loves* you very much."

"I feel the same," Benji whispered, ignoring her slipup.

They settled back into silence after that. Benji had satisfied Rose's curiosity enough for the moment, and I think Rose could sense that he'd only share so much.

As I listened to them breathing, my thoughts drifted to the day I met the Darkness...

...We stepped out of the forest, just a few paces from the Waterfall. It was unnerving, the absolute silence in the Darkness. Not a chirping cricket or a leaf rustling in the breeze. Even the lofty Waterfall was soundless.

My grandmother took my hand and gave it an affectionate squeeze. "It'll be alright, Isa. The Sarrum is fair. He'll help you. I can sense it."

I swallowed, mustering the courage to speak in the void. "We weren't invited. Won't they be angry we're here?"

"Maybe at first." Lifting the hem of her dress, Grandmother stepped in the Waters and motioned for me to follow. "But once we explain why we've come, it'll all work out."

I shook my head and focused on trying not to cry as I stepped in the shallow Waters.

"It will, my precious girl. I promise." She stepped up to the Waterfall and signaled for me to wait behind her. "Hello? We wish to speak to the Sarrum! And we won't be leaving until you've given us an audience with him!"

"Grandmother!"

She flashed a toothless grin and winked at me. "We need to get their attention."

I was beginning to regret letting her talk me into the whole crazy venture when a guard stepped from the Waterfall. She was tall and slender with pointy ears. Her sleek dark hair was pinned up and she was dressed in a fitted black outfit with a sword belted at her side. Eyes narrowed, the elf stepped toward my grandmother. "What business brings you here, woman? You aren't an invited guest."

My frail hunched grandmother chuckled, displaying her perfectly toothless gums. "I don't bother with invitations," she replied in her thick Hispanic accent. "At my age, if I want to go somewhere, I do. And it's my granddaughter who has reason to be here."

The elf's narrowed gaze shifted to me. "What's your name?"

I did my best to keep my voice steady as I answered, "Isabella Salazar."

The elf took a step closer. "And what reason do you have to be here, Miss Salazar?"

"I'd like to see the Sarrum," I muttered.

She crossed her arms and scowled at me. "We don't just allow any girl off the street to walk in and throw herself at the King."

"I don't want the King!" I was too annoyed by her assumption to remember to sound respectful. "The only thing I want is his ear! I've come to ask for protection."

The elf raised an eyebrow. "What makes you special enough to deserve his protection?"

"I don't believe that's your business!" my grandmother barked. "Your job is to protect the palace, is it not? Do we look like dangerous threats to you? A toothless old woman and a young girl? I demand that you grant us an audience with someone qualified to decide whether my granddaughter is worthy of protection!"

Grumbling under her breath, the elf ushered us toward the Waterfall. I followed my grandmother through and stepped into a small comfortably furnished room that obviously wasn't the great hall of the palace.

The guard scowled at my grandmother and pointed to a chair. "Sit!" But when I sat down beside her, the elf shook her head. "Not you. You come with me."

My grandmother sprang to her feet. "I don't think so!"

"I don't care what you think," the elf snarled. "This girl is the one who seeks an audience. So she alone will come with me for questioning."

Grandmother was about to argue, but I smiled at her and took a step toward the elf. "I'll be fine. They're good people, remember?"

My grandmother didn't look happy, but she did sit back down.

The elf led me back through the Waterfall to an even smaller waiting room, instructed me to wait, then turned around and left. And I waited for so long that I started to wonder if she'd forgotten all about me.

When the Darkness stepped from the Waterfall, panic descended like a crushing weight upon my chest. I wanted to scream. But I couldn't even draw a breath.

His harsh expression softened as he met my eyes. "Relax."

I nodded and actually did manage to relax a little, but I still had to fight the urge to bolt when he crossed the room and sat down beside me.

"Be calm." His deep Dark voice was as beautiful as it was terrifying. Why didn't anyone ever mention that when they spoke of him? "No one will harm you here."

I nodded, because I still couldn't find my voice.

"I was told that you've come seeking protection. Protection from what?"

Terrified that he might take offense, I cringed as I whispered, "A shadow."

"Any specific shadow?" he inquired, his tone no less gentle.

"Yes. He works in the same hotel as me."

"And why do you believe you have reason to fear him?"

"Because," I answered in a thready whisper, "he's going to come for the dragon he seeded."

A wave of fury swept through the room, but I wasn't frightened. It clearly wasn't directed toward me. "I'm assuming you didn't consent to," he cleared his throat, searching for a delicate way to phrase the question, "the making of this dragon?"

"No," I whispered, unable to hold back my tears. "I did not."

He reached out and took my hand, his deep voice even softer than before, "You have my word, no one will harm you again and I'll personally see to it that he pays for what he did. We will keep you and your child safe."

"Thank you," I whispered, gripping his hand a little tighter...

...I couldn't hear him breathing anymore. The Darkness must've left the room while I was caught up in the memory, and it broke my heart that I'd missed his goodbye.

23

BENJAMIN

Isa drifted off at the end of my visit. I could sense when she was present enough to hear us and by the time I kissed her cheek and whispered my goodbye, I knew I'd lost her. I rounded the bed with a heavy heart, kissed Rose on the forehead and asked if she felt like getting some air. She declined, like she did every time I asked. So, I crossed the room and exited through the Waterfall.

Doc was waiting for me in the corridor when I stepped out the other side, and it took a substantial amount of effort not to grab him and demand that he heal Isa sooner. "Where's the virgin?"

Doc grinned, no doubt thankful I'd chosen not to manhandle him. "I had to make a house call, so I sent him back to the house on Sycamore."

"Why the house call?"

"The Princess isn't doing well and the Sarrum is losing his patience."

Doc was wrong. The boss never had any patience to begin with. "Can you blame him?"

The witchdoctor busied his hands by fidgeting with the beads and teeth strung around his neck. "I suppose not." He dropped the necklace and looked up at me. "This isn't going to end well."

I suppressed the urge to grab him by the throat. "What makes you say that?"

"She's too far gone," he muttered. Then his eyes widened. "The Princess, that is. Not Isa."

"Well, you'd better figure out a way to bring her back because we're all screwed if you don't." I started to walk away but turned back as his last words sunk in. "You think you can heal Isa?"

"I've no doubt that I can but I'll need Rose's help, and Charlie's too. You need to step up his training."

"I'm on it," I muttered as I walked away. I could've left through the same Waterfall I'd just stepped through, but I needed a walk to clear my head. And the shrieking and whimpering that bled through the walls of the corridors always helped me relax, so I took the long way back, sinking into the darkness and strolling through a few of the cells. By the time I reached the end of the dismal corridor, I felt like a new man.

I stopped and stared at the Waterfall in front of me for a moment. If the boss wasn't with Emma, I wanted to check on her before heading to the house. But I wasn't about to intrude on their privacy. So I reached out mentally. *Boss? You in there?*

All set for the night. Go check in with Brian and the virgin.

Will do. Call if you need anything.

Always.

I stepped through the Waterfall, and sat up in bed. My room was pitch dark and I had no idea what time it was. I was itching for a hot shower but that'd have to wait. Checking in on the Mason brothers and their virgin apprentice was more important.

Tossing the covers off, I slid out of bed and stretched as I moved to the bathroom. I didn't bother with the lights, just took a quick piss, washed my hands and splashed some water on my face. Then I crossed the room and opened the door. The laughter of three dipshits echoed up the stairwell as I stepped into the hall. Shaking my head, I pulled the door shut and followed the sound of merry idiots down the staircase.

The lights were on in every room in the house. How the fuck anyone could stand that much brightness was beyond me. I reached in and flipped the switch in the empty living room, then followed the laughter to the dining room.

Brian and Charlie stopped laughing as I walked through the door. They were sitting at the dining room table dressed in pajamas, which was a good sign. A productive day of training in Draumer was exactly what the virgin needed. Brian could be a smartass, but I could always count on him to get the job done.

A greasy pizza box with a half-finished pizza sat in the center of the table, surrounded by crumb-covered plates and a few empty beer bottles. I moved to the table, grabbed a slice from the box and sunk my teeth into it.

"How's it going, Benji?" a voice like liquid silk murmured behind me.

I turned toward the kitchen door and Tristan winked at me as he sauntered into the room, bare-chested with a beer in each hand. He held one out to me.

I took it and set it on the table. "Would it kill you to put a fucking shirt on?"

"Maybe." The incubus flashed me a mischievous grin. "I'm really hot." He suppressed a laugh as he tipped his beer bottle up to those perfect lips.

"Don't push your luck, pretty boy. I'm not in the mood for your playful banter tonight."

"I'm sorry?" Brian chuckled, grabbing the beer from his brother's hand and downing a sip. "Are you *ever* in the mood for playful banter?"

I tossed my pizza slice to an empty plate on the table. "No."

"How's Isa?" Tristan asked, stealing the beer back from his brother.

I shook my head as I picked up my beer. "No change, but Doc seems confident he can heal her. That's why I'm here. He says he needs Charlie's assistance, so we need to step up his training."

Charlie hopped to his feet. "Great! What's next?"

I downed a swig of beer, then asked, "What did you assholes accomplish today?"

Tristan shot the virgin a provocative grin. "We taught Charlie how to keep from getting wet."

I let out a warning growl. "Can you utter a sentence without making it sound sexual? If you can't, so fucking help me, I will bitch slap you. That's the only warning you're getting tonight."

"I love it when you get all hot and bothered," Tristan murmured without so much as flinching when I slapped him upside the head. "I could go like this all night, shadow. You know I like it rough." He did flinch a little when I slapped him the second time.

"Can we get serious?" I growled. "Or is being an asshole more important to you than getting Isa back?"

"Sorry," Tristan whispered. "Seriously, man. I am. What do you need from us?"

I turned to Charlie. "Are you confident you can move through the Waters without getting wet now?"

Charlie nodded. "Yeah. At least, I did earlier."

"Good enough." I grabbed my pizza slice and took another bite. "We can test that later. Right now, we're gonna work on unmasking."

"Great," the virgin muttered under his breath.

I narrowed my eyes at him. "Something wrong?"

"No." Charlie shot Brian a troubled glance. "It's just… Brian said it's kinda like taking a piss. You can't really explain how to do it because it's supposed to come naturally."

With Brian's coddling approach to training, the kid would never be ready to help Doc. "I might not be able to explain how to take a piss but if I scare you enough, I can still make you do it."

"Yeah…uh…" The virgin combed his fingers through his hair. "You do remember we aren't actually trying to make me piss myself, right? How would that help?"

"Same theory. I'll scare you into unmasking."

"And am I gonna piss myself in the process?"

"Maybe," I answered around a mouthful of pizza. "But that's a chance I'm willing to take."

"Great," the virgin muttered.

Tristan raised an eyebrow. "You know—"

I shot the incubus a death glare. "Say one word about fetishes and I will throw you across this fucking room."

"Roger that," Tristan whispered with a smirk.

Brian cleared his throat. "Can I be the voice of reason here?"

"Sure." I was starting to get seriously pissed off. We were wasting too much time talking instead of doing.

"It wouldn't hurt to start out small," Brian suggested calmly. "Why don't we let Charlie see what he's in for before you start scaring the piss out of him?"

"How exactly would you do that?" the virgin muttered. *And can I go empty my bladder before we start?*

Tristan grinned at Charlie. "Didn't I tell you to go before we left the house, young man?"

"Shit," the kid muttered. "Was I thinking too loud again?"

"**Yes**," all three of us answered in unison.

"Sorry," he whispered. "I'm not sure how to whisper my thoughts."

"It just takes practice," Brian murmured.

"Okay," Charlie muttered. "So... how would you show me what I'm in for?"

"We demonstrate what Benjamin does," Brian put a hand on his brother's shoulder, "on someone else."

Tristan took a step back from his brother. "Seriously?"

I shot the incubus a grin. "What's the matter, pretty boy? Thought you liked it rough."

"Fuck," Tristan muttered. "I did not sign up for this."

"Come on, buddy." Brian took the beer from his brother's hand and started to set it on the table. "On second thought," he handed it back to Tristan, "maybe you better drink up."

Tristan scowled at his brother, then downed what was left in the bottle. "You so fucking owe me, brother."

Brian winked at Tristan.

"So..." the virgin whispered. "What exactly is about to happen?"

Tristan moved to Charlie, put a hand on either side of his head and planted a kiss on his forehead. "Remember this, dragon. You owe me."

"Sure." Charlie's face flushed a deep shade of pink. "Uh, I'm sorry?"

"You should be," Tristan whispered.

"Charlie!" Brian snapped his fingers to regain the virgin's attention. "What Benjamin does is different than what the rest of us do when we unmask."

Charlie's brow furrowed as he muttered, "Okay."

"Brian didn't explain it quite right." I stepped toward the kid as I spoke. "When he told you about shadows, he said we were shape shifting demons."

The kid raked a hand through his hair. "And you aren't?"

"No. My shape never changes. I just change people's perception. Remember the fear you felt when we first met?"

"Yeah," Charlie muttered. "How could I forget?"

"I can project that. I can magnify it. I can make you see me differently or make it so you don't see me at all. I can make it so you don't see anything at all, and I can make you forget every rational thought in your head and replace it with fear and emptiness."

"Shit," Charlie whispered.

"Shit is right," Tristan murmured. "You owe me, dragon."

I grinned at the incubus as I stepped toward him and touched his arm.

"I take it back," he whimpered, clutching his head, "I don't like it rough."

The virgin squinted at Tristan. "What does he see?"

I tightened my grip on Tristan's arm and he let out a petrified shriek.

"Shit," Charlie muttered. "Tristan, what're you seeing?"

Tristan just whimpered.

"He can't hear you," I answered for the incapacitated incubus.

"Why?" Charlie whispered.

"He can't hear anything. He can't see anything. He's losing his grip on who he even is."

"Please! Let me go," Tristan begged as a tear slid down his chiseled cheekbone.

"How is this helping me?" Charlie growled. "Just let him go!"

I released the incubus and he dropped to the floor, sobbing. Stepping past him, I moved to the virgin. "*You* don't make demands on me."

24

CHARLIE

*O*h shit. *What did I just do?* That was my last coherent thought before the Darkness touched my arm. I told him to let Tristan go. *Told him.* What the hell was I thinking? But it didn't matter what I'd been thinking. My thoughts all started vanishing, like they were written on a sheet of paper and Benjamin had dumped a bottle of ink on the page. It didn't all disappear at once. The ink spread slowly, bleeding over my page of thoughts, not erasing, but blacking out. The thoughts were still there somewhere. I could sense it. I just couldn't see past the ink.

What was I saying? Weren't there people in the room with me? I looked for the faces I knew I should re-member, but they were gone. The names. The mem-ories of the faces. All of it, gone. Or maybe I was gone. I couldn't seem to recall where I was, or even who I was. Everything had gone black. The ink had swallowed all of it. The people. The room. The thoughts in my head. All of it, g*one.*

But it wasn't ink. It was Darker. And it wanted to make me disappear, too. Maybe it already had. A wave of nausea washed over me, and with it came terror. I wasn't alone at all. *Something* was beside me in the emptiness. It reached out and touched me. I tried to scream for help, but I had no voice to scream with and there was no one there to help me. Just the *something.* My heart was pounding. My eyes were watering. I might've vomited and possibly pissed myself. But I didn't care. I just needed to run away from the *something,* but I couldn't feel my feet anymore. Did I even have feet? Had I ever been anything more than this? This nothingness in the Darkness?

Come out dragon, commanded a voice inside my head. But it wasn't my voice. It was too Dark.

Show yourself, the voice insisted.

Something growled deep within the Darkness. Something terrifying. I felt it twitch deep in my belly, burning beneath my skin.

Wake dragon, the Dark voice demanded. *There's no need to hide.*

The something inside me twitched again and a rush of Dark thoughts enveloped me, vile filthy thoughts. Urges to do horrible things. Unspeakable desires. I stuffed the something down, told it to keep quiet and willed it back to sleep.

Do not hide from me dragon, the Dark voice insisted. *Come out now.*

"Holy shit!" a faraway voice echoed.

"Zip it," whispered another voice. These voices weren't in my head. They were somewhere outside me.

I tried to call to them for help, but I had no voice. The something inside me growled and I stuffed it down again.

Wake dragon, the Dark voice whispered inside my head, and my blood started boiling in my veins.

"No!" I screamed and opened my eyes. My heart was pounding and tears were streaming down my cheeks. "What just happened?"

"You're magnificent!" Tristan whispered, his voice filled with awe.

Brian was grinning at me.

But unlike the incubus brothers, Benjamin didn't look pleased.

"What just happened?" I looked down, hoping to see wings and scales but I was still just boring old Charlie in pajamas. That explained why Benjamin didn't look happy, but what were Brian and Tristan smiling at? I looked down again, praying to God I hadn't pissed myself. But my pants were dry. *Thank God.* "What're you two looking at?" I muttered, thoroughly confused.

Brian's grin widened. "I'm looking at my prize pupil."

"And I'm looking at some serious bucket list material," Tristan added in a velvety whisper.

"And I'm looking at a disappointment." Benjamin scowled at Brian as he moved to the door. "You've got some serious work to do."

Wow. Thanks for making me feel like shit. It didn't occur to me that I should've tried to whisper the thought, until the Darkness stopped dead in his tracks in the doorway.

He spun around and was in my face in an instant. "You *should* feel like shit, virgin."

"Come on, Benjamin." Brian stepped closer to the shadow. "Lay off him. It was a good effort."

Benjamin didn't even acknowledge the fact that Brian had spoken. "You know who else feels like shit?"

I wasn't sure if the question was rhetorical, but he didn't go on. So I muttered, "Who?"

"The Princess!" Benjamin growled. "You think you're lost? She can't remember who the fuck she is! She doesn't know who she can trust! And she's slipping deeper into the Darkness every fucking day that you're wasting! And Isa! She's lost in a sea of nothingness! Barely clinging to life! But you just take your FUCKING TIME! And keep laughing and joking and half-assing your attempts to be what you were meant to be! You stupid selfish fuck! You have no idea what's at stake! So learn to stifle your fucking thoughts, or I'll reach inside your skull and stifle them for you!"

Benjamin wheeled around and stormed out of the room before I could even process all that, let alone respond.

"I personally think you're doing quite well." Doc smiled at me as he stepped into the kitchen.

"Thanks," I muttered, still feeling vaguely disoriented. "I didn't mean to piss him off."

"You did fine," Brian assured me.

Embarrassingly close to tears, I cleared my throat. "Benjamin sure didn't think so."

"He has a lot on his mind," Doc whispered. "There's an extreme amount of pressure on him. The Sarrum is losing his patience, and Benjamin is bound to him. He not only feels his own rising anxiety as more time passes without any change, but he feels the King's as well and a dragon's fury is a burdensome thing. It's weighing the Darkness down. Still, it's unfair of him to be so impatient with you. We're expecting you to master every skill you should've learned throughout your lifetime in a mere few days. That's a pretty tall order."

"Seriously," Tristan whispered near my ear, making the hairs on the back of my neck stand at attention. "You did great, Charlie. And you're a gorgeous kickass dragon. Once you figure out how to come out of that shell, the world had better watch out."

"Thanks," I muttered. "But right now, I just feel like a huge disappointment."

Brian put a hand on my shoulder. "You did good, Charlie."

"You did," Doc agreed, "and I think perhaps you should begin training with me tomorrow. Benjamin may have too much on his plate to decide whether you're ready. Brian can keep working on the basics with you and we'll figure the rest out as we go along. I'll discuss it with the Sarrum in the morning."

"Right," I muttered. "Because the Sarrum loves me."

"The Sarrum can be practical," Doc whispered. "He's able to detach his emotions from his decisions. And he needs you, Charlie. He'll get over what you said, although I would refrain from calling him a sexual deviant in the future. As you discovered, his actions are much more likely to be governed by emotion where Emma is concerned. It's unwise to get between a dragon and his treasure, and the Princess is what the Dragon King treasures most of all. Go after a dragon's treasure and you'll find out just how venomous he can be."

I raked a hand through my hair. "I'm a dragon, too. How come I'm not like that?"

"You've locked that part of yourself away," Brian answered. "I think that's part of your problem. When it starts to surface, you feel all the Darkness that comes along with it and it scares you. But once you figure out how to let it out, we can work on taming that fierceness."

I let out a loud sigh. "Wonderful. I'm a huge disappointment to the Darkness. I've royally pissed off the King by insulting the relationship he's fiercely protective of and once I finally figure out how to be a dragon, I'm going to be a raging asshole."

"That pretty much sums it up," Tristan chuckled, "but you forgot to mention that any succubus would kill to jump into bed with you once you tap into that inner dragon because you are a beautiful specimen, dragon boy."

"Any *succubus?*" I muttered, feeling detached from my voice. "So I'm not incubus bucket list material?"

Tristan cranked his dazzling smile a notch higher than I'd ever seen it. It was almost blinding. "Charlie, you can be my dance partner anytime you like but I should probably remind you that you're not gay."

"I thought you liked a challenge?" *What the hell was I saying?* It was like someone else was putting words in my mouth.

"Nope," Tristan murmured. "Those are your words, dragon boy. But if you'd like someone to put something in your mouth, I'm sure I could think of something."

"My words?" I muttered. "Why are my words so *gay* all of a sudden?"

Tristan grinned at me. "That's the dragon in you, Charlie. Don't tell me you didn't feel all those ravenous desires when your mask flickered. If there's one thing I'm tuned into, it's desire, and dragons are greedy possessive predators. You have no idea what's inside you."

"Yeah, but..." *What was I trying to say? Oh yeah.* "I'm still not gay."

"Neither am I," Tristan whispered.

Fabulous. So in addition to being a huge disappointment, I was a greedy possessive gay predator deep down inside.

25

DAVID

I saw to it that Emma made it safely back to the waking world but there was no reason to leave my office once I woke, except perhaps for coffee, a task I'd delegate to the housekeeping imp. My Princess would likely be heading to the kitchen for her morning caffeine fix soon. She didn't want to see me, and I needed to respect that no matter how much it infuriated me. Despite all that I was holding together, I couldn't right the wrong I'd done her. To his credit, Benjamin hadn't once said "I told you so." But he certainly *felt* it often enough, and he had every reason to. If I'd listened to him and severed ties with Emma back when I should have, Isa would be fine. Emma would still be Sighted and living a fairytale life in the sunlight. But I'd be in agony. If I wasn't such a selfish bastard, I might've done what was best for everyone else.

But I *was* selfish. And the thought of letting Emma go, of some other man putting his hands on her, was too great a price to pay for her happiness. *She was mine.* Better for her to be miserable with me in the Darkness than happy with someone else in the Light. If I'm truly being honest, a part of me had always known it would end this way. I never really intended to let her go.

It'd all been so much simpler when she was just a child…

… We sat at the edge of the lake squishing our toes in the sand, each wave bathing our feet as it washed ashore. Our vacation was all too swiftly coming to an end. Albert and Judy had gone off for one last romantic lunch and my Princess and I were enjoying our final afternoon together in the waking world, lazily searching the clouds for shapes.

"There!" Emma's innocent eyes glistened with enthusiasm. "Do you see it?"

"See what?" I whispered, feigning ignorance.

She looked away from the heavens and frowned at me. "An elephant! It was right there, but it's gone now. You missed it." She looked positively devastated that I had.

I smiled at her, a true manifestation of joy. She was the only creature who could conjure such sincerity in me. "Look," I whispered, tipping her chin up with my index finger. "Do you see that one?"

An astonished gasp burst from her lips and the wonder in her eyes made my heart swell. There wasn't anything I wouldn't do for this child in either world. "It's a unicorn!" She pushed my finger away from her chin and fixed her eyes on me. "Did you make it?"

My grin widened. "Would that make it less special?"

"No," she whispered. "That makes it more special. I wish we could stay on vacation and I could always live with you."

I let out a regretful sigh. "As do I, Princess but that wouldn't make sense to the Unsighted now, would it?"

She looked down and traced a flower in the sand with her delicate finger. "Who cares? You could just take me anyway."

"No," I whispered, tracing a sun and cloud above her flower. "I couldn't. That wouldn't be fair to anyone."

Apparently placated by my vague response, she nodded. "Do you think we'll ever go someplace like this together again?"

I traced a heart around our masterpiece. "I'm sure I could find a way to make that happen."...

...The ringing of my cell phone rudely interrupted my reminiscence. I snatched it off my desk with an irritated sigh. "Hello?"

"Good morning," Jeremy's annoyingly cheery voice replied. "I was hoping I might have a word with you today."

"You just did," I answered flatly. "What were you hoping to have words about?"

The witchdoctor cleared his throat. "I'd like to bring Rose over to meet you."

"I could certainly fit that into my schedule," I agreed, mentally reaching out for the imp's attention. "I can speak with her while you meet with the Princess."

"Yes, I suppose you could." Doc cleared his throat again. "I was also hoping you and I might discuss Charlie's training."

"Were you?"

I felt Sara's focus shift to me. *What can I do for you, sir?*

Coffee.

Right away, sir.

"I was," Doc muttered in my ear. "I believe he would be a tremendous help to me."

"Really?" I answered dryly. "And slandering my good name helps you how exactly?"

He let out a loud exhalation. "That was stupid of him."

"That, we agree on." The imp knocked on my office door. *Come in.*

The door swung open and Sara stepped into my office with her fist clenched around a coffee cup. I nodded to her. And she walked to my desk and sat the cup down in front of me. *Can I get you anything else, sir?*

"That's all for now." I curled my fingers around the cup and added, "But keep the coffee coming."

Of course, sir. Sara dipped her head and exited the room as noiselessly as she'd entered.

I sipped my coffee and waited for Doc to continue.

There was a momentary silence before he muttered, "We need him."

Smoke billowed from my nostrils as I sat the cup down on my desk. "What you *need* is to fix what is broken."

"I realize that," Doc whispered, "but I require the boy's help."

"Bring Rose over in a few hours and we'll talk." I ended the call without waiting for a response and tossed the phone on my desktop. Then I wrapped my fingers around the coffee cup and continued reminiscing...

...I stepped out of the cave with one hand covering Emma's eyes and the other resting on her shoulder to guide her forward. After several steps, I knelt beside her in the grass and removed my hand from her eyes. "You can look now."

Her eyes welled with tears as he slowly turned around and surveyed the clearing. "It looks just like vacation."

Nodding, I whispered, "Now, we never have to leave."

She turned toward me. "How did this get here?"

"I made it." I stood and took her hand in mine as we started toward the Water.

But her eyes were still on me. "You made all this for me?"

"I did." I gave her hand an affectionate squeeze. "What do you think?"

A tear slid down her porcelain cheek as she whispered, "I never want to go anywhere else."

"Then you'll never have to," I murmured, wiping the tear from her cheek with my thumb.

After several coffee refills, a shave and a long hot shower, I spent a few hours attending to cases I'd somewhat neglected as of late. Before I knew it, Sara was knocking on my office door. "Yes?"

The imp hesitantly opened the door and spoke in a mousy whisper, "The doctor and Rose just drove through the front gate. Where should I take them?"

I shut the file I was reading and slid my chair back from the desk. "Send them in here."

"Yes, sir." Sara collected the empty coffee cup and crumb-covered plate from my desk. Then she promptly left the room, shutting the door behind her.

A few minutes later, there was another knock on my door.

I swiveled my chair toward the doorway. "Come in, Doctor."

The door opened. Doc gestured for Rose to enter. Then he followed her in and shut the door. "Sarrum, this is Isa's daughter Rose."

I stood and greeted her with a smile and an outstretched hand. "Hello, Rose. It's nice to finally meet you."

Smiling politely, Rose shook my hand with a sub-servient bow. "It's an honor to meet you, Sarrum." She kept her head bowed and her eyes on the floor.

I let go of her hand and lifted her chin until her eyes met mine. "That's not necessary, Rose. You're family."

"As you wish, my King." She obediently held my gaze, but it clearly made her uncomfortable to do so.

It was no surprise that Louise had drilled such formality into her. "Your propriety is recognized but Louise isn't here, so loosen up. We do things a bit differently around here."

"Yes, sir," Rose whispered.

I gestured for her and Doc to sit, and they dropped into the two chairs facing my desk. I met Rose's eyes and grinned at her. "Did the imp offer you something to drink?"

"Yes, sir. She did," Rose muttered, then shook her head. "I'm all set though."

I looked to Doc and raised an eyebrow.

"I'm fine too, thank you. Will you grant me per-mission to discuss Isa's treatment, Sarrum?" I nod-ded and he continued, "I believe I've found a potion that will bring her back."

I leaned forward, resting my elbows on the desk-top. "That's excellent news. When will you begin concocting it?"

Doc cleared his throat. "I'll require assistance. Specifically, Rose and Charlie's assistance."

"And why is that?" I leaned back in my chair and folded my arms across my chest. "I have plenty of employees who could assist you."

"I appreciate that, sir," Doc muttered, "but I strongly suspect that Rose has a proclivity toward sorcery and Charlie will undoubtedly be skilled at potion making once I've trained him."

"There are plenty of individuals who possess those talents. Why are you so keen on the two of them assisting you?"

Doc cleared his throat again. "Well, they're both dragons and the potion calls for three drops of dragon's blood."

"You may use mine," I growled, "and I'm sure Rose would be willing to donate her blood to the cause."

"Yes, but the potion requires three drops of blood from three different dragons," Doc croaked, "I was hoping Charlie could donate the third."

"Ah. Well, there it is then. It's his blood you're after, not his innate talents."

Doc shifted in his seat. "It's both, actually."

"And am I just supposed to overlook the virgin's insolence?"

Doc swallowed. "Yes, my King. I think you should. His help may well be invaluable to my efforts."

I narrowed my eyes at him. "Which efforts?" If the virgin's blood could save my Princess, I'd personally drain every drop from his veins.

"Well," Doc muttered uneasily, no doubt suspecting where my train of thought had headed. "First off, my efforts to heal Isa. And if that's successful, we can take it from there."

"That's an awful lot of *if*, Doctor. You don't intend to disappoint me, do you?"

Doc took a handkerchief from his pocket and wiped the sweat from his brow. "No, Sarrum. That certainly isn't my intention, but the Princess will be more difficult to heal. And if we restore Isa, she can probably help us."

I stood from my chair and rounded the desk. "I believe it's time for Emma's appointment, Doctor."

Nodding, Doc glanced at Rose as he stood.

"Run along now." I mentally nudged him from the chair, then sat down in it myself. "Rose and I have a lot to discuss."

Brow furrowed, the doctor frowned at Rose.

"Good bye, Doctor," I growled, nudging him to the door. I watched with narrowed eyes as he pulled the door open and exited the room. Mentally extending, I pushed the door shut and turned to Rose. "I do agree with the witchdoctor about one thing. You can be of great service to me."

26

CHARLIE

Too exhausted to jump in the Waters, I fell into bed and instantly drifted off to sleep. The Waters must've read my thoughts and decided to be kind to me for once because I woke up on the weathered dock where I first met Call-me-Art. Not near it, but awkwardly curled up on it. Stretching the kinks out of my muscles, I fished for the stone in my pocket. But it wasn't in the pocket I remembered shoving it in. Panicked, I stuffed my hands in my other pockets. As my fingers connected with the cool surface of the moonstone in the third pocket I tried, I breathed a sigh of relief and yanked it out. I stood up and moved to the edge of the dock. Then I took a deep breath and braced for the cold.

"That's not necessary," a British voice murmured behind me.

I turned, expecting to see Call-me-Art, but a younger man stood in his place. Dressed in a white button down shirt and gray pants, he had the same pale blue eyes and the same charming smile but his face was clean-shaven and his wavy hair was a light chestnut brown. Confused, I muttered, "Arthur?"

His charming grin widened as he nodded.

"How?"

A soft chuckle erupted from his mouth. "I do apologize, Charlie. I thought you might be more inclined to trust an older stranger the first time we met, but it seemed silly to keep the ruse up any longer."

"Okay." I took a deep breath. "So you're Art? And... what? This is the real you?"

Amusement twinkled in his pale blue eyes. "You catch on quickly. So now that you see the real me, do you think you might still be able to trust me?"

"It's just... um. It's kind of a big surprise. But all things considered, it isn't the weirdest thing I've seen lately."

He chuckled again. "They're keeping your education interesting, are they?"

"You could say that." I raked a hand through my hair. "So what happens now? Do we both jump in the Waters?"

Art shook his head and motioned for me to follow him off the dock. "No need."

I followed him to a set of cushioned chairs that weren't there before we started toward them. He sat down in one and I settled into the other. "So we can talk here? I thought you wanted to meet somewhere more private."

Perpetual laughter seemed to flicker in young Art's eyes as if he was constantly chuckling over some inside joke. "This is as private as it gets, Charlie. I got the distinct impression you weren't all that comfortable in my desert scape the last time we met. So, I switched the scenery to something a bit more familiar."

I considered the view from a fresh perspective. "Is this the same mirage?"

Art grinned and crossed his legs. "It is. Do you feel more comfortable in it now?"

"Yeah." I leaned back in my chair. "Stupid, huh?"

"Not at all," he murmured. "We all have our comfort zones. You feel more centered near the Waters. It makes you feel less trapped having a clear means of escape in sight."

"That kinda makes me sound like an ass."

Art grinned. "That wasn't my intention."

"Yeah. I know." Suddenly thirsty, I cleared my throat. "Have you got any more of that red stuff we drank last time?" It was probably a stupid question since he seemed to pull whatever he wanted out of thin air. "It was delicious."

Eyes dancing with laughter, he turned toward the table that appeared between us and picked up a pitcher of iced red stuff. I grabbed a glass and held it out to him, and Art grinned as he filled my cup. "I'm glad you like it. I don't often get the opportunity to entertain guests."

I took a satisfied sip. And the familiar tingling sensation slid down my throat and heated my insides, despite the drink's cool temperature. "That's too bad. You're a good host."

Chuckling, he filled his own glass and sat the pitcher back on the table. "Thank you, but I doubt you came here to sip cool drinks and chat about the weather."

"Actually, I didn't come here on purpose. I just woke up here."

Art swirled his glass and absently watched the ice cubes clink together. "But you fell asleep intending to come see me. Am I right?"

"Yeah." I downed another decadent sip. "So who brought me here? Me or you?"

Art sat his glass down on the table. "A little of both I think. I meant to touch base with you to see how you're holding up and you meant to come see me."

Grinning, I raked my hair back from my face. "I guess it was fate then."

"Alright," he murmured, his voice ripe with amusement. "So I imagine you have some questions for me now that you've learned a bit more from the Sarrum's happy little family."

I let out a frustrated sigh. "Yeah. I kinda screwed things up with the Sarrum."

Art cocked his head sideways. "How so?"

"I was talking about what a massive pervert he was, and he walked in and overheard me."

Art raised an eyebrow. "And you're still in one piece? He must have very special plans for you."

"Sure," I muttered, setting my empty glass on the table next to Art's. "That's why he slammed me up against a wall, choked me half to death and told me to get the fuck out of his house. Because he thinks I'm special."

Chuckling, Art lifted the pitcher and refilled my glass. "You're looking at it all wrong. Do you have any idea what the Sarrum does to his enemies?"

"Yeah," I muttered, lifting my cup with a nod of gratitude. "I took a tour of some of the cells in his dungeon."

"Did you?" he replied with a devilish grin. "Before or after you pissed him off?"

"After. Benjamin was showing me what happens to people who piss off the King."

Art refilled his own glass. "Then you ought to realize how lucky you are to be in one piece. You befriended his wife, his most beloved treasure, and comforted her when he wasn't allowed near her. You insulted him in the basest way possible in his own home. And yet, you still live under his roof and his best teachers continue to train you. Why do you suppose that is?"

I shrugged. "No idea."

"He needs you, Charlie. You're far more valuable than you think."

"Valuable? I pretty much suck at everything they try to teach me."

He shook his head. "I highly doubt that's true."

"Well, you shouldn't."

Art's gaze shifted to the Water. "Have you seen the Princess yet?"

"No," I whispered. "We were going to talk about me visiting, but I insulted the Dragon King's character and got myself kicked out of the house before we got to it."

"But they haven't stopped training you?"

"No. They're actually working extra hard on it. The doctor wants me to train with him because he thinks I might have a knack for potion making, but Benjamin won't okay it until I master the basics."

"I suppose that's sensible," he murmured. "Crawl before you walk."

"Yeah. But I suck at crawling. So I don't know why they're so convinced I'll be great at walking."

Art took a sip of his drink. "You haven't asked me any questions yet. Isn't there anything you want an outside opinion on?"

I blew out a breath. "How awful are things for Emma?"

Frowning, he uncrossed his legs. "What do you mean?"

"She's a prisoner in her own house," I muttered. "Her husband kidnapped her when she was a baby, and now she's lost her Sight and has no idea what's even going on."

"That pretty much sums it up, doesn't it?" Art leaned forward with a resolute sigh. "She's dying, Charlie. A little each day. A creature of Light was never meant to be kept in the Darkness. Being there is literally draining the life from her soul."

"That's kinda what I figured."

Art nodded. "You care for her, don't you?"

"That's a dangerous question." Even inside the mirage, I was too afraid to say it out loud. "I haven't seen Emma yet but I saw Isa, and Doc said her room is in a portion of the palace that's woven with a special magic to allow a creature of Light to live in the Darkness."

Art sank back against the cushions of his chair. "They trust you quite a bit if they're letting you in there."

"Nah. Benjamin just took me there because he didn't have time to take me back after my tour."

"The Darkness took you to see Isa?" Grinning, he shook his head. "You couldn't possibly get a bigger pat on the back than that. No matter what reason he gave you, he wouldn't take you there if he didn't trust you."

"How do you know that?" I whispered, afraid to let myself believe it.

"Isa is the Darkness's soul mate."

"Soul mate?"

Art nodded. "There's nothing tricky about the term. It means they're a couple in this world where our forms are referred to as *souls*. It's one of those phrases that the Unsighted actually picked up from us. The funny thing is how often they use the term correctly. Somehow, they just sense it. To them it simply means their connection is incredibly special. And it truly is. To find that one perfect person for you in both worlds? That's a rare occurrence."

"But Isa and Benjamin aren't a couple in the waking world. Are they?"

Art shook his head. "No. But that's often the case with the Sighted. It's too dangerous for us to mate in the waking world."

"Why?"

Sorrow drifted over Art's features. "Haven't they taught you what happens when two Sighted individuals conceive a child?"

"Yeah. They have a dragon baby."

"Yes," he replied in a rough whisper, "and why do you suppose dragons are so rare?"

"I don't know. Is it harder for them to conceive?"

"No," he whispered, eyes misting. "It's nearly impossible for the mother to survive the birth."

My stomach knotted as I remembered how surprised David looked when I told him my mother was alive, before I learned she wasn't really my mother.

"The odds of the mother surviving a dragon birth are roughly twenty percent."

The number turned my stomach. "Is that why Isa's daughter thinks the Sarrum wants to impregnate her instead of Emma?"

Art nodded. "I'd imagine so. Emma's chance of survival would be nearly zero. She's far too weak already, and she's a creature of Light. Carrying that much Darkness inside her would rip her apart."

"So the King's just going to let his heir rip some other woman apart?"

"He loves his Princess far too much to risk losing her."

"That doesn't make it okay to risk someone else's life," I whispered hoarsely.

"No," he murmured. "It certainly doesn't. But right and wrong never factored into his other decisions where the Princess was concerned. So why should it now?"

"Good point," I muttered. "Rose seemed to think the Sarrum might want me to, um... make an heir for him. Do you think she could be right?"

Art took a deep breath before answering. "No. The Talbot family would never allow that to happen. The notion of a dragon without Talbot blood in its veins sitting the throne is blasphemous."

I raked a hand through my hair. "And the notion of the Sarrum making an heir with Rose?"

Art grimaced. "Far more likely. The Talbot family never approved of the Sarrum's marriage to a creature of Light and they certainly wouldn't consider her a suitable mother for the future king. Rose may not be a royal dragon, but she's a dragon and the child of two dragons would be a much more powerful creature."

"So," I whispered uneasily, "you think the Sarrum would cheat on his wife under certain circumstances?"

Art studied me closely as he answered. "I think the Sarrum would stop at nothing to protect his little Princess. She's his soul mate after all. Screwing another woman to protect her from a deadly fate could hardly be considered cheating. What other options does he have?"

The whole situation made me sick to my stomach. "Okay. I'll give him that, I guess. But do you think he'd cheat on her under other circumstances? Like, if a succubus seduced him?"

Art narrowed his eyes at me. "Are you referring to Sophie Turner?"

"Yeah. I am." The fact that he'd pulled her name out of nowhere wasn't exactly reassuring. "She told Emma that she was sleeping with David, and Emma was so devastated she couldn't think straight. That's the reason Emma slit her wrist and stabbed Isa."

"Have you ever met a succubus?" Art whispered.

"No. But I've met an incubus. So I get what kind of effect they have on people."

"Yes," he murmured. "I forgot about the bartender. He's a prime example, but it isn't just the charm. A dragon can resist that if he chooses to, but the Sarrum's wife is a fragile creature and a dragon has a ravenous appetite. They aren't gentle lovers by nature. It's understandable that he'd seek an outlet for his baser desires. A succubus has no sexual limits and they crave dragons like an addict craves a fix. They get bored with sexual playthings who'll bend to their every whim. Dragons are dominant predatory beasts in every way, and sexual acts of a Dark nature with a partner capable of dominating them are every succubus's ultimate fantasy."

"You're dancing around the question," I growled, a little angrier than I meant to. "Do you think the Sarrum cheated on Emma with Sophie?"

Art shifted in his chair. "I hardly danced around the question, Charlie. I plainly spelled it out for you. I do believe he cheated on his wife with the succubus. I also believe he did it to protect her from violent tendencies that he couldn't entirely contain. If she hadn't lost her Sight, the Princess probably would've thanked him for satisfying those needs with Sophie. In fact, she might even have known about it before she went blind."

"I don't believe that. Emma wouldn't be alright with anyone else sleeping with her husband. She loves him more than anything. The idea of him touching someone else sickened her."

"Of course it did," Art whispered. "He's her soul mate. I don't agree with many of the Sarrum's choices, but I'm afraid I do agree with those decisions. He has no choice but to impregnate another dragon. Sacrificing your greatest treasure to fulfill an obligation to the next generation is unthinkable. All his infidelities are intended to protect his precious wife."

I hopped to my feet and moved toward the dock. "Cheating is cheating."

Art stood up and stepped toward me. "What if it was you, Charlie? Would you impregnate Emma, knowing it'd kill her to give birth to your child? Or would you find another vessel for your heir?"

"She's not mine," I whispered. "You were the one who told me I shouldn't ever think of her as *my* anything."

"It's a hypothetical question," he murmured, taking a step closer. "Why is that so unthinkable?"

"Because," I growled, "I don't get to touch her. Ever. She belongs to a monster who can justify cheating on her, even though it's killing her. I'd castrate myself before I'd ever dream of breaking her heart. You can't justify what he does! He doesn't deserve her!"

"And you do?"

"More than him," I growled, despite the fact that I shouldn't have answered.

"Then where do you go from here?" Art whispered.

"I don't know."

"If sleeping with Rose would save Emma, would you do it?"

"What kind of choice is that?"

"An impossible one. And that's exactly what the Sarrum's forced to make, impossible choices. There must be an heir." He closed his eyes and took a deep breath. "I'm not saying I agree with all of his decisions, Charlie. Some of us disagree with the way he's done everything. Just keep that in mind." With that, he stepped onto the dock and headed toward the end.

Recalling something I'd forgotten, I stepped after him. "The Sarrum killed your sister."

Art froze but he didn't turn around. "Yes. Thank you for reminding me."

"I'm sorry," I muttered, hating how wounded he sounded. "How did she die?"

"We're done talking," Art growled...

...The next thing I knew, I was sitting up in bed. Stomach churning, I jumped up and rushed into the bathroom. I flipped the lights on and sunk to my knees in front of the toilet. And the second I lifted the lid, I was puking. I would've been better off if I'd never left the facility. I hated every one of these people. *Except Emma.* I had to get her away from all of this.

27

EMMA

I woke up in bed with no idea how I'd gotten there. The last thing I remembered was sitting in the chair across the room talking to Jeremy. I couldn't remember how my therapy session had ended, but I remembered him commenting that my bed *looked well used.* He'd wanted to find Sara and have her change the bedding. Now the sheets were clean. My bathrobe was draped over the chair I must've fallen asleep in and I was dressed in a nightgown. How had I slept through all that? And who'd stripped off my robe and dressed me in the nightgown? It had to have been David. Sara wouldn't get that close to me and the doctor would be too afraid to touch me. He knew my husband well enough to know that'd be a death sentence. I'd told David not to come to bed, and he'd angrily agreed that he wouldn't. Maybe I should've been mad that he'd carried me to bed and changed my clothes, but I wasn't. Those were loving gestures. And he clearly hadn't slept in our bed. His side was still perfectly made.

I sat up and flipped my hair over my shoulder. There didn't seem to be any point in getting out of bed anymore. I looked down at my wrist and traced a finger over the scar. What other options did I have? There were no pills in the medicine cabinet, neither of us took any. We didn't own a gun and I wasn't sure how to hang myself. A breeze fluttered the curtains across the room, flagging my attention and I stood up and moved to the screen door to the balcony. It was a beautiful day, not morning though. The sun was too high. I'd slept through half the day, but it didn't matter. There was nothing in my life to wake up for. The breeze swept the hair off my shoulder as I slid the balcony door open. I stepped out and closed my eyes, reveling in the breeze and the sunshine for a moment. Then I moved to the railing. Was this high enough to be a fatal fall? I stepped on a lounge chair, hoisted myself up and sat down on the railing. I'd always loved the view from the balcony, but it didn't make me smile anymore. Nothing made me smile. And I had no one left to turn to. David had hurt me too deeply and lied to me for too long, and I couldn't confide in my new doctor.

"Emma," the doctor's voice whispered from the doorway. I started at the sound of his voice and he lunged toward me, then stilled when he realized I wasn't about to fall. "Please come down."

I shook my head and looked down at the beach below. "I don't want to."

"Please my dear," he pleaded in an anxious whisper. "You don't want to fall."

I let out a frustrated laugh. "Don't I?"

"No dear." I heard him take a few steps toward me. "You don't."

I turned my head and looked at him. "What've I got to live for Doctor?"

"Call me Jeremy," he whispered, freezing in place.

Eyes tearing, I let out a bitter laugh. "Does it matter what I call you?"

"Yes." I could've sworn I heard his thoughts shouting in my head. *You're needed upstairs, Sarrum! Immediately!*

Great. Now I was imagining whispered nonsense. I looked back at the water. "There's nothing left for me here, Jeremy."

"That's not true. There are people who love you."

"No one I can trust," I sobbed, aching at how true it was.

"What about your friend from the facility, Charlie? Did you trust him?"

"It doesn't matter. I'll never see him again."

"It *does* matter," David whispered as he stepped out onto the balcony.

Tears streamed down my cheeks as I looked at him. "Do you even know what we're talking about?"

"Yes," he whispered, taking a step toward me. "Come down, and I'll have your friend here within the hour."

"You're just saying that to get me to come down."

"Give me your phone," David growled to the doctor as he took another step.

The doctor stuck a trembling hand in his jacket and pulled out his cell phone. Then he dialed a number and I heard it ringing as he handed it to my husband.

Lifting the phone to his ear, David took another step and touched my leg with his free hand. His eyes hadn't strayed from mine since he'd stepped out the door. They were tearing as Brian's voice answered, "What's up, Doc?"

"It's me," he replied in a throaty whisper. "I need to speak to Charlie immediately."

Why would Charlie be with Brian? Pain flared at my temple and the world around me blurred.

"Brian's been training him," David whispered, tightening his grip on my leg. "I still intend to hire him."

The blurring worsened and the world tilted as Brian's voice asked, "Can I call you back? I'm not sure where he is."

"I don't care if he's taking a shit!" David snarled. "Find him and put your phone to his ear! Now!"

"On it," Brian's voice answered.

I clutched my head as the pain throbbed at my temple and David dropped the phone and wrapped his other arm around my waist. I tried to jerk away from him, but the world tilted and I lost my balance. As I started to fall, David pulled me to his chest and dropped into the lounge chair I'd used to climb up onto the railing. I wanted to push him away, but my head was throbbing and everything was a blur. So I squeezed my eyes shut and dropped my head to his shoulder.

"Hello?" Charlie's voice answered from the floor.

Jeremy bent, picked up the phone and handed it to David.

I squinted against the pain and watched my husband put the phone to his ear. "Hello."

Charlie's voice sounded strained, "What do you want from me?"

"My wife wants to see you."

"Okay?" Charlie's voice muttered. "Are you telling me this to hurt me?"

"No. I'm telling you this because I just pulled her off the railing of our balcony," David growled through gritted teeth. "And she needs to see a friendly face. So if you can fit it into your busy schedule, I need you and Brian to get the hell over here."

Tears streamed down my cheeks as I buried my face against David's chest. I knew how much it killed my husband to ask another man to comfort me. Why did he have to be so selfless? Why couldn't he just let me hate him?

"We'll be there as quick as we can." In a broken whisper Charlie added, "Can I talk to her?"

Without responding, David put the phone to my ear.

"Charlie?" I whispered.

"Hey, Em. We'll figure this out, alright?"

Hearing Charlie's voice made my heart ache almost as much as my head, but not just because it was good to hear him. It broke my heart that David was letting him comfort me. It meant that he'd given up on me.

"Em?" There was a lot of shuffling in the background as Charlie whispered, "You still there?"

"Yes," I sobbed, clinging to the collar of David's shirt. I wanted to scream. *Don't give up on me! Dear God, don't let my husband give up on me!* I wanted to take it all back, rewind the moments since I got out of bed, stop myself from climbing onto the railing. I lifted a hand to my mouth, suppressing the urge to vomit.

David took the phone from my ear and held it to his. "We'll see you soon." He ended the call and handed the phone back to Jeremy. "Shhh," he whispered, brushing the hair from my face as the doctor left the balcony. "I'm not going anywhere, Princess. You can't get rid of me that easily."

I let out a laugh, despite the pain in my head and my heart. Then I burst into tears. "I'm sorry. Please. Forgive me."

He kissed my forehead and tightened his hold on me. "You don't have anything to be sorry for, Emma. Just relax."

I lifted my head from his chest and met his beautiful eyes. "Why don't you hate me?"

He took a deep breath and exhaled through flared nostrils. "How could I ever hate you?"

"I keep pushing you away. What are we even doing at this point?"

"You can push me all you want," he murmured, wiping the tears from my cheeks. "I'll never give up on us. You're everything to me, Emma. You always have been. Have you forgotten that?"

Another flare of pain exploded at my temple and I dropped my head to his chest. "I feel like I've forgotten everything."

He cradled the back of my head in his palm as his thumb brushed my temple, and the pain seemed to dull with his touch. "It's all there, and I won't rest until we've fixed this."

I winced as the ache flared again.

He kissed my throbbing temple. "Just relax. I promise you, we'll fix this and everything will be alright."

Too exhausted to think, I squeezed my eyes shut as his kiss warmed my temple. It was terrifying, the depth of my hatred for David. And the depth of my love. I'd die if he ever let me go. My heart would have no reason to keep beating.

28

BENJAMIN

The virgin's voice plucked me from my visit with Isa, and I would've ripped his throat out if it weren't for the urgency in his tone. I sat up and rubbed the sleep from my eyes. "What is it?"

"Brian told me to get you," the kid practically shouted. "The Sarrum needs us to come to his house. He just pulled Emma off the railing of their balcony."

"What?"

"We need to go," Brian hollered from the hall. "Now!"

For Brian to yell at me and for Charlie to wake me, it had to be bad. I threw off the covers and grabbed the pants I'd left folded on my dresser. Hopping into them, I grabbed a shirt from the closet and tugged it on as we raced down the stairs. I narrowed my eyes at Charlie as he tossed me the keys on our way out the door. "Who exactly did the boss ask for?"

"Me! He specifically asked for me! I talked to her! And she sounded terrible! So can we argue about what a disappointment I am some other time?" The virgin all but shoved Brian out of the way to sit shotgun as the three of us piled into the car.

I grinned at him as I settled into the driver's seat. "Yeah, kid. We can."

I broke every speed limit and ran every light, and we made it to the boss's house in record time. The guard opened the gate the second he saw us coming, and it wasn't long before we were hopping out of the car and rushing into the house.

Doc was waiting for us as we stepped into the foyer. "Thank God," he muttered. "They're upstairs." He started up the stairs and the three of us followed, taking the steps a few at a time.

Doc crossed his arms and looked at me as we reached the second floor. "He asked for Charlie."

I gestured for Charlie to take the lead, and Brian fell into step beside him. Doc and I followed the two of them down the hall and as we entered the room, Doc pointed to the balcony. Brian stepped out while the rest of us hung back, but his words wafted in through the open door. "Hey, Emma."

I took a step toward the door and watched Brian kiss the Princess's forehead. She looked pale and there was something hollow about her as she sat there on the boss's lap. Now I knew why Doc said this wouldn't end well. She was too far gone.

Brian dragged a chair close to Emma and the boss and sat down. "I've missed you, sweetheart."

Emma's eyes were dull and lifeless as she grinned at him. "I've missed you, too."

The boss dropped his mouth to her ear. "Would you like me to leave?"

She clutched his arm and shook her head. "Don't go." It was heartbreaking to see her like that, looking so lost.

A sorrowful smile spread across the boss's face. "Never. Not unless you ask me to."

The boss settled back in the chair, and the Princess gripped his arm even tighter as she looked at Brian. "Did Charlie come with you?"

"Yeah." The kid stepped out onto the balcony. "I'm right here, Em."

Tears slid down her cheeks as she whispered, "It's really good to see you, Charlie." She reached a hand out to the virgin.

Charlie tentatively stepped toward Emma but instead of touching her, he looked at the Sarrum and raised his eyebrows. Only after the boss nodded, did Charlie take her hand. "Rough day?"

She chuckled and wiped the tears from her cheeks. "I've had better."

The boss let out a slow sigh as he lifted the Princess from his lap and sat her down in the chair. She looked up at him, and he nodded. "I'll let you two talk alone." Flames flickered in his eyes as he turned to Charlie. "Let anything happen to her, and I'll make you wish you'd never been born."

"No worries," Charlie whispered. "If I let anything happen to her, I'd want you to."

A puff of blue smoke wafted from the boss's nostrils as he glared at Charlie.

And the kid shook his head at his own stupidity. "I swear, nothing's gonna happen to her on my watch."

The boss knelt and kissed Emma's cheek. "I won't go far."

"Promise?"

"On my life." The Sarrum stood and tapped Brian on the shoulder, and the two of them left the balcony together. As they moved past us, Doc fell into step with them and the boss nodded to me. *Do not let her out of your sight.*

Of course. I slipped into the shadows and silently joined Emma and Charlie on the balcony. Charlie stiffened as he felt my presence, and I felt a rush of pride. It wouldn't be long till he embraced what he was. Ignoring me, Charlie slid into the chair beside Emma.

She dropped her head to his shoulder. "I don't want to live anymore, Charlie. It hurts too much."

The kid wrapped a comforting arm around her. "What does?"

"Everything," the Princess whispered. "Every breath. Every time I look at his face. I can't do this anymore."

"Don't say that."

Emma lifted her head off his shoulder. "What did you see, Charlie? Back at the facility when you attacked David?"

The kid shook his head. "It doesn't matter, Em."

"I shouldn't trust him, should I?"

Charlie tugged a hand through his hair. "He's your husband."

"Is he the monster you always saw near me?"

Charlie squinted in my vicinity. *How am I supposed to answer that?*

With the truth. She needs to remember who he is.

Charlie didn't look sure about it but he still whispered, "Yeah. He is."

A tear slid down Emma's cheek as her eyes locked with his. "What is he?"

"A dragon."

Emma let out a whimper as she squeezed her eyes shut and dropped her head in her hands.

Charlie laid his hands on top of hers. "Em?"

Face pale as a corpse, she lifted her head and I could've sworn she looked straight at me. Then she pushed Charlie away and stood up.

Boss! The Sarrum reached her before the kid even had a chance to stand. He touched the small of her back. "Emma? Talk to me."

"No," she whispered. "Get away from me."

"I'm sorry," he murmured, "but I can't do that. You need me here."

Her eyes were cold and dead as she turned to him. "What do I need you for?"

"You need me to keep away the Darkness."

She took a step back. "You're the one who locked me away in the Dark. You made me need you."

"Yes, but I had no choice. You stole my heart and you pushed me to it."

With a ragged sob, Emma took another step back from him. "I should've left you when I had the chance."

"Yes," he agreed, stepping toward her. "You should have, but it's too late for that now. You belong to me and I'd never let anyone take you from me."

"It's your fault," she muttered. "I'm like this because of what you did."

"Yes," he whispered. "But I won't apologize for that. I had my reasons. I'm just sorry you had to see it."

"Why couldn't you just let me die?"

"Because," the boss whispered, "you're my heart. I could never let you go."

"I feel like such a pathetic fool."

"Everything I did, no matter how horrible, all of it was to protect you from harm. You have no idea what your life could've been like."

"You're a monster."

"No," the boss whispered. "I'm *your* monster."

She took a step back, searching his eyes. Then her body crumpled.

The Sarrum caught her in his arms and carried her to the bed. "Get out! All of you!"

Charlie just stood there looking stunned. So I grabbed him by the arm and yanked him off the balcony and out of the room. As we moved toward the stairs, he muttered, "What the hell just happened?"

Doc stood waiting for us at the top of the stairs. "She's starting to remember."

29

DAVID

It was nearly impossible for Emma to pass through the Waters lately. Their pull on her grew stronger each day, and it was no wonder. In the Waters, all of it washed away. The memories. The heartache. The guilt. She wanted to stay there. She wanted her life to end, but I would never let that happen.

As Benjamin and Charlie rushed from our room, I plunged into the Waters after her. And I wasn't silent about it. Those senseless creatures loved to play dumb, but I was in no mood for games. If my tone wasn't enough to convince them of that, I'd have no qualms about sacrificing a few of them to make my point. The Water creatures were an unruly bunch to begin with and now that their monarch was dead, there was no one to enforce their laws. Fuck the whole lot of them. I'd take out as many as I had to and I wouldn't lose a moment's sleep over it. *SHE DOES NOT BELONG TO YOU! SHE IS MINE!*

The insolent little pricks actually had the gall to *push* her to me and I had half a mind to push them back *harder,* but I needed to get Emma to dry ground as soon as possible. *MANHANDLE MY WIFE AGAIN AND YOU'LL ALL BURN! WOMEN! CHILDREN! AND I'LL TAKE THE MEN LAST, SO YOU CAN SPEND YOUR FINAL BREATHS WATCHING YOUR FAMILIES BURN! DO NOT FUCK WITH WHAT BELONGS TO ME!*

They didn't respond but I could taste their fear bleeding through the Waters. Message received, for the moment anyway. Their tiny water-logged brains didn't seem capable of retaining information for long. It was no matter. I'd keep reminding them as often and as harshly as I had to.

Limp and lifeless, Emma fell into my arms. I waded out of the lake at the edge of our clearing, hoping the fresh air would rouse her. But as I stepped onto dry land, my wife watched me through emotionless eyes. No love. No hatred. Not even sorrow.

I hugged her to my chest and dropped to the grass, heart aching as I searched her eyes for any flicker of emotion. "Who am I, Princess?"

There was no response, not the slightest twitch of a facial muscle.

I'd refused to see what everyone had been telling me for months, but it was impossible to ignore the emptiness in her eyes. Perhaps it wasn't all locked away inside her. Maybe too much of my Princess had washed away in the Waters. If I lost her, I'd see both worlds burn for my loss. I was reputed to be a fair ruler who treated his subjects with compassion, but compassion wasn't in my nature. All the kindness came from her. Without my Princess, I'd rule the world with madness and rage. I shook her gently and repeated the question, "Who am I?"

A soft whimper escaped her lips. It was a frail hopeless sound, but it was something.

I put my hand to her cheek. She felt too cold. Inhaling deeply, I drew the Darkness from her. "Who am I?"

Confusion replaced the emptiness in her eyes as she blinked at me. "What?"

Cradling the back of her head in my palm, I lifted her toward my mouth and kissed her pale lips. And for a moment, it was one-sided. But as her lips warmed, she kissed me back with needy desperation as though she sensed my touch could strengthen her. I drew her bottom lip out between my teeth and when her mouth opened, I pushed my tongue inside. She moaned softly, the sound muffled by my mouth. And I gently bit her lip to break the kiss. "Who am I, Princess?"

"You're my King."

"What else?"

Confusion flickered in her eyes again. "What else is there?"

"What else have I been to you?" I murmured, brushing my lips across hers.

"You're everything to me."

"Yes." I stroked her bottom lip with my thumb and her lips parted, eager to accept whatever part of me was offered. "But more specifically, what do you remember?"

"I don't understand," she whispered, caressing my thumb with her lips as she spoke. "What am I supposed to remember?"

"You need me. Do you remember that?"

"Of course. How could I forget?"

I lowered my mouth to her ear. "Are you angry with me?"

She let out a breathy sigh. "Why would I be?"

"Don't you remember the things you just said to me in the waking world?"

She bit down on my thumb, not playfully. Painfully. "I don't want to talk about that."

"Why, Princess?" I moved my mouth to hers, inviting her to bite again.

Anger flashed in her eyes as she bit my lip hard enough to puncture the flesh. "Don't make me talk about that."

"Why?" I whispered, licking the blood from my lip. "What do you remember?" I'd incite as much fury as I had to, to revive the life in those gorgeous eyes.

Without warning, she swung a hand back and struck my cheek. Tears pooled in her eyes as she pushed me away. Then she stood and turned her back to me. "I remember I should hate you."

I stood up behind her, swept the hair off her neck and kissed her sweet flesh. "*Should* hate me? Does that mean you don't?"

She spun around. Her face was only inches from mine, and the war between her head and her heart raged in her eyes. "I don't know what it means."

"Hit me again," I whispered. "It'll make you feel better."

Fury flashed in her eyes as she lifted a hand, but it froze in midair as her heart gained control and a tear slid down her cheek. "Why did you lie to me?"

Intent on milking her fury for all its worth, I whispered, "I did it for your own good." Planting one palm between her shoulder blades and the other at the small of her back, I drew her toward me.

She pushed against my chest, but I could hear her heart racing and the scent of desire pooling between her legs was irrefutable. "You orchestrated my entire life, and you played me for a fool!"

I slid my hand to the back of her head and pushed her mouth toward mine. A warning flashed in her eyes, but I ignored it and smothered her lips with a kiss. She tried to push away, but only for a moment. At first, she just stopped resisting but when my fingers fisted in her hair, her lips parted for me. And as my kiss deepened, she returned the kiss with unbridled enthusiasm. I lowered the hand at the small of her

back, coaxing her ripened flesh against my arousal so she could feel how much I wanted her. "You
chose this, Princess. Don't deny your part in it." She
pushed against my chest again, but made no attempt
to break our contact below the waist and when I lifted
her off the ground, she wrapped her legs around me.
"Which is it, Princess?" I rasped in her ear. "Shall I let
you go? Or make you scream my name?"

A groan escaped her sweet lips, equal parts frustration and arousal. And her eyelids lowered as she
touched her forehead to mine and responded in a
throaty whisper, "I hate you."

Fueled by a carnal sense of urgency, I pressed
her tighter against the erection that was desperately
straining to get inside her. "That's not an appropriate answer to my question. Do you want distance?"
I hastily bunched the hem of her dress, slid a hand
between her legs and pressed my fingers into her
through the wet fabric of her panties. "Or do you
want me here?"

A soft moan escaped her lips as her teeth clamped
onto my earlobe.

"Answer me, Princess." I slipped my fingers inside her panties and slowly sunk them deep inside
her. "Is this where you want me?" Her head tipped
back with a feral whimper as I dropped to my knees
with her limbs still wrapped around me. I fell back
in the grass and withdrew my fingers. "Or shall I let
you go?"

A brazen mix of lust and fury danced in her eyes as she sat up and straddled my legs. "You arrogant bastard! You don't get to win this round." She pressed her palm against the aching bulge in my pants and her eyes locked with mine as she traveled up the length of it, unfastened my pants and stuffed a hand inside. Soft fingers coiled around me and stroked, and she licked her lips as a low growl erupted from my throat. No longer devoid of emotion, triumph now flashed in those hypnotic green eyes.

I gripped her waist to draw her onto me, but a wicked grin spread across her angelic face as she pushed my hands off and sprang to her feet. "You should let me go." With that, she turned and headed toward the cave.

Thrilled with the amount of life I'd breathed into her, I watched her saunter halfway to the cave before I stood. But it was only a matter of seconds till I caught up to her, wrapped an arm around her waist and threw her over my shoulder. "That's no longer an option."

A shiver coursed through me as her lips moved to my ear. "Then make me scream your name."

30

CHARLIE

We stuck around after the Sarrum kicked us out of his room. Leaving the house never even crossed our minds. Instructing us all to "stay the fuck away from him unless it was urgent," Benjamin took the living room and jumped back to Draumer to visit Isa, and I followed Brian and Doc to the lounge. Brian fixed three stiff gin and tonics without asking either of us if we wanted one but considering the circumstances, maybe that was just a given.

Drink in hand, I plopped down on one end of the couch by the fireplace. Brian settled onto the other. Doc took the chair across from us. And for a while, we all just sipped our drinks in silence. When the quiet got to be too much, I cleared my throat. "Is Emma ever going to get better?"

Eyes tearing, Brian shook his head. "It doesn't look good." Then he turned to Doc. "You're our best shot. Is there any way to bring her back from this?"

Doc let out a troubled sigh. "Honestly? I don't know. I think healing Isa is our only hope. I need her help."

Brian sat up a little straighter. "Then what are you waiting for?"

"I need Rose and Charlie's assistance, but the Sarrum isn't ready to forgive Charlie."

Brian sank back against the couch cushions. "He specifically asked for Charlie when he called me. That has to be a good sign."

Doc shook his head as he sat his glass on the table beside him. "The Princess had just stated that she couldn't trust anyone. I asked if she trusted Charlie, and the Sarrum called while she was teetering on the balcony railing. He would've done anything to talk her down. It had nothing to do with forgiving Charlie."

Too pissed at my own stupidity to look either of them in the eyes, I looked down at the ice cubes in my glass. "So how do I fix things?"

Doc picked his drink back up and stared at it for a few seconds before taking a sip. "Perhaps we should begin working on Isa's potion without waiting for permission. The Darkness and the Sarrum may be too preoccupied to make rational decisions."

Brian glanced toward the hall. "If I were you, I wouldn't say that to either of them."

Doc let out a low chuckle. "No shit."

"Can I ask how Emma lost her Sight?" I whispered. "I know that doctor in the cell blinded her. But how did it happen?"

Doc cast a wary glance at Brian. When my number one guide nodded, the doctor turned to me. "The Sarrum has enemies, Charlie. Not everyone agrees with the choices he's made, and some even argue that he isn't the rightful King."

I already knew he had enemies because of Art, but I'd promised not to mention him. "Who disagrees with his choices?"

Brian was quiet for a minute before answering, "There's a growing faction of creatures, mostly Dark creatures, who call themselves the Purists. The Sarrum's uncle is their leader, and he refers to himself as the rightful King."

"Why?"

Brian absently drummed his fingers on the rim of his glass. "Because he *was* supposed to be King. There's always been a Talbot on the throne and their spouses have always been strategically chosen from the other royal families throughout the world. All of them are pure-blooded dragons, and their marriages have always been carefully orchestrated to prevent any genetic familiarity."

"Any what?"

"Inbreeding," Doc whispered, shifting in his chair.

Brian nodded. "The Sarrum's uncle was intended to wed his Aunt Louise."

Yeah. He lost me there. "Wait, how is that not inbreeding?"

Brian suppressed an amused grin. "His uncle Henry is a member of the Godric family and his Aunt Louise is a Talbot. When Louise contracted an illness that prevented her from ever conceiving a child, she couldn't fulfill her obligation. So rather than find another royal to wed Henry, they arranged a marriage between his younger sister and Louise's younger brother. Henry was furious with the decision but there was nothing he could do about it. So he did the only thing he could do. He moved into the palace to watch over his little sister. Dragons are fiercely protective of their treasures, and Henry treasured his sister above everything else. So he stayed by her side, despite how much the whole arrangement pissed him off. When she died giving birth to David Talbot, Henry snapped."

I raked my fingers through my hair. "Snapped?"

"He snuck into David's nursery to kill him. And if the King's shadow hadn't been watching over the little Prince, he would've succeeded."

I blew out a loud breath. "Wow."

Brian sat his empty glass on the coffee table. "Henry fled the palace and went into hiding after that. Nobody knows where he is in either world but every now and then, we do hear whispers about him.

And we know he's been building an army of dragons, patiently waiting for an opportunity to strike."

"Building an army of dragons?" *Was that why the Sarrum invited me to join his family? So I wouldn't join the Purist army?*

All three of us jumped when Benjamin's voice thundered from the doorway, "The Purists refer to Sighted females as incubators or eggs. They view them as disposable shells to hatch new dragons and since they don't get a whole lot of volunteers, they usually take the women. That's how we met Isa. She came to us for protection after a shadow forced himself on her."

My chest tightened as I whispered, "Rose?"

Benjamin nodded.

"Is the shadow who uh... made Rose still around?"

Waves of fury radiated from Benjamin. "No. I took care of him."

"So uh... What does all of that have to do with Emma losing her Sight?"

Brian cleared his throat. "To take the throne, the Purists need to destroy a king who has no weaknesses."

Benjamin took a few steps toward us. "He has one. The Sarrum treasures the Princess above all else, and everyone knows it. So Henry's most recent attempts have been focused on her. The Purists launched an attack along the fringe. When they started moving down the coast, torturing and killing the

Unsighted, the Sarrum and I led the effort to crush them. While we were away, a group of Purists lured Emma from the safety of the King's lair. As soon as she stepped beyond the protections, they attacked her. The King felt it immediately but by the time we reached her, things had happened. The Sarrum rushed her to the royal healer, but the Purists had already gotten to him and threatened him into giving Emma the potion that blinded her. It was meant to kill her. Thankfully, the Sarrum was able to save her from dying, but he couldn't restore her Sight."

"Darkness," Doc whispered. "Would you consider allowing Charlie to assist me with my work now? I believe he can help me heal Isa and once we get her back, I'm hoping she can help us restore the Princess but we're running out of time."

The glare that Benjamin shot the doctor would've made me piss myself if it'd been directed at me. "Then what the fuck are you waiting around here for?"

Doc flinched but his calm expression never changed. "The Sarrum hasn't given me permission to train Charlie yet."

"I'm giving it to you now," Benjamin growled. Then he turned to me. "Do not fuck this up."

Yeah. No pressure. All I had to do was be great at something I knew nothing about, heal the Darkness's soul mate and oh yeah, save the love of the Sarrum's life. And I was worried their expectations were too high.

31

ISABELLA

It was getting easier to stay near the surface lately. There was more to listen to and a positive energy had replaced the somber one. Doc seemed confident that the potion he was concocting would bring me back. Rose was assisting him, along with a young man whose voice and name I didn't recognize. Benji referred to him as "the virgin" but he clearly didn't appreciate the label. Doc was a patient teacher and it warmed my heart to listen to him instructing my daughter and her fellow apprentice.

They were heating the ingredients they'd been painstakingly mixing for the last several days in the fireplace on the other side of my room. Benji was sitting beside me, holding my hand and occasionally criticizing the young man...Charlie. The young man's name was Charlie. "When you're finished here, we're going back to the house to work on unmasking."

Charlie let out an exasperated sigh. "Seriously? Again? I'll still suck at it. I can barely do it when you're scaring the crap out of me, let alone on my own."

"That's why you need to practice. If you were proficient, there'd be no need. But like you said, you still suck at it. So yes, we're working on it again."

"Brian said the Sarrum agreed to meet with me today," Charlie stated in an uncharacteristically somber tone. "When will I be doing that?"

"*After* you practice unmasking."

Across the room, Doc cleared his throat. "And this time, may I suggest you refrain from calling the King a pedophile?"

"Yeah. Thanks," Charlie grumbled. "That hadn't occurred to me."

Benji gave my hand an affectionate squeeze. "You'd think it wouldn't be necessary to mention, but we thought that the first time and look how well that turned out."

"Trust me," Charlie muttered. "Getting thrown against the wall and choked half to death got the point across. I'll be on my best behavior."

"If it's all the same to the two of you, can we get back to the task at hand?" Doc heard the question in Charlie's head and added, "I plan to take you along when I go to the Sarrum's house for the Princess's appointment this afternoon."

"Thanks."

"You're quite welcome. Now can we get back to the potion?"

"Yeah," Charlie whispered. "Sorry."

"It's alright." Doc's voice sounded closer to my bed. "I need you both to take a seat. We need to discuss the final step of the potion. I'll need everyone's consent to proceed."

Charlie's question echoed loudly through the silence. *What kind of final step requires informed consent?*

As usual, the other three ignored his mental comment. "The final ingredient of the potion is three drops of dragon's blood from three different dragons."

Crap. Is that all they really needed me for?

I didn't know how the three of them could ignore such self-deprecating thoughts. If I could speak, I'd have offered the poor boy some encouraging words.

Doc cleared his throat. He was clearly uncomfortable with Charlie's unspoken question, but apparently not enough to respond. "The blood must be added immediately before the potion is administered, and the dragons must all give it willingly. The Sarrum has agreed to provide a drop. And Rose, I assume you'll be willing to donate?"

"Of course," Rose whispered.

"So Charlie, the only remaining question is whether you'd be willing to donate the third."

"Sure. Of course. Why wouldn't I?"

Benji gave my hand another squeeze. "The blood of a dragon is extremely powerful. When another creature ingests it, a connection is formed. The Sarrum is obviously well aware of that and he's more than willing to contribute. Rose understands the severity of the donation, but she's donating to her mother."

"Still," Charlie muttered, "why wouldn't I want to help?"

Benji's grip on my hand tightened. "Because a bond will be formed, a bond that you don't fully understand. That's one of the things the boss plans to discuss with you today. Only a dragon can adequately explain what that bond entails."

"Can you *inadequately* explain? I'd rather not be totally clueless when he talks to me."

"There are risks," Doc murmured.

"I'm willing to take a risk to save Rose's mother."

"The risk is on the recipient's end," Benji growled.

"Sorry," the boy muttered.

"The Sarrum really is the best one to explain it," Doc agreed softly. "Now why don't we check on our potion?"

Chairs screeched across the stone floor as Charlie and Rose stood up. Footsteps moved to the far end of the room. I heard metal scrape against metal as someone stirred. I was definitely close to the surface because I actually caught a whiff of the work in progress. It smelled God awful, but I'd ingest just about anything to interact with my family again. I was dying to talk to Rose and from the bits of conversations I'd heard, I knew Emma was in pretty rough shape. They needed my help to heal her. Together, Doc and I could figure it out. We had to. And hopefully, the simple fact that I was alright would help her a little. It'd at least lessen Emma's guilt to know that I didn't blame her for what happened. I wished they could bring the Princess in to visit me, but she'd stabbed me in the waking world. Her soul wouldn't understand why I was broken and if a flicker of memory did strike her, she'd be traumatized by it. I remembered that much from before. Any mention of events in the world she wasn't in caused her crippling physical pain. Being so powerless to help her had to be tearing the Sarrum apart. It wouldn't surprise me if he was even worse off than Emma by the time I woke.

Across the room, Doc inhaled loudly. "Excellent. This smells perfect."

Charlie let out a snort of laughter. "Smells like crap to me."

"Yes, well potions often do," Doc replied in his usual pleasant manner. "They're brewed for potency, not taste. And this smells exactly as pungent as it ought to."

"I'm just glad I don't have to drink it," Charlie muttered.

"Well, I doubt Isa will mind," Doc murmured. "She must be quite anxious to join us again."

Benji's hand stroked my cheek. "She is."

"How do you know that?" Rose whispered.

"I can feel it when she's listening, and she's been present more often lately."

"Is she listening now?" Rose's voice sounded closer to me.

"She is."

"Hi mom. I can't wait to meet you."

It was torture not being able to tell my daughter how long I'd dreamt of meeting her. I just hoped to God Doc's potion would work.

32

CHARLIE

After finishing up with Doc, I spent three torturous hours with Benjamin and I swear I sucked even more at unmasking by the time we were done. I was never going to get it. I'd forever be the idiot dragon who was too stupid to figure out how to do something as natural as taking a piss. Seriously. I was hopeless, the worst dragon in the history of dragons.

I shook myself out of self-pitying mode as Benjamin pulled the car into the Talbots' garage. Doc was riding shotgun and I was in the back, sandwiched between Brian and Tristan. We'd all come because we were all feeling restless. Everyone needed some good news, and getting the Sarrum's permission to donate my blood to the potion would at least be a step in the right direction.

Their housekeeper was waiting for us when we stepped into the foyer. I'd never seen her unmask but Brian said she was an imp. Imps must be jumpy little creatures because she was about the antsiest person I'd ever met, and I'd spent a lot of time around paranoid mental patients.

Doc stepped toward the imp with a cheery grin. "Is Emma ready for her appointment?"

"Yes, Doctor. She's in the living room." As Doc started down the hall, the imp turned to the rest of us. I'd gotten a lot better at tapping into my dragon instincts lately, and I felt a certain sense of accomplishment hearing her heart beat faster and smelling her fear as her eyes met Benjamin's. "The Sarrum would like the rest of you to wait for him in the lounge."

"Thank you," Tristan murmured.

Fear wasn't the only scent the imp was giving off as she blushed at Tristan's silky voice. "You're welcome, sir."

Tristan cranked his killer smile up a notch. "You don't need to be so formal. Call me Tristan."

If he lays a finger on her, she's gonna pass out.

Tristan winked at me as he took a step closer to the poor defenseless housekeeper.

Her cheeks flushed and her voice shook even more than usual as she whispered, "Right. Tristan it is then."

Tristan touched the small of her back and a rush of air escaped her mouth as he leaned closer. "I just came along for the ride. Would it be too much trouble to ask you to entertain me while my buddies conduct their business?"

The imp's body heated and her heart raced even faster. "I'd be happy to, sir."

"Come on, Sara," Tristan murmured. "What'd I ask you to call me?"

"Sorry," she replied in a breathy whisper. "Follow me, Tristan. I'll keep you entertained."

"Lead the way." Flashing me a mischievous grin, Tristan followed the housekeeper down the hall.

Benjamin shook his head as they turned the corner. Then he started toward the lounge without waiting to see if Brian and I would follow, but of course we did.

Brian and I headed straight to the couch, and I shifted toward him as we sat down. "I don't get it."

Brian's eyes followed Benjamin as he paced by the bar. "What don't you get?"

"Tristan."

Grinning, Brian looked away from Benjamin. "My brother's a pretty open book. What's not to get?"

How should I put this?

His grin widened. "Put it honestly. I can hear your thoughts anyway, remember?"

"Right." I shot a glance at Benjamin. He was still pacing in front of the bar. "Tristan is drop dead gorgeous and not that I want to sound shallow or anything, but he could be a lot choosier about who he flirts with."

Brian's raised eyebrow suggested that he wasn't impressed with my shallow question, but he answered it anyway. "Tristan's an omnivorous suitor, Charlie. He'll flirt with anything that's got a pulse. But I've got to tell you, the nervous quiet types like Sara..."

"Yeah?"

"More often than not, they're insatiable and *very* open to experimentation."

I couldn't help cracking a smile. "Sounds like you speak from experience."

Brian flashed a devilish grin. "Does that make you think less of me?"

"No," I muttered, dropping the smile, "but I'm not just talking about the housekeeper."

"Okay?"

"What about that warty troll at the tavern? Tristan called her beautiful, kissed her on the cheek and flirted with her like crazy. Was that all just part of his charm demonstration?"

Brian let out a snort of amusement. "She's a swimsuit model in the waking world."

"Yeah, right."

Brian traced a cross over his heart. "Fine. Don't believe me. But it's true."

I was about to say that he was full of shit—*He had to be*—but the Sarrum walked in.

All three of us turned toward the King as his presence filled the room, making the spacious lounge feel overcrowded. "I'd like to speak with Charlie alone."

I swallowed the lump in my throat as Brian hopped off the couch. "You got it, boss. I'm gonna go find something to eat. Holler if you need me." Brian gave me a pat on the shoulder, then headed to the door.

The Dragon King nodded to Brian as he left the room. Then his eyes locked with Benjamin's and the two of them stared at each other in silence for several seconds. Then Benjamin moved to the door and left the room without even looking my way.

The Sarrum stepped behind the bar, took out two glasses and a ridiculously expensive-looking bottle of scotch and poured some in each. Then he crossed the room and handed me one without asking if I wanted it.

But based on the little I'd begun to sense about people lately, I figured he knew darn well that I did. "Thanks."

"You're welcome." Holding me steadily in his gaze, the King sat down in the chair across from me.

I took a sip of my drink and waited for him to start the conversation.

His eyes stayed fixed on me as he absently swirled the glass in his hand, creating an elegant whirlpool of scotch. "What have they told you about donating your blood to Isa's potion?"

"Not much. Benjamin just said there are risks on the recipient's end."

"Yes. There are." His icy stare and curt responses made it pretty clear that he didn't intend to make this discussion easy on me.

I took another sip of my drink and forced myself to relax as it warmed its way down to my stomach. "What kind of risks?"

"The donor's intent when the drop is taken can have ramifications."

"Okay?"

"Ingesting dragon's blood can drive another creature mad."

"What does the donor's intent have to do with it?"

"If you purely intended to heal and protect that's all that would come of it. But if you had other intentions, you could manipulate the recipient's mind and sway them to do things that they normally never would."

I lifted my glass to my mouth but lowered it without taking a sip. "I don't have any intention of brainwashing Isa."

"It can be done unintentionally. Any stray thought that crosses your mind as the drop is drawn could pollute the blood."

Shit. No pressure there.

The Sarrum raised an eyebrow. "If you aren't up to it, I'm sure we could find another donor but for some foolish reason, Doc seems quite intent on collecting a drop from you."

"Some foolish reason?" I sat my glass down on the coffee table a little harder than I meant to. "So you don't think it's a good idea to use my blood?"

The King's nostrils flared but his aloof stare never faltered, and his tone remained impassive. "I *think* it's a risk that we don't need to take."

I tugged a hand through my hair. "If I'm such a *risk*, why did you ever invite me to join your family?"

He cocked his head to one side and narrowed his eyes at me. "Do you regret coming?"

"No."

"And I don't regret inviting you. It's a foolish waste of time to regret actions that can't be undone."

That's a copout answer.

If you are going to refrain from opening your mouth when you speak, then mind your manners when you THINK.

Shit. Uh, sorry. I don't think my thoughts out loud on purpose.

Yes. I am well aware of that. Brian should work on that with you.

Okay. But for right now, can we talk out loud? This is freaking me out.

Good. You could do with a little "freaking out." You don't seem to grasp the severity of the situation.

Isa may well be Emma's only hope of recovering. So I'd APPRECIATE it if you would take this a bit more seriously.

Right. Sorry. I really do want to help Emma, and Isa.

You still think me a deviant, don't you?

How am I supposed to answer that?

Truthfully. I can read your thoughts anyway.

Truthfully? I don't get the age difference between you and Emma. How do you go from reading a little girl bedtime stories to sleeping with her?

You have not yet unlocked the dragon inside you. So how would I begin to explain my actions to you?

Truthfully.

The King's nostrils flared. *You are an insolent little bastard.* Standing from his chair, he rounded the coffee table.

I couldn't stop myself from flinching when he sat down beside me on the couch.

Amusement flickered in his brilliant blue eyes as he sat his glass down on the table. *If we're to begin a lesson, I'd prefer to relocate to the palace.*

"Okay. How do I get there?"

David Talbot's icy stare stayed fixed on me as he snapped his fingers, and the Waters immediately appeared before us. When I moved to jump in, he grabbed my arm and yanked me to my feet without the slightest show of exertion. Then he casually gestured toward the Waters, barely a flick of the wrist, and the Water *parted,* forming a perfect path down the center. Still gripping my arm like I was a naughty child he was stuck looking after, he started down the tunnel he'd created.

I moved along with him, too fascinated to be irritated that he was treating me like a toddler. The tunnel was nothing but Water, under our feet, above our heads, all around us, and it didn't take more than a few seconds to reach the other end and step out dry as a bone. I turned back to look at the tunnel we'd come through and saw a silent Waterfall flowing from ceiling to floor. We were in the great hall that Benjamin took me to the night he showed me what happened to the King's enemies. I just hoped we weren't headed to an empty cell.

The Sarrum arched an eyebrow as he released my arm. Then he sauntered across the black marble floor and gracefully climbed the wide set of steps to his throne.

I followed him up and sat down in the chair beside the throne.

"How much have they taught you about dragons?"

I let out a discouraged sigh. "Honestly? Not much."

"Do you know why dragons are the most skillful predators in all of Draumer?"

"Uh," I stammered, a little shocked that he was actually going to teach me something. "I have no idea."

"We don't have to chase our prey."

"Okay."

"When you sense the desires of the treasures you wish to acquire, be it to love or to feast on, there's no need to chase after them. They will willingly come to you when you offer what they desire most."

I suppressed a shiver. "Alright."

"Once you embrace what you are, you will truly understand what that means. For now, you'll just have to trust me. Dragons are possessive creatures by nature and once we acquire what we're after, we do not let go."

I nodded, unsure what to say.

"I treasured Emma from the moment I first set eyes on her. And once I made her mine, I had no intention of letting her go, which made it necessary for the nature of our relationship to evolve over time."

"And she was just okay with that?"

Brilliant blue flames danced in his eyes as a wicked grin spread across his face. "She was far more than *just okay* with it."

Shit. I needed to change the subject before my big mouth got me into trouble. "So have you forgiven me for being an idiot?"

"Absolutely not," he replied, his voice just as icy as his stare.

"Then… where does that leave us?"

"You're going to donate that drop of blood."

"I thought you said it was stupid to use my blood."

"Yes, but the doctor believes your blood will best suit his purpose." Standing from his throne, he started back down the steps.

I practically had to chase after him to keep up. "So how do I stop myself from thinking the wrong thoughts when he takes it?"

"You think about your friend, Nellie."

That came out of nowhere. Shit. I kept meaning to visit her, but I still hadn't gotten around to it. "Why would I do that?"

"Because her mind was poisoned by dragon's blood."

"What?" *How the heck did he even know about Nellie?*

"Pay the old woman a visit and ask her about the consequences of drinking a dragon's blood."

"Okay," I barely kept my balance as he stopped short in front of me, "but how will that help me think good thoughts?"

"Trust me. It will."

I blinked and took a disoriented look around. I was back on the couch in the lounge, and David wasn't even in the room.

33

DAVID

I headed to my office before returning the virgin to the waking world. I'd given him enough to ponder and once he paid the dragon mother a visit, he'd have plenty more. I was so lost in thought that I didn't sense Benjamin's presence until the door creaked open.

He let out a heavy sigh as he stepped in the room. "Can we talk?"

I gestured for him to take a seat.

And he pulled the door shut, then sat down in the chair in front of my desk. "Do you think the kid's capable of giving his blood without fucking it up?"

"Yes." I leaned back in my chair and crossed my arms over my chest. "He'll be paying Nellie Godric a visit soon, most likely tonight. I told him to ask her about the consequences of ingesting dragon's blood."

An appreciative grin spread across Benjamin's face. "That makes me feel a lot better."

"Yes. I should hope so."

"Do you want me to drive Charlie back to Sycamore? Brian can give Doc and Tristan a ride when they're ready."

"No." I slid my chair back from the desk. "I'm going to let the virgin visit with Emma."

"Really?"

"Not alone of course. Brian will accompany him and you'll stay close in case there's a problem."

"What about you?"

There was a quick knock before I could answer. Then Brian pushed the door open. "Doc's almost done with Emma's session."

I turned toward Benjamin with a melancholy smile. "Then we should go."

Brian headed off to the lounge to fetch Charlie while Benjamin followed me to the living room.

Doc was sitting on the couch beside Emma when I entered the room. He stood as I approached. And Emma looked up at me, her lovely green eyes swimming with tears.

I sat down on the couch beside her as Doc left the room.

"What are we even doing, David?"

I took her hand in mine. "We're getting through this one step at a time."

Her eyes dropped to the floor as she whispered, "I don't think I want to."

Bile rose up my throat as I drew her into my arms. She didn't hug me back, but she didn't push away either. "We'll get through this, Princess. I promise."

She let out a sob as her head dropped to my shoulder. "How can I ever trust you again?"

I brushed my lips against her forehead. "You have no reason not to trust me, Emma."

"Really?" Her bitter tone stoked the fire inside me. "That's not what Sophie said."

I meant to whisper but my response came out more like a growl, "Forget about Sophie."

"That'd be convenient for you," she sobbed, pulling away from my arms. "Have you found a new mistress yet?"

I suppressed the surge of heat in my gut. "There's never been anyone but you, Princess. I'd never hurt you, and I'll keep reminding you of that as often as I have to until you believe me."

Her only response was a muffled sniff.

I kissed her forehead as I stood from the couch. *Come back to me, Princess.* "You have visitors."

She lifted her head without meeting my eyes. "Who?"

You may come in now.

Heart torn to shreds, I left the room as Brian entered and it took every iota of self-restraint in me to step past the virgin without tearing him apart.

34

EMMA

Brian smiled at me as he crossed the living room floor. "How's my favorite girl?"

"I've been better," I muttered as I dabbed my eyes with a crumpled tissue. "How are you?"

He sat down next to me and gave my free hand a squeeze. "Happy to see you."

I let out a laugh that sounded more like a sob. "Sorry I'm not better company."

"What are you talking about, gorgeous?" he whispered, graciously ignoring my puffy eyes. "You're always good company."

I dropped my head to his shoulder. "Liar."

"I wouldn't lie to you," he whispered, touching his head to mine, "and I brought somebody to cheer you up."

"Who?"

"Hey, Em." I couldn't help tearing up all over again as Charlie walked in and sat down on my other side. "It's gonna be okay."

I lifted my head off Brian's shoulder as he stood from the couch. "You don't know that."

"Yeah, I do."

I sniffed back my tears. "Really? I didn't know you were psychic."

"Yeah?" Charlie touched his head to mine as I sagged against his shoulder. "Did I forget to tell you that?"

I chuckled despite my broken heart. "Yeah. It must've slipped your mind."

"Everything's gonna be okay, Em. I just have this feeling it'll all work out."

"I'm not so sure about that."

"Then it's a good thing I am."

"Why did David hire you, Charlie?" I lifted my head off his shoulder to look him in the eye. "It doesn't make any sense."

"Well—"

"He wanted to thank Charlie for looking out for you at the facility," Brian answered from the doorway.

"That doesn't make any sense." The throbbing in my head was so intense it was starting to turn my stomach. "Nothing makes sense anymore."

"What about our friendship?" Charlie whispered. "Doesn't that make sense?"

"Yes," I whispered, "but David letting you near me doesn't make sense."

"He trusts you, Em."

I squeezed my eyes shut, fighting back tears. "It doesn't even matter. I don't trust him. I feel more trapped in this house than I did at the facility."

A tear slid down my cheek and Charlie brushed it away with his thumb. "But this is your home."

"It doesn't feel like home anymore," I answered in a broken whisper. "And David might as well be a stranger. I don't want to do this anymore."

"What do you want?"

"I want to die."

I heard Brian step closer to the couch. "When was the last time you went outside?"

I pressed my hands against my temples without opening my eyes. "I don't know. A few days ago maybe."

"Then that's where we're going," Tristan's silky voice purred from the doorway. "I'm going to ask Sara to fix us a picnic lunch."

I dropped my head back to Charlie's shoulder. "I'm not hungry."

I heard Tristan move to the couch and drop to his knees in front of me. "Look at me, sunshine."

I forced myself to open my eyes and cringed at the pain.

Tristan stroked his fingertips over my temples. "You need fresh air." The pain eased a little at the warmth of his touch and the sweetness in his voice.

"I don't feel like it," I sobbed.

He gently massaged my temples as he planted a kiss on my forehead. "All the more reason to go out." I relaxed against Charlie's shoulder as Tristan lessened the pain. "Just breathe," he whispered. "I'm not asking, I'm telling. We're going out for a picnic. You know me. I won't quit pestering you until you say yes."

I chuckled softly as he eased my tension. "You say that to all the girls."

"Yeah." He kissed my forehead again. "But you're my favorite."

I felt Charlie's shoulder tense beneath my head. "Why don't you go get the food, Tristan? Brian and I can walk Emma out."

"Sure." Tristan winked at me. "But if you don't come out, I'll come back in here and throw you over my shoulder. You need sunlight."

"Bossy." I felt a pang of disappointment as he took his hands off my head, but my head felt a hundred times better.

"None of the other girls complain," Tristan murmured, kissing the top of my head as he stood.

"But I'm not the other girls. I'm your favorite, remember?"

"Yes you are, sunshine, and I'm not kidding about throwing you over my shoulder." He stroked his fingertips over my cheek. "So don't even think about ditching me."

Charlie's shoulder twitched as my head tilted up toward Tristan. "You don't have to say that very often, do you?"

"Nope. That's why you're my favorite." Arching an eyebrow, he added. "You've got fifteen minutes. Don't make me come after you."

Tristan was right. The sunlight did make me feel a thousand times better, and the picnic lunch was the best meal Sara had fixed since I'd come home. She clearly liked Tristan a lot more than she liked me or David, which wasn't surprising. All the girls liked Tristan. They blushed at the sound of his voice and melted when he smiled, but none of them really saw him. They were all too distracted by his looks to notice how beautiful he was on the inside. That's why I was his favorite. I didn't blush or grow weak at the knees when he spoke. Only one man would ever have that effect on me, and I was a broken mess because our marriage was crumbling.

"It's great to see you again," Charlie whispered as we sat on a blanket watching Brian and Tristan play Frisbee in the sand.

A twinge of pain flared in my head as I asked, "What exactly did David hire you to do?"

He flashed me a regretful smile. "I don't know. To play errand boy? Or be his human punching bag, maybe?"

I shook my head. "Stop it. What've you been doing?"

"Stupid stuff," he whispered, then quickly changed the subject. "Tell me something, why is your super jealous husband okay with you hanging out with the romance-novel-cover brothers? I'd expect him to string Tristan up for the way he flirts with you."

I grinned as I watched the brothers play by the water. "There's nothing for David to be jealous of. Tristan and Brian are like brothers to me. I don't think of them that way."

Charlie let out a laugh. "*Everybody* thinks of them that way, especially Tristan. And David's okay with him calling you his favorite girl?"

Brow furrowed, I turned to Charlie. "Why do you think I'm Tristan's favorite?"

"Because he *said* you were."

"That's not what I mean," I whispered, wondering if it was jealousy that I saw glinting in Charlie's eyes. "Tristan likes me because I don't swoon every time he smiles. Most people fall in love with his pretty face and never notice how beautiful he is on the inside. I guess I can kind of relate to that."

Eyes tearing, Charlie whispered, "I see how beautiful you are on the inside."

"You have no idea how much I've missed you."

He grinned and wrapped his arms around me. "Ditto, Em. I was afraid I'd never get to see you again."

"Me too," I whispered, hugging him back. "I still can't believe David hired you."

"I don't get it. If your jealous husband is okay with you hanging out with Brian and Tristan, why would he care about keeping me away?"

"Because," I whispered, "what I feel for you is different."

Charlie was about to say something, but Tristan plopped down on the blanket and wrapped his arms around both of us before he got the chance.

35

CHARLIE

For the first time since I'd started my training, I was going to be on my own in Draumer for the night. Benjamin said I deserved a break from all the lessons, but I was pretty sure the Sarrum had asked him to give me the alone time. Message received. It was time to pay Nellie a visit. I flopped down on my bed and draped an arm over my face. I didn't feel like talking to Nellie. Something about it felt wrong. Why was everybody so intent on me learning her story? Art wanted me to ask what her dragon did to her, and the Sarrum wanted me to ask how dragon's blood poisoned her mind. First of all, how the heck did those two even know about Nellie? And second, wouldn't drudging up all those painful memories upset her? But I couldn't see any way around it. I needed answers, and for some inconceivable reason Nellie had them. *So who exactly was Nellie?*

I let myself drift off to sleep with Nellie's shore on my mind. I'd been trying to fall asleep naturally ever since Brian taught me that jumping through the Waters expended a lot of energy. I didn't want to be any weaker than I had to be. I was still hoping I'd miraculously figure out how to unmask at some point, although I definitely didn't want to do it around Nellie. She was terrified of dragons. If she found out I was one, she'd never trust me again. The shore that Nellie inhabited was guarded by my friend Bob. A hero in both worlds, Bob had survived a gunshot wound to the head in the waking world. He saved the lives of two kids and lost his mind in the process. When he was awake, he had a hard time controlling what popped out of his mouth but in Draumer, Bob was an honest to goodness knight in shining armor. When Nellie feared her life was in danger, I took her to Bob's shore and he was more than happy to protect her and her daughter, Lilly. I still had no idea what Lilly was. In the waking world, she was only visible when Nellie unmasked and she wasn't visible at all to the Unsighted. But in Draumer, she seemed just as real as anybody else. Nellie had lots of secrets, and apparently they were more important than I'd figured because the Dragon King knew about her and so did Art, who I was pretty sure was a Purist. I still had no clue which side was the good side. The more I learned, the less I seemed to know about anything...

...I opened my eyes, stretched and sat up. I was only inches from the Water. The sun was shining in a cloudless blue sky and a thick line of trees stood behind me. I'd actually woken up on Bob and Nellie's shore. Brushing the dirt off my clothes, I stood and started walking toward the forest. My whole life, I'd been terrified of entering the trees and all the while, there'd been quaint towns and towering castles and massive silent Waterfalls on the other side.

As I reached the trees, Nellie stepped from the forest looking young and lovely in her soul form. She had rust-colored curls and a pretty smile, when she wasn't pissed at me, which she was a lot of the time. She lifted a hand to her forehead to shield her eyes from the sun and smiled at me. "Charlie?"

"Hey, Nellie. Long time no see. How are you?"

Her smile widened. "I'm good. How're you?"

"Never better." I followed her back to the Waters and when we were close enough to wet our toes, we sat down on the ground. I glanced back at the trees. "Where's Bob?"

Nellie smoothed her sundress over her legs. "He's teaching Lilly how to fish."

It made me happy to hear that. When I first met Bob in Draumer, he lived alone. And in addition to being one of the toughest guys I'd ever met, he was one of the loneliest. "Where are they fishing?"

"There's a little stream inside the trees, not far from here."

"So things are good?"

Tears pooled in her eyes as a wistful smile spread over her face. "Things are perfect. Thanks for bringing me here, Charlie. I don't think I ever thanked you for helping Lilly and me."

"You're welcome," I muttered, suppressing a grin. "So I came because I have some questions."

"I know," she whispered, shifting toward the Water.

"You do?" I waited a few seconds before asking, "How?"

"You were bound to."

I nodded even though she wasn't looking at me. "But I don't want to upset you."

Grinning, she turned back to me. "That never stopped you before."

"Well, I guess I've matured."

She narrowed her eyes and looked me over. "I think you have. Something about you seems different. I can't put my finger on it, but you seem more confident."

"I am. Learning you're not crazy helps you stand a little taller."

"So ask your questions," she whispered, smoothing her dress despite the fact that it was already wrinkle-free.

I let out a heavy sigh. "I really don't want to hurt you."

"You can't make me hurt more than I already do," she whispered, glancing back at the trees.

She seemed less nutty than she used to. I got the feeling that living with Bob grounded her. "Will you tell me about your dragon, Nellie?"

She nodded, then closed her eyes and smiled. "I can still see it like it was yesterday."

I was confused to see her smile until I remembered she'd fallen in love with her dragon. "What happened?" I whispered, hoping I wouldn't break the blissful trance she seemed to have slipped into.

"I met Dr. Godric in a facility in Pennsylvania. It was a small hospital in a small town, and I was bitter and broken and all alone..." Nellie painted such a vivid picture, I lost myself in her story...

"...I usually kept my head down during group therapy and listened while the others drudged up their problems like it'd somehow make everything better, but something about the new doctor made me want to pour my heart out to him. All the other doctors had always made me feel like a science experiment. But Dr. Godric looked at me like he actually cared, like I actually mattered, and I shared everything during our first group session with him. My agony over a life spent locked away in mental institutions. My deepest desires to live a normal life, get married and have children. It'd all come pouring out.

After the session, they sedated me to calm me down. As the needle sunk into my flesh, the Waters came and carried me off to the Dream World. The only place where I was free. I sat near the Water savoring the warmth of the sun on my face, listening to the songbirds chirping, a gentle breeze blowing through my hair. That was where I belonged. The other world was just an ugly place where no one remembered the real world and no one saw the truth.

I was so deep in thought, I didn't hear him until he was almost close enough to touch. Without a word, he sat down beside me. And God forgive my rudeness, but I just sat there staring at him. And he just watched me, not quite smiling, except maybe a little with his eyes. His eyelids were lowered in a way that made my insides tingle. His dark wavy hair wasn't as neat as it was in the other world. It looked wilder and more fluid in the breeze. I'd never study his face that blatantly in the other world, but there in the Dream World at the edge of the Water where no one else existed, it didn't seem wrong. Something in those lovely blue eyes invited me to stare at every sculpted feature, his cheekbones, his chin, those perfect lips that seemed just on the verge of smiling. He was more beautiful than any creature I'd ever set eyes on in either world.

'Penny for your thoughts,' he whispered in his charming British accent.

'Do you know me?'

His almost smile crept closer to an actual smile, like an orgasm on the brink of exploding into being. 'Of course I do, Nellie. I thought you might appreciate a little friendly reassurance after exposing yourself so completely the way you did today.'

Something about the way he said 'exposing yourself' sent a shiver down my spine, and all I managed to whisper was, 'Thanks.'

That smile finally blossomed on his lips, in his eyes and in places deep inside of me. 'You needn't be so shy. What fun would this world be if all the rules and restrictions of the waking world applied? Don't hold back. Tell me what you're feeling, right here, right now.'

His words and the way he watched me beneath those partially lowered lids made my heart pound, but I had to be misinterpreting. It wasn't a sexual advance, just a concerned follow-up visit from my new doctor. Still, words just came tumbling out of my mouth, 'You make my heart beat faster, and I feel naked and vulnerable and more alive than I've ever felt before.' This man clearly remembered the world he wasn't in. I'd wake the next day and look at him and know he knew things he shouldn't, but I didn't even care.

Smiling, he stood and held a hand out to me. 'That's much better.'

I took his hand, not knowing what to think, not wanting to think at all.

Eyes dancing wickedly, he tugged me to my feet. 'Let's go break some rules.' Without letting go of my hand, he started walking toward the forest.

I didn't let go of his hand, but I hesitated. And when he felt my resistance, he stopped and waited for me to speak. 'I shouldn't go into the forest,' I muttered. 'It's a dangerous place to venture into alone.'

He moved so close I think I stopped breathing. 'Then it's a good thing you aren't alone. I promise you'll be perfectly safe with me. I won't allow any harm to come to you.'

I nodded, and he started moving again with a hint of a satisfied smile on his lips. I knew it wasn't safe. I'd always been warned never to go into the forest. But I would've followed him anywhere—the heart of the Dark forest, the mouth of a volcano, the fiery depths of Hell. If he led, I'd follow. I'd willingly pay any price to have him look at me the way he did. I just had no idea how great that price would be. Honestly? Even if I did, I might've followed. I would've gladly burned to be with him.

As we moved deeper into the forest, the thick canopy of leaves above choked out most of the sunlight. Eerie echoes bounced off massive weathered tree trunks. The breeze felt hotter and the air seemed too thick to breathe. Every now and then when I felt a desperate need to turn back, he'd stop moving, pull me close and smile. And the warmth in his eyes melted my desire to flee.

Just when the Darkness seemed almost absolute, we stepped through a cluster of rotting trees and suddenly, the trees were young and virile and blossoming with flowers. Beyond them our feet sunk into pure white sand without a single footprint or track. It was as if we were the first creatures to ever set foot there. The Water beyond the sand was crystal blue like the doctor's eyes. Realizing my mouth was hanging open, I turned and smiled at him. And he chuckled, never taking his eyes from me, never raising those hooded eyelids.

A laugh more gleeful than any sound I'd ever made sprung from my mouth. 'Thank you for bringing me here, Doctor.'

Eyes fixed on me, he shook his head. 'You are a curious little thing, aren't you? You open up to me, expose the most vulnerable parts of yourself, follow me blindly through the Darkness and still call me by my proper title. You've followed me far beyond the boundaries of propriety, Nellie. Now I want to hear you call me Henry.'

'Henry,' I whispered his name like a prayer. 'I'd follow you anywhere.'

His grin widened and something wicked flashed in those blue eyes. 'That's my girl.'

And I was his girl, his to do anything he wanted with. There was nothing in all the worlds that I wouldn't give him, nothing I wouldn't let him do. Henry gave me that beach. And I gave him my heart, my soul and my virginity in the Dream World. After giving me more pleasure than I'd ever imagined possible, he listened and I shared all of my fears and dreams. He explained that I wasn't crazy. I had Dream Sight and I just happened to be one of the unfortunate few Sighted individuals born to Unsighted parents. No one around me had ever seen the Dream forms that I saw. No one in my life remembered the world they weren't in, no one until Henry.

Henry said our actions in the other world had to make sense to the Unsighted. So we couldn't let on that we knew each other intimately when we were there. Each night, I'd lie in his arms and he'd tell me what to do and say the next day at the facility. And little by little, in the eyes of the Unsighted, I made amazing progress in my therapy. Every interaction between us was strictly professional, even when we were alone in his office. But it was always there in his eyes, that smoldering stare and wordless encouragement to stick to our plan and keep up the charade. And before I knew it, the day came when Dr. Henry Godric declared that I was mentally fit enough to be out on my own in the world.

For several months after that, I only saw him on our beach in the Dream World. Eventually, Henry said enough time had passed for us to meet during a chance encounter and strike up a friendship, but we had to be cautious. Our relationship in the Dream World could never be mentioned. That was the way of the Sighted. It could all be discussed quite openly in Dream but awake it had to remain unspoken, nothing more than a knowing twinkle in the good doctor's eye.

I was sitting at a table outside my favorite coffee shop when I heard his voice behind me. 'Nellie?' I turned and watched the doctor sit down in the empty chair across from me. Those knowing eyes studied me with enchanted curiosity like he hadn't seen me in a while and was delighted to find me looking well.

I returned the knowing grin, watching him just as intently. 'Hello, Doctor. It's nice to see you again.'

His eyelids lowered as a devilish grin curved his lips. 'I suppose there's no need to be so formal now that you're no longer my patient. Please, call me Henry.'

I could barely keep from laughing. He was too good at this, pretending he'd never seen me naked, never made me scream his name out in the night. 'Alright, Henry. What happens now?'

Wicked curiosity flashed in his eyes as he answered, 'I suppose I ask you to dinner. I don't see any harm in us becoming friends now that I'm no longer your doctor.'

'I'd love to have a friend like you,' I whispered with a coy smile.

He actually managed to blush. 'Excellent.'

We took it slow just like we'd done at the facility and we never mentioned the Dream World. For several months, it was strictly a friendship but I flirted with him shamelessly. How could I not, when he'd done things to me that'd make a whore blush? I wanted him like I'd never wanted anything. Even though I spent every night in his arms on our beach, I was still a virgin in the waking world and my waking body screamed for his touch. I told him so all the time in the Dream World, but he always reminded me how important it was to keep up appearances for the Unsighted. A psychiatrist jumping into bed with a recently released patient would seem scandalous. So I let him take the lead and painfully slowly, our relationship evolved into something more than friendship.

We courted innocently for a long time and only his eyes ever hinted at the savage hunger he attacked me with each night on our beach. Then one day he proposed to me at our favorite restaurant. I wore his ring and remained a virgin until our wedding night. After that, life became just as magical in the waking world. He made love to me just as passionately as he did on our beach and he always looked at me like he couldn't quite believe it was real.

After five months of wedded bliss, I fixed him a candlelight dinner and told him we were going to have a baby. All my dreams were coming true and I'd never seen my husband happier. My pregnancy was a difficult one. For several months, I wasn't supposed to leave our bed, but he doted on me like no husband had ever doted on a pregnant wife before.

When I went into labor, Henry was bursting with joy. The labor lasted more than a day and I swore my body would rip apart from the pain, but he never left my side and when I drifted off to sleep he was right beside me on our beach. 'It'll all be over soon,' he'd murmur. 'I promise.' And in that reprieve from the pain, he made love to me and thanked me for giving him everything he'd always wanted.

I was so exhausted by the end. I gripped Henry's hand with what little strength I had left. His silent reassurance helped me to go on and with one final agonizing push, our baby entered the waking world.

'It's a girl,' the doctor announced.

I turned to Henry to rejoice over our little miracle, but his smile was gone and the warmth had drained from those beautiful blue eyes. Heart racing, I whispered, 'Henry?'

Whatever melancholy he momentarily felt slipped away as he smiled at me. 'Sorry, love. I think the lack of sleep is catching up with me.'

'We should name her Lilly,' I suggested, hoping he'd be pleased I wanted to name her after the sister he'd lost.

Eyes spilling with tears, he nodded but didn't speak.

As our Lilly grew strong and healthy and lovely, Henry grew distant. He started working longer hours and the brightness in his eyes began to dull. Lilly was just old enough to scoot around in the sand when Henry told me he had business to attend to back in the forest. He assured me that Lilly and I would be fine. And I worried, but I trusted him.

Lilly and I were fine, until the night something howled deep inside the forest. She was playing in the sand a few feet from me and I jumped up to protect her. But as I moved toward her, she turned to the sound and howled back louder and angrier than whatever lurked inside the trees. I took a step back and watched my baby disappear as a monstrous creature took her place, with claws and wings and flaming eyes. It rose a few feet into the air and howled again. Then my child sunk back to the sand and went back to playing like nothing had happened."

"Shit," I muttered. "He didn't tell you your baby would be a dragon?"

Tears glistened in Nellie's eyes as she shook her head.

Reliving her story seemed to be breaking her heart all over again. I really wanted to tell her to stop, but I needed to hear the rest. "What happened after that?"

Nellie wiped her eyes as she whispered, "When Henry came back from his trip, I told him what'd happened and he said he didn't believe me. It took about a month for it to happen while he was there. After it did, he told me there was only one way to save our little girl."

I swallowed the lump in my throat. "What?"

"Henry said the only way to protect her from eventually becoming nothing but a mindless monster was to bind her to the Dream World."

A queasiness settled in the pit of my stomach as I whispered, "What does that mean?"

"I had to hold her underwater in the waking world," she muttered, voice breaking, "while Henry waited in the Dream World to bind her there."

My eyes filled with tears as I pictured young Nellie forcing sweet little Lilly's head underwater.

"Henry said it'd work better if we were apart in the waking world," Nellie continued in a trembling voice. "So we planned to do it while he was off at a medical convention."

I couldn't stop myself from cringing. "Didn't that seem suspicious to you?"

"It probably would've if he hadn't been poisoning my mind with his blood."

I blinked back the tears and waited for her to go on.

"He'd been slipping it into my wine for God knows how long. I didn't learn until much too late that it'd distorted my perception of everything."

Too sick to my stomach to speak, I nodded.

"So while Henry was away, I filled our bathtub with water and made a quick call to him at the hotel like he'd instructed me to. Then I took Lilly into the tub with me and I held my sweet baby girl under the water... until she stopped moving." Nellie's body crumpled as she sobbed the last words.

I wrapped my arms around her and sobbed right along with her. It was a good twenty minutes before our tears dried up and even longer until she spoke. Straightening and wiping her cheeks, she whispered, "Henry was kind enough to grant me an enchantment that activated when our daughter died."

"So that's what Lilly is now," I whispered, "an enchantment?"

Nodding, Nellie sobbed, "She isn't real, Charlie. I know that deep in my heart, but I tuck it away and embrace the insanity because anything else is too horrible to remember."

"What happened with you and Henry after that?"

Nellie let out a bitter laugh. "Henry called the police from his hotel room. He told them he'd gotten a terrifying call from me and he was concerned I might hurt our child. Then he caught a flight home and acted devastated when he came to see me in the psych ward. When I screamed that it was all his plan, he looked horrified and after I recounted everything he'd ever said to me in the Dream World, he told me I was delusional. He said my mind had concocted the whole scenario and I'd convinced myself never to speak of it because somewhere deep inside, I knew none of it was true. He convinced me that I was a monster and none of it had ever been real."

"When did you learn that it was real?"

"After the trial was all over and I'd been committed and Henry had fled the country. Five men came to see me in the hospital. My doctor said they'd come from a nearby university. Two of them were professors, a doctor and a lawyer and the other three were their students. But when my doctor left the room, they turned into monsters. I started screaming that they weren't real and it was all in my head. One of the students was still in human form. He was clearly in charge of everyone, including the professors. He explained that they'd come to judge me for killing my dragon child. When I wouldn't stop screaming, he sat down on my bed and calmly whispered that no one could hear my screams. The next thing I knew, the two of us were sitting on my beach. He told me his father was the King of the Dream World and he'd been tasked with sentencing me to death, but he showed me mercy because he didn't believe I was to blame. He sentenced me to solitary confinement and sealed me inside my beach, but he let me keep Lilly. After he finished sentencing me, the prince brought me back to my hospital room and warned me not to judge all dragons by Henry's actions. Then he turned into a dragon."

"The one that shadows Emma," I whispered.

"Yes."

"If you knew Emma's dragon was the prince who showed you mercy, why were you so afraid of him?"

"Because," Nellie whispered, "I'd suppressed those memories for decades. I'd convinced myself that I was just a crazy old woman and none of it had ever really happened. But when I saw that dragon, it all came back to me and that's when I truly grasped what I'd done."

"But the Dragon King never hurt you. He spared you."

"Killing me would have been merciful," Nellie muttered. "Forcing me to endure a lifetime of remembering was far worse."

As much as I wanted to stop torturing her, I had to know. "What about the scars on your shoulder blades? Emma has them, too."

Nellie nodded. "Emma's tale is similar to mine. We're both fairies, fragile creatures of Light. Forcing us to dwell in the Darkness is a lingering death sentence. It weakens our bodies and slowly drains the Light from us, and our weakness becomes our Dark lover's strength. Since our wings are the most delicate part of us, they're the first thing to wither and die."

"So your wings *fell off*?"

"Yes."

Why would the Sarrum want me to learn that? Art's words suddenly came back to me. *The Sarrum is like a naughty little boy who pulled off a butterfly's wings and kept her in a jar.* The Sarrum didn't want me to find out. Art did.

36

BENJAMIN

The kid had come back from his night off a different man. His somber demeanor made it clear that he took his role in Isa's healing very seriously. There wasn't a doubt in my mind that he'd gone to see the dragon mother, but I didn't want to think about that too much. She'd violated the conditions of her sentence by leaving the mirage. She'd also put herself at risk. Godric was still out there somewhere and without the protections that the Sarrum wove over her mirage, the old woman was an easy target. But addressing those issues would mean sentencing her to death for fleeing her prison. I felt too sorry for the old woman to do that and frankly, I didn't have the time to deal with it. My plate was full enough already.

Charlie and I were on a balcony of the palace that overlooked the Waterfall. I'd been sitting at a table watching the virgin pretty fucking patiently but it'd been almost ninety minutes and despite being drenched in sweat from his efforts to unmask, he hadn't made a damn bit of progress. I kicked the chair across from me out from under the table. "Give it a rest before you hurt yourself, kid."

"Too late." He wiped the sweat off his face with a shirtsleeve as he moved to the table and collapsed in the chair. "Is there such a thing as a mental hernia?"

"No."

"Well, I think there is now. I just gave myself one."

I shook my head as I poured him a glass of water. "Man the fuck up, kid. You're a dragon."

He downed a big gulp of water before responding, "What? Dragons don't get hernias?"

"Not from *thinking* too hard, asshole. Seriously. Man up. You're embarrassing yourself."

"Yeah. You said that already. I get it." He chugged the rest of his water and his expression grew somber as he sat his empty glass on the table. "Can I ask you something?"

"Sure, kid. What is it?"

"You know I went to see Nellie last night, right?"

I nodded and refilled his glass.

"What happened to her was horrible," the kid muttered, "but there are still some things I don't get."

"Such as?"

"Why does everybody know her story?"

"Didn't you catch her husband's name?"

Dr. Henry Godric? "Oh…shit," he muttered. "Nellie was married to the Sarrum's uncle?"

"Yes she was. Most people refer to her as the dragon mother. What Godric did to her is common knowledge among the Sighted and despite the fact that he poisoned her mind with his blood, her actions are considered unforgivable. What else don't you get?"

Charlie took a swig of water before asking, "Why did Godric spend all that time getting Nellie to trust him, releasing her from the facility and marrying her, just to have a kid with her and trick her into murdering it?"

I was starting to feel claustrophobic with my legs cramped under the table, so I slid my chair back for some legroom. "His plan backfired. He wanted her to give him a son he could train to fight at his side and he expected her to die giving birth to him because the odds of the mother surviving a dragon birth are only about twenty percent. When a dragon mother dies during childbirth, the newborn dragon absorbs most of her power. But when she doesn't, the baby draws power from both living parents. So instead of a powerful new son, Godric gained a daughter, lost some of his power and was stuck with a wife he never really wanted. It broke Godric's heart when his sister died giving birth to the Sarrum, so there was no way he was going to love this baby girl just to watch her grow up and die bringing another dragon into the world. And when his wife named the baby after his precious sister, it pretty much sent him over the edge, so he came up with a plan that'd solve all his problems. Once the baby died, he'd regain the power he'd lost along with some of his wife's. She'd get locked away, and no one would blame him for leaving a wife who'd murdered their child."

"And Nellie fell for his insane plan because she'd been drinking his blood?"

"Yeah. It all sounded rational to her because he'd poisoned her mind to blindly believe anything he told her."

The kid traced his finger around the rim of his glass. "That's so fucked up."

I had to laugh at his choice of words. "You've been spending too much time around me."

Charlie was trying to come up with a clever response when Rose stepped out through the Waterfall. "Doc's ready for us."

The kid looked up at Rose as she moved toward our table. "You nervous?"

She exhaled a tense breath. "Horribly. What if my mother doesn't like me?"

I stood up and put a hand on her shoulder. "She's going to love you."

There were tears in her eyes as she whispered, "How can you be so sure?"

"Trust me." I wiped a tear from her cheek. "I know your mother better than anybody, and she's going to love you."

"Thanks."

I motioned for Charlie to get off his ass without taking my eyes off her. "You don't have to thank me for the truth, Rose. Now come on, let's go wake your mother up."

Calm as I was acting, my stomach had been churning all morning. Too much was riding on this. Doc's potion had to work.

As the three of us stepped through the Waterfall into Isa's room, Doc greeted us with a pleasant grin. If he was nervous, he hid it well.

We'd gone over the plan a hundred times. We couldn't all be in Isa's room the whole time. Someone needed to stay near the Princess because she was too unstable to be left alone. Though I didn't want to leave Isa's side, Doc obviously needed to stay there to oversee the whole thing, the Sarrum had to donate a fresh drop of blood to the potion and the only other person authorized to watch over the Princess was lying on the bed. So, I was going to stay with Emma just long enough for the boss to slip in and donate his blood. Then he'd return to the Princess, and I'd rush back to hold Isa's hand while Rose and Charlie added their blood and administered the potion.

My throat felt too tight as I walked to Isa's bedside and took her hand. *Today's the day, Isa. We're bringing you home.* I kissed the top of her head, crossed the room and exited through the Waterfall.

The boss was waiting for me when I stepped out the other side. *This will work, my friend.*

Thanks, Boss.

He clapped me on the shoulder, then stepped through the Waterfall.

Where the hell was Emma? I needed to stay near the Waterfall, but I couldn't very well keep an eye on her if I had no idea where she was. "Emma?" My heart was slamming in my chest. I didn't have time to search for her. The final step of the potion was time-sensitive, and I needed to be by Isa's side when they administered it. "Princess?"

Emma stepped out from behind a cluster of flowering bushes. "What's wrong, Benji?"

I took a deep breath to slow my pounding heart. "What're you up to over there?"

Studying me curiously, she smiled. "Painting. Why did you sound so worried?"

"I don't know. Rough morning. Guess I'm a little off."

She bent down and kissed the top of my ridiculous stuffed animal head. "Well, I hope your day gets better."

"Me too," I muttered, wondering if the boss had been gone too long.

"If you're alright," Emma murmured, "I'm going to go back to my painting."

"Yeah. I'm good. Go do your thing."

Today was a good day. She had no memory of the waking world or the traumatic events that'd occurred in Draumer. "I'm sure it'll all turn out okay, Benji."

I shook my head as I watched her disappear behind the bushes. *I hope to God you're right, Princess.*

"You're up, my friend." The boss's voice startled me as he stepped from the Waterfall and I didn't exactly startle easily.

Fuck. This was too real now. I couldn't pretend it wasn't killing me.

She'll be fine, Benjamin. My blood is strong and my intent was sincere.

Thank you, Sarrum.

I stepped back through the Waterfall, and Rose stood from the bed as I sat down and took Isa's hand. *I'm here, Isa. And soon I'll be holding you in my arms.*

Doc carefully handed the vial to Rose. Then he took hold of her other hand, nicked her finger with the tip of a blade and added one drop of her precious blood to the vial.

As Rose sat down on Isa's other side, Doc moved to Charlie. "Your turn."

Nodding, Charlie took the vial from Doc and extended his hand. No one breathed as Doc lifted the blade. Heart in my throat, I zoned in on the kid's thoughts. *Take my blood and heal Isabella. I wish her well and I can't wait to meet her.* I breathed a sigh of relief as the final drop of blood dripped into the vial.

The room was dead silent as Doc moved to Isa. Rose stood from the bed and tipped her mother's head back, and I held my breath and squeezed my soul mate's hand as Doc poured the foul-smelling mixture down her throat. *Come back to us, Isa. You've been away too long.* Every heart in the room was pounding as a wisp of vapor wafted from Isa's throat. I wanted to ask Doc if that was normal, but keeping the silence in tact felt important. So I just prayed to God it was. *Come home, my love. We need you.* Isa's breaths began to escape her in uneven spurts, but she was only breathing out. Why wasn't she breathing in? *Please, Isa. Come back to us.* Should she have woken by now? I glanced up at Doc's face. And my heart sank.

There were tears in the witchdoctor's eyes and his boney features had contorted into a mask of horrified terror. *Fuck.* I squeezed Isa's hand as her chest began to rise and fall erratically. *Come back to me, Isa! NOW!*

With one desperate inhalation, my soul mate sprung up to a seated position. But there was no exhalation, no second breath. Eyes wild with panic, she clutched at her throat. *FIGHT YOUR WAY BACK TO US, DAMN IT! DON'T LEAVE ME! I'M NOTHING WITHOUT YOU.* Hopelessness flashed in her eyes as they locked onto mine, and tears slid down her cheeks as the color drained from her face. *Don't leave me, Isa! Fight through this and breathe! You're the strongest woman I've ever met! You survived a dragon birth! You can fight through this!*

Isa's eyes rolled back in her head as her body went limp and fell into my arms.

Lost in a torrent of grief, I clutched my soul mate to my chest and ignored the frantic noises in the room around us. My world would never be the same. Slim as her chances of recovery had been, I'd always believed we would bring her back.

A hand gripped my arm and pulled at me. I snarled and tried to swat it away, but it didn't budge. Instead, it flung me off the bed.

I hurried to my feet and watched the Sarrum kneel on the bed above Isa's lifeless body. ***Wake now, Sorceress! It is not time to rest! Your King needs you!*** He tipped her head back, then he opened his mouth and breathed into hers.

Seconds became minutes, and nobody breathed as the boss knelt over my soul mate and breathed life into her body. *Fuck.* It'd been too long.

I forbid you to go, Sorceress! You pledged to serve me and I require your assistance!

Nothing. On the other side of the bed, Rose's quiet sobbing shattered my heart.

You are not finished here, Isa! WAKE NOW!

Isa's back arched off the bed as she drew a deep shuddering breath.

The boss planted a kiss on her forehead, then stepped off the bed.

My soul mate locked eyes with the Sarrum and spoke in a frail whisper, "Thank you."

He grinned at her. "Welcome back." A second later, he was gone.

I sat down on the bed and smiled at the love of my life.

And for the first time in far too long, she took my hand in hers. "I've missed you, Benji."

Too afraid to lift her, I bent and touched my forehead to hers. "I knew you'd come back to us."

She let out a weak laugh as she reached up and touched my cheek. "Then why are there tears in your eyes? This will forever be remembered as the day the Darkness wept."

On Isa's other side, Rose whispered, "I'll remember it as the day I finally met my mother."

Isa reached up and took her daughter's hand. "So will I."

37

DAVID

Cursing under my breath, I stepped back into the clearing. Expending more energy was the last thing I ought to be doing. I was barely holding the mirage together as it was, but I'd felt Isa dying on the other side of the Waterfall and I couldn't very well just sit back and let that happen. I just prayed that Isa could help Doc cure Emma. My wife was slipping away a little more each day and I had no choice but to sit back and watch it happen. Godric would pay for what he'd done to her. I'd make him suffer like no man had ever suffered before, and I'd enjoy inflicting every second of his agony. It was a fantasy I'd entertained often lately.

The scent of wildflowers mingled deliciously with the scent of my Princess as I neared the bushes she was painting behind. It'd been a good morning, all of her suffering momentarily forgotten. Finding her untroubled was such a rarity lately that I'd lingered as long as I possibly could. With each step I took, her scent grew stronger and my appetite increased. Nostrils flared, I rounded the bushes. Emma's easel and paints were still there. But she wasn't. *Damn it.* I'd hardly been gone long, no more than a few minutes. Chest tightening, I looked toward the cave but I didn't sense her there. *Where the hell was she?* The Waters had a hypnotic effect on her lately, ever since I'd pulled her from them half-dead without a lick of recognition in her eyes. And her morbid desire to return to them was getting stronger. Steeling my nerves, I headed toward the lake. My mouth felt utterly devoid of moisture as I called out to her, "Princess?"

Deafening silence was the only answer to my call.

Heart pounding, I roared, "Emma!" As I neared the Water's edge, I picked up her scent. Forcing myself to remain calm, I followed the juncture where the Water kissed the land and with each step, her scent grew stronger. When I caught sight of her tucked behind a patch of cattails, I breathed a sigh of relief, but it was short lived.

She was sitting beside the Water with her knees drawn up to her chest, her arms hugging them to her trembling frame and her chin resting on her knees. Fear and confusion hung like a heavy fog in the air around her. When she felt my eyes on her, she lifted her head. "I remember."

I sat down beside her and stroked her cheek with the backs of my fingers. "What do you remember, Princess?"

Her vacant eyes glistened with tears. "I heard him calling my name through the Waters. Who was that man? Why did he say I belonged to him?"

"You know." I brushed her hair back from her face and touched a hand to each temple. "Somewhere in here you know who he was."

A spasm of clarity gripped her, and she cringed and pushed my hands away. "No. I don't."

I slid closer and wrapped my arms around her, and she only resisted for a heartbeat before sagging against me. "You may not want to, but you do. And you'll have to remember soon. This can't go on forever."

She dropped her head to my chest. "What can't?"

"Your memories are still there. But if we don't unlock them soon, they'll be lost for good and I can't have that."

"It hurts too much."

I kissed the top of her head. "I know, but you need to fight past that."

A shuddering sob escaped her lips. "I don't want to."

"I know, Princess." Each time she denied the memories, the mirage weakened a bit more. I felt each fracture. The weight of it crushed me, robbing the breath from my lungs. Isa's healing should've lessened my burden. Instead, I'd had no choice but to lend my strength to the process. And the burden had grown heavier. "But I need you to try."

She looked up at me and answered in a hollow whisper, "His blood was all over me. On my clothes. In my hair. I can still taste it in my mouth. Why did he say I was his?"

"You're mine, Emma." I dipped my head and touched my forehead to hers. "You've always been mine, and you always will be."

Tears spilled from her eyes as she shook her head. "But I knew him. Who was he?"

"It doesn't matter." I drew a deep breath and exhaled slowly before adding, "He was no friend of ours."

"I remember him hurting me," she whispered. "And you stopping him."

"Yes." I brushed the tears from her cheeks with my thumb. "I stopped him for good. He'll never hurt you again."

"No. Not here," Emma whispered, jerking her head away from my hand. "This was a long time ago."

"Yes. Where were we then?"

She squeezed her eyes shut as the pain flared in her head. "I don't know. It's not a clear memory. More like a dream. But you were there to stop him."

"Yes," I whispered, stroking her temples to ease the pain. "I've always stopped him."

"I don't want to talk about it anymore." She pushed my hands away and jumped to her feet. "I need to lie down until my head feels better."

I stood up beside her. "I'll come with you."

"No," she sobbed, turning her back to me. "I can't look at you right now."

She'd be the death of me. If she only knew how poisonous each word from her lips could be. "At least let me walk you to our room."

She shook her head and started toward the cave. "I need to be alone. I can't stop seeing his blood when I look at you."

"Then I won't stay," I murmured as I followed her, "but I will see you safely there."

She let out a defeated sigh and nodded her head.

We didn't speak, and I didn't lay a hand on her. I just walked beside her to the cave, through the Waterfall and into our bedroom.

I could feel her heart aching as she moved to the bed. She truly didn't want me there, so I walked her to our bedside and kissed the top of her head. Then I turned around and left through the Waterfall without uttering a word.

But I'd be damned if I'd leave her alone. Unmasking, I settled on the stone floor in front of the Waterfall. As I listened to her sobbing on the other side, I was reminded of tears that she'd shed as a child...

...We were sitting by our lake, skipping stones and discussing the traits of dragons and shadows. The defining characteristics of particular types of souls was a subject she'd recently taken a keen interest in.

She giggled as my stone skipped clear across the lake. "That's not fair!"

I raised an eyebrow and grinned at her. "I haven't the faintest idea what you're talking about."

"You're not allowed to use magic to make yours go farther!"

"No?" I feigned a look of innocent surprise. "And who made that rule?"

"Me!" she insisted, laughing.

"Ah," I whispered. "But that's not fair, either. You can't make up new rules when you're dissatisfied with the outcome."

Barely able to contain herself enough to get the words out, she giggled, "Yes I can."

Suppressing a smile, I asked, "And how is that fair?"

Her brow furrowed as she considered the question. "It keeps things equaler."

"That is not proper grammar," I whispered. "And more often than not, things aren't equal in life. Asking me not to use magic is like asking you not to be lovely. It's simply what we are."

"You are magic?"

"As much as you are lovely, yes. It's unchangeable."

"No it's not. I could make myself ugly and you could refrain from using magic."

"Clever girl." I grinned at her and touched a finger to her nose. *Then I skipped a stone the old fashioned way. "But how do you suppose you'd make yourself ugly?"*

"I could wear a mask."

"Hmm," I murmured. *"You've an answer for every-thing, don't you?"*

"Yup."

I raised an eyebrow.

"I mean, yes."

"Better." I skipped anther stone and flashed her a devilish grin as it hopped more than halfway across. *"So go ahead and ask."*

She frowned at me. *"Ask what?"*

"The question you've been so anxious to ask me," I whispered. *"Go ahead and ask it."*

Her frown deepened. *"You promised you'd never read my thoughts."*

"I didn't. I simply sensed your desire to ask a ques-tion. So ask."

She bit her lip as she turned toward me. *"There are three Sighted girls in my class at school and one of them is having a sleepover in the forest this weekend. Can I go?"*

My heart sank as I let out a troubled sigh. *"If it were possible, I would deny you nothing. But I'm afraid I can't let you go."*

Her gorgeous green eyes filled with tears as she whis-pered, *"Why?"*

"It wouldn't be safe, Princess."

"Yes it would. Her parents will be there."

"Unfortunately, that isn't sufficient. You require more protection than most children."

"Why?" she whispered. "I'm not a baby."

"No," I agreed, wiping a tear from her cheek. "You aren't, but there's a great deal of danger out there and I can't allow you to go anywhere near it."

"Then can I invite them here another time?"

"No, Princess. That wouldn't be safe either."

"Why not? This is the safest place in all of Draumer."

"It is," I agreed softly, "but we mustn't share the location with others."

"Why?"

"I have enemies out there, and they would seize any opportunity to attack my weaknesses."

"But you don't have any weaknesses."

With a heavy heart, I stroked her cheek with my fingertips. "My sweet girl, if only that were true."

38

EMMA

I wasn't really tired, but needing to rest was the best excuse I could come up with to get some space. Something was seriously wrong with me and they all knew it, but no one would tell me what was happening. There were times when everything seemed clearer. But more often than not lately, I couldn't shake the feeling that I didn't know who I was. I was a Princess and the Sarrum had raised me. *I was his.* I'd always been his. *So who was that man?* He'd called my name and for some reason, I'd followed his voice through the Waterfall. *I knew him.* But how? It didn't make any sense. I had this extra set of memories of a life that wasn't mine, and the man was a part of that life. I willingly stepped beyond my protections when I heard him call my name. *But why?* He came to hurt me…

...I was sitting by the lake painting a picture of the sunset. Across the clearing, Isa was tending to her flowers. We were both immersing ourselves in our favorite pastimes to take our minds off the battle our husbands were fighting. The Purists had been raiding the fringe for the past several days, hurting innocent souls in unspeakable ways, and the Sarrum and the Darkness had led the counterattack to send a clear message. Harming the inhabitants of the fringe was forbidden and those who broke the law would be swiftly put to death.

Isa and I knew our husbands were more than capable of squashing the raids, but staying behind while your soul mate went off to battle was still terrifying. The Purists were getting bolder. Given the opportunity, they'd gladly run a blade through my husband's heart.

Forcing myself to focus on the landscape, I dipped my brush in a fresh glob of red paint and scooped some into an empty inkwell on my palate. After a quick glance at the sky, I added a scoop of yellow and mixed the colors with my brush. When I was satisfied with the result, I smeared a few brilliant streaks of orange across the blue of the sky. Then I scooped some white into another inkwell and dipped my brush in the red again but before I could blend them into the perfect shade of cotton-candy-pink for the clouds, an agonized shriek echoed through the Waters.

Dropping my brush, I stood and moved toward the Waterfall at the edge of the lake. And I heard it again—a shriek of desperation from outside the mirage. "Emma! Please! Help me!"

I reached a hand into the Waterfall with detached curiosity.

"Emma! Please! Come help your father!"

It was the urgency in his tone that drove me to act before I truly processed what I was doing. Heart racing, I stepped through the Waterfall.

I hadn't seen my father since the day he caught me in bed with David. I was eighteen at the time, and David was my father's business partner and closest friend. My parents had gone out of town for the weekend. They weren't supposed to be back for another day, but they ended the trip early and came home in the middle of the night. When my father walked in my room to tell me they were back, he found me naked in his best friend's arms.

He yanked me out of bed by my hair and I woke up, disoriented and terrified with my father's hands around my throat. At first, I just feared the consequences but as his grip tightened, I started to fear for my life. A thick vein bulged on his forehead as he screamed, "You filthy little whore! What the hell did you do?"

Desperate to cover myself, I made a weak attempt to grab the sheet from my bed. I was fading, and I didn't want to die naked.

"What the fuck are you doing?" Spit flew from my father's lips as he shrieked, "I MADE you! But you cover yourself from me and spread your legs for my partner? You fucking whore!"

It was only a matter of seconds but naked and humiliated and terrified that I was about to die, they were the longest seconds of my life.

Everything beyond my father's reddened face was a blur. I didn't see David get off the bed, but I heard his fist slam into my father's face and the resulting crunch of breaking bone. Somehow, David moved quickly enough to catch me when my father lost his grip on me. Gently setting me on the bed, he grabbed his shirt and wrapped it around me. Then he slipped on his pants, while my father lay curled on the floor clutching his broken nose.

Without the slightest sense of urgency, David stepped toward my father. Giving him a swift kick in the ribs, David growled, "Lay a finger on her ever again, and I'll kill you."

My father didn't say anything. He just looked up at David in wide-eyed disbelief as blood seeped through his fingers. Then his gaze shifted to me.

David kicked him again as he snarled, "No! You are not to look at her ever again. I'm taking her with me. You don't deserve her, you sick fuck. You never did." With that, David scooped me into his arms and we left my father bleeding on the floor.

I hadn't seen my father's face since that night. Yet there he was, my Unsighted fairy father standing in the heart of the Dark forest.

Seconds after I stepped out, Isa raced through the Waterfall after me. Two Dark creatures immediately grabbed her, but I couldn't tell what sort of creatures they were. Shocked as I was, I couldn't turn to look.

"I've missed you, Emma." My father's gaunt face looked much older than I remembered. When I didn't respond, he took a step toward me.

"How are you here?" I whispered. "And how do you know who I am?"

A bitter laugh escaped his pale lips. "How could I not after all the years your precious King kept me chained up in a damp cell?"

"What?" A queasiness settled in the pit of my stomach as I muttered, "Since the night you choked me?"

"No." He stepped closer, and the stench of fermented cider on his breath almost made me vomit. "Since the day you were born, you filthy whore."

It felt like the ground was crumbling out from under me. "What?"

"Every day of your precious little life, he'd torture me and remind me that fathers don't touch their little girls. He said it was necessary to cause me enough pain that my Unsighted mind would still fear the consequences of touching you when I woke. And the whole time, your self-righteous King was just keeping you for himself. He raised you like he was your daddy and he fucked you like you were his whore. He's a daughter fucking hypocrite! You were supposed to be mine!"

I was too stunned to react when he grabbed me by the shoulders and pushed me to the ground.

Isa's distant screams echoed in my ears as he crouched over me. "Don't touch her, you son of a bitch! Get your hands off her!"

"You were always supposed to be mine, Emma." An ugly smile spread across my father's face as he whispered, "And I have a lot of lost time to make up for."

His voice grew distant, until the only sound I could process was the pounding of my own heart. I was too numb to fight as he pinned me beneath him. Immobilized by shock and fear, all I could do was squeeze my eyes shut as he tugged up the hem of my dress.

"I TOLD YOU I'D KILL YOU IF YOU EVER TOUCHED HER AGAIN!"

My eyes flew open at the sound of my husband's voice. I watched him unmask as he towered above my father. His massive claw plunged into my father's back and tore its way out the front of his chest. Blood trickled from my father's lips as he stared wide-eyed at his own beating heart in the Sarrum's clawed hand. The King squeezed, dousing us both in my father's blood, and his lifeless body fell to the ground beside me.

His blood was everywhere. It soaked the front of my dress. It was in my hair and on my skin. It was even in my mouth. I barely managed to roll to my side before vomiting.

Returning to his human form, David lifted me and hurried toward the cave. I heard him tell Benji to fetch the doctor, but everything seemed distant and out of focus. It was all just too wrong to process...

39

I dropped into bed, still dressed in the clothes I'd worn all day. I'd earned another night of shore leave or whatever you'd call a night off from my training, but I had no idea what to do with it. I could go back and see how Nellie was doing after I'd drudged up her nightmarish past, and I did consider it. It'd be nice to see Bob and Lilly again. It actually took me a second to remember that Lilly wasn't real. Call me an ass, but I couldn't bring myself to go back. I'd already had more than enough drama for one day. Isa was finally awake, but she'd come dangerously close to dying. If the Sarrum hadn't rushed in to save her, I doubted she'd still be breathing. But helping her had taken its toll on the Dragon King. I saw it when he was kneeling over her, breathing life into her body. It'd drained the hell out of him. He'd rushed back to Emma, weaker and more exhausted.

I don't know how I knew that. I just sort of sensed it, but it wasn't a guess. I *knew* it was true. I must've been tapping into my dragon instincts. Benjamin would be proud to hear that. He got this sly satisfied grin on his face every time I accomplished something dragonish lately.

I yanked the covers up over my head. Where the heck was I supposed to go? Visiting Nellie would be too depressing. Benjamin and Rose were busy making up for lost time with Isa. The Sarrum and Emma had their own stuff to deal with and even if they didn't, I doubted the King would want to have me over for dinner or anything. I thought about going to the Dragon's Lair but I was too chicken to visit the tavern on my own. I was no Tristan, and I never would be. Tagging along with Brian and Tristan was also out of the question. They'd gone off to deal with some family business. So by sheer process of elimination, I decided it was time to pay Art another visit.

Too keyed up to drift off to sleep naturally, I silently called out to the Waters and they instantly appeared. Not bad, but I couldn't help wishing I could just snap my fingers to call them like the Sarrum did. *Was I so sure I couldn't?* I nudged the Waters to take a hike so I could give it a try. Then I took a deep breath to center myself. I could do this. I was a dragon. The Waters had to listen. Feeling pretty confident about my awesomeness, I snapped my fingers and... absolutely nothing happened. Well, didn't I feel like an idiot. Still, a second try wouldn't hurt. Trying my damndest to ooze confidence, I snapped again and...nothing. Tail between my legs, I called out to the Waters again, but they resisted this time. And why wouldn't they? I was a sorry excuse for a dragon. *Damn it, get out here!* The Waters returned and just for the hell of it, I flicked my wrist like the Sarrum did when he parted the Waters. I could almost swear I heard the Waters laughing at me. At the very least, I think they told me to go fuck myself. Or maybe I'd just been spending too much time around Benjamin. I let out a defeated sigh, then took a deep breath and plunged in.

I ignored the icy cold and mentally shouted, *I better not be wet when I emerge!* The Waters spit me out dry, on the ground beside the dock where I first met Call-me-Art. Or maybe I was in the mirage he'd created to look the same? Either way, I was dry. I stood up and brushed the dirt off my clothes as I moved to the dock. Art wasn't around, so I slowly made my way to the end of the weathered dock and sat down. The sun was setting like it always was when I visited this shore. Brilliant pink and orange streaks sliced across the darkening sky along with the occasional pink-tinged cloud and the air felt heavy, like the clouds might open up at any second. Somewhere in the distance, a chorus of chirping insects welcomed the approaching darkness. Mirage or reality, it wasn't a bad spot to sit and collect my thoughts.

Nellie's story scared the shit out of me and according to her, Emma's story was pretty similar. That scared me a whole lot more. Emma's words at the beach had been echoing in my head since she'd said them. *What I feel for you is different.* I'd have to be a complete moron to explore the possibility of her feeling something more than friendship for me. The Sarrum wasn't the sort of guy you wanted to piss off and I had the bruised neck to prove it. But what kind of man would I be if I left Emma trapped in a jar with her wings torn off? Everything was just so screwed up.

"To what do I owe the pleasure of this visit?" Art's sophisticated British voice asked behind me.

I turned and watched him stroll to the end of the dock. Noting that the boards didn't creak, I decided we must be in the mirage. "Are we in your mirage again?"

Art exhaled a tired sigh as he sat down beside me. "It's our mirage."

"I didn't make it. Why is it ours?"

"Because," Art answered with a charming grin, "it didn't exist until we needed it."

I raked a hand through my windblown hair as I turned toward the Water. "But I didn't make it."

"In a way, you did."

I pulled the moonstone from my pocket and traced a finger around the edge. "I'm too tired for guessing games. Can you just tell me what that means?"

Chuckling softly, Art took the stone from my hand. "Rough day?"

"Yeah. You could say that." I really wanted to take the stone back but he was the one who gave it to me, so I figured he had a right to take it back if he wanted to. "I just feel so lost. I'm not even sure who the good guys are."

Art's fingers curled into a fist around the moonstone. "What does your heart tell you?"

I would've laughed if I wasn't so damn frustrated. "No idea."

"You must have some sort of gut feeling about all of it."

I turned away from the Waters and looked him square in the eye. "Are you one of Henry Godric's followers?"

A knowing grin spread across Art's face, and his eyes punctuated it with wisdom and kindness as he shook his head. "I'm no one's follower, Charlie. I'm just one man following my own heart and trying to do what I believe is right."

"I finally got around to visiting Nellie."

"I know," he murmured, swapping the stone to his other hand.

"How?"

"There's a somber wisdom in your eyes that wasn't there before. Nellie's story convinced you of the gravity of Emma's situation."

"How the hell do you know so much?" It was a little unnerving spending all your time with creatures who could read you like a book. *Shit.* "You read my thoughts, didn't you?"

Art's charming grin widened. "No. I wouldn't do that, but it's hardly necessary. Your thoughts can be easily read from your expression and your body language."

"Well, not everyone has a perfect poker face like you."

Art chuckled as he handed the stone back to me. "Is that what I have?"

Thankful to have it back, I slipped the stone in my pocket. "Yeah. It always seems like you're laughing at some private joke that no one else is in on."

Art reached behind us and grabbed a carafe that wasn't there a second ago. It was filled with a deep crimson-colored liquid. "I tried a slightly different recipe this time and since I know how fond you are of this, I was hoping you might lend your opinion?"

I turned, not at all surprised to find two glasses on a silver tray behind me. I grabbed a glass and held it out to Art. "I'd love to."

Grinning, he filled my glass almost to the top. "Excellent."

I downed a big gulp of the drink. It was even better than the last batch, spicier and sweeter at the same time. But instead of being ice cold, this new concoction was warm, and the heat enhanced the flavor and warmed my insides as it slid down to my stomach. "This is amazing," I practically moaned. "What is this stuff?"

"It's my own creation," Art murmured, looking pleased by my response. "It doesn't have a name yet. What would you suggest I call it?"

I swallowed the heavenly sip in my mouth. "How about liquid ecstasy?"

Chuckling, Art poured himself a glass. "That good?"

I took another swig before answering, "Hell yes. You should bottle and sell this stuff. You'd make a fortune."

Art grinned at me as he swallowed the sip in his mouth. "Thank you. But I'm sure I could make better use of my time. You said you went to see Nellie. How did that go?"

I sat my empty glass down on the tray. "It was painful, and I still don't get how Godric tricked her into all that."

Art's expression was somber as he refilled my glass. "He's a dragon, Charlie. How much have you learned about dragons?"

"Not enough." I took a sip before adding, "I know they're possessive and greedy and they don't part with their treasures."

He reached back and sat the carafe down on the tray. "You make them sound so awful."

"Aren't they?"

Grinning, Art whispered, "Have you forgotten that you are one?"

"No. But I'm barely one. I can't even unmask. Whatever dragon tendencies I have are buried pretty deep inside me."

"Then you can't know what you're talking about."

"Alright?"

"The first time we met in the mirage, you asked if I was a dragon."

"Yeah," I muttered. "And you told me that was rude."

Art chuckled and almost choked on the gulp of ecstasy in his mouth. "It was, but we've gotten to know each other better and I believe I can trust you."

"Thanks." Maybe it was the ecstasy talking, but Art's words warmed my heart a little. "That means a lot. I don't hear a whole lot of praise these days."

"They undervalue you," he replied, dropping the grin. "They shouldn't. They're lucky to have you. But we've gotten off topic. Dragons aren't as horrible as you make them out to be."

"No?" I swirled the liquid in my glass and stared, transfixed by the whirlpool of red. "What makes you so sure?"

"I am one."

I put my glass down on the dock. "So never mind what I know about dragons. Tell me what you know."

"They must have at least taught you the first lesson. What makes dragons such skillful predators?"

"They don't have to chase their prey," I muttered, echoing David Talbot's words.

"Yes. We sense the desires of our prey. So we know how to give them exactly what they want, and *prey* doesn't necessarily equate with *victim*. We also happen to be extremely skillful romantic suitors."

"Maybe you do," I muttered. "I think I lack the gene for that."

Chuckling softly, Art murmured, "You don't."

"What makes you say that?" Feeling sort of awkward, I picked my glass back up and downed another swig.

"Why do you suppose the Princess was so drawn to you at the facility, Charlie?"

"I don't know," I muttered, shrugging. "I offered to keep her safe."

"Because you sensed that she needed to feel safe. Some part of her recognized the dragon in you and she was desperately missing her dragon, so you swooped in and offered to be everything she was missing."

"I was a sad substitute for the Dragon King."

"If you were," Art murmured, "she wouldn't have grown so fond of you. You're more dragon than you realize. I suspect Emma brought that out in you, because what she desired most of all was her dragon."

"Okay?"

"You asked how Godric was able to trick the dragon mother into doing the horrible things that she did. He spent a good deal of time making himself her perfect match because he knew *exactly* what she wanted, even when she wasn't consciously aware of it herself. He gave her everything she'd always desperately longed for. Sanity. Love. A family. How could she not trust him entirely?"

"I don't know and honestly, I don't even want to think about it. I just wish I had a way to help Emma. She's falling apart. You said it yourself. She's a butterfly with its wings torn off trapped in a jar."

"She may be too far gone to help," Art whispered. Instead of laughter, remorse glinted in his eyes.

I turned toward the Waters, fighting back tears. "I don't want to believe that. There has to be something I can do to help her."

"It'd be a fool's mission," Art whispered. "The only way to help her would be to get her away from the Sarrum, and I don't see how you could possibly accomplish that and live to tell the tale."

"Then maybe I need to die trying."

Art let out a thoughtful sigh. "She's too well protected. You'd never even reach her. The Dragon King keeps her locked away deep within his lair. Only a handful of creatures have ever even seen her in this world."

"I've seen her."

Art studied me through narrowed eyes. "When?"

"When we were both at the facility. She snuck into my room one night when she couldn't fall asleep."

He arched an eyebrow. "Well, you're still breathing. So I assume the Dragon King is unaware that you took his wife to bed?"

"Yeah. No. I mean…it wasn't like that," I muttered. "She just fell asleep in my arms, and somehow I pulled her into the Waters with me."

"And then what happened?"

"We ended up on Nellie's beach, but Nellie totally freaked out when she saw us. We didn't stay long, just long enough to take a walk on the beach."

Art sat up a little straighter. "You need to tell the Sarrum about that."

"What?" I asked a little louder than I meant to. "Didn't you just say I'd end up in pieces if he knew?"

"Charlie," Art whispered. "Did the Princess know who you were when you were on that beach?"

"Yeah. Of course. Why wouldn't she?" *Holy crap.* "She knew who I was in the world where she'd never met me."

"Yes. That just might be the key to retrieving her lost memories."

"Great," I raked a hand through my hair, "but the Sarrum will kill me if I tell him Emma crawled into my bed."

"Maybe I need to die trying. Isn't that what you just said a few minutes ago? If this information could help break through Emma's blindness, isn't it worth the risk?"

"Yeah maybe. Damn it. Why do you have to be so helpful?"

"Sorry," Art chuckled.

"So say they let me see Emma and it does heal her. What then? She'll still be trapped in the Dragon King's lair."

Art poured himself a second glass of ecstasy. "Once she regains all her memories, she may realize she'd rather be with you."

"That's insane," I muttered.

"Love usually is."

"Who said anything about love?"

"I can read your expressions and your body language, remember?"

I dropped my head back and looked up at the starry sky. I'd barely noticed that the sun had set.

"It's a fool's mission, remember? Besides, Emma's madly in love with her husband."

"Yes, but her husband isn't exactly a saint. He spent a great deal of time screwing another lawyer at his firm."

My heart sunk as I whispered, "How do you know about that?" For Emma's sake, I'd really wanted Sophie's accusation to be a lie.

"That lawyer was my sister."

I woke up early the next morning feeling like shit. *That lawyer was my sister.* The first time I met Art, he said he tried to kill the Sarrum because the Sarrum had just killed his sister. Damn it. David Talbot *was* unfaithful and he *did* kill Sophie. I needed to get Emma the hell out of there. But Art was right, it was a fool's mission.

Not quite ready to face the new day, I decided to take a shower. Hopefully, that and some strong coffee would get me feeling halfway human. I showered on autopilot, numbly going through the motions. Then I headed downstairs in desperate need of caffeine. The scent of fresh coffee greeted me when I hit the foyer, and I eagerly followed the heavenly smell down the hall to the kitchen.

Rose and Tristan were sitting at the kitchen table drinking coffee. Shirtless as usual, Tristan was wearing blue plaid pajama pants and his smile was cranked up to the irresistible setting. Dressed in a purple tank top and little matching pajama shorts, Rose was drinking in the view and blushing like crazy. I felt a twinge of jealousy but I couldn't decide which of them I was even jealous of. Then I remembered Rose was a virgin, and Tristan could sniff them out. I cleared my throat as I stepped in the room and Rose stopped leaning so close to Tristan. Flashing me a devilish grin, Tristan stayed exactly where he was, but his smile didn't make me feel weak in the knees. All I felt was a fierce need to protect Rose from the walking talking virgin-detector. Without a word, I marched to the coffee pot, grabbed a mug from the cupboard and poured myself a cup. Glaring at Tristan, I marched over and sat down in the empty seat between them at the head of the table.

Not the least bit intimidated by my stare down, Tristan grinned at me. "Morning, sunshine. Rough night? You look like hell."

"Wow. Thanks a lot." *Guess he doesn't have any charm to spare on me. And why would he? Sweet innocent Rose is a dragon AND a virgin. Next to that, I'm chopped liver. Shit. Am I jealous of Tristan? Or Rose?*

"Doesn't matter," Tristan murmured. "We'd make a gorgeous threesome."

"What the fuck?" I blurted, then realized they'd probably both heard what I'd been thinking. *Fabulous.* I pivoted toward Rose with an apologetic frown. "Sorry...for my language and my stupid thoughts."

Rose dropped her eyes to her coffee mug as her cheeks blushed a deep shade of pink. "It's alright."

Damn it. I felt like such an ass. I'd probably embarrassed the hell out of her. The unmistakable scent of female arousal snapped me out of my self-deprecating thoughts. Well, this was awkward as hell. An incubus and two dragons sitting at the kitchen table, all fully aware of Rose's sudden mood change. The scent wasn't there when I walked in the room. So she wasn't just reacting to Tristan. When did the scent hit me? *After Tristan said we'd make a gorgeous threesome.* Well, that didn't make it less awkward.

Tristan not so subtly kicked my leg under the table as he frowned at me. "Why're you such a wet blanket this morning? We're all grownups. Maybe you *should* both come crawl in my bed."

Instead of the exhilarated rush I usually felt when Tristan spoke like that, my heart was thudding with a fierce need to protect Rose. I looked at her and realized she could probably sense that too. *Crap.* I wished I could just crawl back in bed and start the morning over again.

Sliding his chair back from the table, Tristan stood up and stepped behind the two of us. He put one hand on my shoulder and the other on Rose's. I was about to bite his head off but a wave of elated relaxation washed over me, turning my limbs to

Jell-O. "Holy crap that feels good," I muttered before I could censor myself. "What're you doing?"

"Same thing I did to the Princess's head," Tristan answered in a voice like liquid silk. "Easing the tension from your muscles."

Rose didn't say anything but when I shot her a glance, her eyes were shut and her lips were parted. She looked hot as hell, like a woman on the verge of an orgasm. *Shit.* Maybe that was *exactly* what she was.

Tristan squeezed my shoulder. *Relax, dragon boy. I have no intention of stepping on your toes. She's your virgin. Not mine.*

I turned my head and shot him a puzzled look because I had no idea how to direct a thought to just one person, which was exactly what he'd just done. It had to be. Rose was still lost in a pre-orgasmic sea of pleasure. *Pre-orgasmic sea of pleasure?* Yeah… I'd been spending too much time with Tristan.

We've all got our talents, Charlie. There's no denying how you feel about sweet little Rose. I can sense it, and that scent didn't hit the air till you came in here.

Thankfully, Brian came in at that point and Tristan's hands dropped to his sides. Brian shot his brother a disapproving glare as he made a beeline to the coffee pot.

As usual, it didn't faze Tristan in the slightest. "Morning, big brother. What's on the agenda for today?"

"Coffee," Brian grumbled. "That's as far as I've planned today."

"Amen," a woman's voice lilted from the doorway. It took me a second to realize who the voice belonged to. Smiling at each of us in turn, Isa stepped in the room and headed toward the coffee.

Benjamin followed her into the kitchen, and I just about fell over from shock when he shot us a pleasant smile. Isa handed him a cup of coffee and he kissed her cheek, then sat down at the opposite end of the table from me. Brian sat next to him, and Tristan sat on his brother's other side. Isa sat beside her daughter, and we all just savored our coffee in silence for a few minutes. Brian seemed uncharacteristically grumpy, and I think we all wanted to give him some time for the caffeine to kick in.

As soon as Brian sat his empty cup on the table, Benjamin dropped the smile. "Now that Isa's back with us, healing the Princess is our top priority. I want everyone involved with this. She's running out of time, and we're not just going to stand by and lose her."

"I'll be brainstorming with Doc today." Isa reached over and squeezed her daughter's hand. "And Rose will be helping us."

Benjamin cleared his throat. "If anybody's got an idea about how to bring Emma back, no matter how farfetched, I want to hear it."

During the silence that followed, I mentally kicked myself about a hundred times. I wanted to help Emma, but admitting that she'd snuck in my room and slept in my bed was a death sentence. Damn it. *Save her or die trying.* "I've got something."

40

BENJAMIN

All eyes were on Charlie the second he announced he had a suggestion for helping the Princess, but he dropped his eyes to the table without elaborating. I prompted him to continue in a tone that made it abundantly clear I had no patience for games, "Let's hear it."

Fear seeped from the kid's pores as he looked up at me. "Uh…what if we could jog Emma's memory by having somebody she only knows in this world visit her in Draumer?"

I narrowed my eyes at him. "What do you mean?"

"She needs to remember both worlds at the same time, right?"

"Right," Brian agreed, encouraging him to keep talking.

The fear leaking from the kid doubled as he muttered, "What if I visited her in Draumer? If she recognized me, it might help her make the connection between the two worlds."

I let out an aggravated sigh. For a second there, I thought the kid actually had something. Why else would he be so damn nervous? "She had no memory of Doc when she met him in Draumer."

"Yeah," Charlie whispered, "but that was Doc. I mean more to her." The kid's heart was pounding, and for good reason. You didn't say shit like that about the Sarrum's wife, not if you wanted your heart to stay in your chest.

I shook my head in disbelief at the utter stupidity of his words. "What?"

"She said it herself the other day," Charlie muttered without meeting my eyes. "The Sarrum doesn't want me around because I mean more to her."

Brian shot the kid a cautionary glance. "If you're suggesting that you mean more to Emma than the boss does—"

"You're an idiot," Tristan chimed in, finishing his brother's sentence. "You don't say things like that about the Princess. Didn't you learn your lesson when he slammed you up against the wall and choked you half to death?"

Charlie shrugged his shoulders. "I'm not saying I mean more to her than the Sarrum. I'm just saying she might recognize me. That's all."

I was tired of wasting time. "Why the hell do you think she'd recognize you?"

"Because," Charlie shrunk in his seat as he whispered, "she has before."

I didn't even have to say it. Everybody at the table knew to clear out of the kitchen, and it was only a matter of seconds before the kid and I were the only ones left in the room. "What the fuck do you mean she has before?"

"When we were at the facility," Charlie muttered, dangerously close to shitting himself, "she came to my room one night when she couldn't sleep. I accidentally pulled her into the Waters with me. We ended up on Nellie's beach, and Emma knew who I was."

I couldn't decide whether to kill him or kiss him, but I was damn sure which one the boss would choose. "Fuck."

"I know," Charlie whispered. "The Sarrum would rip me apart if he found out about it but if it could pull Emma out of this, it'd be worth it."

I pushed my chair back from the table and carried my cup to the coffee pot for a refill. "You care about her a lot, don't you?"

"Yeah. I do and I hate seeing her suffer like this. She just seems so lost."

"Fuck." I abandoned my empty cup on the counter and started pacing the floor. "We're almost out of time. If there's even a chance it'd work, we've got to try."

"I know." The kid stood up and carried his cup to the sink. "But the Sarrum's going to kill me."

I stopped pacing beside him. "That's a definite possibility but if you can save the Princess, he just might forgive you."

We all spent the morning doing our own separate things. Isa and Rose were brainstorming with Doc in the dining room. Brian and Tristan had gone to the office to deal with a problem client. And Charlie and I were in the backyard on Sycamore working on unmasking.

The kid had gotten stronger. He was picking up on a lot more than he even realized. He'd gotten the hang of moving through the Waters without getting wet. His technique wasn't pretty, but it was functional and he always ended up where he meant to go. But he still hadn't made a damn bit of progress with unmasking, and it was frustrating the hell out of him.

He attempted to unmask for about the hundredth time and when he failed, he flopped down on the grass. "This is hopeless. I'm never gonna get it. Why are you even wasting your time on me?"

I stood from my lounge chair on the deck, descended the steps and walked across the lawn to him. "I don't waste my time. I invest it. Now keep trying."

The kid stood up and shook his head. "What makes you think I'll ever figure it out?"

"I don't think. I *know* you'll figure it out. You just need the right motivation."

The kid threw his hands up in the air. "Great. And what would that be?"

I motioned for him to follow me back to the deck. "Remember the first time I watched you command the Waters?"

"Yeah," Charlie muttered, dropping into the lounge chair beside mine. "You mean the day you drove off a bridge into the Waters and tricked me into thinking our lives were in danger?"

Despite his frustration, I couldn't help laughing. "I didn't trick you into anything. Our lives *were* in danger. If you hadn't manned up, the Waters would've killed us."

The horrified look on the kid's face was priceless. "Are you kidding me?"

I did my best to stifle my laughter. "Have you known me to do a lot of kidding?"

"What the hell?" Charlie muttered. "You really are insane."

"No. I had faith in your abilities. You just needed the right motivation to tap into them."

Charlie shook his head. "You're still insane."

"Your dragon tendencies are buried deep," I lowered my voice, forcing him to focus on my words. "And Isa's pretty sure that wasn't your doing. Someone locked away what you are and as far as I can tell, the best way to draw it out is to up the stakes."

"Okay?" The kid swatted a mosquito hovering above his arm. "So what am I supposed to do, put my life in danger until my inner dragon decides to make an appearance?"

"I have no doubt that you'll be able to unmask when you really need to."

"Great," the kid muttered, shooing another mosquito by his ear. "So… what? I should go play in traffic until my dragon comes out?"

"No." I smacked a bug on the side of his head and grinned at his pissed off scowl. "That'd be idiotic. When the right situation presents itself, it'll happen. And it's going to happen soon. I can feel it."

The kid dropped his head against the back of the chair. "So do I have to keep practicing?"

"No. We're going to pay the Sarrum a visit as soon as Brian and Tristan get back. Go get ready."

"Okay." The kid started to stand, then sunk back into his seat. "Do you think the Sarrum will let me visit Emma in Draumer? Or is he just going to rip me to pieces for suggesting it?"

I stood up and gestured for him to do the same. "There's no way of telling. We'll just have to throw it out there and see how he reacts."

"That's not very comforting," Charlie muttered as he hopped to his feet.

I moved to the back door, pulled it open and stepped inside. "If you wanted coddling, you came to the wrong guy."

"Yeah." The kid grabbed the door and followed me into the house. "No shit."

41

DAVID

I'd just polished off my fourth cup of coffee and the platter of pastries on the dining room table was looking more appetizing by the minute. With a frustrated sigh, I sat my cup down and pushed my chair back from the table. I had hoped that Emma would come down to join me for breakfast before everyone arrived, but after an hour and a half of waiting that no longer seemed likely to happen. *To hell with it.* I'd wait another half an hour, then give up.

"Here's the morning paper, sir," Sara squeaked as she stepped from the kitchen.

I motioned for her to bring it to me. She scurried over and placed it in my hand, and I pulled the chair next to mine back from the table. "Sit."

"Yes, sir." Lips trembling, she obediently dropped into the seat.

"I assume you've heard that Isa is awake?"

She kept her eyes glued to my coffee cup as she whispered, "Yes."

I cleared my throat, prompting her to look at me. "And?"

She flinched slightly as she met my eyes. "And what, sir?"

"Do you believe you've served sufficient time to pay for your crimes?"

Her eyes widened and her heart began to thud. She clearly wanted me to make that decision.

And I already had, but I wasn't about to let her off the hook that easily. "If you're waiting for me to answer the question for you, you'll be waiting a very long time."

"I will serve you for as long as you wish, my King."

"*King?*"

Startled by my wife's accusatory tone, the skittish housekeeper was on her feet in an instant. "Good morning, Mrs. Talbot. Can I get you some coffee?"

"No," Emma whispered, her glare oscillating between the two of us. "Why did you just call my husband *your King*? Did I interrupt some sort of role play?"

Heart racing, the imp inched toward the kitchen.

"Where the hell do you think you're going?" Emma demanded. "Stay here and explain what the hell I just walked in on."

The imp froze dead in her tracks. "I'm sure you'd rather hear that from Mr. Talbot. It's not my place to get in the middle—"

"Get in the middle of *what*?" Emma hissed. "I asked *you* the question. Do I need to grab a knife from the kitchen to get an answer?"

Perhaps I should've intervened. The imp was certainly anxious for me to come to her rescue, but I wanted to see how this would play out. The knife was an empty threat. Even if she truly did intend to stab someone, it would be me.

"I...uh," the imp shot me a pleading glance.

"Don't look at him," Emma shrieked. "Tell me what the hell I just walked in on!"

Sara dropped her eyes to the floor. "Do you really think I'm your husband's type, Mrs. Talbot?"

"I couldn't tell you what my husband's type is these days, but I'm pretty sure he has a thing for his employees." Emma's death glare shifted to me. "Is it the whole subservient thing that does it for you?"

The imp rushed toward the kitchen while my wife's attention was focused on me.

"Are you going to make me tackle you, Sara?" Emma hollered without taking her eyes off me. "You know what? You can keep him. He's all yours." With that, she spun on her heels and stormed out of the room.

I drew a deep breath, debating whether to chase after her or give her time to cool off first. Then I realized the imp was still frozen in place. "Go. You've served your time but if I ever discover that you're stealing from the inhabitants of the fringe again, your next sentence won't be nearly as pleasant."

"Thank you, sir," Sara whispered, bowing her head. "I won't disappoint you, and I'm truly sorry if I caused you further trouble with the Princess."

I tossed the newspaper on the table as I stood from my chair. "Don't be. She's clearly not in her right mind because you are absolutely correct—you're not my type."

Cracking the first smile since her arrival, Sara nodded. "Thank you for showing me mercy, Sarrum."

"Now *there's* your mistake. You'd do well to remember to save those titles for the world they originated in. Here, you're to call me *boss* or *sir.* Now go," I snarled, "before I change my mind."

Without another word, Sara scurried from the room and rushed off to gather her belongings, and I left the dining room to deal with my wife.

It wasn't difficult to track her. A trail of fury crackled through the air in her wake. As I drew closer, the energy intensified and I make no apology for being aroused by the sensation. This clearly wasn't the time to act on it. However, the fact that she still cared enough to fight a rival female for me was promising. It was unnecessary, but arousing nonetheless.

I followed her trail of fury up the stairs and down the hall to the terrace. Drawing a deep breath, I pulled the French doors open and stepped outside. My bride was seated on a lounge chair, hugging her knees to her slender torso. Her head was bent but when she heard the doors open, she looked up at me.

Neither of us spoke as I moved to her and sat down at the foot of her chair. For a while, we just watched each other in silence. Eventually, I asked, "What do you want from me, Princess?"

"What?"

"Tell me what you want from me," I whispered, resting my hands on her knees.

"I don't know what I want." She leaned back against the cushions, but made no move to push my hands away. "I'm not even sure who we are anymore."

I dropped my chin to her knees and drew a deep breath as I watched her. I could feel the ache in her heart. It was an unbearable agony that twisted my insides and turned my stomach. "Have you any love left for me?"

A tear slipped down her cheek as she whispered, "I wish I didn't, but I don't know how to stop loving you. The only way to stop the heartache would be to stop my heart."

I gripped her knees a little tighter. "You might as well stop mine first."

A bitter laugh escaped her lips. "You've hurt me enough already. If one of us is left behind to grieve, it should be you."

My eyelids felt heavy, as though they bore the weight of both worlds. I squeezed my eyes shut and whispered, "You hate me every bit as much as you love me, don't you?"

"No." When I opened my eyes, tears were streaming down her cheeks. "That's always been my curse, hasn't it? To love you more than I have any right to."

Leaning against her legs, I reached out and wiped the tears from her cheeks. "You have every right to love me, Princess."

She pushed my hand away. "What the hell did I walk in on in the dining room? Why did Sara call you her King?"

I reached out again and stroked a thumb over each temple. "You know why."

She squeezed her eyes shut and lurched to the side, and I had just enough time to grab a potted plant and stick it in front of her before she vomited. I slid forward and pulled her hair back from her face as she whimpered and heaved. When she finished, she dropped back against the cushions. "If you love me, you should just let me die. There's no place for me anymore."

I shoved the vomit-soaked plant aside. "Your place is with me."

"It was never supposed to be with you," she whispered. "I didn't ever belong there."

"Where Emma?" I smoothed her hair back from her face. "Where didn't you belong?"

When she looked up at me, her eyes looked wrong. Her pupils were far too dilated for the sunlight. "I don't know why I said that."

"You belong with me," I whispered. "You've always belonged to me."

"No," she whispered. "I don't think that's true."

"It is," I replied, perhaps a little too forcefully. "How we found each other is irrelevant. You belonged to me from the moment you first looked in my eyes. Everything else is beside the point. You are mine, and you were always meant to be mine."

"And you're slowly killing me."

42

EMMA

My conversation with David didn't last much longer after I said he was slowly killing me but he wouldn't leave the terrace without me, probably because he feared I'd jump. Honestly, I couldn't say the fear was unwarranted. So, I begrudgingly followed him back to the dining room and I'd been staring at my untouched breakfast for a ridiculous number of minutes. I figured he'd eventually give up and leave when I wouldn't eat or speak to him, but he was just as stubborn as I was. So we'd been sitting together in silence for an uncomfortably long time.

He cleared his throat and I jumped a little at the unexpected break in the silence. "I have some business to attend to with Benjamin and the Mason brothers whilst you meet with Doc this morning."

My throat felt painfully dry but I wasn't about to give him the satisfaction of watching me drink the juice he'd poured for me himself, since I'd scared his little housekeeper off. "Doc can go fuck himself."

"Since when are you so crass?"

"Since you started fucking your employees." I let out a forced laugh. "Or were you always doing that? Maybe I was just too naive to notice."

Unruffled by my words, he replied, "The vulgarity doesn't suit you."

His calm tone ignited a fire inside me but I ignored the tightness in my chest and fought the urge to scream at him, refusing to let him see how broken I was. "You're so ridiculous."

"Am I?" His voice was cold, and the mask of control remained in place.

I focused on keeping my voice steady as I asked, "Are we done?"

"No," David growled as he grabbed the arm of my chair and dragged me back from the table. "We'll never be done! Don't you get that? I will never let go of you, and I'm getting rather tired of your accusations!"

I felt a certain satisfying measure of power watching his control unravel. He deserved to ache like I ached. "Good. Because I'm getting tired of you."

For one terrifying split second, fury flashed in his brilliant blue eyes. And for the first time in my life, I was truly afraid he might hit me but the mask slipped back in place as he stood from the table, perfectly in control. "Doc will be here soon and he's bringing a visitor to see you."

I was about to protest, but he didn't give me the chance. "Trust me. You'll want to entertain this visit." With that, he headed to the door and left the room without looking back.

Refusing to let him win even after he left, I skipped breakfast and spent the next half hour glaring at the dining room wall. Bored to tears but too stubborn to move, I was still sitting at the table when Doc came looking for me.

He briefly surveyed the spread of food on the table and my untouched plate before greeting me with a warm smile. "Hello, Emma. How are you this morning?"

I crossed my arms and shifted away from him. "Never better."

He rounded the table and sat down in the chair beside mine. Then he helped himself to a cheese Danish and took a large bite. "Why do I doubt your sincerity?" he mumbled around a mouthful.

I shook my head at his utter lack of table manners. "Why should I care?"

"Because," he paused to swallow the food in his mouth, "if you don't make progress, you'll end up back at the facility."

I wasn't an idiot. I knew David would never let that happen. "You don't scare me."

Doc leaned across the table to pour himself a glass of juice. "I don't intend to, but it's time for you to stop being so rude."

"Says the man with no table manners."

He let out a boisterous laugh. "Well, you're in an exceptionally foul mood today."

"Then maybe you should take the hint and leave."

"And what would your husband think of that?"

I squeezed my eyes shut. "I really don't care what he thinks about much of anything."

"I don't believe that for a second," a female voice answered from the doorway.

A chill raced down my spine as I turned toward the voice.

Isa grinned at me as she stepped in the room. "Hello, sweetheart. It's good to see you."

All my indifference melted away as I watched her walk toward me. I wanted to jump up and hug her, but I was too afraid to move. She should be dead because of me. How could she not hate me?

She bent down and wrapped her arms around me. "It's alright, Emma. Everything is going to be alright. I promise."

Tears streamed down my face as I hugged her back like my life depended on it. "I'm so sorry," I sobbed. "I'm so sorry for hurting you."

She sat down in the empty chair beside me and stroked my hair back from my face. "There's no need to be sorry, Emma. You weren't yourself. I know you'd never hurt me intentionally."

"That still doesn't excuse what I did. You should be dead because of me."

"But she isn't," Doc whispered.

Isa leaned toward me and kissed my forehead. Then she settled back in her chair and smiled at Doc. "Could you give us some privacy, Doctor?"

Nodding, Doc stood and left the room without a word.

Isa waited until he was out of earshot before whispering, "I hear you're not doing very well."

"How could I be?" I muttered. "I almost killed you."

"That's old news." She picked my plate up and held it out to me.

But I shook my head. "I'm not hungry."

"It doesn't matter. You need to eat."

Since she wouldn't put it down, I took the plate. "Why don't you hate me?"

"There's nothing to hate, Emma. You weren't yourself."

I balanced the plate on my lap. "Why do you keep saying that? Who else would I be?"

"Sophie was a liar," Isa whispered.

It didn't escape my attention how vague a statement that was. She didn't specify *what* Sophie lied about. "And now she's dead."

"So I heard." She took the plate off my lap and sat it on the table. "Why don't you and I go for a walk?"

"You don't seem very upset about Sophie's death."

Isa stood and held a hand out to me. "Sophie was a heartless bitch, Emma. She deserved to die."

43

DAVID

Seething with fury, I left the dining room and headed for my office. I had planned to wait for Benjamin and the others in the lounge but after my exchange with Emma, I needed time to stopper my emotions before receiving visitors. Otherwise, I was liable to tear the virgin's head off at the first asinine comment that spewed from his mouth. My burden was growing heavier by the hour. Most men would've crushed under the pressure by now, but I didn't have that luxury. If my strength faltered, so would the walls that protected my Princess from the Darkness beyond her mirage and I would never let that happen. I'd protect her till my dying breath, regardless of whether or not she ever regained her Sight.

The emptiness in her eyes was what pained me the most lately. The wife who looked at me through those vacant eyes knew only half our story at any given moment in either world and on those rare occasions when she did remember more, the pain that it caused her was like a knife to my heart. I would bear the weight of a thousand worlds to keep her from hurting. I'd kept her safe all her life, and I didn't intend to stop…

…We'd just finished dinner and I was in the kitchen helping Judy with the cleanup.

After rinsing the last dish, Judy took the towel from my hand and flashed me an appreciative grin. "I can take it from here. Go help Albert and Emma with that puzzle. He'll never fit it all together without another grownup's help."

I kissed her cheek and whispered, "Albert doesn't appreciate how truly lucky he is to have the two of you in his life."

Judy chuckled softly. "Good thing he has you to remind him."

"It is a good thing." I smiled at her as I left the kitchen and headed toward the dining room.

Their voices carried down the hall as I neared the room.

First Emma's sweet voice, "Daddy? Where does this piece go?"

Albert's voice was laced with an odd mixture of joy and frustration, "Darned if I know, sweetheart. You and I weren't graced with the puzzle-solving gene."

"What's that?" Emma's giggle stopped me dead in my tracks. Too giddy a response to his moronic statement, it was more the spontaneous sort of laughter that erupts when one is being tickled.

A rush of heat erupted in my gut but I suppressed the urge to charge in and rip Albert's arms off as I stood frozen in the hallway, listening.

"I don't know," Albert paused, letting Emma's gleeful laughter punctuate his sentence. "You and I just have different talents."

"What talent do I have?"

"Well for one thing, you're more gorgeous than a little girl has any right to be."

It was the tense rasp to his voice that jolted me out of immobility. Bounding around the corner, I entered the room and found my sweet child seated on Albert's lap and it took every ounce of restraint I possessed to refrain from pulling her away and knocking his teeth in. Being dragon was both a blessing and a curse. I was never in the dark as to others' intentions, which allowed me to protect my Princess from danger before it ever manifested. But the curse was having to feel Albert's vile inclinations. The fairies were a nauseatingly self-centered lot. In Draumer, fairy mothers usually wanted nothing to do with their children. They viewed them as a painful reminder of their own fading youth. But fairy fathers were far worse. Given the opportunity to raise their daughters on their own, they were apt to mistreat them *in unspeakable ways. Albert's desire to do things that no father should ever imagine doing to his child swirled in the air around him as my sweet Princess sat on his lap.*

Struggling to hear anything over the furious pounding of my own heart, I moved toward the table and spoke in a measured voice that betrayed no hint of the rage coursing through my veins. "Maybe you both need a break from that puzzle."

Albert hugged my Princess closer as he grinned at me. "Maybe."

I choked back the venom rising up my throat and locked eyes with Emma. "I was hoping your parents might let me steal you away. It's been a while since I took my favorite girl out for ice cream."

Emma responded exactly as I'd hoped she would. Hopping off her father's lap, she ran to me and took my hand in hers. "Yes! Can I, Daddy?"

An ache flared in my chest at the term of endearment. Albert didn't deserve such a title. He deserved to burn. I'd make him pay once he drifted off to Draumer. His cell would be the first stop I made, and I intended to take my time reminding his filthy Unsighted mind to keep his hands off my child. But for the moment, I forced a smile. "What do you say, Albert? Can I steal your daughter for a while and give you and Judy some time alone?"

Albert's grin was equally forced as his eyes traveled to Emma's hand nestled in mine. "Sure. I don't see why not."

"Yay!" Emma dropped my hand, raced back to her father and wrapped her fragile arms around him. "Thank you!"

Albert's unholy intentions echoed through the room as he hugged her back. "You're welcome, baby."

I cleared my throat to mask a growl that I couldn't entirely hold back. "Come on, Emma. Let's go get that ice cream."

She giggled with delight as she let go of the monster who created her and raced back to me.

With a quick kiss on the cheek from both of us, Emma and I said our goodbyes to Judy, left the house and hopped in my car. It took every bit of restraint in me to keep from driving off and disappearing for good. I hadn't realized how much stronger Albert's urges had grown. Now that Emma was getting older, my nightly reminders were scarcely enough to keep his hands off her. I needed to take immediate action to protect Emma when I wasn't around. I stole a glance at her in the rearview mirror. "Why don't we have ice cream at my house?"

She met my eyes in the mirror and flashed an innocent smile that positively melted my heart. "Do you have chocolate chip?"

"Of course. Did you think I wouldn't have your favorite?"

"Nope," she replied, but I was far too preoccupied to correct her speech. "What about sprinkles?"

"What about them?"

Giggling, she asked, "Do you have them?"

I smiled at her reflection. "Of course."

"Chocolate?"

"Now you're just hurting my feelings," I answered softly as I winked at her in the mirror. "Who do you think I am?"

"You're my King," she giggled, winking back.

"And you are my Princess. I always keep your favorites on hand."

"Even when you don't know I'm coming?"

I nodded. "It's best to always be prepared. You never know when an opportunity to spend time together might present itself."

"I love you," she whispered absently, as if thinking aloud.

"I love you more," I replied.

Neither of us spoke again until I pulled the car into the garage. As she unbuckled her seatbelt, I twisted in my seat to look her in the eye. "There's something I need to do before we have ice cream."

"Okay," she answered, content to blindly agree to anything I asked of her. "What is it?"

I exhaled a guilty sigh. "It's going to hurt a little, but it's necessary."

Tears glistened in her eyes as she whispered, "Why do you want to do something that'll hurt me?"

I hopped out of the car, opened her door and held a hand out to her. "I don't want to hurt you, Princess. But I need to protect you, and this will be the best way to keep you safe."

She placed her hand in mine, slid out of the car and moved to the door without letting go of my hand. "What do you need to protect me from?"

I gave her hand a gentle squeeze. "Let me worry about that, alright?"

"Alright." She looked up at me as we stepped into the foyer. "But you're scaring me a little."

Isa grinned at me as we entered the house. Then she bent down to Emma. "Hello, Princess. What a nice surprise! What brings you here today?"

"Ice cream." Her delicate hand twitched in mine. "And something scary."

Isa's eyes moved to me as she straightened.

Albert's urges have gotten much worse than I'd realized. Threatening him in Draumer won't be adequate for much longer. She needs something more of me to protect her.

Disapproval glinted in Isa's eyes as she nodded.

Stay with her while I speak to Benjamin.

Of course, Sarrum. Isa held her hand out to Emma. "Why don't you come with me, Princess? Benjamin needs to talk to the Sarrum for a minute."

Emma nodded and took her hand, but she looked back at me as Isa led her from the foyer and the fear in her eyes nearly stopped my heart.

Benjamin was already waiting for me in my office, and I didn't have to say a word. There was no hiding anything from your own shadow. Unlike Isa, Benjamin made no attempt to mute his disapproval. "She's too young for this, and you know it."

I exhaled slowly, gathering my thoughts. "I don't intend to do it without her consent."

"Which she's too young to give," Benjamin countered, glaring at me.

"Mind your tone," I snarled. "Don't forget who you're speaking to."

"I never do," he whispered, "but I vowed to protect the Princess with my life and I intend to do just that, even if the threat comes from you. If there are consequences, so be it."

"I don't need your permission."

"Good. Because you won't get it. This shouldn't be happening. She's not old enough, and you're too blinded by rage to think straight."

"And what would you suggest I do? Stand back and allow her father to strip her of her innocence?"

Benjamin dropped into the chair beside my desk. "There's no taking it back. Once you do this to her, it can't ever be undone. Will you be able to live with that?"

"Yes," I growled. "And you and Isa are going to assist me. It'll be less traumatic for her if both her guards are present. Do you have a problem with that?"

"Yes," he growled, "but I'm bound to aid you anyway."

We found Emma and Isa sitting on the living room floor, coloring in one of her coloring books. When Isa looked up, doubt clouded her eyes.

I ignored it. This had to be done. If I waited too long... I'd never forgive myself if Albert laid a hand on her. *I moved into the room and sat down behind them on the couch. "Isa, will you give us a moment?"*

Isa stood and whispered, "Of course."

Emma's lip quivered as she watched Isa exit the room. Once we were alone, she looked up at me.

"Come sit down, Princess. We need to talk."

Her heart was racing as she moved to the couch and sat down beside me. Watching my eyes through the tears in hers, she waited for me to speak.

"Do you trust me?" I whispered, fighting back tears of my own.

A tear slipped down her cheek as she nodded.

For a moment, doubt immobilized me. Wiping the tear from her cheek, I whispered, "A nod won't do. I need to hear you answer my questions."

"Yes," she whispered, voice trembling. "I trust you."

"Good. You have no idea how much I worry when you can't be with me."

"What do you worry about?"

"Harm coming to you when I'm not there to protect you."

Her voice was small and uncertain as she asked, "Who would harm me?"

"No one," I took her hand in mine, "if I protect you well enough."

"How?"

I drew a deep breath and barreled past the guilt, "If I give you a part of myself, you'll never be alone. Part of me will always be there to watch over you, no matter how far away I am. Even the Unsighted will sense that you belong to me, and they won't touch you."

"How would you give me part of yourself?" she whispered, looking equally intrigued and terrified.

"That's the part that's going to hurt," I whispered, brushing a stray strand of hair from her face. "But this temporary bit of pain will protect you for life."

"And you'll always be a part of me?"

"Yes, my sweet child. But you must agree to let it happen. I'd never do this without your permission."

"I don't understand."

"I know," I whispered. "Once I explain properly, it will be entirely your decision."

She bit her lip so hard it was a wonder she didn't puncture the flesh. "Do you want to do this?"

For a split second, the room blurred and all that existed was the rapid beat of her innocent heart and the unconditional trust that she placed in me. I wanted to warn her not to let me inside her. I wanted to scoop her into my arms and take off in my car and disappear somewhere Albert would never find us. And God help me, I wanted to do this because the thought of any other man laying a hand on her was unbearable. She belonged to me and I'd never let anyone touch her.

Emma's delicate hand touched my cheek, bringing the world back into focus. "It's okay," she whispered. "Whatever it is, I trust you."

I covered her hand with mine. "It will bind us forever."

"Good." She dropped her head to my shoulder. "I always want to be with you."

I mentally extended to Benjamin and Isa, calling them back to the room. "Then let's get this messy bit over with so we can get to our ice cream."

As Benjamin and Isa walked through the door, Emma squeezed my hand...

...It wasn't until my office door swung open that I realized someone had been knocking. Benjamin stepped in first, studying me with knowing eyes. There were times when our connection was incredibly beneficial. And then there were moments like this, when it was an absolute pain in the ass. *Bygones, boss. You need to focus on today.*

My eyes remained locked with his as the others filed into the room.

"Well this is cozy," Tristan murmured in that perpetual bedroom voice of his.

"*Private* would be a more accurate description," I replied curtly. "At least it would be if any of you knew the definition of the word."

Benjamin dropped into one of the two unoccupied seats in the room. "No time for privacy."

I narrowed my eyes at him. "Well, thank you for enlightening me."

Doc cleared his throat and stepped toward my desk. "I don't believe the Princess has much time left. If she's ever to regain her Sight, we need to act quickly."

I kicked back from my desk and sprung to my feet, making everyone in the room cringe. "Brilliant, Doctor. But what is it that *we* need to do?"

Doc cleared his throat again. "Isa and I believe our best shot at restoring her Sight would be to administer a memory potion, then bombard her with reminders of everything she's forgotten."

I stepped toward him and ignored the pounding of his feeble heart. "And are you *aware* that every time she's reminded of things she's forgotten, the pain in her head becomes unbearable?"

"Yes, sir. I am, but I don't think you fully grasp what I'm saying. She can't go on like this much longer. I'd say she has days at the most."

"Days until *what*?"

"Until her condition becomes permanent. She needs to snap out of this now."

Benjamin motioned for Charlie to sit in the empty seat beside his. "Charlie has another idea."

The virgin refused to meet my eyes as he walked to the chair and sat down.

I moved back to my desk, leaned against it and crossed my arms over my chest. "Then *Charlie* can express the idea himself."

The virgin's stomach was churning. Whatever this idea of his was, he clearly didn't expect me to like it.

"If time is of the essence," I snarled, leaning toward him, "then speak. My Princess is fading away whilst you sit there trying not to piss yourself."

44

CHARLIE

As if it wasn't bad enough that everyone was staring at me waiting for an answer, the Sarrum was eyeing me like a starving predator. He was getting desperate, and that wasn't a good state for someone as powerful as him to be in. He was leaning against the edge of his desk, towering over me. His nostrils were flared. I swear to God his teeth were bared. Flames flickered wildly in his intense blue eyes. And for the first time, I could sense his intentions. He was just a heartbeat away from tearing us all to pieces, especially me. But below that fury was a desperation that didn't sit right on the regal dragon. Emma's blindness was killing him, *literally* killing him. Benjamin said the King was carrying the weight of the world on his shoulders, and I could sense it now. The burden was crushing him. The fire in his eyes flared as he snarled, "Take your time. The Princess is slowly dying in front of us, but don't let that rush you."

The fury in his voice sent a chill down my spine. This was a horrible idea. *Save her or die trying.* "I'd like to pay Emma a visit in Draumer. If she recognizes me there, I think it might help kick start her memories."

A puff of blue smoke wafted from the Sarrum's flared nostrils. "And what makes you think you're so special?"

"She said I was," I muttered, dropping my eyes to my lap and choking back a desperate need to vomit.

"Did she?" he snarled. "How nice for you. And how exactly do you expect your specialness to restore her Sight?"

This was such a bad idea. "She saw me in Draumer, and she knew who I was even though she'd never met me in that world."

A low growl erupted from the Dragon King's throat. "What do you mean *she saw you?*"

Such a stupid idea. I should've written a will before coming. That is, if I had anything to leave to anyone. Or anyone to leave it to. When I looked up, the King was glaring down at me. "She snuck into my room one night when we were at the facility," I muttered, voice breaking as I finished the sentence.

Another growl erupted from deep in the Sarrum's chest. "I hope you intend to be cremated, because I'm going to burn you to nothing but a pile of charred flesh."

A surge of bravery rushed through me as I growled, "Before you do, why don't you *listen* to me? Or is hurting me more important than healing your wife?"

The Sarrum didn't even twitch but my chair flew backward, knocking me on my ass. *You insolent little prick! Don't you dare presume to know the first thing about my feelings for my wife!* Raging heat flared inside my head as if he'd shoved me headfirst into an oven and I doubled over, clutching my head in my hands. *I could kill you now without ever laying a finger on you.*

But you won't. If there's any chance I'm right and I could help Emma, you can't ignore it. The heat intensified and I was sure my brain was melting. In a few seconds, it'd be oozing out my ears. A desperate whimper escaped me as a rush of piss soaked my jeans.

Don't let me stop you. Finish your story. What happened when MY WIFE snuck into your room?

Stop melting my brain, and I'll tell you.

I'm going to enjoy killing you slowly.

No, you're going to fall apart when you lose her for good. Now let me go and listen for once! The heat in my head flared hotter and everything went black...

...I opened my eyes and found myself in a cave that looked similar to the one I'd first met David

Talbot in. But this one was darker and it smelled foul, like stale body fluids.

That would be the puddle of piss you're marinating in.

I blinked my eyes as I sat up and looked around. The Sarrum was seated behind me on a massive chair with black silk cushions. He was in human form, dressed all in black and pissed as hell. I looked down at my pants as his piss puddle comment registered. *Awesome. Way to take a stand. Who wouldn't listen to the suggestions of a guy soaked in his own piss?*

You reek of weakness and fear.

Thanks, boss. You're a real morale booster.

Don't call me that. I doubt you'll ever work for me. If I were you, I'd be more concerned about getting out of here alive.

"Spare me," I growled. "I get it. You've got the biggest balls in the Dream World and we should all cower at your feet. If you're gonna kill me, then kill me. But maybe we should focus on saving Emma before we finish the pissing contest."

"There's no contest," he replied in a frigid tone that made my teeth hurt. "You clearly win in the pissing category."

I looked down at my soiled pants. "Did I piss myself in the waking world too?"

The Sarrum raised an eyebrow and nodded.

Great. I'm sure Rose is super impressed with me now.

"Rose is not your concern," the King snarled. "And if I find out that you've touched her, I'll make certain you live to regret it."

"Blah. Blah. Blah," I growled, ignoring the flames in his eyes. "Isn't that beside the point, right now? Doc said we've only got a couple days before Emma permanently loses her Sight. I don't know about you, but I figure everything other than saving her should go on the back burner and that includes all your *don't-touch-what's-mine* bullshit. If I think I can save Emma, why don't you just let me try? You can kill me, or castrate me, or do whatever your evil heart desires after that, but at least let me give it a shot first."

The Sarrum didn't move a muscle but the brilliant blue flames in his eyes flared even brighter. "So finish your story. What happened after my wife snuck into your room?"

I suddenly realized how dry my mouth and throat were. Without the cushion of all the Sarrum's employees around me, I wasn't sure I could do this. "She snuck in because she couldn't fall asleep and she didn't want to be alone. So I invited her to stay and she fell asleep next to me."

The King didn't speak, but the temperature in the cave skyrocketed until I was drenched in sweat. But I couldn't have cared less. I'd already pissed myself. There wasn't any dignity to worry about preserving.

"Uh." I swallowed, wishing my throat wasn't so dry. "Once she fell asleep, I decided to jump in the Waters and somehow I pulled Emma in with me. We landed on Nellie's beach. We didn't stay long, but she knew who I was and she remembered Nellie."

The Sarrum's voice was bitter calm as he asked, "What else can you tell me about that visit?"

"I don't know... Nellie was pissed that I brought Emma there, and we jumped back in the Waters as soon as a thunderstorm hit."

The King cracked a humorless smile. "That was me, venting frustration."

"Seriously?"

"Yes, seriously. That was the first night the Princess didn't show up in our clearing."

"Yeah," I muttered, "but uh...Emma pushed away from me in the Waters after we left Nellie's beach."

"And when she woke?" the King asked, studying me closely. "Did she remember what'd happened?"

"No. She didn't remember any of it."

"So you're basing your entire theory on a single brief encounter."

"Yeah." I swallowed, in a pointless attempt to work up some spit to wet my mouth. "But it's still worth a shot, isn't it?"

The Sarrum's nostrils flared. Aside from that, he remained motionless. "We haven't got many viable options. This goes against my better judgment, but I suppose we haven't got much to lose at this point and we are running out of time."

I exhaled a heavy breath. "Does that mean you're going to let me try?"

"Yes, but you won't be alone. Benjamin will accompany you to the clearing. Have they taught you anything about mirages?"

They hadn't. Call-me-Art had, but I wasn't stupid enough to mention that I'd been hanging out with Sophie's brother on my days off. "Yeah. I know a little about them."

The Sarrum nodded. "The clearing is a mirage. It's been heavily warded to protect the Princess from the Darkness beyond its borders."

"Protect her from the Darkness?" I whispered. "Or from what *lives* in the Darkness?"

"Demons lie in wait around the entire periphery. As the Princess weakens, they're able to sense her more clearly. Letting you enter that space doesn't sit well with me but I'm desperate enough to give it a try at this point, mostly because Benjamin has such faith in you."

It was a wonder I didn't die of shock. "He does?"

The Sarrum smirked at me. "Shocks you as much as it does me, does it?"

"Yeah. Kinda."

The Dragon King shook his head, probably because he was so darn impressed with the virgin dragon who pissed his pants and couldn't believe someone actually had faith in him. "Time is of the essence. We'll do this tonight and I'll expect all of you to stay at the house until morning."

"Great. But I kinda need some dry clothes."

The Dragon King's nostrils twitched. "I'm sure we can find you something to wear and you can clean up in one of the guestrooms."

"What are you going to tell Emma? Isn't she going to wonder why you're having an employee sleepover?"

"Let me worry about the Princess," the Sarrum replied icily.

"Sure." I raked a hand through my sweat-soaked hair. "You said Benjamin would be going with me to visit Emma in the clearing. Will you be there, too?"

He flashed a terrifying grin. "It's probably best if I don't join you. I'd be extremely tempted to rip your throat out with my teeth."

I touched a hand to my throat. "Okay."

The Sarrum stood up.

And I had to ask, "So what happens when this is all over?"

He took a step closer to me. "I'd say that rather depends on the outcome."

"Meaning?"

"If you help save the Princess, I'd be more inclined to forgive your idiocy."

"Thanks."

He stepped so close that I could smell the dark spicy-scented smoke on his breath. "But if anything goes wrong and my wife is harmed, I'll make you wish you'd never been born."

I blinked, and he disappeared before I even had time to *think* a smartass response.

45

ISABELLA

For the rest of the day, the Talbot home was about as cheerful as a funeral parlor. Emma was running out of time. Everyone knew it, and everyone was on edge because of it. She did seem slightly less troubled after our walk on the beach. Knowing that I was alright and that I didn't hate her seemed to give her a small measure of comfort, but she was still falling apart. And the Sarrum wasn't in much better shape than his wife. Saving me had depleted strength that he didn't have to spare. It was all crumbling—Emma's mind, the Sarrum's strength, the walls of the mirage and their marriage.

We all decided that it'd be best to try one tactic at a time. Once Emma drifted off to sleep, Benjamin was going to bring Charlie to the clearing for a visit.

We were all praying that seeing him would jog her memory but if nothing came of that, Doc and I would administer a memory potion and start bombarding her with reminders of her past in the morning.

We all had a lot of waiting to do until Emma went to bed, and Charlie needed to clean up so I found some spare clothes of Tristan's for him and showed him to one of the guestrooms so he could shower. The poor boy was mortified about losing control of his bladder in front of everyone, but none of us thought any less of him. The Sarrum had that effect on plenty of people, and so did my Benji. Laundering visitors' soiled garments was nothing new to me and honestly, it felt good to get back to my normal routine. The boss had sent the imp packing and from what I could gather, no one was sorry I'd taken her place. Benji hated having to tiptoe around the jumpy creature and the boss despised what she'd done to warrant the sentence. Brian and Tristan didn't really seem to mind her, but those two could find the good in anyone.

I was setting a platter of sandwiches on the coffee table in the lounge when Charlie stepped into the room. His hair was a damp tangle of unkempt locks and his shirt was unfortunately fitted to show off the physique of a Greek God. Charlie was a fine looking boy but no one could fill that shirt quite like Tristan could, except maybe his older brother. Charlie's grin was apologetically bashful, no doubt because of his accident earlier.

I welcomed him in with a comforting smile. "The men are all in the boss's study but they'll be in shortly. Why don't you have a seat and test one of these sandwiches for me?"

Charlie's grin widened as he sat down on the couch. "Sure. Thanks."

I sat down in the chair across the coffee table from him. "You're very welcome."

He grabbed a grilled chicken and Swiss from the platter and settled back against the couch cushions. "And uh, thanks for the clothes and the room to clean up in."

"Don't mention it," I whispered. "No one thinks any less of you for what happened."

"Right," he muttered. "I'm sure they're all super impressed that I wet my pants like a three year old."

"You've no idea how many people the Sarrum and Benji have had that effect on."

He smirked at the mention of my soul mate. "I've heard the Darkness threaten to break Brian's jaw for calling him Benji."

Chuckling softly, I whispered, "Yes. I wouldn't suggest that you call him that. Emma and I are the only people who use the nickname. It's what we've called him since the Princess was a toddler. Benji is a fine name for a little girl's sock monkey."

Charlie took a bite of his sandwich and shook his head. *That form doesn't exactly fit him.*

But it did when the three of us spent our days painting pictures and having tea parties by the lake. Benji is a completely different creature around the Princess. He'd give his life to protect her without giving it a moment's thought.

Charlie grinned and took another bite. *Benjamin's a completely different creature around you, too.*

Yes. He is, and I'd be a different woman without him. May I change the subject?

Sure.

You're doing quite well with your training. From what I understand, you've come a long way in a very short period of time and I don't believe your teachers give you enough credit for that. I'd also like to thank you for donating your blood to heal me.

Yeah. You're welcome. And thanks for the pat on the back. Benjamin doesn't exactly give a lot of those out. Can I ask you something?

Certainly.

What do you think about Emma's relationship with the Sarrum? Isn't it kinda twisted that he raised her like a daughter and then married her?

Who am I to judge anyone's relationship? Let alone the bond between a king and a princess. It's not my place to approve or disapprove, and it certainly isn't yours. You care very much for the Princess, don't you?

Yeah.

That's good. She needs every friend she can get right now, but you need to watch yourself. The Princess belongs to the Sarrum.

I know. It just doesn't sit right.

"What doesn't sit right?" Benjamin's Dark voice thundered from the doorway.

The color drained from the boy's face the instant he heard Benji's voice. "Uh…how lost Emma is. I just hope we can pull her out of this."

Benjamin didn't look at all convinced that Charlie was being truthful. "Watch yourself, virgin or you'll end up getting your throat ripped out before you ever get a chance to pay her a visit."

I was surprised to see Charlie roll his eyes. Even though his back was to Benji, it's not something most creatures would ever dream of doing. My soul mate must've gotten quite close to the boy. "Can I at least finish my sandwich before the throat ripping starts?"

Benji sat down on the other end of the couch and narrowed his eyes at the boy. "You'd better deliver some miraculous results tonight if you're gonna keep being such a smartass."

"Can't we lighten it up a little?" a voice like liquid silk murmured from the doorway. "This is going to be a hell of a long day. Do we really need to up the tension?"

Charlie smiled at Tristan as he plopped down on the couch between the two men. "I'll second that."

Leaning past Tristan, Benjamin eyed the boy. "You don't get a say."

Tristan turned to Benji and planted a kiss on the crown of his bald head. "Lighten up Darkness. What's wrong with having a little fun while we wait for night to fall?"

As Benji was glaring at the incubus, Brian walked in and sat in the chair next to mine. "This is a dark situation, brother. Lightening the mood wouldn't be appropriate."

My Darkness let out a deep chuckle. "Right, because the incubus is all about propriety."

"If no one minds me asking," Charlie muttered, "where's Emma?"

"She's with Doc," I whispered. "He intends to spend most of the day with her."

Swallowing his last bite of sandwich, the boy asked, "Won't she wonder why all of us are hanging around here all day?"

"No," a seductive female voice replied behind me. "I plan to keep her busy after Doc's done with her."

I had to bite my tongue to keep from laughing at the look on Charlie's face as Aubrey walked into the lounge.

46

BENJAMIN

The troll winked at Tristan as she strolled into the lounge. Then she sat herself down on Brian's lap. I half expected the virgin to piss himself again as his thoughts blared in our heads. *Holy crap. I think I'm in love.*

Subtle as always, Tristan burst into laughter as he wrapped an arm around Charlie's shoulders. "Aubrey, you remember the dragon boy?"

Twisting a strand of her silky brown hair around an index figure, the voluptuously curved beauty nodded. "Of course. How could I forget?"

Charlie squinted, like it'd help him recognize her. "Uh, I'm sorry...but when did we meet?" *I'm pretty sure never. I wouldn't forget someone that hot.*

Brian slipped an arm around Aubrey's trim waist and grinned at the kid. "Come on Charlie, I know you didn't forget the swimsuit-model-waitress we met at the Dragon's Lair the day Tristan charmed those two fairies."

The kid looked like he was about to swallow his tongue. Lots of Sighted men swallowed their tongues when they met the troll in the waking world. She was a pretty extreme example of the variations that could exist between a body and soul. The kid's eyes widened as he stared at Brian. *Holy shit. You really weren't kidding!*

"Kidding about what?" Aubrey asked innocently, although I knew damn well there was nothing innocent about the troll. Not from personal experience, but the incubus brothers weren't exactly followers of the don't-kiss-and-tell philosophy.

Face reddening, Charlie cleared his throat. "Sorry. I haven't mastered the art of keeping my thoughts to myself."

Aubrey shot him a seductive grin. "That's okay, dragon boy. Feel free not to keep anything to yourself." *Thoughts, eyes, hands.* The troll blew Tristan a kiss as she melded her supple body to Brian's.

Tristan leaned closer to the kid and whispered, "The four of us could definitely have some fun while we wait for the sun to set."

"Four of us?" the kid muttered, even though he knew damn well who that foursome would include. Isa and I weren't into group shit, and I doubt anyone assumed that we were.

Aubrey let out a throaty moan. "That sounds wonderful, gorgeous. But I'm here to entertain the Princess until nightfall, remember?"

The kid's thoughts took a loud plunge into the gutter, and I reached around Tristan and smacked him on the back of the head. "Aubrey and Emma are old friends. She's here to visit, so the Princess will be too busy to wonder what the fuck we're all doing here."

"Which is somewhat unnecessary," Brian added. "The boss has conducted most of the firm's meetings here since Emma came home. I doubt she'd think twice about us being here."

The troll touched her head to Brian's with a seductive pout. "So I'm not wanted?"

"You're always wanted, angel." Tristan murmured, flashing his signature fuck-me-grin.

"Did I miss a memo about turning this house into the playboy mansion?" Isa asked in a stern maternal voice that made all three naughty children sit up straighter.

Brian shook his head and smiled at her. "No, mam. You didn't."

"Then behave," she whispered, "before I have to turn a hose on the bunch of you."

"Yes, mam," Tristan whispered in a dreamy tone.

The years had done nothing to diminish my soul mate's beauty. Her Hispanic accent coupled with her curves, full lips and chocolate brown eyes still turned heads, and I didn't take kindly to the incubus charming her. Fixing him with a glare that he felt enough to turn toward, I let out a warning growl. *Use the fuck-me-voice on my soul mate again and we'll revisit Charlie's lesson on the unmasking of shadows.*

The incubus stiffened beside me. "Yes, sir. Message received loud and clear."

Isa shook her head, but the slight tug of a grin at the corners of her mouth and the twinkle in her eyes conveyed how she really felt about my warning. "Why don't we make productive use of our time while we're waiting for nightfall? Charlie, do you have any questions about what you've learned so far? We might as well sneak in a lesson."

"Yeah. I've got a few questions." The kid's brow furrowed as he wracked his brain to come up with them. "What's the deal with Light and Dark creatures? I know a Light creature gets weaker in the Darkness, but is the opposite true? Do Dark creatures get weaker in the Light? Or is it a one way thing because pure souls are weaker than tarnished ones?"

Brian fielded the first question. "First of all, you've got to ditch the notion that Light equals good and Darkness equals evil. There are Light souls who wouldn't bat an eyelash at committing horrific crimes, and there are Dark souls who are utterly selfless and devote their lives to helping others."

"Huh," the kid muttered. "So, why are Dark souls called demons and Light ones called angels?"

"Those are just terms that the Sighted adopted," I answered, taking over for Brian. "Dark souls typically dwell in areas with little or no illumination. Lots of us look scary as shit and are capable of nightmarish deeds, but just possessing the ability doesn't make us evil. How you choose to use your abilities is what matters."

"That makes sense," Charlie muttered.

I leaned forward to look the kid in the eye. "To answer your original question, Dark souls don't get weaker in the Light but it's painful for us to stay there for extended periods of time. Our eyes were meant for the Darkness. Being bombarded by all that color and sunlight is torture for us. We also scare the shit out of most Light creatures, so we tend not to feel overly welcome in their sections of the forest."

"I've got another question," Charlie muttered. "Why is the King always a dragon? Isn't that kinda racist? And why is there a King at all? Don't the Sighted believe in democracy?"

I grabbed a sandwich while Tristan tackled that question. "You can't compare Draumer to the waking world. Things aren't as linear and logical there. You can't necessarily get from point A to point B by moving in a straight line and most creatures' actions are more primal in Draumer than in the waking world. Sighted creatures can make rational choices about whether or not to act on their natural inclinations, but the Unsighted are mostly governed by urge and impulse. And many Sighted creatures purposely let their bestial urges guide their behavior, just because they can. A logical democratic government wouldn't work in an often-illogical world. You have to think of Draumer as being more like a jungle. The lion rules because he's the most powerful creature. To keep law breakers in their place, you have to be stronger than they are. A dragon is always King of Draumer because he can kick every other creature's ass. Unruly creatures only obey laws out of fear and sometimes not even then, so the Sarrum has to be powerful enough to follow through with the punishments."

The kid tugged a hand through his hair. "So what exactly do the Purists want to change?"

I swallowed my last bite of sandwich in time to field that question. "Well first off, their nutcase leader believes he should be King. He also believes we should go back to doing things the medieval way."

Charlie arched an eyebrow. "Meaning?"

"He believes that the breeding of new dragons should be accomplished through the use of breeding females."

"Huh?"

"Sighted females kept in captivity to be used solely for pleasure and the making of new dragons."

"Holy crap," the kid muttered.

Isa nodded. "The Purists are a bunch of animals. They also don't approve of the fact that the Sarrum chose his wife because he loved her. They believe he should've wed the dragon he was intended to."

"Who was that?" the kid whispered.

"There are royal families of dragons living in every country in this world," Isa answered. "The Sarrum came to America to attend college because his intended bride's family lived here, but he chose not to go through with that marriage long before Emma was even born and the Purists don't approve of his choices."

"How come nobody's ever found Godric," the kid asked, "or rounded up his followers?"

Brian grabbed a sandwich off the platter and handed it to Aubrey as he answered, "He has powerful supporters all over the place in both worlds. They've aided in his identity changes and relocated him to remote places where he isn't likely to be found. He really only messed up once. The incident with the dragon mother put him on everybody's radar but while she was being tried for murder, his supporters were busy hiding him someplace new. As far as rounding up the supporters goes, it's tough to pinpoint exactly who's aligned with who. They usually only associate with each other in one of the worlds. They could be neighbors who conspire together in Draumer and total strangers in remote parts of the waking world. So a job offer or a group venture orchestrated by two seemingly unconnected people wouldn't set off any bells or whistles."

The kid started to reach for a sandwich but stopped before picking one up. "Why can't the Sarrum fly?"

Tired of feeling confined beside the incubus, I stood up and moved behind Isa's chair. "He's shouldering the weight of the world, remember?"

Charlie slouched against the back of the couch. "Right. Like Atlas. That's what you said before, but what does it mean?"

"All the throat-crushing-chair-throwing-piss-inducing strength that you've witnessed is only a fraction of what the Sarrum is actually capable of. He's literally shouldering the weight of the sky in Emma's mirage and the weaker she gets, the heavier that burden becomes. On top of that he kept Isa alive for months with his magic and he pulled her back from the brink of death the other day. As strong as he appears, you have no grasp of how powerful he truly is. If he ever let go of everything he's holding together, you can't imagine how much he'd be capable of."

"So he can't fly because there's too much weighing him down?" the kid whispered.

I put a hand on Isa's shoulder. "Yeah. That pretty much covers it."

"And the Purists want him weak," Charlie muttered.

"Yeah, kid. They do.

47

We spent the hours till nightfall doing stupid stuff. Before Aubrey took off to hang out with Emma, Tristan suggested we all play strip poker. Knowing Tristan, he probably would've played it even after she left with just about anybody who agreed to. Benjamin shot the strip poker suggestion down pretty quickly, so we settled on regular poker. Even Isa and Benjamin played a few rounds before dinner. After dinner, we all just settled into an anxious silence. The TV was on but none of us were really watching it.

I was a million miles away, lost in my own thoughts. The Sarrum had agreed to let me visit Emma because he was desperate and she was running out of time, but what if I couldn't deliver what I'd promised? Just because Emma recognized me once when she traveled through the Waters with me didn't guarantee that she'd know me when I came strolling into her mirage. And if I failed, I'd probably end up burnt to a crisp. Worse than that, I'd have wasted time that could've been spent bombarding Emma with old memories. No pressure, just the king of the freaking world expecting me to heal his broken princess, or die trying.

In my zoned out state, Doc's soft voice took a few extra seconds to register. "Emma is turning in for the night."

This was it. I looked up at him, heart racing, hands shaking. *Please let this work.*

Doc smiled, acknowledging my fears with his sympathetic eyes. "Come on, Charlie. Benjamin asked me to bring you to him."

I barely felt my legs as I stood and followed Doc out of the room. "I'm not sure I've ever been this nervous before."

"That's understandable," Doc whispered as he led me down the hall.

I followed him up the stairs and down the hall to a spacious guestroom. A massive vase of yellow roses sat on top of the dresser and the whole room smelled like a rose garden. Brightly colored paintings hung on the muted-green walls. A plush comforter with a yellow and green flowery pattern covered the king sized bed, and Benjamin was seated in an armchair across the room with his feet propped on a footstool. It felt like a flashback to the night we took our fieldtrip to the palace but instead of being nervous about what Benjamin might do, I was terrified of what I had to do.

I turned back to Doc. He winked at me, then stepped out of the room and closed the door.

I took a deep breath to steel my nerves. "I'm nervous as hell that this won't work."

"Me too," Benjamin whispered, "but we have to give it a shot."

"Easy for you to say. The Sarrum isn't going to cook you alive."

"You've got this," Benjamin promised. "Just remember, confidence is key."

I let out an unsteady laugh. "Confidence can't work miracles."

"You'd be surprised." Benjamin dropped his head back against the chair and closed his eyes. "No time like the present, kid. Lie down and sleep."

I flipped off the lights, moved to the bed and pulled back the covers. "There's too much adrenaline coursing through me to just fall asleep," I muttered as I crawled into bed and pulled the covers up to my chin.

"You don't want to expend extra energy tonight."

"Right. So are you gonna sing me a lullaby or read me a bedtime story?"

"No," he grumbled from the darkness in the corner, "but I'd be happy to knock you out."

I let out a laugh. "Why don't you scare the crap out of me anymore?"

"Because I don't have any reason to." Benjamin's voice sounded rougher than usual. "Believe it or not, you've earned my respect."

"Words I never thought I'd hear the Darkness say," I whispered.

His deep chuckle was the last thing I heard before drifting off to sleep…

…When I opened my eyes, Benjamin was standing next to me and the silent Waterfall that led to the Dragon King's lair towered in front of us. It was lighter out than the day of our fieldtrip. Our surroundings were clearly visible in muted shades of black. I looked up as a faint rustling of leaves high overhead announced the presence of some sort of creature at the top of the canyon, and a pair of pitch black eyes blinked at me. I turned to Benjamin. "How come it's so much lighter here tonight?"

A proud grin spread across his face. "It isn't."

I craned my neck, knowing a massive castle looked down at us from the other side of the Waterfall, and I wondered if anyone was watching us.

Benjamin touched my shoulder. "Ready?"

I felt like I'd forgotten how to breathe. "Not at all."

"You've got this," he whispered. "Now let's go. Time is of the essence."

Following his lead, I stepped into the pitch black pool at the base of the Waterfall. "Yeah. Thanks for reminding me."

Benjamin didn't respond. He just shook his head and stepped into the Waterfall.

I took a quick glance at the top of the Waterfall, not expecting to see the palace but needing to look anyway. Those black eyes blinked at me again, but I couldn't make out the creature they were attached to. I waved to the floating pair of eyes, then stepped into the Water.

When I stepped out, I wasn't in the great hall of the palace. I was in a dimly lit cave that smelled like the Sarrum and Emma's exotic spiced scent. Faint voices whispered from nowhere and everywhere. I turned around, looking for the source of the noises. I didn't see one but the voices grew louder. They echoed inside my head with a maddening intensity. Some begged me to put an end their agony, others to join them and increase their suffering, but I did my best to ignore their taunts and pleas. It was humid as hell in the breezeless space, and my hair and shirt were instantly matted to me.

Benjamin's deep voice bounced off the stone walls, "What the fuck are you doing?"

I turned, expecting to see a sock monkey. But he was still himself, dressed all in black and looking like a total badass, even more than usual. "How come you're not a monkey?"

He scowled at me. "We aren't in the warded section of the palace yet."

"Where are we then?"

"Somewhere between here and there."

"Thanks. That clears it all up."

He gestured toward a stone corridor that I hadn't noticed until he pointed it out. "Shut up and walk."

"Yes, sir." We moved down the narrow corridor, with me in the lead. The air grew even hotter and thicker and the voices started whispering in my head again. "What is that?"

"Demons mostly."

I stopped and looked back at him. "Could you be more specific?"

"Later," he growled. "Right now, we need to get to the Princess." We reached a wider portion of the corridor and Benjamin fell into step beside me.

"I know everyone keeps telling me not to ask about the Sarrum's relationship with Emma, but why am I the only one who's bothered by the fact that everyone still calls her *the Princess*? Doesn't anybody else think it's sick that he still talks like his wife is his daughter?"

Benjamin stopped moving and narrowed his eyes at me. "That's not why we call her that."

I combed my fingers through my sweat-soaked hair. "What?"

"She *is* a princess of Light, a real live fairy princess, and we've always called her that to acknowledge her title by birthright. She's a queen because she married a king, but she was *born* a fairy princess. The Sarrum has always used it as a term of affection and the rest of us use it to show respect for her heritage."

"Well, now I feel like an ass."

Benjamin started walking again and motioned for me to do the same. "Yeah, you should."

"Wow. Way to make a guy feel better."

The corridor narrowed as it took a sharp turn to the left, and Benjamin took the lead. "It's not my job to make you feel better. It's my job to help you grow a pair and become the dragon you're capable of being."

"What if I'm *not* capable?"

He shook his head without looking back at me. "You are. Steel your confidence and focus."

"So I was wrong about the princess title, but that doesn't mean he isn't a pedophile. He coerced an innocent girl into a relationship she was way too young for. Tell me that's not wrong."

Benjamin stopped moving as we reached the Waterfall that silently spilled from ceiling to floor at the end of the corridor. "You've got that backwards." He stepped into the Water before I could ask what he meant.

I followed after him and stepped out in a brighter corridor. It took my unadjusted eyes a second to make out the sock monkey in front of me, but I was too preoccupied with his last statement to find the humor in it. "Are you saying Emma forced *him* into a sexual relationship?"

It was impressive how much emotion his stuffed monkey face could convey. He stood there with his toy arms crossed and his knit brows furrowed into an oddly terrifying scowl. "Now you're getting it."

"That doesn't make any sense."

Sock monkey Benjamin shook his head as he marched down the short corridor toward the entrance of the cave. "It's also none of your fucking business."

I followed him, trying to process his words and come up with a response but the view outside the cave stopped me—Emma's clearing. It was exactly like the vision I had at the facility. I shook off the twinge of arousal that the memory ignited. She was naked in that vision. She was also staring up at me like she wanted me desperately. *Not me* I reminded myself, *her husband.* Outside the cave, a full moon hung low in the star covered sky and a lake sparkled in the distance, reflecting the radiance of the moon and stars. It was breathtakingly serene, and it shouldn't exist in the heart of the Dark forest. No wonder the Sarrum was exhausted. Holding all that together couldn't be easy.

I stepped out of the cave ahead of Benjamin. "Where's Emma?"

"She's with Isa," he whispered, stepping beside me.

"Is the Sarrum here, too?"

Monkey Benjamin shook his head. "He's close enough to sense how she's doing but not close enough to rip out your throat."

I touched a hand to my throat. "Where are Emma and Isa?"

"By the lake."

With each step I took toward the lake, my throat felt drier. The pounding of my heart drowned out the peaceful chirping of nocturnal birds and insects. Sweat broke out on my forehead and the back of my neck, and other places I won't mention, as Emma's words echoed in my head. *What I feel for you is different.* What if she didn't recognize me? There'd be no good reason for that to hurt me. But I knew if it happened, I'd be crushed. I swallowed as I spotted Emma and Isa on a bench by the lake.

China doll Isa looked over her shoulder at me. I turned to say something to Benjamin, but he was already retreating toward the cave so I turned back and waved. Isa waved back, then said something to Emma.

I stopped breathing as Emma turned around. This was it. *Save her or die trying.*

48

EMMA

Isa and I were sitting on a bench by the lake. She was telling me how much she'd missed me while she was away on her trip but for the life of me, I couldn't remember where she'd gone. Whenever I tried, my head started aching so I just nodded and pretended I knew what she was talking about. I got the feeling she wasn't convinced but she didn't call me out on it. Isa was in the middle of a sentence when the world stilled. The breeze died off. The night creatures stopped their distant chirping and buzzing. Even the surface of the lake grew quiet. Isa twisted sideways to look behind us and grinned. "You have a visitor."

A visitor? I didn't get visitors. My circle of family was pretty small and it wasn't safe to let anyone outside that circle into the clearing. Confused, I turned around and the breath escaped my lungs in a rush. "Charlie?"

Isa kissed my forehead as she stood from the bench. "I'll leave you to your visit."

When I turned to ask what was going on, she was already gone. I turned back toward the clearing and watched her enter the cave with Benji. Then I stood as my unexpected visitor reached me.

"Hey, Em," he whispered.

"Charlie?"

A huge smile lit up his face. "You remember me?"

"I, uh…yes." The rest of the world seemed to go out of focus. "But I don't understand." He was a memory from that other life I kept remembering, the one I'd never lived. None of this made any sense.

"You and I knew each other at the facility," he whispered. "Remember?"

I looked back at the cave, not really sure what I was expecting to see. "I do, but…I don't understand. Why do I remember things that never happened? Have I lost my mind?"

Charlie shook his head. "No. You just lost some memories, and I came here to help you get them back."

"How?" I struggled to ignore the ache in my head. "This doesn't make any sense."

Charlie took my hand and started toward the lake, gently pulling me along with him. "It does make sense. Trust me."

"I do," I muttered, numbly moving beside him. "I don't know why I trust you or how I know you, but I do trust you. You and I are pretty close, aren't we?"

Charlie squeezed my hand. "Yeah, Em. We are."

I tried to fight back the tears, but more kept coming as the ache in my head intensified. "Why do I remember a life I never lived?"

Charlie stopped walking. "You did live it, Em. You just didn't live it here."

It felt like my stomach had tied itself in knots. "That doesn't make any sense. I've always been here."

He let out a troubled sigh. "No, you haven't."

"What do you mean?" I whispered, unable to keep my voice from shaking.

"You've only lived half your life here."

"No." The pain in my head was almost unbearable. "I've never been anywhere else and I've never met you before. So, why do I feel like I could tell you anything?"

"Because you can," he whispered, wiping a tear from my cheek.

I reached up and touched his hand, half expecting not to feel it. "But I don't know you."

"Yes, you do."

"But..." I struggled for words and when the right words escaped me, I whispered, "I shouldn't."

"I'd be hurt if you didn't." He took my hand in his and lowered it from my face. "You're the closest friend I've ever had, and I came here to help you get over this."

"Over what?" I muttered, pulling my hand away.

"Your blindness."

I squeezed my eyes shut, bracing myself against the pain. "I can see just fine."

"You're only seeing half of what you should," Charlie whispered, "and that's all you're remembering."

"What are you talking about?" I opened my eyes and tried to search his for a grain of logic in this insanity.

"We know each other in the waking world, Em."

"What?" Even as I questioned him, I knew it was true.

"Those other memories of yours are from the waking world. That's where you live the other half of your life."

"I don't—." This was all too much to process.

"Yeah," Charlie whispered, "you do."

The knots in my stomach tightened. The world started spinning and before I even realized I was falling, Charlie was catching me as a rush of memories washed over me... *A man from that other world showing up and calling me his daughter... David stopping him from hurting me... His blood drenching my skin and my clothes... David carrying me into the palace, everything hazy and distant as the doctor poured something sweet down my throat... Everything I'd ever been slipping away in the Waters... A fierce creature with angry features carrying me off... David setting the Waters on fire and killing that creature, killing everyone who got in our way...* "I'm scared, Charlie."

As the clearing came back into focus, Charlie smiled at me but a rush of hot air stole his attention.

And time stopped.

49

DAVID

S itting inside the palace while the Princess was out in the clearing with the virgin was killing me. Brian had come to my study armed with an ample supply of paperwork, matters I'd been neglecting. He meant well, but nothing could possibly take my mind off what was happening beyond the Waterfall across the room. I pushed back from my desk, stood and started pacing the floor like a caged animal. As I moved, my thoughts drifted to the day I stole Emma away from the Reeds with a promise of ice cream...

...As Benjamin and Isa walked back into the living room, Emma squeezed my hand.

I threaded my fingers through hers. "Don't be frightened. You're safe with me. You'll always be safe with me."

Her lower lip quivered as she whispered, "I know."

I drew her closer to my side.   "Would you like me to explain what I intend to do?"

The Princess bit her lip and nodded.

"It pains me to let you out of my sight," I whispered. "I worry a great deal about your safety, which is why I want to leave something of myself inside you to watch over you."

"How?"

"Do you remember your lessons on enchantments?"

"Yes," she answered proudly. "They're dragon magic."

"Very good," I whispered, tilting her chin up so I could look her in the eye. "And how are they created?"

"With a dragon's blood."

Nodding, I whispered, "More specifically?"

"The dragon's blood is inked into the recipient's skin," she recited verbatim, "and the dragon's intent when the blood is drawn determines how the enchantment will function."

"Excellent," I whispered. "My intent is to protect you when I can't be there to do it myself. A piece of me will remain bound to you."

"What will it do?"

"Whenever you feel frightened, the enchantment will awaken. You'll see it, and other Sighted individuals will see it. The Unsighted won't, but they'll feel it if they intend to harm you."

"What will they feel?" she whispered, more curious than fearful.

"The enchantment will hurt them," I answered softly. "And the more severe the hurt they mean to cause you, the more severe the pain they'll feel. If need be, it will kill them."

"That's kind of scary," she whispered.

"It shouldn't be. It will be a piece of me and it would never harm you in any way."

"What if someone wants to hurt me, but I don't know it?"

"It will still sense danger and eradicate the source."

"What if I just want to see you? Or I can't fall asleep and I don't want to be alone in the dark?"

"You can call it forth at any time. It will always come for you."

"How do I call it?" she whispered. "Do I touch the tattoo?"

"You can, but you don't have to. It will come simply if you wish it to."

"Neat."

I couldn't help smiling. "I'm glad you think so, but you must understand that the enchantment can never be undone. This part of me will be with you for the rest of your life."

"I'd like that." She looked up at me. "Is it going to hurt a lot?"

"We must both be awake when the process begins. Isa will ink the tattoo and as soon as she begins, I'll draw you into the Waters. We'll stay in the clearing until she's finished."

"And then we can have ice cream?"

"Yes my sweet girl, you can have all the ice cream you'd like."

"How do you plan to keep her family from noticing that you've marked her?" Benjamin growled from the doorway.

Mentally warning him not to frighten the Princess, I replied, "The mark needn't be much larger than a pin-prick. If we place it on her scalp beneath her hair, no one will be the wiser."

As Isa slipped out of the room to gather the necessary supplies, Emma and I moved to the floor to color a picture in her coloring book...

...Benjamin was waiting for me when I returned from driving Emma home that night. I didn't take more than two steps in the house before he came storming into the foyer.

I slipped out of my shoes and started down the hall. "It's been a long night. Can this wait until morning?"

"No," Benjamin growled as he followed me down the hall to the lounge. "Did you think I wouldn't notice?"

I stepped behind the bar, grabbed two tumblers and a bottle of single malt and poured us both a drink. "I'm sure I don't know what you're talking about."

"Cut the crap," the shadow growled. "We both know you can't hide anything from me."

I handed him one of the drinks, then carried mine to the couch. Sinking back against the cushions, I took a slow sip before answering, "What exactly are you taking issue with now?"

"All of it," he growled as he sat down in the chair across from me. "But you knew that already, and you know exactly what I'm talking about."

I propped my feet up on the coffee table. "Indulge me. Pretend that I don't, and say it to my face."

"Your intent," he growled. "Did you think I wouldn't notice?"

"Notice what?" I snarled, tired of being badgered by my own shadow.

"You intended the enchantment to prevent any man from laying a hand on her."

"AND?"

Setting his drink on the coffee table, Benjamin glared at me as he leaned forward. "You didn't specify for it to happen only if what the man intended was against her will."

"Are you suggesting that a child would want to be touched in that way?"

"You know damn well what I'm suggesting. She won't be a child forever, but that enchantment will be with her for life."

"Then are you implying that I mean to touch my own child in an inappropriate way at some point?"

"I'm not implying anything. I'm flat out saying that dragons don't give up their treasures, but you know damn well you can't keep her forever."

"Do I?"

"The mirage was woven with the magic of childhood innocence. You can't expect Emma to stay innocent forever, and you shouldn't want her to. She deserves to grow up and live a normal life."

"This discussion is pointless," I growled. "She is still a child now and she will be for quite some time. When she's ready, I fully intend to let my little bird fly from the nest. My intent was quite open to interpretation and you are well aware of that. Now, this conversation is over and I don't want to hear you speak of it again until the Princess is no longer a child."

"You won't want to hear it then either," Benjamin muttered. "Whether or not you admit it, I know you'll never give her up." With that, he hopped from his chair and stormed out of the room...

..."I'm not helping at all, am I?" Until he spoke, I'd almost forgotten Brian was in the room.

I returned to my chair and forced an apologetic smile. "I'm not sure there's anything that could take my mind off what's happening in the clearing.

Brian shut the ledger he'd been pouring over. "Charlie's a good guy."

"I'm afraid I haven't yet come to that conclusion just yet."

"He cares about the Princess."

I turned toward the Waterfall to view the clearing beyond it. "I'm not sure that makes me feel better about leaving him alone with her."

"I'd trust him with my life," Brian muttered, "so would Benjamin and Tristan."

"Yes, I know. That's exactly what Benjamin did the day the boy insulted my integrity and called me a pedophile."

"Yeah." Brian turned toward the clearing. "I'm not saying Charlie can't be an idiot. I'm just saying that I believe his intentions are good and I trust him to do the right thing."

"And what is the right thing?"

"Today? It's healing Emma."

I was about to reply when a wrongness writhed in the pit of my stomach, and then my worst nightmare came true.

50

CHARLIE

Emma remembered me. I felt like I could do anything. Heal her. Save her. Fix all the wrongs in her life. She swooned, and I caught her in my arms and lowered her to the grass. My temperature skyrocketed as I looked at the pained expression on her face. I would endure years of torture to spare her that suffering.

As her eyes met mine, she looked so fragile and lost. "I'm scared, Charlie."

A sheen of sweat erupted all over me as I answered with a reassuring smile. I was so focused on her that it took a few seconds to grasp why I felt so warm. As the realization struck me, I shoved a hand in my pocket and the moonstone seared the flesh on my palm as I yanked it out. A massive heat wave sucked all the air from the clearing, stealing the breath from my lungs. The ground shook, and the stone fell from my hand.

"Remarkable," Call-me-Art whispered. "They really do undervalue you, Charlie. You have no idea how long I've been trying to penetrate this mirage." The way he eyed Emma as he said the word *penetrate* turned my stomach.

Still struggling for breath, I barely managed to choke out his name, "Art?"

That familiar perpetual laughter glinted in his eyes. "Surprised to see me?"

"Yeah." I hugged Emma a little tighter. "What's going on?"

"Come now, Charlie," Art murmured, his eyes still fixed on Emma. "You're a smart lad. Figure it out."

"Who are you?" Emma asked in a trembling whisper.

A sinister grin spread across Art's face. "I'm delighted to finally meet you, Princess. You're every bit as beautiful as the rumors proclaim you to be, which is remarkable in its own right as that's so often not the way of things."

Dread rose in my chest as I growled, "You didn't answer her question." I heard shouting in the distance but my tunnel vision remained focused on Art.

"Sorry," he murmured, "but I'm afraid I haven't got much time to chat." He took a step toward me, knelt and touched my shoulder. And every muscle in my body locked.

As much as I strained against it, I couldn't stop him from taking Emma into his arms. He must've immobilized her too, because she didn't even try to fight it. Powerless to help her, all I could do was whisper, "Why?"

Art grinned at me as the distant shouts drew nearer. "Because I want the Sarrum to hurt like I've hurt. I want him to know the agony of losing the one creature who's more precious to him than anything else could ever be."

Time seemed to be moving faster for the three of us, because the shouting voices still hadn't reached us. "This is to get back at him for killing Sophie?"

The laughter in his eyes blazed brighter. "I don't give a damn about that whore."

"But…" I muttered, desperately struggling against whatever he'd done to freeze me, "she was your sister."

Chuckling softly, he murmured, "Let me give you a piece of advice, Charlie. Don't believe everything you're told. I played you like a fiddle, told you everything you wanted to hear and led you toward the conclusions I wanted you to reach."

"What?" My chest was aching from my desperate efforts to move. *Emma was right there* but all the adrenaline pumping through me still wasn't enough to unlock my muscles and help her.

Art took a step back from me. "Tell your Dragon King that I'm going to enjoy ripping his Princess to shreds from the inside, just as he did to my sister."

"But…" *Why did their shouting still sound so distant?* "You just said Sophie wasn't your sister."

His grin widened as he took another step back. "You still haven't figured it out? My sister gave birth to the King who sits the throne. He tore his way out of her body like a reptile from a useless shell, drained every bit of life from her and gorged himself on her magic. And I've been waiting his entire life for this precise moment."

"You said you weren't with the Purists," I whispered, hoping to stall him till the others could reach us.

He laughed like he didn't have a care in the world. "No. I said I wasn't one of Henry Godric's followers. I follow no one. The Purists follow me."

I fought against my invisible bindings so savagely that it's a wonder my muscles didn't rip from the bone, but I still didn't move an inch. "Don't do this."

All the laughter drained from Henry Godric's eyes. "I did enjoy our little chats, Charlie. If the Sarrum doesn't tear you apart, perhaps one day you can join me."

Another massive heat wave barreled through the clearing, knocking me backward before I could answer. When it was gone, so was Godric.

And he took Emma with him.

The instant they vanished, a thunderous roar shook the ground. The magnitude of its fury was incomprehensible, but it didn't scare me. All my fear was focused on what would happen to Emma. I'd never loathed myself this deeply before. I wanted the Dragon King to tear me to pieces. Even that would be less torture than I deserved.

A second later, Benjamin was yanking me to my feet. "What the fuck did you do?"

"I uh... I swear I didn't do anything on purpose." Tears pooled in my eyes as I muttered, "Henry Godric took Emma."

As Isa caught up to Benjamin, she crouched down and picked up the moonstone. "Where did this come from?"

"Godric gave it to me," I whispered, choking back the need to vomit. "But I didn't know it was him until now. He introduced himself as Arthur, before I even came to Sycamore Lane. He warned me not to trust everything I was told and offered to give me another point of view when I wanted one." Panic gripped me, sinking its claws deep in my chest as Benjamin glared at me. "Oh God!" I muttered. "What did I do?"

A surge of molten fury rammed into me, and I flew backward several feet and landed on my back with the wind knocked out of me. *I will rip you apart for this, you traitorous piece of filth!* In the blink of an eye, the Sarrum was towering over me. *Where did he take her?*

Without laying a finger on me, the Sarrum was constricting my throat so I could only answer with my thoughts. *I don't know. I swear to God, I didn't know who he was. I would never do anything to hurt Emma.*

YOU JUST DID! The Dragon King turned to Isa. "Go back to the waking world and rouse her! And do not let her sleep until I've found her!"

"Of course." Isa dropped the stone and took off running toward the cave.

A furious growl rumbled in the Sarrum's chest as he bent to retrieve the discarded stone. "You'd better pray he doesn't lay a finger on her!"

"Sarrum." Benjamin stepped toward us as he spoke. "You'll never get her back with the burden you're carrying."

Sapphire flames danced in the King's eyes as he snarled, "And what would you suggest I do? Let the world I aim to bring her back to crumble?"

"No," he whispered. "Charlie will hold it together for you."

The flames in the Sarrum's eyes grew brighter as he bared his teeth at Benjamin. "You must be joking!"

"He fucked up," the shadow replied calmly. "There's no denying that, but he did it out of stupidity. He'd never hurt the Princess on purpose. Let him make up for it."

"YOU EXPECT ME TO PLACE TRUST IN HIM AFTER WHAT JUST HAPPENED?" the Sarrum's voice thundered aloud and inside my head.

"Yes, I do." Benjamin took a quick glance at me. "Charlie can do this, and you need to get the hell out of here with your full strength."

The King exhaled, and I felt the heat of his breath on my face. "Need I remind you that it's not just the mirage that I'm holding together?"

"No," the shadow replied softly, "but he can handle it. He wouldn't let the Princess's strength slip, not for anything."

The Dragon King's nostrils flared as he placed a foot on my chest. "Fuck this up and I'll make you regret it in ways too horrific for you to imagine!"

"If I fuck up," I managed to croak, "I'll want you to."

The flames in the Sarrum's eyes grew so blindingly bright that I had to shield my eyes, and his breath felt hot enough to blister my face as he growled, "Do you promise to shoulder this burden and guard it as I would?"

"Yes," I whispered. "Please, let me help."

He took his foot off my chest and I hurried to my feet and looked him square in the eye, which wasn't an easy task. Staring into those brilliant flames was like staring straight into the sun.

He gripped my shoulder with a claw that I felt but couldn't see and snarled, "Do not fail."

"I won't—"

"The burden is yours dragon. Guard it with your life."

As he spoke the words, the weight of a mountain fell on me, crushing me to the ground face first, squeezing the air from my lungs and splintering my bones. And I ached with an intensity that I never would've imagined possible. *This was what he'd been carrying the whole time?*

Somehow, I managed to turn my head enough to watch the Sarrum step toward his shadow. "If he fails, it's on you."

I could feel Benjamin's fear, but the shadow didn't flinch. "He won't."

The King's voice was low and furious as he growled, "Watch him."

Benjamin nodded. "I won't leave his side. He's ready for this. I'd bet my life on it."

A puff of blue smoke escaped the Dragon King's flared nostrils. "But you aren't betting your life, you're betting the Princess's life."

"All the more reason I'd never fail you," Benjamin whispered. "The kid can handle it. Give him the rest of the burden."

The rest? My body was already crushed beneath the weight of a mountain. *How much more could there be?*

I craned my neck just enough to watch the human King advance two steps. Then in one fluid movement, he seamlessly transitioned into dragon form as he gracefully took to the sky. The beat of his monstrous wings shook the trees and whipped the quiet surface of the lake into a violent torrent of waves. With a bellow that rattled the bones inside me, the Dragon King exhaled and ignited the heavens in a blaze of blue flames. Then he tore through the burning fabric of the sky, leaving a gaping black hole. It sealed behind him almost instantly and the weight on top of me tripled, crushing me with such force that the ground beneath me sunk several inches.

51

ISABELLA

I sprang out of bed the second my eyes opened, raced to the hallway and started pounding on Doc's door. "Doctor! Wake up! The Princess needs you!" I didn't wait for an answer but as I rushed into Emma's room, I heard Doc's door open behind me.

"What's going on?" he muttered as he followed me through the door.

I sat down on the bed beside the Princess's soulless body. "We need to wake her, and we can't let her sleep until the Sarrum's found her!"

Doc moved to her bedside and whispered, "What happened?"

"Godric took her!" I grabbed Emma by the shoulders and shook her. "Emma! Wake up!"

She let out a whimper but her eyes didn't open.

There were tears in my eyes as I looked up at Doc. "We have to get her out of there!"

Doc rounded the bed. "Keep shaking her and shouting."

"Where are you going?"

"Shake and shout!" Doc marched into the bathroom and quickly returned with a wastebasket full of water.

Dread churned in my stomach as a tear slid down the Princess's cheek. I shook her a little harder. "Wake up, Emma! Open your eyes!" Thankfully, fairies disappear from Draumer when they wake in this world. If we could just keep her awake, Godric wouldn't be able to harm her. But until she woke, she was in that monster's hands. And God only knew what he'd do to her.

Without asking me to back away, Doc moved to Emma's bedside and tossed the water from the wastebasket in her face.

Emma's eyes were wild with terror as she bolted upright. "Why did you do that?"

Doc shot me a sideways glance. *Charlie's visit didn't work?*

Apparently not.

Then it's time for plan B.

I combed the wet strands of hair off Emma's face with my fingers. "You need to stay awake." The Princess looked at me like I'd lost my mind, and I mentally reached out to Doc. *How am I going to explain this?*

Leave that to me. "I'm afraid I miscalculated the dosage on your medication this evening. It'd be dangerous for you to sleep until it's out of your system. So we need to keep you awake for a while."

Emma's eyes darted back and forth between the two of us. "You didn't give me any medication."

Doc's brow furrowed as he nodded. "Short term memory loss. It's a common side effect, especially with the dose you ingested."

"I don't understand," Emma muttered. She couldn't remember her abduction but she still seemed agitated, as if some dormant part of her mind recalled the trauma.

"You won't be alone," I whispered. "We're going to wait this out with you."

"How?"

"Well for starters," Doc answered as he started toward the door, "I'm going to make some strong coffee." *Thank heavens we brought the memory potion with us.*

As he stepped out of the room, I moved to Emma's dresser and grabbed a dry set of clothes. Then I moved back to the bed and held them out to her. "Why don't you change into these while I grab a movie for us to watch?"

"Alright." Looking thoroughly confused, Emma took the clothes and moved to the bathroom.

As soon as she shut the door, I opened the armoire that concealed a flat screen television, DVD player and an eclectic selection of movies. I grabbed the horror movie that hadn't been viewed since the Princess was a teenager and whispered, "Sorry, Princess."

"Sorry for what?"

"Nothing," I muttered. "I was just talking to myself."

Emma crossed the room and took the DVD from my hand. "Why did you get this out?"

Because I'm praying it'll jog your memory. "I figured a horror movie would be the perfect thing to help keep you awake."

"I hate scary movies."

"But you've watched this one before, remember?"

Emma cringed and squeezed her eyes shut. "Well, I don't want to see it again."

A pang of guilt gripped me and I had to remind myself that the pain in her head was a sure sign that I was on the right track.

"Sweet," a silky voice murmured from the doorway. "You didn't start without us!" Tristan stepped in the room dressed in a fitted t-shirt and pajama pants and Brian walked in after his brother, also wearing pajamas and carrying a large ceramic bowl full of popcorn.

I let out a sigh of relief and grinned at the brothers. *Thank you.*

We're in this for the long haul. Tristan winked at me as he sat down on the bed, but he bolted back up the second he realized the bedding was sopping wet.

Emma stifled a laugh and shook her head. "Doc's idea of a wakeup call. Why don't we go to the living room?"

Emma was laughing! Tristan was a Godsend.

Brian smiled at the Princess and motioned to the door. "After you, my dear."

Emma tossed the DVD on the foot of the bed and started toward the door.

As Tristan moved to follow her, I grabbed his arm. *We need to play THAT movie. There are powerful memories attached to it.*

With a slight nod, Tristan grabbed the DVD. Then he caught up to Emma and held it out to her. "Why'd you toss it? I've always wanted to see this movie."

She shook her head without slowing down. "You're welcome to borrow it."

"No time like the present," Tristan purred.

As she led our procession down the stairs, Emma shook her head. "I don't want to watch it."

Brian raced ahead to descend the staircase beside the Princess. "Come on, I'm in the mood for a horror movie, too."

Emma's voice sounded strained as she answered, "Then maybe you boys should watch it in the lounge."

"No way," Tristan murmured, stepping off the stairs. "We're here to help you stay awake."

Emma led our procession into the living room without slowing down. "I don't like that movie."

"Then why do you own it?" Brian asked as he settled onto the couch beside her.

"I wanted to watch it once," she whispered, squeezing her eyes shut, "when I was almost sixteen. My mother said R-rated movies were off limits until I turned seventeen, but my father had no problem with me seeing it. So David bought it for us to watch while my parents were out of town for the weekend."

Brian sat the popcorn bowl down next to him. "And you didn't like it?"

"I, uh…" Emma winced and touched her hands to her temples.

Kneeling on the floor in front of her, Tristan placed his hands over hers and she slipped hers out and dropped them to her sides. As Tristan's fingers worked their magic on her temples, he whispered, "You're a big girl now. I'm sure you can handle the movie. Who knows? Maybe you'll even like it now that you're older."

"I don't—"

"Shhh," Tristan interrupted, kneading her scalp with his magic fingers. "Come on, sweetheart. Watch it for me? I'll keep working on your headache."

She chuckled softly without opening her eyes. "Does any girl ever say no to you?"

"Only you," he whispered, planting a kiss on her forehead, "but tonight, you're going to say yes."

He was laying his charm on so thick that I was beginning to feel it across the room, but the Princess looked more relaxed than I'd seen her in ages.

"Fine," Emma whispered as the tension visibly melted from her body. "But you owe me."

"Any day. Anytime," Tristan murmured. "Just name your price."

Doc grinned at me as he peeked his head into the room. "Coffee's ready. Can I get some volunteers to help me carry it in?"

As Brian hopped off the couch, Tristan gave me a subtle nod. *I'll stay with the Princess.*

I was about to head to the kitchen when Emma's eyes popped open. "Where's David?"

Damn it.

Tristan stood from the floor and sat down on the couch beside her. "He got an urgent call from a client who found himself into some legal trouble, and he had to go meet him at the police station."

The uncertainty in Emma's eyes was painful to witness. She'd lost trust in her husband. Telling her that he'd slipped out in the middle of the night "because he had to work" might not have been such a great idea, but what were we supposed to tell her? That her husband couldn't be disturbed because he'd turned into a dragon and flown off to rescue her from the monster-who-would-be-King?

52

CHARLIE

I'd majorly fucked everything up. Emma was gone. The Sarrum's worst enemy had her, and it was all my fault. I tried to suck in a breath but it's hard to breathe when there's a mountain crushing your spine. I couldn't last much longer like this. On top of everything else I'd screwed up, the Sarrum would have no safe place to bring Emma back to when he found her. I couldn't have sucked more at life if I purposely tried to.

"Are you done?" Benjamin's deep growl snapped me to my senses enough to realize I'd squeezed my eyes shut. With a massive amount of effort, I lifted my eyelids and found Benjamin sitting on the grass beside where I laid, pinned on my stomach.

I didn't have enough air in my lungs to answer him out loud. *Done with what? Living?*

"No," he growled, "wallowing in your own failure." I was glad I couldn't turn my head enough to see his face. The disappointment in his voice was hard enough to stomach.

I fucked EVERYTHING up! Emma is God knows where with a man who plans to tear her apart! And I'm the moron who brought him to her!

"And how is your whining helping the situation?"

What?

"You don't have time for self-pity. This place is gonna start crumbling soon, and you're our only hope of keeping that from happening."

Well that's a shame because I'm a hopeless failure.

"You're done whining!" Benjamin grabbed a fistful of my hair and yanked my head off the ground so he could look me in the eye. "Now focus! Or I'll kill you before the weight on your back does!"

I can't even breathe!

"You can," he growled, emphasizing the words by giving my hair another tug.

Way to kick a man when he's down!

"This isn't about you!" Benjamin snarled. "You want to fix this? Focus on my words!" He yanked my head up a little farther. That's when I realized he wasn't a sock monkey anymore. Out of it as I'd been, I hadn't noticed that he'd turned into a turbo charged version of scary-as-hell Benjamin. His eyes were pitch black. Not just the iris, his entire eye was black. And the air around him felt cold and *wrong*. I would've pissed myself but any fluids in me had already leaked out when the mountain flattened me, and I was so overwhelmed by excruciating pain that I didn't even care. "Breathe!" he growled.

I can't—

"BREATHE!" he commanded, his voice even Darker. "I'M NOT ASKING YOU. I'M TELLING YOU! I MAY BE A PATIENT TEACHER, BUT I'M AT THE END OF MY FUCKING ROPE. SO OPEN YOUR MOUTH AND BREATHE!"

There was a fury in his tone that I didn't dare question. Pointless as it was, I tried to suck in a breath. *And I did.*

He didn't wait for me to catch my breath before yanking my head back farther. "Look at the sky."

The flames that the Sarrum had breathed across the sky were dying down. Now the night sky looked transparent and I could actually see the massive invisible dome that encompassed the mirage.

Benjamin gave my hair another tug. "LOOK CLOSER!"

When I did, I saw the cracks. Thin fissures blacker than the black sky were spreading all over the dome.

"LOOK BEYOND THE WALLS."

I squinted and tried to focus beyond the fractures, but I couldn't see anything past the cracks in the darkness.

"You can't hide any longer dragon," the Darkness growled in a bestial tone. "It's time to take your place in this world."

I *felt* his words more than I heard them. They slid down my throat and ignited deep in my belly. Somewhere in the distance, a low growl answered Benjamin. My heart skipped a beat. My chest tightened and a rush of desires coursed through me, filthy primal animalistic urges. I wanted to be disgusted by them. Really, I did. But the Dark desires aroused me. I probably should've felt ashamed by that, but all I really felt was raw bestial greed. *What's happening to me?*

"DON'T FIGHT IT, DRAGON!" Benjamin's Dark voice commanded.

That fierce growl answered him again. *Where the hell is that coming from?*

"COME OUT DRAGON! YOUR TIME TO HIDE IS OVER!"

The growl came again, lower and angrier than the last. And Dark primal need gripped me. I needed to find Godric and rip him to shreds. I ached to sink my teeth into his throat and tear his chest open with my bare hands. I wanted to coat the mirage with his blood as a warning to other demons to stay the fuck away from her! Another growl snapped me to my senses. *Where did all that come from? Sure, I hate Godric and he deserves to die. But—*

"FOCUS, DRAGON!" Benjamin demanded. "LIS-TEN TO MY VOICE AND FIND YOUR WAY OUT

OF THE DARKNESS. IF YOU DON'T EMERGE, THE PRINCESS WILL BE AT RISK. IT'S YOUR DUTY TO GUARD HER HOME NOW."

Another growl rumbled, shaking the earth beneath my chest. *No.* The growl *came* from my chest.

"WAKE DRAGON!" Benjamin's voice no longer sounded human. This voice was all demon. Dark. Furious. And terrifying. "LOOK AT THE WALLS, DRAGON!" the Darkness commanded, yanking my head back by the hair.

I saw the night sky and the fissures that covered it, but I could see *beyond* that now. All along the perimeter, demons were waiting to come in. Some clawed at the walls of the mirage. Some gnawed at them and licked them. Winged beasts were perched on top of the dome, drool dripping from their lips as they stared down into the Princess's home. Their collective growls filled my head. They all wanted in. They all wanted *her*. They'd been waiting years to claim her. The Light creature had offered herself up to the Darkness a very long time ago and they'd been patiently waiting for this moment ever since. The Dragon King wasn't there to stop them. They'd take her as soon as she returned and they'd tear each other apart fighting over her.

A deep growl rumbled in my chest, a warning growl. *TOUCH HER AND I'LL BURN YOU ALL ALIVE!* Horrified, I looked up at the Darkness.

He didn't look any different but he *felt* different. Fear prickled the air around him. I could sense it enough to be disturbed by it, but the demons beyond the walls were writhing in agony. A gruesome smile spread across the Darkness's face as he watched them. Then he turned to me. "COME OUT DRAGON! THE PRINCESS NEEDS YOUR HELP! OR WOULD YOU STAY HIDDEN WHILE THESE MONSTERS VIOLATE HER?"

I sprang to my feet with a ravenous growl. *NO ONE WILL ENTER THIS SPACE! AND NO ONE WILL TOUCH HER!* They were my words. I felt myself *think* them and I could tell the beasts beyond the walls heard them. Some clapped their hands over their ears. Some whimpered and lowered their faces to the dirt, draping talons or claws or long crooked fingers over their heads.

"You're standing," Benjamin whispered.

"Yeah," I muttered. "I guess I am."

"How do you feel?"

"Like I've got the weight of the world on my shoulders."

The Darkness's laugh was deep and terrifying. A few of the beasts beyond the walls backed up when they heard it. "Then it's time to stop walking like a man."

"I don't—"

"Come out, dragon." It was a calm invitation but Benjamin's calm voice was terrifying enough.

The request slipped down my throat and spoke to the Darkness in my belly. It *wanted* to come out. I looked up at Benjamin. "What do I do?"

"Just let it."

Come out. A thunderous roar barreled from my chest the instant I finished the thought and the creatures beyond the walls backed away yelping. Pleased with their reaction, I let out another roar and the ground beneath my feet shook. I looked down at my body. *Dragon. Holy crap! I did it!*

Benjamin flashed me a proud grin, which was terrifying in his current form. "Now seal the cracks in the Princess's home."

I was about to ask how, but somehow it just came to me and I knew exactly what to do. I let out another thunderous bellow, satisfied with the way that every living thing trembled at the sound. Then I drew a deep breath and breathed fire, igniting the sky with orange flames. The flames melted the fissures, sealing them shut and the creatures beyond the walls cowered.

I let out another deafening roar. *ENTER THIS SPACE AND ALL OF YOU WILL BURN!*

53

DAVID

It's curious, the boundaries we create for ourselves and the limits we fear surpassing because the consequences are so unthinkable. Once we lose what we treasure most, all of those boundaries shatter. I'd kept myself bound for ages but now that the Princess had been taken, there was nothing I wouldn't do. There was no boundary I wouldn't decimate to retrieve her.

The sound of my wing beats sliced through the silence in the Darkness, punctuating the furious pounding of my heart. There was nothing left to hold me back in either world. If Godric harmed her, I'd burn both worlds to ash and if her heart stopped beating, every creature alive would feel my pain.

Could I have prevented all of this from happening if I'd been honest with Emma once she was old enough to understand? My intention was to spare her the pain. Better to think your father cold and uncaring than know him to be a sexual deviant but if she'd known what a monster he was, she never would've followed his cries beyond the mirage. When all was said and done, my efforts to spare her pain had led to a jarring realization when her father attacked her, followed by the equally jarring experience of witnessing his death at her own husband's hands. The Purists had orchestrated the entire incident perfectly. They'd scooped Albert up as soon as I released him from his cell. I'd seen no need to continue torturing him once the Princess was well beyond his reach in both worlds. I never dreamed Godric would come upon him and meddle with his mind, bestowing him temporary Sight. How did I know that's what he'd done? Sophie Turner told me when she was pleading for her life...

...I'd waited by the lake all night but Emma never came to the clearing. In a torrent of frustration, I breathed my fury into the atmosphere. And in the midst of the storm, I left to pay the succubus a visit.

The musky scent of hallucinogenic candles hung heavy in the breezeless air as I neared her dwelling. Nostrils flared, I barreled through the vulgar haze. The compound had no effect on me. It was nothing more than an offense to my senses. But for the droves of hedonistic creatures that flocked to her territory, it was a powerful aphrodisiac luring them closer, hungry for sin.

As I stepped toward the open-air dwelling that would've rivaled the entrance to Sodom and Gomorra, an orgiastic chorus of whimpers and grunts echoed through the Darkness. The succubus sat lounging on a cushioned chaise on a raised platform, watching her addle-minded miscreants perform various deviant sexual acts. This was nothing out of the ordinary. Sophie often tired of being the dominant in her sexual encounters. Though she orchestrated every depraved act that the dominants below her performed, watching allowed her to fantasize about taking the submissive role. She'd role-played the submissive countless times, but truly being dominated was nearly impossible for a succubus. Only a creature immune to her charms could ever truly dominate her, and dragons are the only such creatures in existence.

She'd begged me for years to give her the release she so desperately craved, begged to be the vestal I poured all my unadulterated fury and frustration into. Eventually, I grew tired of her pleading and began declining in less polite ways. In retrospect, perhaps I should've been more understanding. Pointing to my gorgeous bride and asking Sophie what I could possibly want with her when I had Emma had left Sophie wounded and jealous and ripe for the taking by a rival dragon.

As I ascended the steps to her pedestal, the succubus rose to her feet. She was clothed in a filmy black gown that left little to the imagination, yet she still felt the need to part the slit and offer a glimpse of her thigh. "What brings you here tonight, my King?"

A puff of smoke escaped my nostrils as I cast a displeased glance at the orgy below. Many of the participants were Unsighted and all of them were drugged out of their fucking minds. "I want no audience for my actions."

The scent of her arousal flooded the air as she stepped to the edge of her pedestal. She stood there watching her pornographic puppets for a moment before addressing them. "Leave us. Your animalistic behavior displeases the King."

Many of them groaned, expressing their frustration at being asked to stop before the climactic moment, but all of them ceased their fornicating and slunk off to the shadows of the forest.

Sophie stepped toward me as the last of them disbanded. "To what do I owe the honor of your presence?"

I arched an eyebrow and regarded her with detached coolness. "I miss my wife."

A devious grin spread across her face. "I'd be delighted to ease your frustrations."

Nostrils flaring, I growled, "Get on your knees."

The succubus licked her painted lips and obediently dropped to the floor at my feet.

When she reached out to unfasten my pants, I didn't temper my fury in the slightest as I backhanded her across the face. "Did I tell you to do that?"

Licking the trail of blood that trickled from her lips, she shook her head. And yet, she continued to smile.

A low growl resonated in my chest as I wrapped a hand around her throat, forcing her head back. "What the fuck are you smiling at?"

She immediately dropped the smile, but her eyes still glistened with anticipation. Unable to answer aloud with my fingers constricting her windpipe, she thought her response. Do you prefer your submissive to fear you? Perhaps you should punish me.

I tightened my grip. "I intend to." As the scent of her arousal bled through the air, a twisted part of me couldn't help but be curious. How long would it take this foolish whore to realize this was no game?

I tightened my grasp and her eyes widened as a wheezing sound escaped her mouth. Yet even as she feared my actions, a rush of heat pooled between her legs and tightened her nipples. Disgusted, I grabbed a fistful of her hair with my free hand. When the move merely heightened her arousal, I snarled and yanked her head back. Even then, it wasn't until I tore a patch of hair from her scalp that she truly felt fear.

Grinning wickedly, I released her throat. "Do you know why I came here?"

Eyes filled with tears, she touched one hand to her throat and fingered the bald patch on her head with the other.

I grabbed another fistful of hair. "Suddenly shy, are we?"

"No," she whispered, clutching my fist in a vain attempt to detach it from her head. I gave her hair a fierce tug and she let out a strangled cry. "Please, Sarrum! What have I done to displease you?"

"Isn't this what you've always wanted? To be completely at the mercy of a man you couldn't control? Tell me, succubus, how does it feel to be powerless?"

"Horrible," she sobbed. "Please! You're scaring me."

My answer was more bestial growl than human voice, "Good."

"What have I done to anger you, my King?" she pleaded, desperately trying to free her hair from my fist.

"Did you really think I wouldn't find out?" I snarled, dragging her toward the staircase by the hair.

She let out an agonized shriek as the hair began to rip. "Please stop!"

I yanked her down the staircase and when the fistful of hair tore from her scalp, I caught her by the throat and descended the remaining steps with her feet dangling beneath her. "What did Godric pay you?"

In her panic, she couldn't focus enough to answer. I released my hold on her neck and a desperate whimper accompanied the thud as her body hit the ground.

"What did he pay you?" I snarled, planting a foot on either side of her crumpled body. "What price was worth betraying the dragon who took you in off the streets, put you through law school and gave you a respectable job? I fed and clothed and protected you, you fucking whore! And you turned on me for the first dragon who crawled between your legs!"

Heart racing, she whimpered, "I don't know what you're talking about."

I exhaled through flared nostrils.

And she shrieked as her flesh blistered from the heat. "Alright! Godric promised to make me his queen when he took the throne if I helped him destroy the Princess! He offered to give me everything you'd always denied me! And the pleasure of being with him was worth every bit of this pain!"

I bent and wrapped a hand around her bruised throat. "Was it?"

No longer able to speak because of the damage to her windpipe, she answered in thought. Yes!

"Then I haven't caused enough pain yet."

No! Please!

"How did he do it?" I snarled, squeezing harder. "How did he bring an Unsighted man into the heart of the Darkness with a head full of memories that he shouldn't possess?"

Godric's sorcerer altered his mind, gave him temporary Sight and filled his head with stories about how the Princess should've been his. He told him she'd be his to keep if he did what Godric asked and Albert was too stupid to realize that complying was a death sentence.

I tightened my grip a little more. "As were you."

Please Sarrum! Show me mercy! I didn't want to do it! Godric's followers abducted me from the forest. When his demons delivered me to him, he was torturing an Unsighted girl. When he was done with her, he handed her over to the demons. They dragged her out of the room and the whole time he was speaking to me, I could hear the girl screaming.

He said my choice was simple, suffer the same fate as that girl or earn a place in his bed.

I let go of her throat, unmasked and towered above her on four legs. "That's a filthy bunch of lies! You know damn well I could've protected you. All you had to do was call out to me. You did it out of jealousy, to hurt the girl who had what you wanted! You were envious of her youth and beauty, and you were envious that she was everything I desired, everything you could never be!"

You're right. I hated that little cunt! I always had. Even when she was a child, no other female could turn your head. If you'd fucked me even once while she was still a little girl, I could've accepted it. But I couldn't compete with your precious treasure even when she was your innocent daughter. Think whatever you like, but I know the truth. You're every bit as perverted as I am! You were always obsessed with her.

I lowered my head so my face was inches from hers, and she winced at the heat of my breath. "Of course I was." I sunk my teeth into her throat, bathing us both in her blood. Then I spit her flesh to the ground beside her and snarled, "I am dragon. Obsessing over our treasure is what we do. In time, I will mend my marriage but I'm afraid your time is up." I lifted my head, never taking my eyes off hers. "Nothing more to say? No final clever words? I regret to inform you, this death won't come easily. Even as that gaping wound drains the life from your body, my venom attempts to mend you. Quite vainly, I'm afraid. But you won't go quickly. Are you certain you've no last words?"

Her only response was the wet gurgle of an open throat futilely attempting to breathe.

"I'll mend the Princess's mind eventually. In her heart, she knows I'd never hurt her. All will be forgiven in the end and Godric will suffer for his actions, but you won't be around to see any of that."

For hours, I watched her soul teeter the line between life and death. Her panicked eyes never strayed from mine, and she pleaded with me several times to show her mercy.

When I grew tired of listening to her beg, I moved closer and crouched above her. "You're boring me," I whispered. "You always have."

Her eyes widened as I plunged a hand into her chest and ripped out her beating heart. "You sided with the wrong dragon." As I snarled the words, I squashed the pulsing organ like a piece of overripe fruit and watched the life drain from her eyes...

...This was not the end. I wouldn't rest until I found my Princess. And once I did, Godric had better be ready for a war because I intended to give him one.

Damn the boundaries. Damn the innocents. I'd destroy both worlds if I had to.

Godric was going to burn.

Turn the page for an excerpt from DREAM SIGHT
Book Three of the Dream Waters series

1

BOB

Watching Nellie dredge up all the heartache from her past was torture. What was the point of this? Hadn't this bastard caused her enough suffering? What purpose could forcing her to pour her heart out to Charlie possibly serve? Even at a distance, I could feel how much it pained her. But hard as I fought against it, I couldn't free myself from the spell that bound me. I couldn't move a muscle, couldn't call out to Charlie and warn him of the danger. I couldn't do a damn thing to help the woman I'd vowed to protect with my life. Keeping me immobilized just inside the forest, close enough to witness her anguish but powerless to help her, seemed intentionally cruel. Not that Godric's cruelty came as a surprise. Nellie shared her story with me soon after Charlie brought her to my shore. I knew what a monster her ex-husband was, and it killed me that I hadn't prevented him from getting to her.

Laughter danced in Godric's cruel eyes as he watched me. "You're a noble man, Robert. I can see why Nellie is so fond of you."

"Why are you doing this?" I managed to choke out through gritted teeth.

"That doesn't concern you, my friend."

"You're no friend of mine," I whispered, sweat beading on my brow from the effort.

Henry's amused grin widened. "I suppose that's true."

Exchanging words with this monster was a waste of energy, so I ignored him and focused on fighting the invisible bonds that held me frozen in place.

My life had become something magical the night Charlie washed up on my shore with Nellie and her daughter, Lilly. Before them, I walked that shore alone and my life had lost all sense of purpose, but they breathed new life into me. They became my purpose and my one goal in life was to keep them safe from the dragon that Nellie believed was coming for her but after enough time passed without incident, I suppose we'd both gotten careless. There didn't appear to be anything to worry about. Neither man, nor beast had come searching for Nellie or her sweet child so we settled into a comfortable routine, spending our days playing with Lilly and our evenings learning everything there was to know about each other. Nellie was hesitant to share the details of her past at first but as we grew closer, she began to trust that she could tell me anything and eventually, she opened up and shared the nightmarish details of her past. A weight seemed to lift from her as soon as she did and she truly began to enjoy life again. That's when Henry Godric showed up on our shore.

Determined as I'd been to slay Nellie's demon, I couldn't even touch him. The instant I stepped toward Godric, he paralyzed me. Then he took sweet little Lilly and sealed her in an elaborately ornamented cage. If I'd been able to speak, I would've warned Nellie not to cooperate with that monster but he made certain that I couldn't tell her anything. He froze my vocal chords as well as every muscle in my body. Then he told Nellie that Charlie would be paying us a visit soon and if she didn't do exactly as he said, he'd take the lives of the two people she loved most in this world. He didn't ask her to lie or deceive Charlie. He simply instructed her to tell her tale as it'd truly happened, but that was torture enough. Nellie kept those memories buried deep inside. Allowing them to surface was agony for her and for the life of me, I couldn't imagine what reason Godric could have for making her do it.

Utterly spent and useless, I struggled to draw a breath as I watched Nellie drop into Charlie's arms. For a short eternity the two of them wept, locked in that embrace. I spent those torturous minutes

ERIN A. JENSEN

fighting to regain control of my voice and holler a
warning to Charlie but for all my efforts, I didn't accomplish a thing. They spoke a bit longer after Nellie
straightened and shortly after that, Charlie departed
none the wiser.

I died a thousand times over as Henry dragged
Lilly's gilded cage and my immobilized body out
of the forest. My heart ached as we approached
the spot where Nellie's body laid crumpled by the
Water's edge. She lifted her head as we neared her,
and I wanted nothing more than to take her in my
arms and dry her tearstained cheeks.

Henry let out a maddeningly cheerful laugh.
"You did well, Nellie."

I ached to throttle him, but I still couldn't budge
an inch or even verbally defend her.

"Then leave us alone like you promised," Nellie
whispered.

"I'm afraid there's been a slight miscommunica-
tion," Godric murmured as he took a step toward
her. "I never promised to leave you alone."

A frail sob escaped Nellie's trembling lips.
"What?"

"I simply promised to spare the lives of the people you loved."

A fresh tear slid down Nellie's cheek as Godric
moved toward Lilly. "What are you saying?"

"Your knight in shining armor truly is a noble
man." Henry's grin widened as he turned to look at

me. "He's honest and decent and selfless, everything that I despise. Did you really believe I'd allow him to keep what belonged to me?"

Try as I might, I couldn't even choke out a response.

Nellie stole a worried glance at me as she numbly repeated her question. "What are you saying?"

"Dragons do not part with their treasures."

Nellie dropped her head as if it'd suddenly grown too heavy for her neck to support. "You never treasured me."

"True," he agreed, his voice cold as ice, "but you belong to me, and I can't allow another man to keep what's mine."

"I did what you asked," Nellie whimpered. "Please. Let me go."

"I'm afraid I can't do that." Grinning like he didn't have a care in the world, Henry took a leisurely step toward me. "I thank you for your hospitality, Bob. However, I can't allow you to keep on screwing my wife, now can I? What sort of man would that make me?"

"You...are...no...man," I choked the words out in a broken whisper as Nellie's sobbing shattered my heart.

"Enough tears," Godric whispered, rattling Lilly's cage with his foot. "If you behave, I might consider allowing you to keep this lovely little enchantment."

Nellie instantly stilled.

With hardly any effort, Henry lifted Nellie and tossed her over his shoulder. Then he picked up Lilly's cage. "It's been a pleasure, Bob."

As they moved toward the Water, Nellie lifted her head to look back at me and mouthed the words, "I love you."

Then Godric stepped into the Water, and the Waters promptly swallowed them.

The moment they vanished, my invisible chains fell away. Heart pounding, I dove into the Water after them...

...I startled myself awake with a groggy holler and a loud snort, rubbed my eyes and looked around the room. I musta dozed off on the couch again. I couldn't remember what the hell I'd been dreamin about, but I was definitely havin a nightmare. My old heart was beatin a mile a minute. Somehow, Nellie'd managed to sleep through my outburst. She was still snorin away with her head on my shoulder. I brushed the wiry pieces of gray hair off her face. That's when I saw the tears on her wrinkled cheeks.

I gave her a little shake. "Wake up, woman. Naptime's over."

She didn't wake up, but her eyelids twitched and she let out a whiny squeak. Guess I wasn't the only one havin nightmares. What the fuck were we watchin when we nodded off? I squinted at the television. Two sour old bastards were flappin their gums about fly fishin, not exactly my idea of quality programmin but it wasn't the stuff nightmares were made of.

Nellie let out another nervous squeak.

I shook her a little harder. "Hey! Wake up. You're startin to worry me."

She jerked her head off my shoulder, and her eyes were wide as hell as she looked up at me. "He's planning to take the Princess."

"Shhh." I'd gotten pretty used to Nellie's looniness. In fact, I usually found it kinda charmin. But her face looked too pale this time. "It was just a bad dream, that's all. Everything's okay."

"No it's not," she whispered. "You need to find Charlie and warn him that Godric's coming for the Princess. You'll find him with the Sarrum. They've been training him at the palace."

I narrowed my eyes at her. "What the hell's gotten into you, woman? You're startin to scare me."

"You need to find Charlie!" Her crazy eyes widened as she grabbed ahold of my arm. "Tell him Godric took me and he plans to take the Princess!"

"Charlie checked outta here, remember? The kid ain't here anymore."

"Not here," she squeaked, "in the Dream World."

"I think that oversized retard fucked up the dose on your medication." I flagged the slow kid over to us. "Hey, numb nut! Get your fat ass over here and make yourself useful!"

He stomped across the room and dropped to his knees in fronta Nellie with a blank stare on his re-tard face. "What's goin on?"

"I'll tell ya what's goin on," I growled. "The old bat woke up talkin nonsense, so either somebody laced her oatmeal with LSD or she's havin a fuckin stroke."

The retard motioned for a skinny broad by the door to come over, then he turned to Nellie. "We're gonna take you for a walk and have the doctor take a look at you."

"Fuck off, troll," Nellie snarled. Then she grabbed my hand. "You need to remember, Bob! When you fall asleep, find Charlie! Have him take you to the Dragon King, tell him his Princess is in danger and tell Charlie you need his help because Godric took me!"

"Relax, Hun." The skinny broad was all smiles as she pulled a syringe outta nowhere and jabbed it into the saggy skin on Nellie's arm.

Nellie looked up at me as she slumped sideways. "Find Charlie... You have to save me... and they need to protect the Princess."

I felt useless and guilty watchin them wheel in a gurney and lift her lifeless little body onto it. They wheeled her out the door and I dropped my head back against the couch, concentrated on slowin my breathin and tried to convince myself I did the right thing. I'm embarrassed to admit, it didn't take long for me to nod off again...

…I bolted upright and sprang to my feet a few inches from the Water's edge. The last thing I remembered was diving in the Water after Godric took Nellie and Lilly. What had I been thinking? I couldn't travel through the Waters like Nellie and Charlie could. I was just a simple man with simple memories of a single world and no special abilities to speak of. I'd failed the woman I'd sworn to protect, but I'd be damned if I would ever give up searching for her. If the Waters would rather spit me out than take me to them, I'd just have to find another way to reach her.

Adrenaline coursed through my veins as I marched toward the forest. My axe was just inside those trees. I'd chop down enough of them to build a raft, travel the Waters and search until I found her. No… not her… *Find Charlie.* I wasn't sure how or why I knew, but I'd never been more certain of anything in my life. I needed to find Charlie. The only trouble was, I had no idea where to even begin looking for him.

Praying for a miracle, I entered the forest, grabbed my axe and swung it at the nearest tree trunk.

90701157R00293

Made in the USA
Columbia, SC
11 March 2018